Thundered

Hearts

Thundered
Hearts

RAE Z. RYANS

Published 2014 By Fictitious Publishing
www.fictitiouspublishing.com

Thundered Hearts
Copyright © 2014 Rae Z. Ryans
ISBN 978-0-9916654-6-4
www.raezryans.com

Cover and interior design: Raven Tree Design
www.raventreedesign.com

In remembrance of Baby Kitty; my inspiration for Zoro.

Contents

Chapter One

"*Burn the fire bright and keep the locha at bay. Bask in the daylight where the locha won't play.*"

Strangeness encompassed Beth's life. She slurped her latte and leaned in her chair, gazing at the busy Abbeville street. Locha existed; stories passed through the generations and kept the anxiety alive for some in the quaint community. Many of those people shuffling along the streets had shunned the ancient ways of the Creek people and those born with gifts from The One Above. Movement caught her eye, reflecting in the hardware store's glass, but she shook the shadow away.

Bethany Ann McCallister was a Spirit Walker, and she would have given anything to fulfill her birth rite as a huntress of the locha, yet the panic and her family had stopped her. Beth had witnessed the locha living in the shadows.

Stubby fingers tapped out her reply. "*Sure. Am I bringing anything home?*"

Her phone buzzed with a list of herbs, the same list her aunt had given her before leaving that morning on her delivery route. Jemma gathered them from the shops as Beth enjoyed her daily ritual of coffee and people watching. No one spoke to her unless they had to. A deep breath filled her lungs, and the air pushed through her clenched jaw.

She muttered, "More like bleached blonde monsters with venomous tongues."

Some kids might have been forgetful, but Beth was not a kid, and her memory was like that of an elephant. Blue eyes blinked at her across the street. She did not forgive either and tilted her jaw, forcing her gaze away. As the owner of said eyes drove off, Beth peeked in his direction and inspected the driver of the slow moving hybrid, waving to the girls seated behind her.

Beth giggled because laughter was preferred over tears. Too many had fallen for Lucien Brown, both tears and girls. How many nights had she wasted, sobbing over the bastard responsible for ripping her heart out?

"What is she laughing at?" someone whispered a few tables over, and Beth bit the inside of her cheek. Sparks emitted from her fingertips. "Beth's so bizarre." Uncaring about its hefty calorie content, she ignored the person, slurped her iced latte, and closed her eyes. "All those McCallister's are strange."

Cracked lips twitched. Coffee sizzled as burnt plastic crinkled her nose. *One day they will learn and respect me.* Beth thrust their whispers and snickers aside and enjoyed a deep, cleansing breath. All the pain bubbled toward the surface of her skin. Within her mind, she buried their hatred and ridicule where no one else dared to find it. A cozy spot marked on her black heart right next to *him*. Beth's shoulders straightened.

Sun rays washed warmth over her skin, and sweat formed on her brow. Beth's pants squeaked as pleather leg slid against pleather leg. Aunt Vivian kept the McCallisters on a tightened leash. Yes, a bit twisted at times, but the family was as old as the red Alabama clay. Secrets bred secrets until they had alienated themselves from the other Creek families and the American townsfolk. Being niece to the tribe's medicine woman did not help matters when more and more Creek turned their backs on natural treatments. Beth chewed her lip contemplating her deliveries. Every week they seemed lighter as people departed the world.

A howl cut through the muggy early evening, hazel-brown eyes opened, and she jumped from the bistro table. Already outstaying her welcome in the sun, the white salt—a side effect of the electricity in her body—dusted her bronzed skin. Snorts of laughter reached her ears, but Beth again ignored the banter. She brushed the dried salt away. Blazed in a rolling fire of purple and orange, the last rays filtered over the treetops. Beth covered her eyes and peered along the street, searching for Jemma. Summer nights meant longer excursions and extra noise to cut threw her brain. No one else heard the odd howling as her head tilted from side to side. Tossing the melted cup over her shoulder into the waste bin, Beth's booted feet stomped toward the whining. Fingers pattered over thick thighs as the caffeine fueled her steps and worked over her pounding heart.

Beth paused and inhaled; the wind whipped tonight, and a charred odor curled her nose. Locha held a certain stank, and of that fact, she was surer than rain and sunshine. Spirit Walkers held keener senses than humans, a gift from the six elements: earth, air, fire, water, animal, and ancestor. Squinting, she scanned the greenery for signs of moving shadows. The locha played in the shade.

Beth's gift was the rarest. Few Spirit Walkers developed the power to draw electricity from objects and nature. A hand shielded her eyes as her stomach churned. Spirit Walkers held many weaknesses though. Beth understood her limitations as well as what set her apart from other humans. She studied the shadows but saw nothing out of the ordinary. Bound in human bodies, Spirit Walkers were also mortal. Mortality sucked, but the mythical beings were fallible and susceptible to the dark forces of the night. A humid breeze did little to cool the heat spreading across her neck. Locha—the Creek called those twisted and grotesque, who had fallen to evil as did their folklore snakes and horned beasts.

"Beth," Jemma called from behind, rattling her shopping bags, and cussing under her breath. Rules sucked too. Her baby cousin knew Beth's aspirations, what she too had tried to become, but the magical gifts had not run through her veins. "Wait up, Auntie called again. We gotta go before sundown."

Instead Beth ran. A quick glance over her shoulder was unneeded, but her curvy frame stumbled. She brushed the grime from her delicate hands. Pressing onward, she jumped the short park fence in a single bound, landing and tumbling through the soft Bermuda grass. Raised to fear the dark shadows and the twisted nightmares birthed in the universe's underworld, she halted, crouching near bushes as the huffing and puffing of Jemma's struggled breath neared. Her cousin winced as a hand touched her thundering heart; the other handed over her phone.

"Stand down, Beth." Beth shot a glare towards her cousin, but Jemma only offered a light shrug, and stuffed her hands deep into her pockets. Sweat beaded on her forehead, and for a second Beth despised her normality. "Did you hear me young lady?"

Beth's attention zipped to the phone. She blinked at the word speakerphone scrolling across and flinched at the name. "Yeah, Auntie, I hear you."

But her stare trailed and followed the ricocheting sounds around the deserted park. A swing creaked. Without another word, Beth hung up the phone and jogged toward the groaning sway of metal. The park closed at dusk and silence bathed in the area, at least human silence. What creature lurked within its walls and gardens?

A thick voice whispered her name across the wind as Jemma yelled, "Turn around." Auntie this and Auntie that, she cried from her safe distance.

No! Aunt Vivian always ruined her fun; she squashed her dreams. Vision narrowed as she swung the metal gate open to the Abbeville Children's Park—adjacent to the main park but enclosed for child safety. Tall wooden castles steeped high in the sky and created long shadowy passages. Wood chips rustled beneath her feet as she crept closer to the sound, and the strange smoldering aroma returned, but this time it held a familiarity. A flash of dark hair caught her attention as the swing flung into the air. A thud followed, but the swing swung backward, and the person was gone.

"Luce?" Rusted chains groaned and clattered as Beth caught the metal rope. "Lucien, stop playing games and show yourself." The seat radiated heat in comparison to the one next to it. *No, someone had sat here.* She had seen someone even if only for a brief second. Lucien had messed with her head for the last time. Still clutching Jemma's phone, she pressed redial. Auntie answered on the first ring as another wail shrieked through the night.

"Come home now and bring Jemma with you." Beth held the phone away from her ear as her aunt shouted.

"I know it's him; it has to be him," Beth said as her cousin wheezed behind her. Jemma—unlike her—was not active. Yoga and swimming had helped to condition Beth's body, allowing for elastic flexibility and the ability to run without keeling over despite her size. Jems needed a crash course before she toppled over dead. Although no amount of healthy eating or exercise changed Beth's weight or size. Forever stuck in a size fourteen like the other Spirit Walkers in the world. Aunt Vivian said the electricity needed the extra pounds to protect her vital organs, but she could not harness the electrical currents either. Beth ignored her words, as no one alive in their family had the ability, and they all teetered on the heavy side.

The line crackled, and the phone heated in her palm. She dropped the cell, and the once white case glowed red. No, this had Luce written all over it. The pit of her stomach churned. The bane of her existence and source of her rage had a name: Lucien Brown. For three years, she had sworn the man was not human. No man should have held such a woozy effect over girls, inhuman strength and speed, and captivating blue eyes that caused her heart to stutter in addition to her words. To make matters worse, Beth was not immune to his charms. She hated him even more for how he had once made her care. Luce's actions had monster written all over them, and he'd carved a target into her forehead.

"Let's go." Beth tugged Jemma's arm and dragged her from the park, tossing glances over her shoulder into the creeping shadows that chased and swirled behind them. Jemma tried to talk, but she shushed her and kept her senses turned on their surroundings. The whispers started again, and they chanted her name, not her real name, but one her familiar often used in his soft purring voice.

"Kolkohkafoosi."

Beth asked, "Did you hear that?" Jemma shot her a puzzled look and searched the park. "Seriously, you don't hear that?"

"All I hear are bugs. You're losing it, cuz."

"Kolkohkafoosi, come to me." A curse flew out of Beth's mouth with a long breath. Beth's pulse skyrocketed as the whisper reached her ears. She yanked harder on Jemma's arm and broke into a light jog.

Her feet scuffled over the dirt. "Beth, stop you're hurting me." No, she could not stop. The shadows arose, and she was not safe. She had to get Jemma home before Lucien struck or worse, the locha attacked again. Vivian would never forgive her if anything happened to her daughter; Beth would not forgive herself either.

They reached the street. Muscle strength was not her forte, but somehow she pushed Jemma's large ass over the four-foot fence. She landed on her rear, huffing and puffing the thickened air, and glared at her.

"What's your problem? Geesh, you almost dropped me in an ant bed." Fire ants were a way of life in the south. Jemma flicked a fire ant from her tennis shoe and hopped from the ground. Streetlights hummed their warning tune, flickering yellow in tune with Beth's heartbeat. Whenever *he* was near it raced. At just the thought of Lucien, her blood pumped and coursed through her body like a sparked wire, emitting a blue flicker from her sweaty fingertips. Beth would have to find another way to release the tension building and flowing through her veins. She shoved her hands behind her back.

Something dark came into Abbeville, and Beth aimed to find out what denizens beseeched their picturesque town. Rules or no rules this had to stop. Running from the locha wasn't how she saw her future. The whispers settled into a dull roar, and the tree frogs awakened. Crickets and locusts joined their chorus. Jemma's sweaty palm grasped a hold of Beth. Sweet innocence reflected in her hazel eyes, and a smile played at her lips. This life was not for her.

"C'mon kid, let's get you home."

They made it as far as the coffee shop. Beth heard the whispers again, but the locha were not to blame. "What'd she forget, her donuts?"

Snickers followed as she spun on her heels coming face-to-face Luce's flavor of the last three years, Amber. Her perfect blonde brow arched as Beth's fists curled and uncurled behind her back. Heat surged into her palms and coiled to her tips, the spark itching to strike her down as ridicule stabbed her ego.

Jemma tugged on her arm and whispered her name as the coffee house door jingled. Blue eyes swept over Beth, and an easy smile dimpled into his ruddy, wind burnt cheeks. As always, her mouth dried, and her heartbeat skipped at the sight of low-slung jeans and the dark blue V-neck tee shirt, showing the dark hair of his chest.

Unsteady breath blew out slow as her cousin tugged again. She allowed gravity to drag her toward her car. Cackles and snorts followed in their wake, but her breath remained ragged, and her cheeks grew hotter than Hades.

"Where's the fire, sunshine? Running home?" Beth gulped and awaited his jibe.

Amber said, "Ew, don't talk to her."

Jemma kept quiet. She understood what Beth had dealt with that night, and every day since their friendship expired. One long sniffle and Beth slid behind the wheel of her car. His mockery stung the most; it always did. After the sacrifices she'd made to save his life, the least he could have done was treat her like a human being instead of a mangy dog. But the insult didn't arrive.

"Shut your mouth, Amber," he said instead, but the roar of the engine drowned out the rest. Luce stepped toward her car. Beth revved the engine, and without looking, she sped away.

Ten minutes later, they pulled up to the gate of their historic home. The tears Beth held at bay threatened to spill as she recalled the prison looming before her. What was worse, Lucien or jail?

To outsiders it was not a prison, but a historic home built in the eighteen hundreds by her family. Outsiders did not know Beth's secrets or Auntie's asinine rules. The plantation house featured private baths and balconies, but the enclosed observation deck was Beth's secret place. At least it had been until Aunt Vivian forbade her from entering the third floor as a punishment for lying about a party three years ago. Every time Beth pushed boundaries, someone had caught her, and the punishment was typically to bar her from something she loved.

Mossy lion statues greeted her, and Beth punched in her security code. Quivering lips settled as she breathed deeply. Prison, her jail cell trumped Lucien, but college would have been better. Vivian had refused despite the acceptance letters arriving. Heck, two colleges awarded her a full ride. Beth had asked why not and received a backhand, as a response, across her cheek. The iron gate opened, as she tried to ignore the distant howls etching a chill into her spine and gunned the gas. Screw the rules. The quicker she disposed of Jemma, the quicker Beth could sneak out again. Her dark braid slapped her in the face; a grown woman should not have to sneak out of her home, but she had to try.

Beth glanced at her cousin. She had to try for her and innocent people like Amber, regardless of her cruelty. The bear tribe was peaceful, but as more settlers had claimed Creek land, more tribes revolted with ancient magic. Legends spoke of a great evil that rose up and swallowed the settlers and sympathizing tribes, but many legends were nothing more than tales meant to frighten children into behaving. The locha, however, were real.

Jemma whispered, "Good luck," as Beth tossed the car into park. The locha were not a fairy tale. Neither were the Spirit Walkers who maintained the balance between the three worlds. She sighed, pushing air through her tight lips. Saving the likes of her warden from the locha fell to her too.

Vivian waited in the open foyer wearing her signature button up embroidered sweater, and polyester tapered pants. A pair of winged glasses perched upon her long bird nose, and her parted, black hair wound into a bun. Beth thanked The One Above nightly for not inheriting her facial genes. Knowing she could not sit in her car all evening and that Vivian would not budge, she sank her teeth into her bottom lip as the final rays settled behind the forest lining the property.

Heavy feet inched toward the front door. Beth's heart had not calmed. Vivian's palm turned over, and her fingers snapped. "Keys. Now," she clipped her words as if she was a slave. Beth hesitated; she faced another night of lockdown. "Bethany Ann McCallister."

Her head hung, and she placed the car keys in her aunt's palm. Vivian's fingers snapped again, and her gaze followed the stiff finger pointing toward the stairs. A sigh tickled her chest, and her ears burned. How many nineteen year olds received scolding and ridicule from their aunt? Beth's parents had refused to intervene, leaving the decisions and punishments to Aunt Vivian.

The walls closed in as Beth shuffled past the old paintings and photographs hanging on the walls. Their eyes followed her, and the beady stares judged her weak stature for not standing up for herself and demanding the withheld birthright. Lead feet stomped up the double staircase, and the steps echoed as they had done every night. If her ancestors could have spoken, Beth wondered if they would have agreed with Vivian.

Did they understand the locha? Had they known why the shadows whispered her name? Vivian, her parents, and even Luce had said she lied, but Beth heard their calls, and why would she lie? Attention was their response. Either way no matter what side she chose Beth was forever wrong. Only Zoro believed her.

Jemma's alto voice carried as she argued with her mother down-stairs, but like all the times before, her support would not change the old woman's mind. The Mandate had spoken; the McCallisters refused to intervene anymore in the white man's world or some crap. Evil was evil, and evil affected everyone no matter their skin color, mystical powers, or beliefs. Heck, if they had wanted to get technical, all Creek Indians had mixed blood. From black to white to red and any other color, she might have missed. The Mandate's job was to protect them, the old ways, and enforce the laws.

Beth threw her handbag on the bed followed by her body. The springs groaned from the impact of her weight. Zoro hissed, and she peeked at the seal point Himalayan taking up residence on the pillow.

"Excuse me, your highness, but get out of my room." As usual, the familiar refused to budge. He yawned, stretching his paws out in front of him. No one ever listened, and that was half the problem. Beth scoffed and stared out the balcony door. Five locks barred the sliding door, and a lace curtain added another barrier. A prisoner in her own home; what else was new?

A knock came on the bedroom door, and it creaked. "How many times have we had this conversation, Beth?" Her eyes closed; every night they'd argued. Vivian closed the door behind her. "*We* don't hunt anymore, thunderbird."

Vivian had not hunted at all, but Beth bit her tongue at the nickname and her emphasis on we. Knuckles cracked as Beth stared out the door, not even bothering to roll over or stand up. The beady eye stare of her aunt reflected in the exposed glass. She did not deserve that much attention. The last rays of the fiery light disappeared behind the tribunal hill. A soft thud rattled the door, and a large shadow formed in the shape of a hunched person on her balcony. Everyone pretended it was not there except Beth. The stranger arrived each night.

Her throat thickened. The creature hid amongst the shadows, but the hairs on her arm stood at full attention. "Something's out there," Beth whispered and noted the slight chatter of her teeth.

"It's not your problem or ours," Zoro said, brushing against her shoulder. Magic was a wonderful gift, and every Spirit Walker received a familiar. Too bad hers chit chatted. His never-ending opinions seldom said anything nice. "Now shut up so I can sleep."

"Zoro's right." Aunt Vivian stroked Beth's long, black braid. Hazel eyes glued to the spot on her balcony. It moved, rising and falling as if breathing. Vivian continued, "The town turned their backs on us, and the Mandate decided long ago to punish them. Those that heed our advice stay safe at night."

Beth and Vivian saw eye to eye on many rules, but she could not wrap her brain around this one. The door clicked behind her. Arguments were of no use. As the head of the family, her word mattered. As a tribal councilwoman, she held weight.

Times had changed, and few listened to the old folk tales of the evil bred in the darkness of night. Years ago, before Beth was even born, something had transpired, and everyone in the family refused to speak about whatever happened. She'd searched the archives and the family treasures, but there wasn't anything to explain the angst against the town. Sure, there had been wars and segregations. But what had drawn the line between them and the tribe?

Beth asked Zoro, "You don't see it?" Two yellow eyes glowed in the shadows. She scrambled from the bed, body trembling as the muffled whispers began again. If she found the truth, the Mandate would see the town needed protection.

Wobbly legs pushed from the bed and crept toward the balcony door. The yellow eyes were gone but not the sense of watching. As she stared out into the courtyard, a plan formed in her brain. Beth would use the daylight hours and search for signs of the supernatural living amongst them in Abbeville. There had to be clues they left behind. She wasn't crazy and imagining the sounds.

"It'll never work." The cat read her mind, but she could not read his.

"Shut it, flea bag." She would make it work, and end the chaos warring inside her soul. A sigh tickled her chest as she stared into Zoro's blue eyes. "You'll help, right?"

"I can only guide you, Kolkohkafoosi. There is a difference between helping you make decisions and telling you the path to follow. Spirit Walkers are both great warrior and great mind." Beth hated when anyone called her thunderbird. Vivian did it often, and the whispering darkness too, but coming from her familiar the name held extra weight. "One day you shall see the truth," Zoro added. "But the truth is a path you alone must walk." A dark brow rose questioning how she could walk a path when Vivian barred her from the outside after sunset. What good was a familiar if he spouted off mumbo-jumbo? "What about the internet?"

Her braid whipped back and forth. Aunt Vivian ran blocking and tracking software on her laptop. She eluded the tactic had benefited security, but the library had computers Beth used. Before now, she had not thought about using them for anything besides school research. Zoro slanted his eyes and lowered his head toward his paws.

"There has to be something."

He glanced to the door and asked her to sit. "Don't seek trouble you're not prepared to handle. You are not ready."

"What are you saying, Zoro?"

"Hush. Not here." A door groaned in the hallway and footsteps pattered over the hardwood floor, halting near her bedroom door. Her insides twisted, forming knots, and bile rose. Someone listened and spied from inside her own house. Zoro's gaze brushed over the stuffed animals on her shelf, settling on an old teddy bear.

Beth had no memory of how it came to be in her room and plucked the deteriorated bear from the shelf. She could have told anyone where the rest came from. Luce had bought them for her over the years they had been friends. Despite his betrayal, she could not throw them out. At first glance, the new comer appeared as nothing more than an outdated plaything, worn and much loved from its scratched eyes and tattered fur. But the weight felt off. She looked over her shoulder. Her hands squeezed the bear, Velcro gave way, and the bottom opened. "What is this?"

"Tread carefully and don't ..." His words trailed as her fingers shoved into the opening, past the stuffing, and clasped a hard object. Zoro hopped onto the desk. "Put it back," he whispered and batted at her arm. Feet tiptoed, pacing in the hallway. The doorknob rattled, and Beth scurried to place the bear back on the shelf. "Someone comes."

Stuffing rested on the floor, and she kicked the white fluff away as the door opened. Jemma poked her head in, and Beth breathed a sigh.

"You all right, Bethy?" Jemma slipped through the door and plopped on the bed to Zoro's dissatisfaction. Luce was the only other person who called her Bethy. "I didn't see you at dinner."

Jemma hid a small napkin her hands. A smile spread over Beth's face as she handed it over, and her heart melted. Although she could be a pain in the side, she had a large heart. "Mom gave me your medicine too."

Vivian withheld meals as punishment sometimes. Without proper food and water, Beth's powers waned. But she kept a snack stash hidden in her room for emergencies. The medicine Vivian designed for her helped balance her after. Every member of the family had one.

Sweet Jemma had risked her mother's wrath and brought her half a sandwich with her pills. By the time she had left, Beth was full, sleepier than usual, and had pushed the teddy bear into the far recesses of her mind. Disturbing, yes, but what could she do about it? No, they could not deny the evidence but Beth required more proof before she acted on it.

The whispers halted too. But the hairs on her arms had not subsided and neither had the prickling over her skin. Satiated and drowsy, she lay her head down and petted her cat.

Chapter Two

*B*eth awoke earlier than usual and worked through a series of sun salutations prior to daybreak. *What happened last night?* Why had she fallen asleep so quickly? Try as she might, Beth pieced what she had recalled together, but all she remembered was the basement.

The energy spent invigorated her, but exercise allowed the electrical current in her veins an outlet too. Salty sweat did not bead on her skin, and it did not dribble. Her skin burned hot enough to evaporate the sweat, leaving behind a crystallized residue. Keeping her noise to a minimum, Beth stepped into the shower. Water sizzled as it poured over her heated skin, dissolving and washing the salt away. Cold water rejuvenated the senses, awakening her mind to the plan it had formed.

Beth seized yoga pants and a tank top from the dresser drawer. Bare feet padded about the bedroom as she prepared for her day. Southern heat meant dressing in light, breathable clothing. Shade became her friend, but her skin still shone a bronzed glow courtesy of her Native American heritage. The same traditions had stopped her from cutting her thick black locks. She rolled the mass into a high bun—a common style among her ancestors long before the name ballerina bun had become famous.

Tiptoeing through the house, the boards whined beneath her feet. No matter how quiet she tried to be, her movements seemed to echo in the old house. Silence blanketed the area as the family slept in their beds, but soon they would awaken. In the kitchen was the door to the cellar. Vivian kept the door locked at all times, but the key hung on the wall, dangling like a golden carrot. Beth warred whether to break to her rules. *How much more could Vivian take away?*

Fresh coffee brewed, trickling into the pot with a gurgled hiss. Her empty stomach twisted as an angel and devil whispered in her ears. Twitchy fingers tapped across the counter as curiosity tore up her insides. A rooster crowed in the distance, announcing sunrise. *What could Vivian have hidden down there?* Perhaps the answers paraded under her nose this entire time. "You'd think I wanted the elixir of life."

All she wanted was the truth.

The clock chimed in the foyer, and she jumped. A chuckle left her lips at her edginess, and she shook it away. Still her gaze fixated on the key to one of the many off-limit rooms in the old house. Over twenty rooms made up the house; the cellar, observatory, and the study remained off limits along with Vivian's outbuilding. She worked out there, and some of the herbs were valuable and rare. Being curious and one to break the rules, Beth had tried breaching into them over the years but never succeeded.

Opportunity had more to do with it than following the rules. Someone was frequently home. Then again, dank basements gave Beth the heebie-jeebies courtesy of all those horror movies Jemma forced her to watch. She shuddered. Hockey masks held a similar effect.

"Screw it," she mumbled and snatched the key from the wall. A quick glance over both shoulders and a keen listen showed no signs that anyone approached. Light footsteps shuffled toward the door. Her hand wobbled inserting the key, and the metal scratched against metal before it popped in. The lock engaged and clunked, and she breathed a sigh of relief.

A hand rubbed against the wall in search of a light switch and using her palm she flicked it on. As the room flooded with lights, she blinked. Rows of fluorescents hummed and hugged ceiling. Beth squinted, allowing her eyes to adjust. Steps groaned beneath her feet as her over sensitive nose burned from the musty scent. A gentle drone filled her ears along with her thumping heart. Vivian would tan her hide if she found her down here. At least she threatened Beth with such, but mostly, she took away her freedom.

A mouthed whoa escaped parted lips. Swords and various weapons lined the basement walls. Tarnished and dusty blades met her widened eyes; resting her hands atop her hips, she blew out a whistled breath. Dust particles pranced under the false lights, and a sneeze tickled the back of her throat. The state of the room washed over her, stunning Beth into silence. As if the Mandate decreed no more hunting and that was that. Someone locked the place up and forgot it existed. Had anyone came down since? She assumed no, but the updated technology said otherwise. The bans had supposedly gone into effect before GE patented the lights. Granted Vivian could have updated the fixtures, but why bother in the unused room?

"This makes no sense." Half-new yet half-old and forgotten did not make any sense.

The floor squashed between her toes, and she stared down. Thick mats lined the floorboards, but a gray layer of grime coated their surface. Boot prints tracked through the grime, but she was barefooted. Beth shoved the thought aside as giddiness rose within her as if finding a hidden treasure. Legs twirled around the room, and her arms spread out wide. Cracked lips drew into a wide smile as if Christmas morning had arrived early. Like a child she danced as images of what she could become resurfaced. *What she should have already been.*

Long swords, broad swords, even daggers and throwing knives graced the dirty walls. Crossbows, long bows, and short bows too. On those walls, her heritage, her birthright, rested as if waiting for her to claim it.

Vivian called, "Bethany?" More like screamed her name, and her heart rate soared. Beth snuck back up the steps and replaced the stolen key on its hook, jotting a mental note to make a copy the next time they left her alone.

"What were you doing?" Zoro asked.

"Nothing ..." Beth glanced away, but the heat dimpled her cheeks.

He rubbed between her legs and purred. "Liar."

"Oh Beth, there you are. Run this over to the Browns straight away." Vivian placed a package in her hand, and Beth gawked at her.

She groaned; Vivian always sent her to *their* house. She slipped the white bag in Beth's other hand. It contained the day's deliveries. *But why the Browns again?* Beth cocked a brow. She had made a delivery two days ago. Was Lucien's leukemia back? Her mouth opened to ask. Vivian pursed her lips and tapped her foot. "What are you waiting for?" Beth snatched the car keys from the hook and bit her cheek. "Oh, Jemma and I are finalizing plans for the Green Corn Festival today at the Mandate. We'll have over ten tribes this year." She shot her a blank stare. Vivian pushed her glasses up. "It's our turn to host the ceremony this year, hadn't I told you?" Beth shook her head, still biting her inner cheek as a new plan unfolded. If she could somehow prove that problems were occurring in Abbeville, then the Mandate would have to overturn their ruling. "Well must've slipped my mind. Go on now, we'll chat later."

As soon as the door closed behind her, Beth grinned. Nothing, not even Lucien Brown, would ruin her day. Dressed in her yoga pants and flip-flops, she whistled a bird song and slid into the driver's seat. *Today was a good day.* A quick glance at her watch and Beth's smile widened, noting the golden skyline. This ought to be fun; her hands rubbed together. The time read six o'clock in the morning. Thank goodness, she had no interest in what Lucifer Brown thought of her anymore, and she looked forward to disturbing him for once.

Lies. Beth cared and always would, but the damage he'd done was irreparable. Lucien did not want to mend their friendship, or else he would have said sorry. Years later and that word still had not left his mouth. She sighed recalling the gentle curve of Lucien's smile. Beth gave up on waiting for his apology, but part of her never let go of her dream, and the future that had involved them together.

The beamer's engine roared to life. Luce thought he was so much better than everyone else was, and he scrutinized her all the time. A time ago, their families had been thicker than thieves. They'd lived in Abbeville as long as her family and were part of the Creeks tribe. At fourteen, Beth had even planned her wedding to Lucien. Young, naïve, and stupid but that was once her fantasy. Heat rose in her cheeks at the blind foolishness. The scrapbook still sat on her shelf; wedding dresses, flowers, and everything else filled the pages.

"Luce doesn't deserve me." She wanted to believe the words leaving her lips, but his opinions and comments reared their ugly head. Worthless, useless, dumb, fat, and other cruel remarks had spouted from his jaws over the past three years. A knife jabbed through her heart because Lucien—the only man she had ever loved—had said them. Beth wiped her eyes, forcing a laugh to shake her belly, and departed the safety of the driveway. His sweetness had disappeared overnight under a shadow of loathing hatred, but Beth was not the cruel, lying bag of scum.

She laughed again as her gaze drifted over the paved street. Woods and farmland made up most of southeastern Alabama, but Vivian only planted what she needed for remedies. The Browns had used their acreage for peanuts and fresh vegetables too, as their ancestors had. Before the falling out, she had seen James and Dana as surrogate parents. Unlike her family, they had cared and without their love, she may have never understood what that felt like. Beth pulled up to their gated drive and smashed the call button on the security box, holding it in for good measure. A bit childish but Luce's parents would have left for work by this hour.

They lived next door on ancient Creek land, but a maintained natural forest, and tall iron fence, separated the properties. Beth did not know who put up the fence, but it had never stopped them from visiting one another. No answer came. Deft fingers danced over the steering column to a beat only she heard, and the hammer resonated from her chest. As the gate opened, Beth pressed the button again, knowing the alert buzzed long and loud.

"Knock it off, sunshine." The speaker crackled.

Her jaw tilted into the air. Lucien Brown had developed from a sickly boy on the verge of death into a girl's wet dream. All right, maybe that stretched the truth. Outward he was her wet dream. Did girls even have those dreams? A breath filled her chest and fought against her pounding heart. Tall, dark hair, handsome, and he had ice blue eyes. Oh, man she had a weakness for his baby blues. But all it ever took to disperse the delusion was for Luce to open his mouth. She slowed, winding up the driveway and willed her thundering heart to settle.

He lounged, resting against a large pecan tree, and a dawdling, easy smile squinted into his eyes. Once a week they performed the same song and dance, but seeing him never became easier. If he would just tell her why … At least he treated her kinder during the visits; he did not have an audience to share in his ridicules. Beth swallowed hard enough the gulp echoed, and Luce opened her door before backing away, forcing her to leave the vehicle.

"Well now, good morning, sunshine. To what do I owe this pleasure?" Her eyes rolled. He had called her sunshine for as long as she could remember. Beth shoved the package in Lucien's hands. Before he could object, she'd started back toward the car. "Now wait up." *Keep walking, do not listen, and just keep walking.* Her feet weighed a gazillion pounds and even forced dainty steps seemed impossible. "Beth, c'mon stop now, sugar."

She spun around and pointed a finger in his face. "What do you want?"

Anger, even forced, helped in his presence. If she kept remembering how much he'd hurt her, she would not fall into his trap. Like the stories of her youth, he was the horned snake or trickster rabbit.

He reached toward her face and tapped her freckled nose. "Well now, you know what I want." Lucien brushed a stray hair behind her ear, and Beth slanted her chin, angling her gaze away from him. "You still owe me a date."

"Nope." Three years ago, she'd given him a chance. He had ruined everything. Oh, such a fool she'd been back then. Was she any less of one now? Arms crossed high on her chest, Beth would not repeat her mistakes.

"What's in the box?" Lucien shook the package as he treaded closer. Vivian said the medicine was for him, so why would he ask.

Beth leaned against the car door, reaching behind her for the handle. "Heck if I know."

"Viv hasn't brought you in yet?" She snorted. No, on a permanent punishment she used her as the errand bitch. Lucien leaned forward, and she froze. His aftershave smelled of the woods and fire. Beth gulped the air swelling in her throat. "Tell her you want to come over tonight. Family's out of town preparing for the Green Corn Festival, right?"

Words whispered against her skin as his hot breath tickled her ear. Stars danced in her eyes as dizziness swept over her, and the blood rushed from her head. Birds sang their morning tunes as thunder rolled in the distance. Electricity pooled in her fingertips but he did not appear to notice as he pierced her against the car with his gaze.

She turned her head a notch, brushing against his rough cheek, and whispered back, "Now why'd I ever go and do a thing like that?"

"Bethy that ain't fair," he whispered as she opened the door and slid behind the wheel. Deep breaths eased the current from her hands. Lucien leaned in the window, but she refused to meet his stare. "You're always mean to me. What'd I ever do to you?"

Her jaw twitched, and fingers sparked again. "How dare you …" Lightning struck the forest despite the clear blue sky. Beth could not finish the sentence as the stinging returned to her eyes. He had broken her heart, all but tore it out and shredded her into bits, and stomped on the poor thing. Even worse, she would have let him do it again if she stayed another moment. Feet gunned the gas, and she tossed the gear into reverse. Tires screeched, peeling out, and filled the air with burnt rubber so thick she gagged on it, but Beth did not care. How dare he act innocent and not like the conceited son of a …*Wait?* Two feet slammed the brakes as she gripped the steering wheel. The brakes screamed. What had he meant Vivian hadn't brought her in yet? Brought her into what?

"Lucien."

"What?" Luce stuck his head in the window, and she yelped. Her hand touched her heart. How had he walked down the driveway so fast? Just one of many reasons Beth swore the man wasn't human. She shook her head. Lucien's gaze connected with hers, and the words fluttered away. "Never mind."

He reached over the wheel; lips hovered close to her. Breath held and constricted inside her chest as the urge to lean in overtook her mind.

Lucien turned the car off. Air refused to fill her lungs as the brush of his words tickled her lips. "I don't buy that for a minute, Bethy."

Keys jingled in front of her face, and as she reached for them, Luce snatched them away with a light chuckle. *Ah, the evil twin surfaced at last.* Would he pull her hair and call her names next? Kindergarten antics might have gone over well with his groupies, but Beth preferred a more direct approach. The games Luce played, she knew them all too well. *Fool her once and all that nonsense.*

An impish grin flashed over his face as she exited the car. A battle for the butterflies tumbled in her stomach, and Beth had to settle those fast. The devil closed in quick, and his fingers unwound her brown hair, fluffing it over her bare shoulders. *Was he flirting?* Hands cupped her cheeks, and her eyes widened. Lucien pinned her body against the car door. Each rigid muscle smooshed into her soft curves. A flutter rippled through her center.

"You're trembling, sunshine. Do I scare you?"

Yes. "No." A lump formed in her throat from the lie. The gleam in his eyes brightened. He knew the affect his closeness held over her. "You asked about Vivian bringing me in, what'd you mean?"

Lucien leaned closer and sniffed her hair, drawing the long strands out in a fan. "Tonight, Bethy, please," he pled, "I'll protect you from the locha."

But who would protect her from him? She chewed her lip weighing his proposition over. Who would defend her from her? Lord knew Luce drove her to a new level of crazy, but could the old enemy become her greatest ally?

"I'll ask." Beth left out the part where Vivian would not be home until after dark. But she planned to confide in Zoro. The familiar did not like Lucien, but the cat never allowed personal feelings to cloud his judgments either, and she needed help.

Lucien pressed her against the car door again, reminding her that he was dangerous. Breath sucked in as the spark coursed through her veins. He groaned, spreading the fire into her cheeks. Thick, full lips hovered, and the energy drew her in like a magnet. "Promise me?"

"Promise," she whispered. Luce held up his pinky and she chuckled. When was the last time they had sworn like that? Beth curled her pinky around his, ignoring the blue spark, and shook on the agreement. Blue eyes rolled over her, down, and up in a dangerous flirtatious game as if daring her to make a move. But she couldn't think straight. Luce would strike her down the moment she eased her guard. In the whole world, no amount of personal strength was strong enough to heal the damage he had inflicted. Twice couldn't happen. Her hand hovered, and she whispered, "Let me get and stop stalling."

Deliveries wouldn't make themselves. Vivian might have been out, but she did not expect her parents to be home from work until after dark. She needed to get in before they did, if she wanted free range of the basement.

The delivery schedule seemed lighter than previous weeks as Beth checked off the final drop on her list. If Vivian's remedies healed those no longer on the route that was a good sign, right? Both her aunt and father had started the business when she was younger, but the healing gene skipped her. Slipping her sunglasses on, Beth cranked up the stereo. Skipping the latte today, she headed for home, tapping her fingers along the wheel to the rhythm of the song. No cars lined the horseshoe drive as Beth parked in front of the fountain. Her heart leapt. An empty house awaited discovery, and she raced through the back door, dropping her belongings in a heap onto the floor, and barreled straight into the basement.

Earlier exploits interrupted, she searched every corner with a twirling gaze. Fingertips ran over the tarnished blades but something was off. The blades appeared unused, like ornaments or maybe they had dulled with age. Somewhere, the truth she sought lay hidden in the McCallister residence. Three years of library and clan research and she had yet to find any proof the Mandate ever revoked the family's hunting bid. Not much existed on the Mandate either, but the library was neither big nor current on Native American affairs. If the family had stored the weapons, who was to say the evidence she sought was not here too. As the clock struck five, a sighing Beth eased up the stairs, one thumping step at a time.

Zoro slept in the sun rays as she tiptoed past him. The doorbell rang as she returned the key, and he peeked at her. Those kitty eyes narrowed, but she turned on her heels. Who had let the visitor through the gate? Beth cursed and padded toward the front door as the bell rang its song again.

One quick glance at the surveillance screen showed a wavering Lucien. A scowl formed over her face but not from his pressed smile or frantic movements. A second glance showed a man trying to hide his distress. He clutched himself, a sweaty sheen plastered black bangs to his forehead, and his coloring tinted green. The whites of his eyes had yellowed, and his lips trembled despite the forced smirk. What game was this? Her brow rose as she disengaged the locks and swung the door open.

"What do you want?" she snapped. Not a game, he was ill. Lucien stumbled past her, his eyes spacious, and the heat cindered from his skin. Beth mumbled, "Sure come on in."

"Where's Viv?" Shoulders shrugged. "She gave … the wrong … package, but she's … not answering at … the shop … her cell."

Beth blinked. "She's out."

Lucien plopped—more like crumpled—onto the sofa in the sitting room. The antique Queen Anne style couch lurched across the floor. The piece had been in her family forever, and she winced. Luce did not look well at all, between the ashen skin and sweaty sheen beading over his forehead.

Beth brushed a hand across his forehead, checking him for fever. "You're burning up."

Luce glowered at her, emotions warring in those heavy blue eyes. "It's back, Bethy." Lucien clutched his stomach, nails digging into his t-shirt. "Oh, God it hurts … help me … please."

Rubbing hands over her face, she breathed deeply. *It was back.* No, it could not be back. She had saved him. The steadiness in her legs gave way, and Beth plummeted to his side. Her own feelings and emotions bubbled below the surface, and she needed to get a grip … fast.

"It can't be … this cannot happen, Luce." *No.* Lucien and she did not always agree, but she was not vindictive. Only a sicko would have wished cancer on their worst enemy. Beth would not have done half of what he had done to her. "How? What do I do? What do you need? Should I call 911?" The questions spewed from her mouth as her heart beat faster with each passing second he did not answer.

How could she help? *Please, The One Above, show me how to save him.* Her forehead touched his, and he closed his eyes, but his face twisted with pain. The sound of her heart beat louder, breaking, and thudding shards into her ears. The ticking clock overpowered the reverberation as she wracked her brain, yanking her hair by the fistful from her bun. Vivian and Dad were the experts with herbs, not her. What did she know about healing him? Last time he had been in the hospital, and the doctors had saved his life with a transplant.

"No … 911." One hand wound around his stomach, and Luce lifted the other, smoothing his thumb over her cheek. Dry lips parted, and his jagged voice cut through the stilled air. "I'm … sorry, sunshine. So sorry. This wasn't supposed to happen. I just wanted to save you, baby."

His eyes closed. "Luce," she cried. "Luce, save me from what? Talk to me. Oh my God, Lucien wake-up." But Luce did not open his eyes again. "Zoro, Zoro come quick."

The cat barreled into the sitting room, taking out a rug with him as he slid across the hardwood floor. "What is it kolko—"

His furry head cocked, and hers shook. "He just passed out." Beth held Luce's shoulders. Lightning flashed; the lights inside flickered as a large boom rattled the house that sounded more like popcorn than thunder. The power outage bathed the house in darkness. "What do I do?"

"Call Vivian." Zoro batted at him, swatted his face, and jumped on Lucien as she grabbed her cell phone. Unsteady fingers swept over the key board as she tried number after number. Beth dialed 9-1-1 but it rang and rang through the static. Abbeville didn't have a cell tower. She wiped the humidity from her skin, but only smeared the sweat of her palms. No matter what the cat did, her Lucien would not wake up. Beth toyed with kissing him but thought against the notion of a reverse sleeping beauty. Luce didn't see her as his princess even if he was her knight. At least he used to be before seeing her as a leper. "Don't stand there, call someone."

"Nothings getting through."

"The storm ..." His head cocked. "It is not yours."

"Of course it isn't me. That's ridiculous." Her head fell into shaky hands. What would Vivian do? A sigh caught in her throat as his color dangled closer to gang green. Beth ran upstairs into the library, falling twice and earning raw, skinned knees, but ignored the throbbing scrapes. Both Dad and Vivian kept herbal lore books and dictionaries there.

Rules or not Lucien was not going to die.

Fingers flipped through pages by candlelight. Paper cuts marred each fingertip. Wax splattered haphazardly along the spine. *No pain, no gain.* Every few minutes Beth rushed downstairs to check on Lucien and call their families again. No change for better or worse. Hope lit within her heart as she stared at an old Native American remedy and recalled Vivian making it for Jemma last time she had the flu. Leukemia didn't compare, but the symptoms were similar enough that she had to try.

Silence blanketed the house in addition to the constant darkness. Luce's rattled breathing and the old wind-up grandfather clock ticking in the foyer were the only constant sounds. No other noises mattered for death arrived if one stopped. Old stories spoke of death arriving whenever time halted. Lucien had not uttered a word or stirred from the chaise lounge, and Zoro had vanished. Beth lit the gas stove with a match and set a kettle to boil. Sore fingers stirred the dried herbs in the mortar and pestle. Beth measured the amounts twice before adding them to the mug. Medicinal healing wasn't her forte. Healers had a knack and not all the herbal knowledge in the world would help her save him.

Water boiled on the stove as more thick clouds settled in. Had she missed the weather report? They were close enough to the Gulf of Mexico. Gulf hurricanes hit them yearly. The emerald blades and olive glades churned into sinister puke before her eyes. Uneasiness thickened the air, electrifying the hairs on her arms. Lightning crackled the hazy skyline, and thunder followed, rattling the old glass windows. Beth bit her tongue, jumping backward from the window, as the kettle whistled.

Vivian's workshop stared at her from the window as she prepared tea, mixing in raw local honey and real cinnamon for flavor. The outbuilding was off limits. Beth chewed on her cheek. She protected it with a security code. As if beckoning her, the shed shuddered, but she did not know Vivian's password.

She hurried to Luce's side as the tincture cooled on the kitchen counter. A cool cloth dipped in witch hazel draped across his forehead. His teeth chattered behind dry lips. "Luce." Her cracked voice broke the eerie silence, and she stared out the front window. The small dogwood swayed, bending toward the ground under the violent winds. "I never thought you'd knock on my door again."

Not after the party where he'd flirted with Amber. Fingertips touched her lips wishing then and now he would have chosen her as his first kiss. Beth glanced away as wetness leaked from her eyes. She did not want him to wake and see her defenses crumble, not because of him. A silent strength survived inside of her. His verbal bullying, and those from the town, had absorbed into her thick skin, but she felt the cut and burn. They just never saw the damage or emotions. No one did but Zoro and Jemma. Despite the broken heart, he had made her prayers. Beth removed the cloth and dipped it again, wringing out the excess, and placed the cotton against his clammy skin. At least one of them had understood what true friendship—and loving one another—had meant.

Hands twisted in her lap. A tear slipped past closed lashes like life dripping through time. Welling, building, and then set free only to plummet into the ground. The foyer clock chimed six times. Once again, she reached for her phone and dialed through the numbers. Only the call to Vivian went through, but Beth received her voice mail. As the tea cooled, she repeated the actions and called 9-1-1, Viv, Jems, and both hers and Luce's parents.

As the wetness splattered on the floor, the sky opened up, and the rain poured from the heavens. The more she tried, the harder and faster the storm became as if the storm itself had not wanted her to save Lucien. Beth wiped her eyes and retrieved the tea, pausing in the hallway, and gazed at the man she had once dreamed of marrying. A silly thought to have after all the hell he'd put her through. Some loves never die though. Neither of them could take back that time; Lucien could not mend the scars he had left behind.

The saucer clattered as she set it on the antique table. To hell with a coaster, he would not die on her. His blood would not coat her hands, and no one would pin his death on her. Bad enough the whole town thought Beth nothing more than a freak of nature. She strained, gritting teeth and groaning, as his upper body lifted enough for her to slide beneath him. Black, sweaty hair rested in her lap, and she ran her fingers through it.

"Why? You owe me that much." Beth reached across his body for the tea, thankful for her long and limber limbs. Lucien shivered. "We've known each other forever. Why'd you turn on me?"

Part of her always expected the other kids to poke fun, and they did. Mom had said kids were cruel, but their opinions did not matter, and neither did their friendships. Luce though, he was her everything, her rock. Heck, she had given him her bone marrow and saved his life. And here Beth was again, saving his life, praying for his survival, but this time he had not earned her love.

"Life is delicate," Zoro said and hopped into the windowsill. The rain splattered, pinging its song against the glass.

"You better get down before Vivian catches you." Beth tilted Lucien's head with her knee. "Open your mouth."

"Isn't that dangerous?" Her shoulders shrugged but she did not glance at him. Unconscious feeding was not exactly a graduation requirement, but she had to try something. Zoro thudded on the floor and pattered to the sofa, jumping onto Lucien's belly. He still did not stir. The cat meandered up his chest and placed his paws on Luce's nostrils. "He'll open his mouth. Dribble the tea in, but aim at his cheek." Beth nodded, sucking in her breath, and releasing the steady stream. It did not calm her. Lucien's lips parted and air drew through his teeth. "Now Kolkohkafoosi."

The spoon slipped past his teeth. "Please Luce, I'll do anything. Just don't die, okay?"

Every word she was true, even if that meant playing nice and putting up with his ridicule for the rest of her life. Worse, never knowing why he had shunned her. The one regret she held was that if he did not wake, he would never know how much he'd hurt her, or how much he'd ruined her, and the crippling ache he caused day in and day out. Or how much Beth cared, despite all he'd put her through. Anyone else in that situation would have let him die. And she was well within her rights to do just that.

"Again," Zoro said. No, Luce's time wasn't over yet, and the thought echoed through her bones. She lifted the spoon to his mouth, and Zoro covered his nose. Every fifteen minutes, they repeated the process. In between, Beth prayed to save her friend as he thrashed or cried out in pain. Poor Zoro clung to him, clawing at his chest to hold on.

"Luce, you have to wake-up and tell me what you need." *I need you.* Beth loved him, but the words refused to leave her lips. Fourteen years of friendship was not enough to forgive and forget. Lucien could never know how deeply she loved him. The man was like a bad habit. Somewhere down the line, she had grown addicted to his verbal abuses, because it meant he saw her. Luce could say anything, but part of her melted whenever he had called her sunshine. For a moment, Beth recalled the old days, those days they had spent attached at the hip as they waited for their young lives to end and their adulthood to finally begin.

Lucien did not wake-up. As each hour dinged, his shakes worsened, and the worry twisted in her stomach. But the phones were still down. The tea was gone. It didn't help. Real sleep eventually overtook him again, and Beth slipped from underneath his body.

The storm raged outside, and the evening hour fell into chaotic darkness. Zoro meowed for his supper, but her appetite was nonexistent. Beth opened a can of tuna, nicking her thumb on the tin can. Nonchalantly she wiped the blood on a towel and placed the dish on the table. Vivian would have thrown a hissy fit if she caught him on the kitchen furniture. He was not some animal, but an animal with a human soul—a Spirit Walker's soul.

Pacing across the dark sitting room, Beth made more phone calls, none of which had gone through. Her eyes fixated on Lucien as his chest rose and fell with shallow breaths. A strange aroma emitted from his body like a cross between dead leaves and fire. Death touched him, and somehow, its presence peppered her tongue.

Luce mumbled, "Bethy." But his lips didn't move.

"Now I'm hearing things." Beth sighed, watching a bundled Lucien on the couch. Tossing her phone down, she crumpled on the inside. "Tell me what to do."

His fingers twined into her shirt, fiddling with the edge as it unraveled a string. Luce's face twisted again; his jaw ground as he clenched it. Such a beautiful man but that made up only a fraction of her attraction. Words like smart and funny described the boy she used to know, but this man lying on her sofa was a stranger. His pale skin shined, reflecting shades of green and yellow. Lightning lit the room. Blue eyes opened. Another flash and his eyes had closed. Eight years ago, she had witnessed the same horrific fright on his face. Lucien's parents had rushed him to the hospital. Such a frail, grey visage he had had then as he teetered on the edge of death. The doctors said he would never leave, and that her best friend was dying.

Beth proved them wrong then. Her shoulders straightened. Her hands shook. A lump swelled in her throat. Glancing toward the hallway her fists curled. "Hold on, Luce."

Out the back door and into the dreary evening she sprinted. Zoro screeched behind her as the screen door slammed in his face. Rain soaked through her thin clothing. Whispers brushed her skin, trailing goose flesh in its wake. "Huntresssss."

Slick fingers pressed codes into the keypad but none worked. Vivian ran a tight ship. A fist slammed against the metal door, and she kicked the obstruction, stubbing her toe. Laughter buzzed around her head as if a cackling spirit swooped past. Prayers muttered from her lips, as she searched for anything to knock the door down. A shovel caught her attention. Could she break the lock? *No.* Fingertips hummed. But...Beth could melt it.

Words hissed in her ear, but the wind muffled the syllables. Eyes closed; hairs stood on edge as the energies rushed toward sparking fingertips. Her mind aimed, envisioning the lock and metal melting in a blaze of white fire. Smoke billowed into her lungs, and heat dried her wet skin. Water sizzled, and her eyes opened to a thick fog. Tears blinded Beth's gaze as the smoke burned. Waving a hand in front of her face, she coughed. Calling the winds forth, she dispersed the air; a massive hole melted into the doorway greeted her. Luckily, those who controlled the electricity controlled all elements.

Metal glowed red, and ash muddied the pathway. Beth waited, glancing over her shoulder, as the edges cooled. Careful not to cut herself on the jagged metal, she crouched, duck walking her way into the safety of the shed. Inside she flicked on the light, but it didn't turn on. Beth blinked allowing her eyes to adjust to the stuffy darkness and took in the space. This building stored Vivian's herbs. Herbs she had not heard of before. Lightning struck and illuminated a large metallic door located in the back. A yellow biohazard reflected as lightning struck again. Her hand ran over the jars on the tables. Pre made tinctures lined up on one side. Another workstation held small empty boxes. Yet another table collected binders and sheets of paper with random names scribbled on its surface. Beth's heart remained unusually calm, but an after effect of using her power was serenity. A finger slid along the list, turning the pages for comparison. Under each name, Vivian had jotted a recipe. Each of the recipes called for the same ingredient.

Her brows scrunched. "What's a BAM?"

Repeated on papers, recipes, and invoices she saw that same word. A pen and pad of paper sat on the station, and she scrawled the word down. Whispers did not halt as hot breath brushed her ear. Beth shoved the paper into her bra and continued searching for anything that would have helped Lucien. The storm raged, rattling the siding. Beth slid her hand over the large metal doors. An ear rested against its cool surface. A loud hum came from inside; she unlatched the door. Icy air blasted forth, and a shiver dimpled her skin. Bags filled with dark red goo piled up to the ceiling, the plastic sacks reminded her of blood, and the bags looked like the ones her daddy had used.

Starting at a young age her parents forced her to donate blood. Dad was a phlebotomist and drew it himself. Hidden in the crease of her elbow was the scabbed puncture marks covered by fleshy

Band-Aids. Dad took blood days ago, typically every fifty-six days. But lately he took it more often than that. With a rare blood type that aided others, she never turned down a chance to lend a hand.

Beth headed for the house having melted a hole in Vivian's shed for nothing. She had written down the herbs, the measurements, and swiped a few empty vials in case she needed to make another tincture.

"Kolkohkafoosi." Zoro's wide blue eyes blinked at her. His fur stood on edge as he twined through her legs. "Did you find anything?" She noted the strained tone but shoved it aside. Even if there were something to tell, Zoro would not have told her. Guides were not endless information banks.

"Any change?" He shook his head, and Beth bee-lined for the sitting room. Luce's chest rose and fell, but his color looked an inkling better.

The stairs creaked and shuddered as she bound up them two at a time, heading again for the library. Zoro followed. "Vivian will punish you," he said of the room's disarray, but she said nothing. *Let her punish me.* Nothing mattered as long as Lucien survived.

The problems compounded as Beth sped through the indexes. BAM didn't exist. Not one author had heard or written of BAM, and she doubted the name referred to the famous Emeril Lagasse.

Lucien called out, "Beth." Her fingers flipped through another medicinal book upstairs, and her muscles froze. His strained voice enunciated each syllable. "B …e … t … h …y."

Hands sparked along the railing as she raced, rattling the house as if a stampede of elephants partied. His eyes were open. "Luce."

A prayer of thanks ran through her mind. The couch scooted as he thrashed, trying to break free of the woven blankets cocooned around him, and swaddled his arms taught. Luce's dull eyes met hers as Beth forced her best smile. He looked like hell, and that was the nice way of putting it.

"You have to tell me what Aunt Vivian made you. What's BAM?" Lucien shook his still rather greenish head, and his teeth chattered.

The clock tolled nine times. Her breath held through each chime. Beth knelt by his side and smoothed a hand over his damp brow, tenderly stroking his forehead. Lucien's heart rate steadied into a loud thundered beat as he squirmed beneath the blankets. Like an animal begging for attention, he nuzzled into her palm, and she chuckled.

"What was in the potion, Luce?" Cracked lips scratched against the cut on her finger. "I'm here. Calm down."

His eyes darted, staring at her skinned knees, and he licked his chapped lips. A whisper whimpered, "Blood."

Beth mouthed the word staring at the corked cobalt vial in his now outstretched, trembling hand. Why would he have needed blood? Whose blood? She pressed her palm to his forehead. Was this his fever talking? Beth eyed Lucien and chewed on her cheek.

"Your bl … ood … sun … shi … ne."

His eyes closed, and the empty vial shattered on the floor. She leaned away and rocked on the balls of her feet, being careful to avoid the shards. Blue eyes blinked open, and he searched the room. Without thinking, she dropped forward and smoothed the dark hair from his clammy forehead.

Why her blood? What else had been in the concoction? Why had Auntie made it for him? How had she stolen her blood? Who drank blood on a weekly basis? She'd delivered the vials every week for him. Lucien's sticky hand curled into her hair; she'd left it down from before, and he dragged her closer.

"Only yours will do." Beth's mouth dropped open, gaping at him. A million more questions raced through her mind, but she hadn't a single answer. Before blacking out she heard him say, "Forgive … me?"

$\mathcal{W}$armth surrounded her in the darkness. She opened her eyes. Piled under blankets, she awoke on the couch. A kink in her neck ached, but not from sleeping on the sofa. A light hummed from the foyer and on sleepy stumbling steps, she investigated the cause. She did not recall leaving a light on. The strangest dream blinked back in shards. Lucien drank blood in his tincture. The thought brought on a soft chuckle as she rubbed her face. Passing the mirror she halted, sliding on the rug. Fingertips pressed against her neck causing a wince as the tender skin ached. Beth rose slowly, still grasping her neck, and drew her hand away. Staring at herself, she gaped at the large hickey spanning her collar.

"He drank you, but I forced him to stop," Zoro said. He hopped up on the table and brushed against her stomach. "Take your blend Vivian made for you. Speaking of … where is everyone?"

Vivian had made an herbal blend especially formulated for combatting anemia. Beth never questioned why she was anemic, but now she had a sneaking feeling as to the answer. All the blood draws her father had done, many lapsing the usual wait time. A tear released as she forced her gaze from the mirror. Did they even donate any of it or did Luce drink it all? Her fingers drummed over the table.

"I hoped you'd know. They should've come back by now." Her parents should have at least arrived. The cat shook his head as the clock chimed eleven times. She'd been out for two hours. Fingertips skimmed the purple bruise again. What had Lucien done to her? There wasn't time to worry now. Beth checked her cell phone, but there were no messages. They were five hours late, and she prayed they were safe.

"Oh, and the inheritor is still here." Zoro licked his paw.

Beth scooped him up, holding him away from her body, and stared into his eyes. "The what?"

Floorboards creaked upstairs, and her gaze drifted toward the double staircase. Lucien hadn't left. He'd taken a shower while she'd lain unconscious, but his color had returned to normal, and he appeared healed again like the old Luce. Beth glanced away. No the old Lucien had died.

"A half breed," he said descending the stairs in his low-slung jeans and a fresh t-shirt. At the sight of him, her chest tightened. Where had he found clean clothes? Each step he drew, Beth took two backwards and clutched Zoro tighter. A slow smile spread over his lips.

"Part human like you, but my distant ancestor was the Jumlin." The wall hit her back. Native Americans had a few names for his ancestor, but Jumlin had not meant a vampire, not like Hollywood painted them. "Put the cat down, sunshine." Zoro jumped from her arms, skittered across the room, and she shot the traitor a glare. Lucien's tone softened as he added, "I won't hurt you."

But he had already hurt her. "You … you … marked me." Lucien's finger skimmed the bruise, but his grin widened as if he'd won some miraculous prize. Hazel eyes narrowed, and her fingers curled at her sides, sparks shattering the stillness. "You … you … bit me."

Blue eyes bore into hers. "Bethy." Luce leaned in close enough to pack her lungs with his campfire fragrance. An old comfort tugged at her belly, but her mind screamed otherwise. Against her lips he whispered, "I'll do it again and again, sunshine, but next time I'll ask." Pain wrinkled his forehead. "You will let me, right?"

"Let you?" Her lips quivered and pressed down. "Let you?" Her tone pitched higher. Beth tilted her chin, lifting it into the air. *No fear*, the phrase repeated in her head, and she slammed her foot on top of his. "Why would I let you talk to me, let alone touch me?"

"Ouch." Was this all she was worth to him? Beth shoved past him and ran for the stairs without looking back. Lucien proved faster and blocked the landing.

"Move," she growled, and her fingertips flickered blue.

The energy of the room yanked free and coursed through Beth's conduit veins. Blue and white streams drew toward her from the walls and electronics. Vivian would skin her hide when she came home. No amount of fireproofing could stop a 54,000-degree bolt of electricity. Nostrils flared attempting to take more air. Paint melted and bubbled on the walls, and the floors blistered under their feet. Beth swallowed hard, tasting the fumes on her tongue. Glass liquefied as she pressed upon Lucien, turning the tides. He hadn't burned, but neither had Zoro. As her familiar, he was immune to her magic. But why was Luce?

His calm demeanor cracked. "Let me explain, please, Bethy."

"There's nothing to explain, Luce." She pushed him and released the electricity straight into his chest. Lucien's body lit up in blue tones, skin cracked, and he tremored as if absorbing her power. She pushed more power, seeking the point it would tear him asunder. "And you have no right to call me that."

Zoro hissed at her feet. "You will kill him. Control yourself child." Smoke and black patches formed over his skin. *Crap. No. Yes. Die.* All those words ransacked Beth's mind. Evil deserved to die.

Anyone who wasn't a Spirit Walker or an ordinary human must die. The Mandate had said so. Drain them dry they had said. "Bethany, you must stop before it is too late; you will kill him."

Lucien moved, and not in the oh-my-god-I-am-being-electrocuted way, but with sure-footed movements, and a devil may die smirk plastered over his dimpled cheeks. He cupped her face; her jaw dropped as the energy poured back into her body. Damaged lights remained off as they stood in total darkness on the staircase. Burnt wood, leather, and a hundred items she could not name assaulted her senses, souring her stomach. Sweat trickled down her forehead, sizzling and tickling along her nose. "Bethy, I am not the rabbit nor am I the snake. I am but a man after his own heart."

She stammered, "How," instead of screaming bullshit. Both the rabbit and the horned snakes showed up in lore stories as typical tricksters.

Electricity should have fried him on the spot. The heat alone should have evaporated him into dust. Zoro was immune, but Luce's heart should have stopped, yet with a single touch he had become like distilled water and neutralized her attack. Beth blinked as her eyes adjusted, and the dim moonlight bathed the world. The storm had ended.

"Easy, I have your blood," he lifted his arms, "inside of me." Beth slapped him across the face. "I'll let that one slide." Lucien winked and staggered forward. His forehead bent to hers. "Every hero needs an Achilles heel. Our world demands balance." She shoved him away, fleeing up the remaining steps and down the hall. "Love a good chase, sunshine."

Beth skidded to a halt a moment too late, barreling right into Lucien's chest. Strong arms engulfed her, and it did not take long before he had her pressed against the wall, pinning her hands overhead. Kicking his shins, he smiled at the feeble attempts. Lucien bent closer, and his lips skimmed hers. A gasp rose as her heart hammered away at her ribcage.

Those devious lips trailed over Beth's jaw as her body surrendered, shuddering beneath his magical touch. Tension and fight trickled away, but memories whispered, reminding her of the damage he had once caused. Ache followed in Lucien's wake and soon enough his venom would engulf her. Could she be strong enough to survive him again? *No.* She barely survived the first time. "Stop, please, Luce."

Lucien released her and stepped aside. Beth's eyes fell to the floor, unable to meet his gaze. The laughter still riddled her ears from that fateful day, yesterdays too, and her neck sweltered.

"Sunshine." His rough voice called, but she still did not look at him. Lucien stroked her cheek, and only then had Beth realized the tears fell. "I never meant to hurt you."

The twinge in his voice struck a nerve. Fists balled and furled at her sides. How dare he apologize now? How dare he act as if he'd learned of her pain for the first time? *No.* "Get out of my house."

"Sugar—"

Beth punched him, and he stumbled toward the staircase. The words ground from her tight jaw as her feet stomped over the antique floor. "Get out of my life."

"—Bethy you don't."

Hazel eyes narrowed as the electricity brewed again and illuminated the hallway and staircase in a glow of blue fire. "Lucifer, ha. Get. Out. Now."

"No, I ain't leaving." She pressed onward as he descended the staircase backward. Oh, he would leave all right, even if she had to leave too. Lucifer yes, no more Lucien or Luce for his evil, conniving ass, not after all he'd done.

"Bethy baby," a brow rose at the pet name, "let me protect you … and … we'll …" Beth backed him against the front door, and his blue eyes widened. Had he thought syrupy but vacant words could fool her again? "Please don't do this." Her body pressed against his, and his breath cut through her. "They'll take you too and … I'm trying to make this right. I screwed up."

A hand constrained his chest. "What do you mean they will take me too? Who the heck are *they*, Luce? Who'd *they* take?" Each pump of his heart pulsed against her palm. Long ago, she had memorized his strange rhythm, but never questioned why.

His thumbs smoothed over the tear stains. "The Mandate. They aren't what you think." She snorted, shaking her head at the absurdity of his accusation. The Mandate watched over Native American affairs.

They did so much for the Native American population. Why would they have taken her family? "She really hasn't taught you a damn thing." Lucien kissed her, and she punched his shoulder, but he pulled away with a big fat grin. *What had gotten into him?* Beth blinked and wondered why he had said they took her family. Rough palms grasped her face and drew her in again. "All this time." Another kiss set the wrinkles in her furrowed brow. He snickered, grinning like a Cheshire cat, and she wanted to slap it off his face. Dipping in again, and again, she found no words of protest as each kiss shocked her heart like static electricity. Too late, as Lucien invaded her mouth, Beth kissed him back, more than kissed as her hands curled into his shirt and dragged him closer.

Groaning—his tongue stirred more than her mouth. Tasting sweet and somehow salty too, he enticed her to delve deeper. Tension building and welling deep in her center, as it never had before, caused her limbs to tremble, and her grip tightened as he yanked a fistful of her hair. Beth wrenched away stumbling backward as the dizziness warred inside her head. Deep breaths filled her lungs but did not settle the fight. She could not kiss the man responsible for her pain and forget.

"Say something, Bethy." Hand hovering, she covered her tingling lips as he stepped toward her. Words did not exist. Brows rose higher as she inched away. A rumble sounded in the distance slowly rolling and rattling the windows.

She said nothing, scaling the steps backwards, and refusing to avert her gaze as he closed in on her. Withdrawing until she had reached her room, Beth closed and locked her bedroom door. No chase. Her head leaned against the door as the sigh released, but she felt his energy through the wooden barrier as she always had in the past. Words did not exist for what she had done or he had said. Kissing Luce was a mistake. Her eyes closed, and she willed her heart to steady, but the throbbing continued as if a hand squeezed it. Nothing would ever erase the damage he brought into her life three years ago. But how long could she withstand him before she had caved?

Luce drank blood too, but Beth found no fault there. Human or not, she saw the frail boy dying when she looked into his eyes.

Everyone deserved a chance at life, right? *Just a kid that grew into a man* .... A sigh tickled her chest as she opened her eyes to the darkness of her world. Zoro slept on her bed, sprawled out in the middle as if he'd owned the place. As if Beth hadn't almost set the whole house on fire. The life of a cat appealed to her if it were only that simple, but she knew it wasn't. Zoro was not any old cat any more than she was an ordinary human. What was Luce? Inheritor didn't define him alone although the Mandate would have used it against him.

Nails tapped over the door as she connected all she had known of her former best friend. The lies started long ago but she never suspected anything amiss until he had shunned her. Beth paced, bare feet sliding over the shag rug. Reliving those days as the memories of her former best friend arose, ransacking her brain with more questions than answers. Her likeness caught in the mirror, and she questioned Lucien's game again. In her nineteen years, no one had ever wanted her, and she could not fathom why he would have shown any interest in her—not after three years of hating her guts. Even with her weight out of the question, and the family name, there just wasn't anything special about Bethany McCallister. Plain Jane, Sarah Plain and Tall, Laura Wilder, all of them had a plain beauty that radiated from within. She had nothing but electricity and blood.

"How could I have been so blind?"

Chapter Three

*L*ucien *needed* her blood. The mirror reflected his only source. He *wanted* her blood. No other reason for wanting her made a lick of sense. A sob swallowed, catching in her throat. The other girls had more to offer—Amber had more to offer. Fingertips brushed her lips; nails cut into the surface. All of her experiences tied back to him from touch to kiss. None of the other boys had paid her any mind except in mocking, but their whispers did not start until he had turned his back on her. The girls at school were always cruel.

The name-calling cut her, but it had stung more from his lips. Lucien had looked at her, though he too had poked fun. Zoro snored, and her brows arched, wondering if familiar life played out any better. Did he deal with this high school crap too when he had been a human?

Invisible scars he left behind had not healed, and Lucien's presence was akin to dousing her wounds with salt and vinegar. But she bit back the tears, burying them deeper than ever before. Why couldn't he leave her in peace and allow her to live out this miserable existence alone?

The balcony locks clicked one by one, as she turned the knobs. Beth slid the door open to the wrap around balcony and stepped into the warm night. A low hum coursed over the wind and caressed her skin. Like a call to her soul, the air rolled in waves and whispered her hopes and fears. It made promises too. Beth closed her eyes as the element slithered, "Huntress."

Trembles wracked her body, and she inched back inside. Wide eyes darted into the shadows with each staggered step. Unknown hands seized her, and she screamed as a rough, acrid palm, covered her mouth. Her elbow flung back, and Beth stomped her foot on the intruder but she connected with air. A scream released as the curtain strangled her, yanking free from the rod.

The assailant released her, electricity sparking in her hands, and she swung around. Lucien pounded on the door, and Beth tripped over herself, landing face first on the floor as he knocked the barrier down. Breath caught, strangling at the wild fire glowing in his eyes and the electrical pulse vibrating in his hand. Those powers weren't of the inheritor. Speed, strength, and drinking blood yes, Beth gulped, mind control made the list too. But she did not know the finer workings of the sub-species. It wasn't as if they studied them in class. Summoning elements and electricity did not make the list.

Vampires did not always have magic in popular books or television shows. Did he lie to her? Wind gusted through the room and ruffled his dark hair as he scanned the space. Four long strides and he slammed the balcony door closed. The air shifted, burning with melted plastic. His muscles twitched as he gazed through the glass. Lucien's attention rained on her.

"Don't scream like that," he grumbled, fabric rustled as he kicked the curtain tangled around his leg, and he faced Beth. A scowl set in his rough jaw as he loomed above her. Strong shoulders uncoiled the tension, and Luce cracked his neck. His hand extended, and she stared at it.

"C'mon." Beth rolled her eyes and hoisted herself off the carpet, dusting invisible dirt from her clothing. Cheeks burned hot, but the cover of darkness hid her embarrassment. "I expected a more gory room, sunshine." Her arms crossed over her chest. Lucien's eyes followed the movements, and she released herself. Hot and cold, night and day, yes that was the new Lucien. "No Goth posters or black walls."

She raised a black brow seeing as she was not anywhere near Goth. Confidences reigned in the light of day but dwindled in the darkened shadows of the locha. Blue eyes pinned her against an invisible wall and his fiery scent curled around her neck. "Unicorns, dragons, faeries, rainbows," and he lifted a stuffed animal from the shelf, "teddy bears?"

The room had survived the surge. A sigh hissed through her tightened jaw as he continued invading her private space. The last time he had been here, he would have only come to her shoulders. Beth stared at her hands, palms facing the heavens. Luce had to go.

"You still have this?" He reached for the photo album, but she swatted at him. "C'mon sunshine …" The video camera crashed from the bear and clattered under her desk. "What was that?"

Beth dove for it, but Luce swiped down, knocking his head into hers, and he grabbed the camera first. A hand rubbed where his thick skull had banged into hers. His dark brows smashed together as a titan grip smashed the camcorder into plastic and metal bits. Its remnants plunged to the floor. They stared at each other blinking. She had forgotten about the camera. Shaky fingers swirled through the debris; she winced, nicking herself. Lucien moved first, leaning in and grabbing her hand. His tongue swirled over the tip and she shivered, sparring against the tightness in her belly. Drawing away, his warm lips brushed her forehead.

"Sorry," he whispered. She shook her head. What exactly was he sorry for: kissing her, breaking the camera, someone entering her space, or for him hurting her?

Beth ripped the bear from his hand, hopped from the floor, and tossed him next to a snoring Zoro. *No. Vivian had not taped her.* Black hair tossed from side to side as she glowered at the evidence lying next to her familiar playing possum. Lucien spoke, but Beth couldn't make out the words. Hands covered her face, fighting the burning rising inside of her throat. How dare they … who else could have planted a camera? To believe her own family had infiltrated the private space and taped her … what else had they done?

"Just proves you don't know me at all," Beth whispered and winced, realizing how true the words were and ignoring the evidence smashed into dust at Luce's feet as if discounting the truth somehow changed the facts.

"What don't I know?" Lucien tore her hands away, squeezing them. She stared at the pocket of his t-shirt and refused to look at him. "Sunshine," his voice strained, "what don't I know?"

Her arms tossed in the air leaving his hold. Cold crept over her sweaty palms as thoughts and words collided within her mind. A finger poked in his chest. "You have no right judging me or my things." Pale cream walls lined with pink and lavender stripes closed in on her, spinning as she wobbled, and Lucien grasped her elbow. To her it was always just a room, some place Beth escaped to. But it was a lie. Her gaze drifted to the empty teddy bear spot on the shelf. That too had been a lie. The one place she felt safe. Beth's lip wavered, and she turned her head before Lucien saw her weakness.

"No one knows you better than me." His hand grasped her shoulder, and every muscle seized. Was the camera his? "No." He scoffed at her thoughts? "Your hopes and dreams, even your hatred and pain," his fingers stroked down to her heart, "I feel you." Lucien brushed her hair to the side. "You can hate me tomorrow, and I'd feel that too."

She gulped; he moved behind her, drawing her against his chest. The beat of his heart quickened, massaging her muscles with every thump. Still he was not making any sense. She chewed her cheek as her mind reeled and digested his words. What did he mean he could feel her? And how did he answer her thoughts?

"If you can feel all that then why are you still here?" Every inch of courage mustered into her throat.

"Still a traditionalist," he whispered combing fingers through her long locks and changing the subject. "I like that." But he wasn't big on traditions. Lucien did not shave his head as their ancestors had or worn a roach—a headdress made from porcupine quills. Slowly she spun, swaying to an unheard beat. Thighs brushed hers, and he bent his head, angling her chin.

"Get a room," Zoro said. Laughter spewed at his asinine statement, and Beth grounded herself on the cat's distraction, refusing to admit any of Lucien's attentions as reality.

She pinched herself, tugging harder with each pull. Beth would not wake-up, and she needed to wake-up now. "Stop that," Lucien whispered in her ear.

Distant eyes connected with Beth. The familiar witnessed all the awful ache she had endured from this man. That same treacherous man's arms encompassed her waist; Lucien held her tighter, plastering her backside against him. Beth's gaze faltered and dropped to the wooden floor. Dust bunnies collected on its surface along with Zoro's fur. Was this a dream? Would her dream-self fight the natural draw to her ex best friend? How could something so wrong feel so right? Beth did not trust herself to say no again. Rough lips skimmed across her shoulder, and her body quaked against him. Saliva flooded her mouth and she swallowed hard. Once upon a time, she had dreamed of Lucien, but he was not the same man clutching hold of her in the darkness.

"Last I checked this was her room." A shiver erupted over her skin as his teeth grazed flesh. Rough hands skimmed her sides as if he was massaging her insides. Every ounce of her wanted to let go, meld with the man she'd dreamed of marrying, but the raw ache seeped from her invisible wounds, burning the reminder as if it had begun yesterday.

His ears plastered against his head, and he swatted the air with his tawny paw. Zoro hissed and growled. "Let go of her, leech."

Lucien let go and Beth stumbled, ripped from her dream, and tumbled face first into reality. Eyes, bluer than the ocean, charged with tiny bolts as she scrambled away. Zoro did not back down, but he asked, "Are you okay Beth?"

Slowly she nodded, glancing between them. On one hand, Luce was right. It was her room, but Zoro knew she wanted him to leave too. Lucien's jaw twitched. "Are we swinging insults now? Do I call you tuna breath? No, perhaps rat is better, because I sure smell one." His gaze narrowed on her feline companion. Beth leaned against her dresser steadying herself as the air crackled and thunder roared outside. The pitter-patter of rain followed as the ions in the air tickled her nose.

"Stop it," she said interlacing her words and laughter. "Good night, y'all may leave." She stumbled toward the bed, shaking her head. "Don't let the door hit your ass on the way out."

"No," he growled low. The cat knew better, or maybe he feared Luce and high tailed it from the room. "You shouldn't trust him. He's keeping secrets."

A snort burned her nose. Familiars told their Spirit Walkers only what they needed to know, of course, they kept secrets. She should not have trusted *Lucien*. Not now and certainly not all those years ago. Beth stiffened. Sounds of beating hearts and breathes filled the bedroom as the wheels within her mind churned. Hands chased the shiver rushing over her bare arms. If he accused Zoro of keeping secrets, did that mean Luce had kept them too? Outside lightning struck a pecan tree in the grove, and thunder followed rocking the house. Its vibration reached from the balls of her feet to the top of her head. She blinked, gazing out the balcony window, her reflection flashing back as he snuck behind her.

"Bethy?"

"Don't," she spun around and shoved him away, "don't you dare tell me who to trust."

Shadows shrouded Lucien, but the creak of his steps echoed in the quiet house. Scooping her up, he leaned her backwards onto the bed, staring into her eyes as her lungs struggled for breath. Deciphering the gleam in his blue eyes, she found lust, but what else warred inside his mind? That she was too hideous, was that why he'd hurt her?

"One day I will take what's mine, but sleep well, sunshine."

"I'm not sleepy." Her mouth dropped as his words registered. "And I'm not yours."

Lucien rose, peeling off his t-shirt, and words ceased as she eyed his flesh illuminated by the lightning. To others he might have appeared imperfect without washboard abs, but he wasn't overweight like her. His dark trail escorted her eyes downhill toward the center of his stomach. Beth tried to glance away, but her eyes ventured further south to the bulge in his dark jeans. Heat and musk radiated from there, and she did not enjoy the effects. *No, not from him, anyone but him.* Her mind and heart howled, but her body betrayed them both. Fire scorched her belly, and the shiver hardened her nipples. And that damn smirk said he dang well knew what he did to her. Jerk.

"Your turn, Bethy." His lashes lowered, but the sultry glance sizzled.

Heat returned to her cheeks, and she glanced away. "This isn't show and tell. Leave." She pointed toward the door and snapped her fingers. Lucien climbed onto the bed and drew the covers to the side. Her lip bled as she gnawed the surface, attempting to sort out her predicament.

An idea slowly hatched. A lazy grin egged her on as he sighed into her pillow. Beth jumped from the bed, gathered pajamas, and readied for bed. The sooner he slept, the quicker he would leave her alone, but if he wanted to play games then so be it.

Lucien's eyes remained on Beth, burning a path along her spine. She lifted her t-shirt. The bra dropped, and his breath hitched. The satin and lace negligee slid over her skin and hugged each curve. The yoga pants were last, but she'd made sure to hike up the back of the nightgown and flash her thong as her feet kicked them down. "Trying to kill me, Bethy?"

Oh, one could hope, not that he would have had any of her. As southerners often said, Lucien had about a hell's chance at getting in her pants. Beth knelt, ignoring his remarks, and said her prayers.

Beth still worried about her family, and what Lucien had said about the Mandate, but he was not exactly forthcoming either. When she finished, he patted the bed as if she was some puppy dog. Fists balled into the edge of the bed skirt. To make matters worse, she had dreamt of this moment too. The moment where they would be alone, and she'd pour her soul out to him. Lucien acted as if he knew pain, but she doubted his view scratched the surface of her scars.

He pulled the covers aside as she stood. Tingles spread as her hormones surged. *Yes, it's just the hormones and having a half-naked man in her bed.* Uttering her reluctance, Beth climbed into bed and scooted under the covers. Again, she thanked The One Above, but this time for the king size bed. Little good it did. Lucien scooted closer to her side. The warmth of his skin radiated into her bones as his arm draped across her belly. Such a simple touch but she hated that it had come from him.

A dream lay inches away, and she would have lied if his presence were not on her mind or affecting her body. Her eyes clamped shut, and her mind forced in every direction but his presence. She failed in the silence as his breathing and heartbeat brought those old memories to the surface. A battle ripped between the dreams she had prayed would become reality versus the truth. Without reason or cause, the man holding her heart had crushed her. Shredded her heart into tiny pieces and even she did not know if The One Above himself could have fixed her or their friendship. Trust did not exist anymore, as it too had dried and withered away. A sigh released with a single drop and the following sob rattled her chest. Dithering between want and need, her thoughts, bumbled and collided.

Beth thought apologies would save them, but he did that already. The deceits and half-truths he had told compounded on her shoulders, drawing her down under the sea of lies. "When did I lie to you?" She froze. Had he answered her thoughts again? What the heck was he? She inched out of bed. Lucien's hands dragged her back and held her hostage. His hot breath tickled her neck as he rolled over her. Even in the dark his eyes lit, casting a bluish glow over his face. "Never. I've never lied."

He still lied. Lucien waited for an answer. Deep down Beth saw the poison in his words. Three years ago, she was naive. "How is it you know what I am?"

"Our family's known each other for centuries." Lucien moved over. "Vivian excluded you, though I don't know why she told me otherwise." He chuckled, and Beth glanced across her pillow. Luce softened, a hand covering his mouth, and he whispered, "You tried to kill me."

Beth snapped, "I saved you. Why would the Mandate take my family? What do you mean Vivian excluded me? You're talking in circles and hurting my head. Start explaining or shut up." He chuckled again. She growled, narrowed her eyes, and heaved him from the bed.

Landing with a thud, Lucien sighed and righted himself, sliding under the covers once more. Unable to make sense of him or why the Mandate took her family, Beth chewed her cheek. Vivian must have done something illegal, but she was always so by the book with all her rules.

"To get to you."

Beth blinked. "Why me? What'd I do?" What could she have had that the Mandate wanted? They already knew she was a Spirit Walker and by extension a huntress. Did they want to train her? Her face pinched as pain shot through her brain. Water, she needed water. Why her, she asked silently again as she retreated to the bathroom and filled a cup with cold water. One, two, three glasses chugged and the water sloshed in her belly. Beth's mind reeled around to the same question: what made her so special?

"You've asked that a lot tonight." She shrieked and a hand covered her heart. Lucien leaned on the door frame behind her. "Sorry."

"Not aloud." She spun and swatted at Lucien for scaring her. Sneaking up on her was not an easy feat due to her superior hearing. Increased vision was nice too. He grasped her hand and squeezed. A new word lingered at the tip of her tongue, swelling like her eyes, but she couldn't ask. Beth feared his answer. Letting her hand drop, his fingers danced up her arm, and traced a path over her shoulder. "What is an inheritor?"

"Me." Lips replaced fingers as a chill swept over her body from the inside out. "That's not what you want to ask, is it?" She said nothing; unable to trust her thoughts she barred it from her mind. "Give me your hand again."

"Why?" The word rolled like ash. All her questions had begun with why. The reflection wavered as he stood behind her. Lucien was not buff by any means but his body was harder than hers was. Buff was not her type, not that she had one. She wanted to know why he said those hurtful things to her. Why he had made her promises, broke them, and then had laughed in her face as if she was a moron for expecting anything from him. Beth dried her hands and slipped from the bathroom, but he tossed an arm in her path.

"You were always a stubborn puss." His breath blew over her shoulders as she stared into the dark bedroom. "Bethy baby, just give me your damned hand."

Grasping the negligee in her hands, she ducked under his arm, twirling from his reach, and lain in bed again. The bed creaked and shifted as he silently joined her, and she nibbled her cheek, waiting for him to fall asleep. "Let me see your hand," he said. Beth sighed and did as he asked. Chapped lips caressed each fingertip, and his tongue teased the tender skin. Each kiss or lick tightened her stomach, but Beth studied Lucien, peering at him over her shoulder. The knowing smile said all she'd needed to know. This was another game.

"Give me your other hand." A statement issued, not a question as he reached across her; Lucien dragged her closer. "You think it's your blood I crave?"

No other reason made sense to her after how he'd treated her. He snaked their joined hands over his chest. The thick forest of hair gave way to a sparse trail as each hair tickled her palms. Before Beth could protest, he had placed her palm on his crotch. She gasped, drawing her hand away, but he tightened his grip, and moaned. Beneath the surface, he leapt and pulsed against her hand. Heat seared her skin, sweeping across her cheeks, and flushing down her neck.

"Your smile, laugh, your scent drives me insane. Always has, even before I understood what it all meant. The blood running through your veins might heal me, but I'd suffer without, just to prove it. If you'd open yourself to me, you would see how much you truly are my sunshine."

Beth yanked her hands away from him. "Just stop it." She threw the covers off and stormed to the balcony door, shivering, and rubbing her arms. "Don't say things you don't mean, and stop touching me." Tears prickled her eyes, and she chided herself for not making him leave, for not marching out the door herself. Breath fogged the window. Odd how tonight the strange watching sensations ended as if Luce chased the dark away. "You don't own me. You don't even like me."

"I don't lie," he growled, grasping her shoulders. A shriek left her lips as he twisted her around, pressing her back to the balcony door. "I want you, every last inch of you." Lucien's lids lowered as the air heated, and he nibbled on his bottom lip. Caging Beth in his hands, they squeaked, as they drew along the glass and she shuddered. "For years I've chased after you. You always shoot me down."

A hand touched his forehead. "What are you doing?"

"Checking for a fever."

Lucien cocked his head. "Why?"

"Because you're talking like a belligerent idiot." Two possible conclusions presented themselves. Either he was the dumbest man on this planet or he hadn't known she was there that night. Lucien's brow creased, and Beth nodded as she withdrew her hand. The night he had claimed illness, but she saw him at the party. Jemma had talked her into going despite the lack of escort and lied to Vivian for her too. Cut number one had burned, but the hushed whispers and giggles he'd shared with his real date burned into Beth's soul. She altered her gaze, staring at his throat as he swallowed hard. "Just go away, Luce. You ... you don't want me. I think we both ... know that"

Beth sniffled as her resolve crumbled, resembling the state of her heart. Prayers ransacked her mind begging that he didn't ask her again. Temptation and weakness stood stoically before her, within her grasp, but she stood too, wounds dripping in an invisible bloody mess. The gashes he had inflicted on her soul, and he said nothing. Breaths passed as she eyed the rise and fall of his chest. Rough fingers stroked her cheek, but she turned her head, starring at the floor. How could she love him so much after all the pain she had lived through?

Silence bloomed between them. Rumors had followed her for years. How she'd actually thought herself worthy of Lucien Brown's attention. Whispers spouted in otherwise silent corridors as she passed through the hallways and streets. How *he* could not stand the sight of Beth. Maybe she could not blame the others. It was not as if they had known of her super hearing. *He* knew. *He* admitted it that tonight. *He* knew what she was and that she was different.

But the Lucien she knew alone and in public were two different people. Like he had not wanted others to know that, they were once friends. Once upon a time, he had planned a future with her. Her gaze drifted to the old book filled with their shared dream. Dust particles shattered into the moon light as if the dream itself burst. Maybe she was being silly for holding on to that dream or any of her dreams. How many kids had grown up and married their childhood sweethearts?

In her mind, she deserved better than a man who lashed out and burned her, but the heart would not listen. Would it listen to her now?

Clouds blocked the moonlight. Those moments relived in his presence. Her hands trembled, and her heart ached something fierce. Somehow, he knew what Beth thought. Wind howled through the trees. No relief came in his learning the truth either, only more pain compounded within her heart and soul, as he said nothing. Thunder rumbled in the distance and lightning flickered to the tune of her heartbeat. Fearing the truth, she stared into the corner, eyes settling on a crack in the paint.

A white elephant ransacked the room, and the satisfaction she received was his silence. No sorry in the world would fix it, not without an explanation of why. Lucien grasped her chin and forced her gaze to him. Out of defiance, she fixated on the scar on his chin; he had received it falling from a tree before his diagnosis.

Confusion and something Beth could not explain crossed his face as he stared into her eyes. Her chin tilted higher, slipping from his fingers, and she matched his gaze. Beth vowed never to fall for his tricks again or anyone else's crap. One day she would find someone who loved her. Someone who did not ridicule her, did not judge her. After that night, Beth had poured her energy, learning all she could from the books on becoming a huntress. The books eventually led her to believe he wasn't human, but they'd not named evil directly beyond the locha. For what he'd done to her maybe, Lucien was both.

"I'm going to say this once more seeing as you ain't listening. I have never lied to you. That wasn't me at the party, and only you have ever mattered to me. Beth, I have loved you for as long as I have known you. I would never hurt you. One day you'll see the truth, and I hope to God it's sooner than later."

Her hand raised, ready to swoop across his face, but Lucien stormed out the broken door as Beth stood there like a mouth-breathing idiot wondering what planet that boy hailed from, because it sure as heck wasn't Earth. *How dare Luce say he never lies and lie right to my face?*

"No. He doesn't get to walk away." Her fists curled, and her head throbbed. A purring sound drew her attention, and Beth found Zoro sitting at her feet meowing.

The cat asked, "Do you really want to know?" She knelt and petted through his long silky fur. Sometimes it relaxed her, but her familiar's comfort served only to fuel the fire.

"I was there." Zoro rubbed his nose against hers. She glanced at the clock. Midnight had come and gone. "I can't trust him if he keeps lying."

Lucien didn't lie to her before that day. At least not that she had known of. What had changed? What did she do or not do? "You did nothing wrong," Zoro said, "He doesn't know how to apologize." All he had to do was tell her why. What was so hard about that? "His intentions were noble."

Breath huffed, vibrating her lips. Only a few hours remained before dawn, and she needed sleep. Explaining wasn't rocket science. With Zoro in tow, she slipped into bed, ignoring the clattering metal sounds resonating from the basement. If that were not hard enough to sleep through, Lucien's constant yelling halted her efforts too. A string of curses left her lips. The covers flung aside, and she stormed downstairs and into the basement.

A whooshing sound filled the dusty space. Lucien swung a sword through the air. His back faced the staircase, and Beth observed him for a spell from the shelter of the steps. Zoro's words replayed in her head, but they did not make sense. Nothing made sense the more she thought about her life. If she had done nothing, why did that make it tougher to clarify?

Words left his mouth with every thrust or swish of the blade, but she made one out. Mandate: he repeated the word along with some colorful adjectives. Arms hugged her legs, shifting to remain hidden. Beth enjoyed watching him move as his dark skin danced and glistened under the florescent lights. Maybe the kids at school were right. She didn't deserve him. Lucien was imported chocolate while she was bobo brand in the clearance bin. Her chin rested on her hands, and she rubbernecked, peeking around the corner. A breathy sigh sounded from within her chest, not so much to his verbal retorts, but at the jeans clinging to his defined hips. Men always had the cutest butts. Muscles arrested along his shoulder blades, and he slowly faced her. Sweat glistened off his hirsute chest; a lazy bead dribbled over his stomach, and her eyes followed. Some girls hated sweaty guys, but a brutal magnificence subsisted in a sweat-covered man. Beth had exhausted many sunny days admiring Lucian from a safe distance, averting her gaze whenever he had glanced her way. He did the same then, but she did not look away.

"I found this room today," she said trying to deter attention from her no good lusty thoughts.

His lips turned up. "I always knew." Lucien rolled his shoulders; strong arms whizzed through the air.

"That we had the room?" Beth blinked wondering why Vivian had told him.

Lucien laughed and shook his head. "I knew you watched me … and the room. I have one too." His gaze rolled over her. "I watched you too, sunshine."

Beth pondered his comment and added up all the times she'd thought he stalked her, all the objects that had moved or emitted sounds when she would have otherwise assumed herself alone. Like the other night in the park. Luce nodded, putting the sword in its holder on the wall. No matter where Beth ended up in town, he would be there too. Another nod issued from his sweat-drenched head. The town was small, but Abbeville wasn't that small.

"I'm not sure what bothers me more, that you've claimed someone impersonated you, that you know what I'm thinking, or that you've spent the last three years being an ass. Either way you're guilty, Luce, guilty as sin." His head cocked, and he glanced at the weapons. Did he find it strange they were tarnished but dull? Nothing in her thoughts would give a hint to the words she wanted him to say. Whatever he hid, she wanted it to come out because he wanted her to know, not out of guilt, but her curiosity won the battle. Her hands wrapped around her belly and squeezed. "Why? I deserve to know."

"You saw me that night, right?" Beth swallowed hard and recalled the pinnacle moment their eyes had connected during the party. "When else?"

"At school, the coffee shop, and just around." Shoulders shrugged as she stared at her fingertips, flicking dust from her nightgown.

"You leave every morning for deliveries and then again in the afternoon and head to the library. At three, you grab a coffee and read on Main Street. Yes," he cracked his neck, "I stalk your every move." Fingers fidgeted, yanking invisible loose threads from her nightgown.

"Bethy, I wish I could take it all back. I wish you would believe me. Do you know why I take the elixir?" She shook her head as he changed the subject. "Your blood keeps my illness under control."

Illness. The shakes and chills made sense, but Beth thought the inhibitor immune to illness and injury. "I have Leukemia, and your dear Aunt Vivian has treated it for as long as I can recall. Do you remember when I was in the hospital?" She nodded and chewed her lip. Hard to believe it now, but in those days they had been best friends. Like peas and carrots or grits and eggs. He had appeared frail and half-dead much like earlier today. Doctors searched for a marrow donor, but his parents weren't compatible. Vivian, her dad, and mom all tested negative too. At eleven years old, she'd begged her family to test her marrow. Beth would have done anything for Lucien. Because they were not a match, the doctors and her family had said no. But she'd thrown one of the biggest fits ever, and they had caved. Turned out they were compatible.

Lucien said, "We never got that far."

A tear slid down her cheek, and she fisted the negligée. A fit full of nerves then and now, but Beth knew in her heart, that she had made the right choice to save her friend's life. Despite the three years of hatred and ridicule, she would never have denied Lucien life. She blinked. Was that it? Had Lucien Brown wanted to die? Her knees popped as she rose from the stairs.

"No," he whispered. "I had much to live for and still do, sweetheart."

Beth stepped toward him but stopped, cocking her head. "I remember the nurse putting me under."

"Vivian gave me your blood; she stole it from the hospital and changed the records. She *knew* your blood would've saved me from the start. Your blood heals ..." He did not need to finished as Beth winced. Luce had been sick for years and *she knew*? Teeth mashed into her bottom lip as heat rose on her neck. All the pain he had endured ... Sparks lit her fingertips ... All the people who had died ... She whispered, choking on a sob, "Why didn't anyone tell me?"

Lucien hurried to her and cupped her cheek, wiping the tear away with his thumb. How did he move so quickly? "I wanted to, but I never wanted you to think I'd only wanted your blood. It hadn't helped that Vivian accused me of using you for that very reason."

Who else had known? "You don't think so?" She pulled away, kneeling at his feet. As the stars lessened, she stared at his bare feet. If she could only make herself smaller maybe, she could disappear from this nightmare. Luce grimaced, wounded by the words she said or the ones rolling through her mind. "I think so." The whisper hadn't left her lips when he lugged her from the ground and wrapped his arms around her shoulders. Beth inhaled the blend of salt and burnt oak. Lucien's lips skimmed the top of her head, and she looked up into his deep blue eyes. *If not my blood then what?* But she did not know the answer.

"I think it's because our lives were tied together from the very start. I think it's because I love you. Feel this." He placed her hand over his sweaty chest. Lucien's heart had never beaten like hers, or anyone else's for that matter. The slow, sluggish rhythm changed, speeding up as her palm rested over the skin. If her blood had saved him then why did he still need to take the medicine? "Your blood neutralizes the cancer but doesn't cure it. She must've left it out by accident today. A drop a week is all it takes."

He lied again. Beth was sick of his lying. But what part was he lying about: Aunt Vivian leaving out the blood or the medicine he still required? Her heart and mind pegged her aunt. If she had allowed him to die ... Had she saved others too? Beth sure hoped so, but why all the deceptions? *Lucien lied. She lied. Her parents lied.* Had anyone ever told her the truth?

"Can I show you how your blood changes me?" Her mouth dried. "Bethy, it won't hurt, but I'm asking ... to bite you," his gaze and tone lowered, "to connect with you."

The thought of linking with a man who'd hurt her and stated he wanted to claim her churned Beth's stomach. If she allowed him, what would that have meant for them? She stepped backward. "No."

He sighed at the rejection, and her heart pained. "One day ..." Lucien's breath sucked in as his eyes raked downward and lingered. "You're beautiful, and I ain't just saying that because you're half naked." Beth laughed as the nervousness bubbled to the surface. She pressed against his chest, but he grasped her elbow. Ice etched into his eyes. Lucien was not laughing. His grip tightened on her elbow, and he said, "Shut up."

Lucien leaned toward her, hovering as if to kiss her. Her mouth shut, clamping, and his lips twitched. Amusement twinkled in his eyes, and she stiffened. The air thickened and charged, twisting and churning around them. Luce whispered, "Relax," as his hands feathered touches across her flamed cheeks. Beth opened her mouth to object, but Lucien shushed the protests with his tongue as it slid over her bottom lip, rippling a shudder through her center. Her body attuned to his and his to hers as they kissed and explored. Pride existed in a man wanting her, but beneath his surface, there lay more, secrets and lies laid in wait. Down to his soul and back again, driving and drowning in her Lucien.

He drew away, and she stole a precious gasp of air through her stinging lips. "Say it again," he rumbled.

"More beneath the—"

"No."

"—Down to your soul?"

"No."

She whispered, "My Lucien."

"My Beth … my sunshine … mine."

Zoro meowed at the top of the stairs. "I do hate to interrupt, but we have visitors."

"At this hour?"

Lucien's eyes widened. "The Mandate's arrived."

When they reached her bedroom she bee lined for the phone, but Lucien was faster. He multi tasked too, and tossed her a bag while he dialed. The moment he had said Dad, Beth knew he contacted his family. Luce tugged her arm as she stared into space listening to the buzzing sound at the gate. Rough hands held her face, gently drawing her attention. "Five minutes and only what you can't live without."

She grabbed Bubba—the first present she had received from Luce, some clothes, and her yoga mat. Nothing else mattered except her familiar and the journals. Zoro watched, but he was not amused if the tail twitching served as any indication. A brow rose, but he closed his eyes and lay down in the doorway.

"What's your gate password?"

"Huntress." Lucien pressed the buttons and placed the phone on the bed. Twitchy fingers drummed over her thigh as she wondered what he planned. He snatched her laptop, and Beth frowned as he held out the phone.

The line crackled, and a hushed voice spoke. "Beth, they're coming for you. Listen carefully." Other voices and noises echoed in the background followed by a scream outside her house. A hand flew to her neck, and she stumbled backward into the dresser, knocking books and journals to the floor. "The Mandate arrested your aunt, and they're detaining your family," James said.

Lucien leapt from the bed and steadied her. "It's a trap right, Dad?"

Beth glanced left and right, but her legs glued to the floor.

"Do not let them in," James said something to Dana, but she did not understand, "Luce, get her out of there now."

Luce righted her fallen books, but halted, running his thumb over her lips. She would lose her resolve quickly if he kept on touching her. "When is the festival?"

She didn't know if he asked her, but she answered, "Two and a half weeks." After another short exchange with his father, Lucien hung up the phone.

"Beth," he warned, striding to her, and grabbing her hands. "Baby, you have to focus now. We ain't got time for you to breakdown." The calm and cool collective stirred her muscles and one by one, they relaxed. Lucien brushed her hair, his hand lingering at her jaw. "I always thought there was more time."

Robotically she moved, forgetting her fear as if he willed it away. Her eyes closed for a moment, recalling the inheritor trait of mind control. Luce chuckled. "I wish it worked like that. It's not true, but many use it as an excuse."

"People will arrive early to the festival," Zoro reminded, primping his fur. "They always do to set up and prepare the ritual areas. The McCallisters and Browns are supposed to cohost this year." Her duffel bag dropped. Vivian had told the cat. Fists smoldered and sparked as she glared at him for not telling her.

Zoro said, "Temper." Beth continued glaring at him but the dang cat merely stretched his legs.

"How do you put up with him?" She ignored Luce's question. Love blossomed for her furry familiar but she did not like that, he seemed to know everything.

"Tell me what to do." Pacing the length of her room, she spoke to them both but looked at neither. "I see only two choices."

"Run, stay for capture, or stay to fight." Okay three choices. "Bethy, you ain't ready to fight, but you ain't the running type either. Two weeks." He ran a palm over his rough face and stared at the doorway. "But we can't stay here. Can you give me two weeks?" As he said here, the gate buzzed again. "Grab the cat and let's go. We've already worn out our welcome." Beth pointed toward the laptop as he closed it up. Blush settled over his tanned cheeks. "Oh, I was changing all the gate passwords on them buying us a bit more time. Figured you'd need it, sweetheart." Swallowing she reached for her phone. Lucien slapped her hand away. "Leave it. No electronics."

Cat carrier in hand and a bag to her name, they scooted out the back door and into the darkness. Whispers assaulted her ears, escalating with each passing second. Lucien took Zoro and dragged her across the backyard, only pausing when they reached the trees. Under the cover of darkness, the trio edged along the natural barrier until they had a full view of the front door. Luce held a finger to his lips. Headlights approached the house. A dark sedan stopped in the cul-de-sac, and two people exited the vehicle, but a dog barked from the backseat. Zoro grumbled; he did not like dogs.

Their eyes swept over the landscape. Her grip on Lucien tightened, and for a split second, Beth thought they had spotted her. A wordless exchange passed between the intruding pair as they nodded to one another. The moment they disappeared into the house, Lucien tugged Beth's arm. "C'mon, we got a long run to safety."

Beth glanced at her bare feet and cursed. Silent prayers muttered as they took off, dashing and ducking through the thick brush of trees separating the properties. The wind whipped past her head, and shadows bred shadows as her eyes saw the darkness she had feared. Branches cracked in the distance and under her feet, but she dared not chase the sounds, or to let go of Luce's hand. Beth's heart hammered, and her lungs screamed. Never before had she run this long or fast, and her muscles revolted. Lucien flashed a smile, but it did not encourage her, and his presence did not offer her solace. The Mandate was supposed to be good, but she ran. James Brown may be Luce's father, but he had no reason to lie or hurt her … neither had his son, but she trusted them both.

The glint, the wideness of his eyes, Beth did not know why, but she somehow knew that this threat was real. Zoro had not objected either except to screech at her jostling his cage. Poor thing but she could not hold him steady. Bile churned her stomach with every forced step, and she heaved, toppled to the ground, and tumbled into the fence. Zoro issued a yowl that cut through the crickets and tree frogs. A hand fell to her enraged heart as it puttered and she blinked at the stars, counting them slowly to settle her heart. Every muscle vibrated with pulse as blood rushed through her body. No sweat, but her skin encrusted in a salty film. In a wordless gesture, Lucien cradled her in his arms and rested the cat carrier on her stomach.

He stroked her grimy cheek as she wheezed. "Don't fret; let me enjoy this moment."

Beth could not have talked if her life depended on it. A wide, toothy grin flashed and she returned it, chuckling to herself. Without warning, he lifted them over the fence. Hands curled around his neck, nails scraping his skin, and she shrieked as they barrel rolled into the woods. Lucien shushed her, placing a hand over her mouth, and glanced over his shoulder.

"Ow," he said as she bit him. "I had to shut you up somehow. They'd have heard those opera lungs of yours woman."

"Opera lungs? I'll show you opera lungs," she replied and opened her mouth, but Luce's glare made her shut it. "Do you think I was that loud?"

"Glass shattered somewhere." Beth ignored his comment and checked over Zoro as her arms squeezed his crate. His wide eyes met hers, and his nose kissed her through the grate. "He'll be all right. Can you walk?"

"Yes … how'd you jump the fence?" Lucien hopped to his feet and dragged her up. Vertigo threatened, but she held onto him, and his quick grin said he had liked it. Heads or tails it did not seem to matter. One day he hated her, one day he liked her, and her brows lifted as confusion drowned her.

His fingers rubbed over her crusty skin, and Beth winced from the rough contact. Sweating salt embarrassed her enough without Lucien seeing all the freakish Spirit Walker angles in one night. "I'll explain everything when you're safe." He wrapped his fingers around hers, and they strolled at an almost leisurely pace through the woods. Beth kept silent, but wondered why they were not rushing, and where would she find safety? His home was not any safer than hers was. But they were not headed toward his home.

Chapter Four

*V*eering away from Lucien's home, at least the home belonging to his family, they weaved farther into the woody depths of the forest lining the properties. As children they used to explore and play out here, but Beth did not recall venturing this far before. Trickling water caught her attention in the distance, but creeks and streams remained abundant in this area, and untouched since the time of their ancestors. Brush strokes of fire warmed the heavens, but fading stars still reigned as they approached a thatched hut. Beth cast a sidelong glance to Lucien.

"Where are we?"

"Home," he said. Wobbly legs turned into bricks as she skidded, sliding into the compacted dirt. Lucien spun around and eyed Beth, trying to contain his laughter, but his shaking belly gave him away. "It ain't that bad."

A snort scratched her throat, and she attempted to swallow the expression. Instead, the noise shot forth as a cross between a pig's squeal and a dying man's groan. Lucien chuckled at her apparent displeasure, gripped her elbow, and dragged her planted heels toward the archaic structure. "My parents don't even know it's here. Think it's the old slave master's quarters, but the place was empty when I found it last year."

Beth hated that part of her history although the Creek tribe had treated their slaves better; she had believed no one should ever own people. Hut—an understatement as the entry steps protested her weight, and the front door sang a croaky tune as it heaved open.

"Next step is building a proper porch." Even shack seemed too fancy. Lucien offered his hand but she stared at it. *Two weeks, it would be like camping.* Beth blinked half-expecting the structure to crumble into dust. It needed more than a porch to become livable. A twinge stirred her belly; he did not have to help her, and she should have been grateful. He scratched his head and shrugged, waving her inside. Cruel and unusual punishment came to mind instead. She nodded to herself; her gaze drifted over the shack. *No electricity. No bathroom. One bed.* Over which one her eyes had widened the most, she had not exactly known.

"The stream gives plenty of fish, and the woods have more than enough game. There's ..."

Tears sprang into her eyes as her body thudded to the floor. *Her life was over.* Two weeks of hell ... with him ... in here. "Bethy, awe c'mon, it ain't so bad. I spend weekends here."

Beth wailed louder and yanked bloodied knees into her chest. Salt scorched the busted scrapes and stung worse than a horde of bees guarding their sweet bounty.

Lucien carried her outside and sat by the creek edge. Beth protested as he lifted the hem of her negligee, and her face burned crimson from the oversight. She'd run all that way in a nightgown and bare feet. He tugged again. "Leave me alone."

"I ain't trying to attack you, dang stubborn woman. I'm trying to clean your wounds."

Her cries quieted, and she peeked at Lucien's naked back. "Close your eyes," she said. He stomped into the house instead, muttering protests, and slammed the door behind him.

"Huh," she said as the little building that could managed not to fall into the abyss. Daytime crept over the sky despite the sun resting behind the trees. Shadows stirred but their time ended as dawn reigned.

Legs trembled beneath her as she knelt forward. Water bubbled and sputtered but not deep enough to submerge a whole body. After dousing her legs with water, she waded into the depths, holding the nightgown around her hips. Fish nibbled and tickled her feet as a smile played at her lips. Aside from the shack, it truly was a majestic place; she could have enjoyed it alone. The satin slipped through her hands and rested on the surface. Clay squashed through her toes as they curled into the murky bank. A glance over her shoulder gave no signs of Lucien, yet his eyes burned through her.

Tender skin cracked, and the white flakes drifted to the surface. The longer the salt sweat remained on her skin the drier her skin would become. Beth peeled the garment over her head and chuckled. The salt stains would have ruined the nightgown, yet she'd tried her best to not get it wet. Despite the aloneness, her body warmed, and her nipples tightened as the cool water spilled over sensitive breasts. With gentle strokes and a sore bottom lip, she washed the remaining salt from her body.

Lucien spied from inside the cabin. Stopping him wasn't an option, but if he saw the dimpled and soft fleshy bits then he'd no longer want her. Living beside him would be easier if he didn't. A shrug dragged her shoulders forward. No wonder she had allowed her family to lock her away. Lucien couldn't hurt her there. She closed her eyes, willing the tears to cease. The thought churned in her mind. There never would have been another even if someone else did want her. He didn't know it yet, but Lucien owned her heart.

She bent forward to rinse her scalp. Years of yoga paid off as her curves folded into herself and held the pose with ease. So-called superior hearing failed her though as water trickled near her ears. "See you're missing spots."

Her heart pounded as he doused her head with water. Another bucketful poured over her head and splashed into her eyes. "Lucien," she growled a warning.

Easing out of a forward standing bend, her chin tilted toward the sky, and her arms covered her exposed breasts. Lucien laughed and poured water over her thigh. "Squat down."

Husky words tightened her belly, but she nodded and complied, seeking to hide her imperfect body from him. He waded behind her and crouched below the water's surface. Strong arms snaked around her waist and dragged her into his lap. She blinked and gasped. Stark naked and harder than a rock was the man sitting beneath her. "Let me hold you; I promise not to hurt you, but I need to feel you in my arms."

Beth squirmed from his grip, slipping and splashing in the creek. He said zilch, but the mood shifted, and the air crackled against her sopping skin. Insects and bugs screamed, and a strange howl echoed through the early morning air. The hammer of her heart drowned the other sounds out as she squeezed her temples, rubbing circles. Her negligee sealed its ruined fate as she used the satin and lace to dry her body as Lucien watched. Her hair still dripped, but nothing short of a towel would have sufficed.

What was he thinking? Did he think the past had never happened? Water splattered as her hair whipped back and forth. Deft feet padded into the shack, refusing to turn around, knowing she would eventually lose the strength to fight his attentions. Inevitable, self-fulfilling prophecy, all that jazz, and glutton for punishment she could have added them all into the pot of her life. Part of Beth truly wanted to forgive, forget, and drown in Lucien. The other part screamed, "*You will not survive.*"

Comfort had not existed in his presence. An itch she could not quite scratch. At least she had Zoro. He'd keep her sane. Someone had to keep her honest and her head out of fairy tales with Grimm brother endings.

Dull light from an oil lamp bathed the cabin, and her lashes flickered, adjusting her eyes. Still a shack, but on a second less shocking glance, the interior was not so bad. Lucien had fixed the place up, but between the size and lack of amenities ... Her eyes flittered to the double bed nestled in the corner. A patchwork quilt rested over the surface, and it appeared vaguely familiar. A sigh tickled her throat as her memory flashed to the day she gave him the quilt. Americana in design of red, white, and blue tickled her heart, and the muscle went from pounding to a dull flutter as her palm smoothed the tattered surface.

Beth had made him this quilt with her momma's help. Sewed the squares by hand, crying over every piece as momma soothed her.

One of the few memories she had of her mother acting motherly too. Most of the time she was distant like her daddy. Beth shook her parents away, narrowing in on the frail boy she had made it for in the first place. Lucien had asked her to bury him with it, wanting to take a piece of her away to heaven. A tear released and dotted the blue square. The hospital and its drab white had frightened him so much.

"What happened to us?" she whispered as Zoro peeked at her. "What happened to you?" By you, she did not mean her cat. He had slept with the quilt every night. Threads had popped, and the poor thing was almost in rags, as if well loved.

"I still sleep with it every night." Beth jumped, and a hand flew to her neck at his voice. "It's all I have left of you," he gulped, "of us."

Before, during, and a few years after his illness they had been inseparable. One day he awoke, and she became the bubonic plague without any explanation. The wince twisted across her face no matter how hard she fought the emotion. Slipping a hand to her mouth, she bit her check hard enough to draw blood. Regret filled her where there should have been love that day, because she hadn't stood up for herself, but allowed him to ridicule her, to hurt her because somewhere deep inside Beth believed it was all she had deserved.

Even now she thought it; he did that to her. Beth loved him so much that she did not care if his attentions were loving or cruel as long as he didn't forget her. *How messed up was that?* That tiny bubble of confidence flared and ebbed as the years ticked by them. No bigger than a pinhead, her hope in them and herself had diminished. After the deepest cuts had scabbed over, she questioned every motive, every word, and every move Lucien had made then and now.

Faced with the whispered words of others hadn't helped paint a picture of a better future. How often had she dreamt of ending up alone like Vivian? She had not married Jemma's father. Jemma did not know her father at all. Would she end up like her mother too? Would Beth?

"Beth," Lucien whispered. "Live in the now." Twirling on him, her hand raised, and sent the palm flying across his face. He rubbed the mark as teeth sunk into her lip.

"Don't you dare ..." Claws dug and ripped through her chest, but the hands owning those deathlike paws were always Luce. He had held her heart in his grasp and what had he done. A ragged breath released. Tore her into tiny bits like the camera, he'd turned her into worthless dust, and she had yet to glue all those pieces together. "You have no right talking about us. And put some dang clothes on."

Pain flashed over his warped face. *He had to know.* How could he not realize? A breeze rushed its shiver over her exposed, heated skin. *Beth* had loved him unconditionally. No judgments over his faults or family and *Beth* let him in. *Beth* had saved his life, continuing to do so without knowing, and Lucien broke hers in return. The thoughts caused her to gasp and clutch, burrowing nails into her flesh. Whatever happened from here on out, she could never forget, and the time for second chances had long ago passed. Hairs stood at full attention on the back of her neck, and she stiffened, waiting for Lucien to touch her. Waiting for an explanation that never came. Steady breaths were the only clue that he was there but, all too soon, they too were gone. Beth faced him, grasping the negligee to her chest to cover her body, but the doorway stood empty. Had Beth imagined him there?

All the thoughts shook away. Like a King, she found her favorite feline sound asleep on the bed. Her fingers ran through his silky fur, and a purr filled her ears. "Promise me, Zoro. Don't let me be a fool."

"You already are Kolkohkafoosi."

*A*fternoon rays streamed through the window and warmed her puffy face. Aside from Zoro, Beth awoke alone. Maybe she had dreamt of the arms too. Her mouth dried from the previous night's sweating, and she required fresh water. Moving with grace, Beth dressed in fresh clothing—a yellow sundress Lucien must have laid out– and tiptoed outside in search of an outhouse. Where the dress came from, she did not know. The oil painting like scene of a faraway place was beautiful. Lush trees surrounded the alcove, and the water trickled down from a small, stony overlook. Serene yet tucked away from unwanted eyes.

Boards shifted behind her, and Beth whirled to find an expressionless Lucien framing the doorway. Her head tilted, she had not seen him inside. Not like he could have hidden in the one room shack. Purple bags rimmed his eyes, showing signs of sleeplessness. A hand caressed his unshaven chin, while the other shoved into his pocket. At least he was dressed again. So unfair that, no matter what state his wardrobe and grooming were in, he was handsome.

Words tickled her parting lips as she gasped. Emotions flashed in his blue eyes, and Lucien rocked on his heels holding all the innocence of a child. "I need answers," she said glancing toward the ground, noting the tremble of her voice.

"You need a toothbrush too." A hand flew to her mouth, and she mumbled about needing a bathroom. "Yellow suits you. Brings out the gold in your eyes." His lids lowered. "And shows off your legs."

Hands tugged the hem lower, not wanting him checking out her legs, and she ignored the compliment. Before she would have thanked him, but his disposal of her had made her insecure, and she did not know how to turn it off. "Inside, Bethy," he shook his head and grinned, "did you think I wouldn't make some changes?"

He led her into what she'd have described as half a closet. Beth plastered against the wall not wanting to touch him. Heat from Lucien occupied the space with his woodsy-fire scent, and she chewed her lip, trying her best to ignore his presence or the changes occurring within her body from the sudden close proximity.

There in the tiny room sat a bucket and a pail of sawdust. A finger pointed, and her black brow rose. "What. Is. That?"

"Toilet." Lucien smirked and lifted the lid. "Do your business, and cover it with sawdust. Close the lid. Ain't rocket science, sweetheart."

Beth swallowed hard and wondered if squatting in the woods would not be easier. Sure, there was privacy here. Lucien's zipper ripped through the air and his jeans rattled, hitting the floor. A gasp released as her wide eyes averted, but they rose and settled on his beefy behind. He sighed as his business released, piddling into the bucket. "See not so hard, sunshine."

Luce hiked his jeans up and the zipper ripped again. Easing past her, he paused, still smirking and daring her to say something with his eyes. As kids, he'd used the woods as his bathroom countless times, but it was different now. The door closed, and she breathed, but no odor came from the bucket. Her bladder screamed as her legs danced; eyes skirted the tiny space. "Geesh, it's just a bucket, Beth." Lucien's snickers filled the shack, and her tongue stuck out, narrowing her eyes. She would show him.

Beth emerged from the bathroom a little redder and a whole lot wiser. Lucien, snickering, directed her toward a washbasin and pointed toward a toothbrush and paste. The blue and white porcelain inlaid the cabinet, and at the top sat a pump. He placed a stopper in the bottom and worked the metal handle.

Beth muttered, "You're enjoying this."

Lucien brushed her cheek and left the cabin without a word. After a quick hand and face wash, she brushed her teeth to fresh breath perfection. An empty cup sat near the basin, and she filled it to the brim with fresh water from the spout. Four chugged glasses later, her tummy sloshed as she ventured outside in search of Lucien, leaving a still snoozing Zoro on the bed. *Must be nice.* Rays brushed her shoulders, but the warmth had not ended her quakes. The tremble of the unknown, and the evening's findings, came rushing back as she swayed, clutching a support beam under the overhang. The dizzy spells seemed worse too. Luce was the enemy, her enemy, and sweet words, glances, touches, and definitely not kisses would change the damage he had wrought.

A chopping sound drew her attention, and Beth strolled to the back to find the devil himself, shirtless and splitting wood. Never one for many words, she silently watched as the sweat beaded on his tan skin, and her mind flashed back to him wielding the sword. Muscles curled and formed along the softer lines of his stomach. If he did this more often he would whip into shape in no time. Her eyes trailed lower as those jeans clung, revealing the lazy V. Dark hair painted the trail, and her fingers itched, wanting to feel the silkiness of the curls and sweltering of his skin.

How could one man have affected her like this? He hated her; they were enemies. She leaned against the house; arms and legs crossed, eyes watched, insides silently swooned, as she all but fanned herself as her insides melted. The dull ache returned, throbbing and slickening between her thighs. How many times had Beth read about this reaction in a book, yet in the shaded moment she finally understood attraction, and she hated that it was due to him. Devilish lips curled into half-cocked grin, and Beth blew out a long, cleansing breath, desperate to wash the impure thoughts from her mind. Too bad her body disagreed. Lucien inhaled, closing his eyes mid swing.

"We can't cook without it," he said in a gruffer than usual tone swinging the axe downward. Shards of wood splintered, raining, and cracking through the air. "Should've done some last night."

Muttering under his breath, Lucien continued his task instead of answering her thoughts. Beth hid in the shade regardless of his refusal to chat. They did not need words as kids either, but she had nothing to say to him that did not involve screaming, and one of Vivian's rules was if she didn't have anything nice to say, she didn't say anything at all.

The wood fractured as his axe jimmied through the center of the last log. He had worked quickly, but there was not any surprise there. Two words that described him well were powerful and fast.

"All set, now to woo you with my spectacular cooking skills." Heck, the man couldn't be any worse than her, right? Even with the summer heat, Lucien set up an outdoor fire. Burning cedar smoke helped to keep the bugs away too. "You were never this quiet. C'mon, lay it on me." Beth rolled the length of her hair into a high bun. "Suit yourself."

While building the fire, he spoke of how these houses used to line the whole area, speaking louder as she retrieved her yoga mat. A snap of her wrists and she rolled the sticky foam mat out on level ground. The houses he spoke of transported her mind as the salt crusted her skin, turning the golden tan into a pasty white mess as Beth ran through her sun salutations. Lucien had always loved history, even as a kid, but if she heard another word about how the thatched roof style remained popular even after the settlers arrived, she would shove mud in her ears. Their people had once lived in a tight knit community and governed themselves. They had answered to themselves too. She knew all about it, and he was yapping to hear himself speak.

Lucien glared at her. "Like I can remember what you know." How different life had progressed from one thousand years ago let alone a few hundred. All Native people had come a long way from those days, yet the simpler life called to her soul. Simple meaning air conditioning, running hot water, and Wi-fi, but bells and whistles were not required to please her. "You need to get out more."

Beth folded onto her belly, rising into cobra, and asked, "What happened to the other houses?"

"Decayed or destroyed I reckon," he said, squinting and shielding his eyes. Beth followed his gaze, and found it ending on her breasts. "This one needed work too. I've put every inch of talent and my allowance went into restoring or upgrading."

"Take a picture."

A lazy lick slid across his lips. "Take the dress off and I will."

Beth hefted herself from the ground and leered at Lucien. "You are an impossible ass." He grinned and reached for her, but she skirted away.

Lucien didn't miss a beat and hopped from the ground. "You'll lose." Beth halted shy of the stream as his arms grasped her waist. Rough lips skimmed her neck, tickling her inside and out. "I'll always catch you, Bethy."

Slowly his hands turned her as if she were a piece of china. Dark lashes fluttered faster than her heart. Closer he leaned, dragging her against his chest. No words released his parted lips. All that needed saying she'd already said to him. Lucien owed her the truth.

Releasing herself from his grasp, she flashed a small, forced smile and ventured toward the blanket. Beth lounged as he followed her movements. This wasn't a game. Her heart wasn't a chess piece. Lucien returned to his spot and stirred the pot in silence. The rise and fall of her chest quickened every time he flinched or twitched. Pain furrowed his forehead, and he couldn't hide the symptoms from her. How much of it was his sickness?

Beth broke the ice. "When do you need another treatment?"

Blue eyes lifted from the pot, but he ignored the question. Her long legs shifted on the blanket, the hem skirting up her thigh. Lucien's hand tightened, knuckles bleeding from tan to white as he stirred their breakfast. Beth eyed the nature surrounding their hide-away, but her mind returned to Lucien no matter how beautiful the trees and birds were. All roads led to the man who had destroyed her.

Lucien dished the mush into bowls and handed one to her. It tasted about as good as it looked, but her growling stomach was not as fussy as her palate. Lucien did not eat, rising and retrieving a can of tuna from the shack. Zoro sniffed it out of suspicion, but his hunger won in the end too.

"I know you eat."

"Not hungry for mush."

"Beggars can't be choosy."

"I ain't begging," he started clearing dishes, "you'll come around. Everyone comes around."

She was not everyone. Beth glanced away and hid her face. What stung worse, his insults or the jibes of his other conquests? Like a fool, she had saved herself, saved herself for a man undeserving. She collected her dishes and headed toward a large kettle of cooling water. Lucien had set the massive cast iron pot over the fire and removed the monstrosity after it simmered.

"I didn't mean it like that," he said, rubbing his neck. Beth con-centrated on the pot. Part of her was like that cauldron and the water her pain. As long as it simmered or boiled there would always be room for more, but left alone the pain would evaporate leaving her alone in the world. The sentiment was almost worth the loneliness. "Bethy baby talk to me."

As she set to work, her mind wandered over the previous day's events. From the toe-curling kiss to her missing family to the rev-elation and confrontations, none of it made any sense. What was his game? What did the Mandate want with her family? How did she play into this?

Lucien lounged on the blanket as Zoro gorged on another tin of tuna. Tranquility washed over her, and blue eyes met her frown. Beth wanted all of this, but at what price? Lucien sighed; she assumed at her thoughts, but his sulking wouldn't change her mind. What if nothing would have altered her decision? A good place to start was the truth. Clean up took no time at all, and she set the dishes to dry on the blanket. The sun made quick work of the task, and Beth hefted the cookware back inside, continuing to ignore Lucien.

"What am I going to do about the Mandate?" Her shoulder pressed into the open doorway, and her arms folded. Lucien's lips pressed together into a thin line as his dark brows furrowed. He rolled onto his knees and patted the blanket, but Beth didn't move. Zoro eyed the scene with interest, but he too remained quiet aside from chasing butterflies. He wasn't an outside cat.

"I didn't know Vivian was giving you my blood." Colored spots tunneled into her vision. Skirts gathered in her sweaty hands, and she sat on the shaded stoop. Food had helped but something in her still felt off. "Daddy's been taking blood for ages."

Lucien blinked. "Before I was sick?"

Sunshine warmed over the hidden beauty, scenting the area with fragrant floral notes, but the early scent of decay wafted on the breeze. Fall approached ready to strip the forests of their vibrant life like a reaper culled existence. Why did her blood matter?

"Around then. Before the hospital." He chewed on his lip and patted the blanket again.

"I'm fine, thanks."

Lucien hopped from the blanket and grasped her hands, yanking her toward the blanket. "You're not fine. What's wrong?" Laughter filled the space.

"Hmm, where do I start?" No matter the distance, he found a way to touch her. He rolled onto his back, stretching until his head wound up in her lap, his hair tickling her bare thighs, and he breathed deeply as a lazy smile crept over those thick lips as if he'd won. Blue eyes peeked at her, shielded by his large hand. Indifference wasn't her forte, but she tried her best, and failed as the blush warmed her face. Lucien, one to steal the initiative, swiped her hand and folded them together. Beth repeated her question again and stared off into the tree line. Judas trees and chestnuts protected them from view, but how far into the land had they ventured?

"We're five miles out. I'll see what I can find out about your family." Lucien shifted and lay at her side, dancing his fingers over her ribs and staring at her. A dark brow twitched as he inched toward her breast, and her mind shouted to stop him. Beth came out here for safety and answers, not to play games with a wishy-washy, mind reading ass wipe.

"I'm not actually reading your mind." A snort rose in her chest. "Thoughts aren't projected, and I can't invade your head." Lucien wiggled his fingers but she slapped them away from her head. "Like I said, there are myths about my kind and most of those are false. Like if I wasn't sick, I wouldn't need blood at all."

Of all the terrible crimes people committed in this world, drinking blood, while disgusting, was the least of her concerns. Her thoughts had mattered the most as well as the secrets. The last three years of her life, he had not known about, because he chose not to be there, but she did not want him to see that pain. Not yet. Lucien Brown would pay the piper, but why force him to relive it if he did not care.

How did he read her mind? Beth had an intuition about Lucien's thoughts, but she knew him and all his little quirks. Like how he fidgeted when asked about the Mandate or her family. A master at changing the subject or distracting her too, but unlike him, she wanted to save her family and not spend her life hidden away in his shack. For a fleeting moment, Beth somehow imagined playing wife, smiling, and raising a cackle of children. But reality smacked her in the face recalling who'd play her husband.

"Why save them?" Tight fists pounded the blanket and she jumped taken aback by his outburst. "Sorry." Lucien flipped over and pressed her back flat against the blanket. His nose rubbed against hers as her insides trembled under his weight. "Am I that bad, sunshine? You'd choose them over me?"

Yes. No. Beth did not know and bit her lip. He lied and made her life a living nightmare of sorts, but so had her family.

"Would you believe I have an evil twin?" She glared at him and pushed back, using the strength of her forearms. A groan slipped from Luce's lips as he leaned into her and slipped between her thighs. "How about a cousin, who looks exactly like me?" Her eyes didn't falter; he'd known about her and even called her sunshine. Lucien snorted. "When you turned your back on me, maybe I confided in him. Up until a day ago, I'd confided in him, but why he'd hurt you is beyond me."

Her nails dug into his biceps as his skin burned blue. Her voice rolled with the shaking thunder. "I never turned my back on you. *Ever.*" Her eyes widened, and the thought of his words caused her head to shake. Black clouds blocked out the sun as lightning danced in the sky. Lucien had tossed her aside for Amber and popularity. Her fists curled deeper into his skin as blood seeped from the wounds; how dare he make this her fault. Beth had to get away from him and fast. "Stop lying to me. God Luce, haven't you hurt me enough?"

He rose from their makeshift picnic as the rain swept from the sky. Coldness crept over her skin, and she shivered, despite wanting to lob off his head and display it on a stake. "Hurting you ..." Lucien touched his heart but her eyes watched the wounds bubble and crust over, slowly healing as her jaw dropped. "It hurts me to even think of it, but I never understood the cause of your pain."

"The cause of my pain?" She pointed toward the shack and snapped her fingers. "Go look in a dang mirror. It is you. It has always been you." On some deep level, she had wanted to believe him. Craved to believe the past all a misunderstanding and that she was not plagued. Her fingers ticked off the reasons why she could not. "You don't have a cousin. You forget I've met your whole family. I saw you with my own two eyes. Heard you with my own two ears." The bitterness soured her mouth as much as his insistence to lie. "Leave me alone, until you're prepared with the real truth."

Even then, Beth wondered was it already too late for apologies. He stomped toward the door, and his broad shoulders slouched as if he was a little boy told no. Lucien turned and glanced over his shoulder, flashing his signature smile. "Haven't I taught you that you ain't known the half of it, sunshine?"

Blue sky disappeared under the cover of storm clouds. Earth rumbled from thunder beneath her feet. Zoro pawed at her leg, but Beth didn't glance in his direction. Her laser eyes trained on Lucien as the wind whipped her tangled hair.

"It's 'don't know'," she shouted, "and at least I'm not a liar."

Seldom had she lost her temper or emotional control unless Lucien was around. The door slammed, and a chill crept over her spine again, but this one crippled and held her shaken body hostage. Weather too seemed to react to the change inside of her, but she brushed the coincidences aside. No one could control the storms, right?

A sopping wet Zoro cleaned himself at her feet. "You're holding a grudge," his tone broke the odd spell over her. So what if she was, she had wanted to say, but he would have ignored her. She couldn't have spotted a liar if they'd held a sign, except Lucien. The man had a tell, a gleam his eyes reflected, almost a glossy sheen. "He's trying."

"Shove a sock in it," she snapped, lightning splintered the sky, and the cat blinked. "How do I forgive someone who hasn't stopped lying? He isn't trying." A hand extended toward the door. "Maybe he's lying to himself too, but I … I don't know." Her eyes closed as the drops splattered her face. Ebbing and flowing like the wind, she connected with nature as its power surged through her veins. Holding her hands towards the heavens, the electricity jolted and released into the sky. Beth gasped as her eyes flew open, and the blue charges attacked the black clouds.

"Beth you must calm down," the cat said, pawing her leg. "The storm is within you. Let it go." Her body collapsed, narrowly missing Zoro as he leapt from her path. One leg crossed in front of the other as she glowered, staring at the soggy blanket. Zoro and Lucien had not been sociable. *Ever.* Over protectiveness or male ego, either way she shrugged her faked indifference. Until someone gave her answers, her fat ass was not budging. Rain, sleet, sunshine, or turning into a pillar of salt didn't matter. Beth refused to move.

How did he know the Mandate captured her family? What did he know about the locha? Lucien said she was full of it as a kid. Did he still think that? Why did she care what he thought?

Zoro stretched his paws and yawned. "You still love him." The dark clouds lessened, but the sunset approached as its orange rays dipped below the trees.

"That's why it hurts so much. I never stopped." A crash sounded from inside the cabin, and her heart jumped. The door slammed open, and Lucien chucked her bag outside. Tension rolled off him in waves, and all her hairs stood from the electrified air. Rain splattered against her cheek. At least she told herself it was the rain.

"You rejected him again. Men don't like that. I didn't like it." Not everyone owned a talking cat, but sometimes Beth forgot he used to be a man—a Spirit Walker like her. After they had died, The One Above made them into familiars if the Spirit Walker chose that path. Most did.

A groan parted her lips as she flung herself on the blanket. A hand shielded her eyes, but she rolled away from Zoro. Beth didn't like others to see her cry. "I can't believe anything until he stops lying."

She smacked a biting mosquito. The fire had died, sizzling under the pelting of rain and releasing a hazy smog that smelled like warm beer. Her gaze tore away; his behavior proved how different they were. How much he hadn't known her. Beth retrieved the duffel bag and rifled through her belongings. The diary was missing, the same one that had planned the life they'd never have together. Seemed fitting for him to see the dreams of her deranged mind after last night's kiss, but Beth guessed that too had been nothing more than another lie. Had he lied about the Mandate too? Was his gang hiding in the woods giggling and having a joke at her expense?

The tears rolled and rolled as dark clouds formed on the horizon again. Lightning crackled, rupturing the sky as if it were a piece of wood. How fitting that the storm reflected the emotions twisting her gut. Zoro kneaded in her lap, content with the weather raging away in the distance. She sniffled, staring into the world, and considering why she was a part of it.

As the sun began its descent, Beth disrobed and bathed the salt from her skin, watching the clouds stall. Words whispered on the howling wind: death meant nothing more than another begin-ning. A new life filled with new adventure. But the memories of this life would haunt her. Zoro did not talk about his previous life, but his soulful eyes spoke the pain he had faced. She glanced over her shoulder hoping to catch a glimpse of Lucien, praying he felt pain—her pain. Would he cry if the lightning struck her down? Her head cocked. Could the lightning strike her dead?

"No."

The forest came alive singing a busy tune courtesy of tree frogs. Her stomach gurgled, craving water and food, but Beth could not bring herself to ask anything more of the devil. Flickers of last night resurfaced, and her bare skin flushed. Did he realize that had been her first real kiss? Fingertips brushed the surface of her lips, no longer swollen from his kisses or parting at his heart-filled lies.

Lucien had not attempted to join her and he'd not assisted her tonight. Fine by her, as she did not desire his help or his company either.

As the final light disappeared, Beth gathered the days clothing, blanket, and Zoro. She headed inside, but Luce had locked the door. Thunder shook the ground, and she yelped, but realized it was her own heart. Her fist curled and pounded on the wood, but there wasn't any answer. No snarky remarks or replies as the night crept around her. Rain drizzled. Darkness brushed the backs of her legs and stroked her cheek. With each whisper, her cries grew frantic. Lightning illuminated the darkness, and a shadowy man crept through the brush.

Her heart boomed louder as he stepped from the woods. Yellow eyes glowed like fire and a sinister smile spread over his lips as he sauntered toward her. "Beth," Zoro cried.

"I see it too … Luce, this isn't funny. Someone's out here." The shrilly voice didn't help her nerves, and her feet backpedaled, stumbling through the muddy ground. Zoro mewed in her arms; his nails stung, gripping her bare flesh.

"We aren't alone." Wide eyes darted as he clung to her. "Kolkohkafoosi, we must get inside."

Each step the shadow man took, Beth took another backward. Bark scratched her skin and she froze, trembling. Flinching, she shut her eyes, bracing for an attack. She gulped but nothing happened. A sigh blew from her lips, and a soft chuckle left her open mouth, but her heart still beat the dickens out of her ribcage. "That was clo—" Icy arms surrounded her, and Beth screamed. Zoro cried and hissed, slicing her skin as he flew from her arms. The door hadn't opened. By her hair, the captor dragged Beth into the stream as she kicked, flailed, and shrieked for help. The shadow man—locha—held her under the water. Laughter—muffled sinister mirth filled her ears.

He hissed, "Huntress." Sharp, yellowed teeth matched his eyes. Beth pushed against the force, barely holding her head above the water and gasped for breath. She choked. Yellow eyes glowed as she struggled to break free. Nowhere to run and nowhere to hide as shadow man pinned her arms down and shoved a knee into her chest.

"Lucien," she sputtered, a strangled gargled cry; water filled her mouth and drowned her lungs. Some say life flashes before a victim's eyes before they die, but her eyes saw a dark, murky shroud tearing at her. Eyes blinked. *This was it; this was how she died.* Her tombstone would read here rests the girl who lived and died. Not loving wife or mother. Not huntress of the locha. Empty and cold described the whole of her world. Zoro, Lucien at times, and Jemma were her only warmth, and none of them knew the truth. She loved them despite the lies or weaknesses. Beth loved them all, even the mother and father who did not care, the aunt who held back her dreams, the cousin who tried, the cat who spied, and most of all the man who had lied.

As the wind gusted across her damp face, her attacker flew into the shadows. A slew of curses rained from above as vibrant blue eyes centered her spinning mind. Teeth chattered as Lucien lifted her from the water and cradled her against his chest. He carried her inside the shack, never breaking eye contact as his brows set into a furious scowl, but he said no words.

Her feet hit the floor as water dripped from her body. Zoro darted in behind them, hissing, and swatting at her rescuer. Words refused to form as Lucien ignored the cat and slammed the door. The tremors rose from her feet, and the whole house shook. He returned to his task and gathered towels.

"Say ... something." Her chattering teeth helped little with her enunciation. He patted her body dry. Beth cupped his cheek and saw what he'd hidden beneath the façade of strength. Lucien trembled as much as she did. He put on a strong front for her benefit alone, and the notion lit a hope from within. If only he could stop the lies. "Luce?"

The towel dropped to the floor, and he engulfed her. "I thought she'd lied about the locha too." Blood oozed from her arms. Scratches burned across her face. "Can I?" Beth cocked her head. "You're bleeding." Lucien's whispered words vibrated like her body, and he clung to her as if she would float away.

"Oh. Guess you don't have a first aid kit," he shook his head, "Okay." Despite knowing the answer, she asked, "Who lied?"

His mouth lowered as Lucien stretched out her arm. Warmth glided over her icy skin as he lathed the bloody scratch. Twinges rocked through her gut and more than one area of her body flooded from the intimate contact. Wracked with tremors her mouth betrayed her inner desires. "Luce."

Hardened nipples brushed against his bare chest. The truth hid behind her cold words and actions. Lucien owned her heart. Despite the lies and deceit, Beth was still in love with him. No wonder each name or ignorance had cut deeper than anyone else. No one could have denied the truth. But how long before loving him came back to bite her? How long before he had some nelly welly excuse as to why he could not have ever loved her?

Her hands rubbed up his arms and snaked around his neck. Baby steps, but she hugged him and rested in the crook of his shoulder. A pregnant pause rested between them as her hot breath skimmed his neck, and she shut her eyes. Vertigo swayed her body or maybe Lucien swayed. Safe in his arms, Beth didn't let their shaky path haunt her thoughts. Life was too dang short to waste. But she wasn't ready to forgive him or cross that line.

"Viv lied to protect her investments." Lucien shrugged, but he held back, and turned his head. "I'm sorry, Bethy." His lips caressed her wrinkled forehead. "So sorry." Why'd everyone think it was their job to protect her? As a huntress, she should have obtained the skills to fight without their help and protect the town from the locha. "Your blood saved those fighting couldn't."

And they rolled around to her blood. She sighed. Vivian had made a judgment call that was not hers to make. How long had she known? The worst of it all was lying to her. They could have reached a compromise. She swallowed hard and drew away as a shudder bowled over her skin. Desire burned in his eyes, and Beth wondered if her gaze reflected the same emotion.

"What about other hunters? Does—" Her words cut off courtesy of his curt nod. "Did the Mandate demand my family cease—" Another no. "So, Vivian refused my birthright in order to use me to save others."

Her brows rose and fell as she stared at the floor. Why didn't Vivian just ask her?

"Money ... thought you knew of her scheme. Not enough to be involved but ..."

Fingers tapped against his chest, resisting the temptation to twine in his hair, and she chewed over this newfound information. Lucien she hadn't blamed. Then or now, she'd have done whatever it took to save his life. Closing her eyes, the ghost like appearance and frailness of his youth haunted her. Heck, she would have given Vivian her blood for him, and the others, as long as it was free. All she had to do was ask instead of lie. Beth glanced to an already sleeping Zoro and called his name. He blinked his sleepy eyes.

"Did you know about this?"

The hesitation spoke enough to cut through her heart. Had anyone not lied to her? *Jemma.*

"She threatened me. I wanted to tell you but wanted to live too."

Electricity sparked in her fingertips, and Lucien lifted her hands. He stroked the digits over his coarse cheek. Skin absorbed the blue-white tendrils, but not before, they had illuminated and burned his skin. Beth pulled away, afraid she'd hurt him, but he smiled.

"Remember what I said about Achilles heel?" Her throat swelled as he kissed her fingertips. "Let's get you changed. Tomorrow, I'll scope out your home; think of anything you left, and I'll grab it if I can."

He kissed her forehead again, and a scowl fought to form. Beth had rather he kissed her like last night. The passion and dizzy sensations held addictive qualities. Lucien slid a thumb over her lips, and she repeated the gesture, caught up in watching him shudder under the feathered touch. A ragged breath sucked into his lungs and voice mirrored the torture.

"Dressed now or you'll tempt me." Her brow rose; he slapped her butt cheek and wrapped the towel around her. "I mean it. Bethy," his face reddened, "you make it ..."

"Hard?"

His cheeks deepened to a crimson red, and he rubbed his neck. "Yes, sunshine."

"Luce, thanks."

"For?" A brow rose.

"Saving me."

"Dressed," he said, straining his voice and shrugged it off. A shaky hand pointed toward the bed. Another sundress lay on the surface, but this one was not hers either. How many women had he brought here before her? Beth refrained from asking its origin. "You're the first."

"Not going to answer the rest?"

"In time." His weight shifted as the towel dropped to the floor, slipping through her trembling fingers as she reached for the paler yellow dress. The heat rose in her cheeks and shot straight to her center as Beth bent forward, exposing herself to Lucien. Those blue eyes, she bet they hadn't strayed after his admittance. When she turned around the fire-lit eyes smoldered. Goose bumps erupted and chased over her damp skin.

Lucien swallowed hard and nodded; at what she had not understood. Want, need, and ache fought in his facial lines. But Beth could not allow his emotions, or the fact that he wanted her, to cloud her judgment. The raw ache within her bled too new, and the fresh wounds needed to heal. Lies still required truths. Confusion within her needed understanding too. Boards creaked under his feet and he sat, facing away from her. Fingers tightened into balled fists, but she empathized with his frustration.

A tear escaped and splashed against her bare breast. The idea of happily ever after, of children and family, exploded and Beth closed her eyes. Zoro pushed at her hand, his wet nose shocking her out of those thoughts. She stared at him. He lied too, but they both held something back. *One problem at a time.*

Her drained body curled into the blankets, wrapping and mummifying the soft quilt around her body. It smelled like her Lucien: spicy, smoky, and woodsy with a touch of wrong. The wrong was his leukemia. Bubba, the teddy bear that he had given her, cuddled against her chest. Invisible tears fell in their silent reverie, but not for the reasons one might think. No tears fell for liars, but for all the people she could have saved.

Why hadn't Zoro told her about the blood? People Beth had not even known, all around the world and innocent children, died every passing second. In her veins, pumping through her shattered heart, she held the power. Not her freakish electrical current, but the power to heal coursed through her. For the first time since learning about the hunters, her mind brought forth a renewed purpose. Beth would find a way to show the world what she could do and save every person until her final breath.

The fire behind her lids died as the lamplight ceased. Springs shifted as Lucien slid under the covers. He kept his distance as she shifted, facing him. Unshed tears rimmed her eyes. How could she have been so stupid not to see what her family did? Did he think she was part of their scheme? That was it wasn't it? Lucien thought she had known all along. In hindsight, Beth should have known but she did not. Between their well-laced lies and life, she did not piece it together.

Beth fell into a fit of tangled dreams. Chanting voices flooded her nightmare; locha chased her through the dark forest. The man-shadow swooped from the sky and held her under frigid water. She kicked, flailed, and screamed, but no one came. A man spoke to her in Muskogee, and his words chilled her bones and soul.

"You have upset the balance," shadow man accused her. "The locha are punishment, purgatory for the soul, and we have a place waiting for you, huntress."

"I didn't do anything wrong," she said back and cried out a name. One name she didn't expect to hear off her lips. "Lucien, Lucien, help me. Tell them I didn't know." His blue gaze caught her attention outside the shack. Their eyes met, but the scowl formed, setting deeper wrinkles into his face. Slowly his skin altered, appearing waxy and then crumpling away like dust in the stiff breeze until only a shade of the man remained behind. But Luce wasn't locha—locha didn't glow azure blue.

Beth shot from bed gasping for air. Salt-sweat crusted her forehead, and she winced as it cracked. The bed was empty. Splashing sounds lured her gaze outdoors. The shack's only door lay open, allowing the northern breeze to cool the tiny space. Sleepy eyes found him by the water's edge, bathing. Powerful thighs squatted, and a sculpted ass flexed in plain view from the shack. He dipped and poured the water over his tanned skin—all of it a soft bronze.

In her short years, Beth had not witnessed the splendor of the naked male body, and her eyes refused to glance anywhere else. Luce stood, flexing and gleaming with wetness. A shadow cast between his thick thighs relayed a shock through her system. A groan left his parted lips as his hand slid over himself. A hand flew to her mouth, attempting to cover the audible gasp.

An inferno rushed to her cheeks, and she should have glanced away, but Beth could not tear her peeping eyes from him. Breath caught in another noticeable gasp, tasting the heavy salt filling her lungs without trying. A strange pulse throbbed inside of her core, more intense than yesterday, and set a steady thrum of her heart. Fingertips gripped the doorway, digging further with each stir of her center. Like the steadiness of the war drums, his hard breaths and moans echoed in Beth's ears.

His hand increased its speed, and the wind carried his breathless cries. Her teeth bit into her lip in a desperate attempt to squelch the ache between her thighs. The crescendo of his voice and movements enchanted her further and all but hypnotized her to approach.

"Bethy." Wide eyes widened. *He knew I stalked him.* "Sweet sunshine." Lucien's body trembled from head to toe, and his head flung toward the heavens.

Like a scrambling squirrel, she skittered inside the shack, and pretended to busy herself. As Beth reached for last night's wet discarded clothing, Lucien's hands circled her waist. His husky breath tickled her neck, and her muscles froze as if doused in ice as he pressed against her.

Chapter Five

"One day I'll stare deep into your eyes and call out your name." Her flushed cheeks blushed even hotter than before. Oh God, had he truly known she was spying on him. "But I can't wait till you scream my name." Lucien's hand trailed down her back and pinched her ass. Beth squeaked, spun, and whacked his arm. He wore his birthday suit and a devious grin.

"Why so red, sunshine?" His tone softened. "By now, if we'd lived back then, we'd be married." His lips caressed her temple, and she elbowed his ribs. What had gotten into him?

Indian culture varied depending upon the tribe. Marriage wasn't anything like marriage today. Beth blinked at Luce and waited for an answer. Once again one did not come. Men and women took multiple partners and could have as many lovers as they could financially support. He tilted her chin and brushed the salt from her forehead. Man or woman, it didn't matter. Unions formed as early as thirteen, but typically no later than twenty for a woman. Maybe she'd become too Americanized, but she hadn't liked the idea of more than one partner or being sold like cattle. Beth snorted and heaved from his arms. Maybe that was why he had enjoyed Amber's company over hers, and the mere thought caused the bile to lurch up her throat. She came with a whole posse of women stupid enough to believe they were more important than the next.

The spittle burned her nose. "Beth," Luce warned as her gaze landed on the door. What were they doing here? Playing house? How long until he chucked her aside again? Was it convenience? Beth shut her eyes, willing the images to disperse. The wind whispered: she would never be enough for him. It shouted: she didn't deserve him.

Beth lunged for the opening. Zoro yowled as she stepped on his tail. She found herself running from the shack and into the woods, heaving and choking on the vomit with no idea which direction she was heading except away from Lucien. Her love for him had not mattered, and the one regret she had was not grabbing Zoro, but she could not turn around. The time for relying on another's opinion had ended. Beth had to do this for herself, free herself of this life, and all the bands that bound her fate to Lucien.

Guilt bubbled and singed her insides as the ire of reality reared up her throat again. The acidic fire rooted and stung as Beth ran. No glances spared; she did not look behind her, and her gaze focused on the world in front of her. No longer a prisoner to the darkness, of Lucien Brown, or her family; Beth was free.

Branches and stones nicked her feet. Scratches sliced into her cheeks and arms as branches swung into her tornado path. Her feet kept on running, crashing, and crunching the earth beneath her. Birds flew into the air, disturbed by her presence. Animals darted from her thundering path, chattering their displeasure. Every inch of her body burned as if his words lit a fuse, her heart pumped their poison, and the thoughts ignited within her soul.

"Bethany McCallister," a woman yelled her name in the far distance. Her course altered and veered toward the voice as she repeated her name. A dog barked in the same location, and Beth assumed the Mandate had searched for her. *I would fare better with them. I'm innocent.* The state of her home, the electrical burns, and melted walls, the disarray she had left behind all pointed to a struggle even though Beth left willingly with Lucien. Tell them she had not known about whatever Vivian and her parents did. Show them Jemma was innocent too. They would believe the truth; they had to believe.

Lungs threatened to give out, and the cramps returned from the previous night's adventure. *Just a little farther*, Beth egged herself on and refused to give-up. The woman's voice grew nearer with every call.

Thunder roared to the south, and the reverberation fueled her steps. The crash rolled over the hillsides and dipped into the valleys like a wavering boom. Wind and rain whipped around the strange sunny sky, and the dense air reeked of rain. Not a dark cloud lain within her sight. Tones vibrated from the tree roots and shook the ground. Beth spun around for another glance and squinted at the brightness. Too late, the fatal mistake sent her tumbling to the earth and grasping her ankle as the pain stabbed up her leg.

Breath caught, and face pinched. Beth lay upon the sandy earth powerless to stand, rocking, and moaning as the tears choked and burned. The storm closed in. Legs scrambled, trying again to rise, but she collapsed to the ground, yelping. Curses flew from her lips. She rarely uttered swears. The tender ankle proved too great to bear her weight. Beth dragged herself, army crawling on her good side across the forest floor, and propped herself against the nearest tree.

"Bethany McCallister."

A deep breath filled her lungs, hands cupped her mouth, and she shouted, "I am here. I am injured."

Whistles blew, and the woman asked her to call out again. She would follow her voice. Her gaze darted around as the sounds of nature stole her attention. Branches snapped. Any one of them could have been Lucien storming after her, but she pushed the thought from her mind. Leaves crunched. A frown tugged her lips. Beth was right. Lucien had been playing a game. Blue eyes glowed in the stormy grey morning. Two pairs greeted her from the direction she had run.

A dog barked again, but closer this time, and Beth asked, "Is that you?"

Chocolate eyes blinked, and tall perky ears pointed upward. Its tail wagged, and it leapt, releasing a high-pitched bark. Beth drew into herself and trembled; she did not know much about dogs and was more of a cat person.

"Bethy." The dog growled and dipped his head, baring sharp teeth. Beth blinked, and Lucien knelt beside her, holding Zoro's crate, but she refused to meet his gaze. He stroked her temple, burning her cuts with salty fingers. The dog lunged, snarling at her or him. *Probably him.* "Beth, don't go with them. They'll keep you from me."

Zoro purred. "He's right."

The dog pinned his ears back, his fur bristled, and his tail stiffened. Lucien cursed as a slender woman approached the dog from behind. She appeared older, grey marring her temples. She patted the dog's head and narrowed her eyes on Beth. Lucien's hand squeezed her shoulder, and he placed Zoro's crate in her lap.

"Bethany McCallister?" She nodded. "Mr. Brown, why are you here?"

"I've known Beth my whole life. Why wouldn't I help search for her?" Beth bit her lip to keep from cussing him out.

His eyes pled for silence as the woman grilled him. "You didn't check in when you found her as per protocol, Brown."

The dog snarled and lunged. *Protocol?* Lucien snorted and sidestepped the dog's attempt. "I stumbled across her heading toward your voice." He cracked his neck and the vein in his jaw throbbed. "Call that mangy mutt off, before I wring its neck."

The woman asked to speak with Beth alone, and she agreed despite Lucien's interjections. He stalked away into the woods, but if his hearing were like hers, he would be listening. A hand ran over her face, wincing at the scabbed scratches, and she took a deep breath. The point of running was to leave Lucien, but another lie had uncovered itself.

He had worked for the Mandate. Made sense seeing as his daddy did too.

She introduced herself as Claire and knelt Beth's side. The German Shepherd lain at her feet and wagged his tail through the felled needles; he eyed the crate. Zoro didn't feel the same about him if his growling had anything to say about his temperament.

"What's this one's name?" she asked and pointed toward the cat. Beth told her and hugged the crate a little closer. A finger wiggled between the bars seeking his soft and comforting fur, but her familiar offered no more advice. "How long have you known Lucien?"

Beth stared straight at Zoro. "For as long as I can remember. We've always been friends." The lie soured her mouth. They'd been friends all right except for the last three years, but the whole town knew that. Claire must not have been from around these parts, or she would know how bizarre this situation was to her. Lucien would not—should not have helped her—and maybe it was not normal for Beth to have saved his life either. After all, they were enemies or was it frenemies.

"Did he hurt you?" She shook her head. "Okay. Where'd you get the bruises and scratches?" Claire whistled a breath and glanced over her body.

"I fell in the woods as I was running."

Claire raised an eyebrow. "Can you walk?"

"Not without help. Don't think it's broken." Beth glanced to her swollen ankle and noticed the speckled bruising settling over her skin. "You from the Mandate?"

The woman removed her badge from the back of her jeans and flipped it over. Claire from Mandated Native American Affairs, she nodded, and forced a smile.

"Am I in trouble?"

Claire pursed her lips, but Lucien spoke, "No." Her almond colored eyes blinked. "We're holding your family for questioning."

We. The woods charged as if Luce overstepped boundaries. Air trapped in her lungs as she sought guidance from her familiar, but there wasn't a decision to make. Beth could not run anymore, not physically or mentally. Hiding like a rat wasn't for her and neither was hiding with a rat's ass like Lucien.

His feet shuffled through the pine needles as if drawn by her thoughts. The slow lull of his heartbeat a reminder of his sickness, and Beth's stomach knotted. The wrong scent was stronger. An offered hand hovered in her face, and she glanced between the two Mandate employees. Fingers flickered, and she stared into his eyes. A blue sheen reflected from the widened irises, mirroring hurt in his welled gaze.

Pieces of her shattered again, and a sniffle caught in her throat, choking her sanity. She should have been proud, but hurting Lucien made her feel like a leeching flea. Beth glanced to his hand; it shook.

"Beth, let *me* help you." The words pled something unspoken.

Swallowing the sob, she grasped his hand, half-expecting for him to carry her. Claire lifted the cat carrier, and the dog sniffed the crate. Zoro growled a warning.

"He's not used to dogs. Might want to lift him higher and hold the crate steady." Clinging to Luce, she hobbled a few steps and winced as her foot struck an exposed root. Lucien reacted quickly and caught her before they had both tumbled.

"Want to tell me about the destruction inside your house? Looks like a fire with no signs of anyone putting it out."

If she got out of this mess, she would owe Aunt Vivian for life. Cinderella servitude came to mind on top of draining of her blood. Beth exchanged a glance with Lucien. He nodded but averted his eyes. "That was my fault too."

"I've heard of those born ... different."

The word rolled from her tongue like a stigma, and Beth's cheeks flushed. Over the years, she'd grown used to the townsfolk thinking she was odd. All her weight leaned on Luce as they limped along slower than snails during a summer storm; he lifted her over root systems but did not carry her.

"The locha attacked," Beth whispered. Luce's body stiffened.

Claire tossed her head back, laughing, and almost dropped Zoro's crate. "Those are superstitions. None of its real."

But whatever attacked her last night was alive. Her hand brushed her collarbone and recalled the hands that held her under the water in both reality and dream. Beth shared a fleeting look with Lucien, and he winked.

"Where did the bruise on your neck come from?"

"Locha."

"Uh-huh." Claire whipped around, and her eyes settled on Lucien. Had she known what he was? Beth wasn't in the mood to ask, and whatever history he had with her wasn't Beth's business. "What do you know about—"

"Not now," Lucien said under his breath. Claire mumbled about a warrant and searching the residence for evidence but kept navigating the forest. "What part of not now ain't you understanding?"

"What about my stuff and clothes?" Beth fingered the borrowed sundress. Luce halted, and air whistled through his teeth. Pain reflected to her, echoing the last few years of her life, but on him, the emotion seemed displaced and wrong.

"Don't you worry now, sunshine. I'll take you shopping." Lucien stroked his thumb over her cheek, lingering the touch as his forehead wrinkled. Birds chirped above them. Tightness formed in her belly as she searched the treetops for them before Lucien drew her into another trap.

Claire cleared her throat. "The McCallister accounts are frozen."

Beth's mouth dropped. Lucien flicked her chin, smiling as he leaned closer. "It'll be all right, Bethany." If he hadn't spent the last three years lying through his teeth, she may have believed him, but the twisting sensation of her gut said otherwise. "Mean it sweetheart," he whispered and kissed her temple. "You'll see soon."

Would it be all right? Blue eyes said no, but his head shook yes. Energy rushed over her bare arms and bumps skittered over her skin. The sky darkened as her stomach reeled. Why did she have to be a fool and run off like that? Her breath blew out as the wind tousled Lucien's black locks. Whatever crime Vivian committed had to be bigger than she'd imagined. Monumental big, but aside from that mystery ingredient and using Beth's blood, she didn't know what could have wrought the wrath of the Mandate on her family.

That which doesn't kill me will make me stronger.

Lucien sat her on a tree stump and talked to Claire. Their hushed whispers overpowered by the storm brewing and approaching them. Beth cracked her knuckles, relieving tension, but the sparks crackled at their tips. He shot her a wide-eyed look, and she slipped her hands behind her back. Luce dipped into his jeans and withdrew his phone. The speakerphone blared over the forest clattering, and his father answered on the second ring. James Brown sat on the Mandate—local and elected official to represent the town—but the memory had slipped her mind before Claire arrived. His momma did too. Was that how Luce knew about her family? He handed Claire his phone. Mr. Brown spoke to her in a stern voice that carried and raced her heart.

Claire nodded, glanced at Beth, and said, "Yes, sir, a person of interest in protective custody." She rolled her eyes as Lucien grinned.

James Brown insisted on recuperation time from the attack and that she received treatment with a doctor before the Mandate could question Beth about her aunt's business dealings. Super hearing rocked. Claire hung up the phone but stared at it, blinking as if confused.

"See sunshine? Everything's all right." He kneeled at her feet and squeezed her kneecaps.

They arrived at the forest's edge after their long five mile traipse. This house was smaller than the mansion, and her dad had said that it used to be the guest quarters, but the Browns purchased it from the McCallisters in the eighteen hundreds along with a parcel for two hundred acres. Fancy cars sat in the driveway, but Lucien's hybrid wasn't there. Dana Brown stepped onto the back porch. She frowned, and Beth gulped. Appearing the same as she had when they were kids, albeit with a tad more grey hair, her hands cradled slender hips, and her hazel eyes narrowed. "Lucien Lewis Brown, you get that girl off her feet this instant."

"Momma's orders sweetheart," he whispered as a yelp left Beth's open mouth. The grin and chuckle said he enjoyed rescuing her a bit too much. "You don't argue with my momma."

Snaking her hands around his neck, her cheek brushed against his beard. The officer rested Zoro's crate on her stomach. Too bad Beth's mother never cared. Neither had her dad, but she had recalled Dana Brown, and used to think of her as a mom even if she was only a surrogate.

"Well I haven't seen you in forever girl." Dana bit her lip. "Wish you didn't look like the forest stomped all over you."

Were the bruises and scratches that bad? Lucien didn't have a mirror at the shack, but her face felt puffier than usual, and pain seared through her body. Beth said her hellos to the Browns and reflected their hovering attention away, not liking being the center of attention.

Officer Claire did not follow them inside the house, and the dirty look Mrs. Brown shared with the agent did not surprise Beth as much as she thought it would have. Lucien carried her over the threshold and set her in their family room. The same old striped couch molded to her body and hugged her tender points. He set Zoro on the floor, bending in his glorious jeans, and opened his cage. Beth's gaze darted over the space, noting the only big changes were in updated photographs on the walls and mantle. Lucien broke her search, kissing her forehead; his lips lingered.

"Told you what they'd do, Bethy." The fur ball hopped into her lap and batted at her belly. Luce drew himself away, and Zoro kissed her nose. *Jealous bugger.* His hands disappeared deep into his pockets. Luce rocked on his heels—his bare, mud covered heels. No smile or grin graced his blank face. "You just made saving your sweet ass harder."

Heat flooded her cheeks, and Beth looked away as he leaned over her again, shoving Zoro off her lap. Voices carried inside as his parents joined them, and she breathed easier as he backed off. Lucien resembled James more than he resembled Dana, especially with his scruffy face making him appear older. Zoro hissed and growled as they approached. All in good fun, she hoped, as James laughed at her finicky feline familiar. Dana disappeared into the kitchen. She'd find a way to shove food down Beth's throat like when she was a kid.

"I'll be back," Luce said and kissed her cheek. "Need to pick up some things for you." Like a zombie, she nodded as her gaze wandered over the old pictures of them as kids again. For years, the Browns were a second family for her. They never minded the time spent with Lucien before or after his illness, but as they drifted apart, so did her relationship with his parents. If he hated her, part of her had figured they did too.

"Bethany," James interrupted her memory lane escapade. "Our home is yours. We owe you more than you'll ever realize."

"Thank you for not turning me over." She shifted trying to find a comfortable position. "Luce told me some but I still don't understand what's going on." He sighed. Zoro sniffed his shoes. James settled himself in a chair and reached for the light. His dark brow rose as he lifted her leg onto this thigh and Beth clenched her jaw to keep herself from crying out as the pain shot up her leg again. When left alone the throb dulled to a tender ache but hurt like the dickens if moved.

"Dana, get me some ice." She brought him an ice pack and a first aid kit. Beth winced every time he touched or moved her ankle; the whole foot had doubled in size. "It's broken, Beth. We should take it for an x-ray just to be certain." He turned to his wife. "Call Lucien and tell him to hurry."

Beth twisted her hands in her lap. Doctors and her did not mix. High stress and pain never turned out well.

"Let's wait for Lucien," Beth said voice cracking, "Maybe the ice will help?" Dana cleared the coffee table and piled pillows to elevate her ankle. She made small talk, asking how she'd been and why she stopped coming around. Mrs. Brown did not need to hear that her son was a lying pain in her ass or that he had broken her spirit and heart. James covered the ice with a towel and applied it to her ankle. Her teeth gritted as he wrapped a bandage to hold it steady.

James asked, "How much has Lucien told you?"

"By admission or because I ran into Claire?" Beth laughed, but the Browns weren't amused. "He showed up sick, looking like death warmed over." Heavy lines laced their foreheads as the couple shared a worried glance. "My blood healed him. It's something special to Spirit Walkers, right, and my family knew about it too. I didn't know." She left out the lying parts, the destruction to her house, and her ability to harness lightning on purpose. If they knew the lore and believed it then they already knew her capabilities.

Her eyes burned thinking about how her family betrayed her. Dana asked, "How did Claire find you?"

Beth chewed her lip for a moment as James opened the first aid kit and laid the contents on the table. Dana retrieved a bottle of rubbing alcohol, and her grimace flashed before plastering into a false smile. Beth told them how Lucien took her far into the woods but did not mention specifics. James doused a cotton ball in disinfectant. Air whistled through her teeth as he swiped it across her skin, repeating the process more times than she could count. The smell was so strong she tasted the alcohol. Her hands twisted in her lap again, gripping the fabric and grinding her teeth. Dana soothed her at first, but wiped her hands on an apron, and excused herself. Zoro jumped as a dish clattered in the kitchen.

James eyes widened as Beth told him about outrunning Luce. A bit of a white lie as she didn't believe he followed her into the woods despite yesterday's claim of chasing her. "You outran him?" Dana's raised voice carried into the room. "That's not an easy feat, young lady."

Slouching lower, Beth prayed wanting to both disappear and turn back time. Stiff shoulders shrugged instead, and she took a page from Lucien's notebook of indifference. "Did you know Vivian's business? I have to ask, Bethany."

"She sold remedies, and I delivered them. It's what she's always done." Her head shook, and a tear slid over her cheek. Beth wiped it away as James patted her knee. "Part of me should know something, but they ... spied on me. Luce found a video recorder in my room." Another tear released. "They never let me out after dark."

Dana scolded, "You leave her be."

"No, I want to know." The sobs didn't relent as warm arms surrounded her. Dana stroked her hair and held her as the dams burst. Beth cried for Jemma, Lucien, and every person suffering without her blood. Her life meant nothing if the people she cared about agonized in pain or from illness; it did not matter if they knew she had existed as the reason or not.

Dana rocked her gently. "You don't need to do this now."

But Beth insisted. James gulped but agreed, despite his wife's protests that she needed more rest. Throbbing under the layer of ice, her ankle screamed, but the pain was a spat compared to her fragile heart. Still she hid it, as she did all agony in her life, a feat most nineteen year olds had not mastered.

"Luce agreed to be our mole," he started. "The Mandate knew Vivian's cures worked, and we let her practice for years without interference. Beth, she saved lives, you saved people and gave them a second chance."

Dana squeezed her tighter. Her heart fluttered like Lucien's heartbeat, but the comfort was different. "I still don't think she should hear this, James," she murmured. "Not from us."

But Lucien didn't tell her. Brows rose, and a sigh tickled her throat. He was protecting her. Beth closed her eyes and sniffled. "Luce never thought … He didn't think …" The words would not leave her lips. Dana shushed her. A car door slammed outside. Heat flooded her cheeks.

"No. He's always maintained your innocence. At sixteen he did a brave thing, a hurtful thing, but he knew your aunt would never … I'm getting ahead of myself," James said and glanced over his shoulder. Another car door slammed, and her pulse quickened. Sobs rattled her chest as Beth gasped for air. Three years … for three years, he hurt her for their investigation. "If a patient couldn't pay, your aunt removed your blood from her tinctures. As long as you and Luce were friends …"

Keys rattled as they dropped but against what she could not see. Hairs stood on her neck, and she gazed over her shoulder. A disheveled Lucien stood in the doorway; his jaw slightly moving, and blue eyes rimmed with tears. Heart breaking again, the simmering anger for him dissipated. Silence fell for a moment as a beacon of light shined over her angel. Answers reflected in her mind and in his eyes, she saw the truth. Broken them to save her and to prove Vivian was a criminal. Lucien had to hate her, and had to make her despise him. She swallowed hard as the twisted conflictions warred within her. James and Dana continued, but she heard all she had needed. The why had haunted her? Beth thought was something she had done without knowing, but it had been him.

"Leaving the key ingredient out of Lucien's potion exposed some of it," Dana whispered. "We saw her workspace and the blood, and we pieced together that it was yours. What happened inside the house?"

She whispered, "After Luce came to, I lost control." Her eyes did not leave him, but Luce had continued standing there frozen like a deer in headlights. Why didn't he tell her this? Beth would have pretended. She would have understood.

He answered her thoughts, staring at the ground. "Would you have believed me?"

"Maybe?" The tone of her voice said no she would not have believed him, not without proof.

"Came to?" Dana fiddled with Beth's hair. "Came to?" The confusion in her voice increased. "You bit her?"

"I was dying, Momma." Lucien's eyes did not leave hers as her heart beat harder, louder, and stronger for him. Her hands itched, scratching over the upholstery wanting to hold him. Lips parted. Sweaty palms wanted to smack him into next Tuesday for not telling her the truth sooner, but she let that one slide off her shoulders.

Dana said something but she could not make out the words. Shaky hands shoved into his pockets. Covered in orange dirt the boy was a complete mess, though she doubted she had fared much better. The edges of his lips curled into a tiny smile. Luce inched closer as if waiting for her invitation. Beth tapped the armrest, tilting her head. Raised brows rose even higher but he leaned on the couch, twining their hands together in a wordless exchange. He slipped between the end and her, squeezing and shifting until Beth sat on his lap.

"You all right, sunshine?" Rough lips caressed her temple. *Yes and no.* How did one react to learning their family sold your blood for profit, denying treatment, and killing innocent people if they couldn't pay. "Meant your ankle."

Dana patted her good knee. "This is how it always should have been." Lucien shifted them toward the middle as his mother departed, heading for the kitchen. Pots and pans clattered. Food sizzled and fried chicken wafted past her nose as they sat in silence. Beth's mind leapt between the lies, wondering if her family had deceived her in other ways. A rumble issued from her belly.

Zoro explored, batting at random objects, and jumping in the air when they moved. Watching him, she could not help but wonder if he had known of this. Catching his curious gaze settling on her, she knew he had also known of this. What else did her familiar hide? Why hide it in the first place?

Lucien was lucky. His family had always been both loving and kind. Honest it seemed too. The only one who had not lied was Jemma. Everyone else deceived her, not just her now, but also the little girl. How could she have been so stupid? Daddy took her blood all the time. Why didn't she question him further? A sob rose; her breath stuttered. She could have done something about this sooner if she had only asked.

"Oh, no you don't," Lucien said. "This ain't your fault, Bethy." The couch creaked and the cushions moved as she stared at the mantle photographs again. Three years … she was as much as fault as he was for the pain and separation. He knelt at her feet. "Baby look at me."

A tremor rolled through her shoulders as thunder rattled the windows. Lightning and rain followed as liquid streamed from her stinging eyes.

James asked, "Is she—"

"Yeah, Dad."

Was she what? Her lids blinked, closing. Deep cleansing breaths relaxed her shuddering body as her emotions tampered under control. Dana said, "Holy moly, the clouds disappeared." Heels clicked over the floors, Beth peeped through slanting eyes. A towel draped over her shoulder, and Dana's mouth hung open. "Oh, my stars girl."

"What?"

"Kolkohkafoosi," Zoro whispered. The Browns gaped at him. "Yes, I talk."

Her fingers rubbed together, and the cat jumped in her lap, kissing her nose as he often did. Luce said, "Zoro is her familiar."

Dana's shaky hands reached for the chair, James grabbed them, and she lowered herself to the armrest of his recliner. Her eyes darted to Lucien, Zoro, and then to Dana. "You didn't tell us this," she gulped, "Kolkohkafoosi indeed." A hand flew to her heart. "Tell me you didn't know, James."

He stuffed his hands in his pockets and shrugged. Like father like son. A snort rose in Beth's throat, but she swallowed hard, burying it with the rest of her emotions.

"Would someone like to tell *me* what's going on?" Lucien shook his head, scowling. Oh, he knew all right too just like his father.

"They can't take her," Luce whispered, still kneeling at her feet, but twisted his torso. "They'll destroy her."

"Will you stop talking about me like I'm not here?"

"No one's taking her. Calm down. We'll move her if we have to." James nodded, staring at his son.

Zoro meowed. "It is not time." Arms crossed over her chest, and she glared at him. "That's not going to work."

His parents exchanged glances with Lucien, but he wasn't opening up either. Her fists curled. Beth hated secrets and lies; she had heard enough of them to spread across the world and still have some leftover. "Tell me something you can then. Vivian broke the law, right?"

Lucien grasped her hand, kneeling still, and placed his chin on her skinned knee. "You are more than your blood to me, to this family. You're a beautiful woman with a selfless heart, but the Mandate will exploit you."

He smiled and patted her hand. "That's not what I meant and you know it." Didn't they work for the Mandate? Beth opened her mouth to ask, but his parents interrupted her, showering more than enough praise, and turned her redder than the dirt. "I'd have helped you even if we weren't friends. After we stopped hanging out …"

Her world had crumbled. Some girls were stronger than that. Beth was not that resilient.

From a young age, she had clung to Lucien as if he were the moon and stars, lighting her path to freedom. Then he fell ill and piece by piece, star by star the lights had faded. It had rained almost daily that summer. Hurricanes had attacked the Gulf of Mexico seemingly one after another, fueled by the falling tears for the future ripped from her tiny eleven-year-old grasp. When her family and the doctors told her no, she could not save Lucien's life, the tornado sirens had blasted.

Every emotional roller coaster ride Beth took, the storms had followed in her wake. Thunderbird—Guardian of Men and protector of life and death— showed up all over Native American folklore. The job never changed, but how they appeared did, and some myths claimed there was only one. But Beth didn't believe them. If it weren't for the lightning, she would not have believed she was a Spirit Walker either.

"Vivian made a lot of enemies, but she has allies too. Many people can't afford her prices or to keep buying the cure forever. Remember what I said?" He drew a palm over his rugged face. "I had to protect you by distancing myself from you, but now the Mandate wants you too, and I ain't letting them touch you, sweetheart."

"But why do they want me?"

James sighed, easing into his chair again. "The rumor is that your Aunt is placing the bulk of the blame on your shoulders." He scratched his neck. "They're willing to cut her a deal for you." Lucien roared, and Beth jumped, crying out as her ankle dropped off the coffee table, and her foot slammed into the floor. Zoro hissed. "Calm yourself, Lucien." James turned to Beth. "I pulled every favor to secure you here, Beth, and we'll do whatever it takes to protect you, even if that means hiding you."

He continued, "Vivian's charged with murder, Beth. Your parent's are charged with larceny."

"Jemma?" A deep breath drowned her lungs, holding it as she discovered the fate of her cousin.

"She didn't manifest powers. They've sent her into a group home." Lucien's hands squeezed her shoulders, and he kissed the top of her head. Torn between the family she'd thought she'd known and the scandalous truth. Beth would have given the blood if ... her head fell into her hands, but her eyes ran dry.

"Dad," Lucien said in a warning tone. "No more."

Every item Vivian bought: her car, belongings, and her clothes, all of it she purchased for her. Supported the entire household and they never wanted for anything. But it was blood money. The thought of it churned Beth's stomach. Luce forced her gaze. Unshed liquid warred in his eyes. "How much did she charge?"

"$3,000 per dose, one dose a week, and she's had anywhere from twenty to thirty customers a week."

A curse flew from her mouth, and she clamped a hand over it. Three thousand times twenty was ... "$156,000 per customer a year? Or 3.1 Mil ..."

Winds howled through the screens and rattled the glass panes. Lightning snapped, hitting their pecan tree, and thunder shook the earth. Her face twisted, and her fists coiled into tiny balls. Sparks and smoke released from her hands. Lucien stroked her cheek, drawing her attention. Beth stared at the char marks on her dress and blinked.

"Look at me, Bethy." He grasped her fists, unwinding the fingertips, and swept them over his rough cheek. Like before, he absorbed the excess power. "That's it sunshine," his blue lips moved as his parents gasped, "she can't hurt me. But I think we're done with talking. You've got to relax and let it out." A surge of sparks crawled beneath her skin, reaching for her fingers. Both magnificent and scarily beautiful watching the sheer power of nature as it moved through her. "That's it, force it out."

When the last charge left, Lucien sat beside her, cradling her limp body as the serenity peaked. Stunned speechless, Dana and James remained silent as he explained why he and Zoro were both immune to her powers. Bit by bit his skin returned to its usual reddish tan, and the blue slowly dissipated. Beth did not know where or how it exited his body, but she assumed to the earth.

A kettle whistled in the kitchen. Dana leapt from the armchair, returning with a pot of herbal tea. She leaned forward, but Luce held up his hand, and poured a cup.

Beth sipped, listening to the gentle thrum of rain matching the cadence of her pulse. Her eyes had dried but inside of her the emotions poured, building and mixing. With each rumble, Luce fidgeted, pacing the living room floor. His dad called him into the hallway, but she heard them.

"She still needs a doctor. I swear her ankle's broken, son." James whispered to Lucien in the foyer. Their footsteps carried as they moved upstairs where she could no longer listen in, but Zoro stayed at Luce's heels.

Minutes passed as her fingertips tapped along the side of the teacup. A dark hole in the middle of nowhere looked better with each passing second. Maybe then, Beth could sort through the lies and confusion spinning webs around her blood. She reached forward, placing the cup on the table when he burst in. Lucien faced her. "You told them no? Why?" Beth opened her mouth to answer, but closed it again. "Out with it, sunshine."

A shiver crept from her toes to her spine as the memory flashed within her mind. As he cringed, she knew he had seen it too. "Last time I was there you were sick. Every time I picture the hospital or a doctor, I see you frail and dying. Remember when I broke the machine?" His smile returned and spread into a massive grin. Beth had her old Lucien back if only for a fraction of a second. "Vivian said I couldn't go to the hospital something about … the electrical current."

Another lie perhaps, another way to keep her under their control, but she still clung to the first reason. Even the memory raced her heart. The clock chimed on their mantle. The storm had settled, but the grey skies remained. "I never wanted to hurt you." He kissed her sweaty palm. "I was trying to figure out how to tell you without worrying you more about your family." A sigh tickled her hand. "Beth, I've been trying for years, but you ignored me."

"Jemma's innocent in all this." Beth needed to clear her name and bring her home. Nothing else mattered. A hand brushed her heart thinking about how frightened she must have been. The poor kid had to be scared out of her wits. Who knows what they would do to her … what she would tell them? "What if she tells the Mandate?"

Her eyes locked with Lucien. "Do you think she'd tattle on you?"

"What if she thinks she's helping me?" A dark brow rose. Jemma did not own a malicious bone in her body, but she would not think twice if she thought she was somehow saving her. "Can you warn her?"

Lucien cursed under his breath. Zoro batted at his thigh—all claws. "Why not call a Dr. Pawl?"

"Because I'm not an animal? I'm fine." Why did they make such a big deal over it? Injured often as a kid, she had healed fine on her own before.

"You ain't fine, Beth." Lucien eased from the couch and withdrew his cell phone. She nibbled on her lip. "Stop your pouting. What's his number?" She swiped it from him and typed in the vet's office number. They also gave the cat his shots and yearly check-ups and she knew the number by heart. As it started ringing, she handed the phone back, pressing her lips together. Luce blew her a kiss and chuckled as the answering service picked up. He walked into the other room leaving Beth and Zoro behind.

"Kolkohkafoosi, I had no knowledge of the money, just your blood as the secret in her remedies." Lucien slid next to her, and Zoro pounced onto his lap, placing a paw on his cheek. Two sets of blue eyes blinked, but only one pair was confused and as wide as the saucer on the table. "You believe me, iyyìnko?"

"Don't you dare call him a heathen," Beth scolded but laughed at the same time. "He is hasi." She leaned against Lucien and brushed her palm over his cheek. "He is my hasi, my light."

"Locha, Bethany, the inheritors came from locha." Locha —the dark– her nose stuck into the air refusing to believe he was birthed from the darkness. Nothing evil would go to such lengths to save another life. His mistreatments, while still painful, she understood better than before. They could have avoided all the awkwardness though.

Lucien lifted her without warning. "Stop that. Put me down." His lips silenced her; no fight remained within her as her lips parted. A groan vibrated her mouth, and her belly knotted, drawing, and squeezing her navel.

"I'm still here," Zoro said.

Chapter Six

The three of them—Zoro refused to stay behind with the heathens—pulled up to the veterinary clinic downtown as night blanketed the sky in hazy darkness. Each day seemed to grow shorter, but in July, the sun should have shined. Storm clouds spanned the horizon, blocking out the sun like a giant inkblot. Wind whipped Lucien's hybrid around the parking lot as if it weighed nothing at all. Her gaze darted following the shadows despite the well-lit streets.

She still could not get used to his sudden movements as Luce opened her door. Reaching over her to unbuckle the seatbelt, Beth held her breath as their skin brushed. A rough hand cupped her face, holding her for a millisecond, yet an hour could have passed. Time halted with Lucien. *Does he want that?* Beth looked out the driver's side window. *Does he want me?* Even with knowing the truth, their shared past was harder to let go than she had realized.

Everyone wanted a piece of her for what ran through her veins, whether it was to take her blood to live or sell it as a cure. How would Beth ever distinguish who was sincere?

"Sweetheart," he said and knelt on the sidewalk. The dashboard dinged. "Baby, if there was a way …" But there wasn't. Luce would die without her blood, and if she found a way to be normal, he'd still die. "What does your heart tell you?"

"That you love me," she whispered, and Zoro flicked his tail.

"Beth, I do love you. Will you look at me?" Lucien guided her stiff chin and forced her gaze. "I've loved you since we were kids, and I ain't stopping just because you think it's your blood." Her lip trembled in time with the dashboard chimes. "There ain't anything in the entire universe that can keep me from you except you. Cancer couldn't separate us, baby. Now quit your stalling, and let's go."

He didn't wait for a response and scooped her from the passenger seat, pausing for Zoro to jump in her lap. Beth did not know what to say. Before a snarky remark or coy tease would have worked perfectly against Lucien, but not anymore. Shadows darted, rustling the bushes as he carried them into the veterinary clinic. Her arm slid around his neck, gripping tighter.

White and green walls encompassed her; the lights hummed and flickered. Her fingers stroked his ear as if Lucien had transformed into her Zoro, but he didn't purr like her comforting familiar. "Now you're playing dirty. Ain't going to work."

Once inside the ill feelings worsened as bile rose in her throat. Sweat-salt crusted on her forehead, and the flaky bits cracked as eyebrows rose at Lucien's statement. White walls painted with green paw prints shifted, closing in on her. Fingernails scratched into his neck.

"You're safe, Bethy." Bleach burned her nose, and memories tried to rise from the wafting scent.

The vet smiled despite his yellowed eyes. Lucien whispered, "Liver cancer."

Beth knew already from chatting with him during her deliveries and vet appointments. Nerves didn't cause his shaky hands either. A smile forced over her lips as Luce made the introductions but refused to put her down. The doctor suffered because of her, but he listened as Lucien explained her fears and agreed to x-ray her ankle.

"What's this?" he asked as the vet handed him a card.

"I can't write scripts for pain relief, and you should have a medical doctor look over her gashes and bruises." The vet brushed his neck, but he didn't accuse Lucien as Claire had. Even after all he had done in the past; she knew he would never physically harm her. The vet knelt; an uneasy feat as Lucien helped him. "What happened, kiddo?"

Lucien bit his lip. Zoro said, "Locha. Kolkohkafoosi."

Dr. Pawl's head cocked as the room silenced. Thickened skin reflected a greenish hue like Lucien had days ago. A wrongness she couldn't place misted from his person. It held no name or flavor existing in Beth's vocabulary, but long ago, she had decided it was looming death. As if the air was sucked from the office and their lungs, a pregnant pause fell over the room. Dr. Pawl stared at her with those sickened yellow eyes; hands twisted in her lap, but Beth met his gaze.

He said, "Many moons ago there were signs the elders spoke of. A girl would walk among us, but she wasn't normal." Dr. Pawl cracked a smile. "She would look human outside, but inside she would be different in bone and organs."

Feeble fingers tilted Beth's chin left and right. "Some tribes believe there is but one Kolkohkafoosi, but others believe them as an ancient race older than humans. But as disease, war, and famine spread, the Kolkohkafoosi disappeared from the world. Many think they died, others think they left for another world, and then there are those who refuse to believe they ever existed."

"What do you believe?" asked Beth, gulping.

"Not the latter, but I cannot say what happened to your race." Cold fingers pressed into her neck as he murmured, "That's odd." Beth flinched.

"You're hurting her," Luce said and grasped the vet's shoulder.

Dr. Pawl's lips pursed as his forehead wrinkled. "She doesn't have a human thyroid gland." The fingers pressed harder against her sensitive skin, and Beth cried out. "Sorry." His hands withdrew, but the wrinkles remained etched across his forehead. "We still look for hope and guidance from our ancestors, but the proof is here."

Zoro purred and brushed his head against her hand. Mindlessly Beth petted him, allowing the vibration to sooth her rattled nerves.

What did Mr. Pawl mean she didn't have a human thyroid? What did her thyroid have to do with her injured ankle? Nibbling her lip, she pushed the words from her mind. Lucien knelt, stroking the wet streak on her cheek, and she fell into his rough palm. When would it end?

Dark tresses fell over her face as the vet studied her. "You have all the signs of Avian Thyroid Disorder. Dull features—"

"Beth ain't dull," Luce snapped. A sob caught in Beth's chest. She saw herself as listless but to hear another agree slashed through her heart.

"—That's not what I meant." Dr. Pawl averted his attention back to Beth. "You've always been overweight too, but there are other symptoms that only a trained doctor would see. When was your last physical?"

She bowed her head and whispered, "Never."

"I see …" But Beth didn't see. She stared at her hands curling into her ruined dress and bit the inside of her cheek. Emotions hid beneath her tresses as the gates flooded, and heat ravished her body, not the good heat, but the red-faced heat she fought years ago. "I am on the tribal council for the Bear Creek, the tribe you were born into," he looked to Lucien, "and you too, young man. Carry her to exam room one, and I'll x-ray her ankle."

The vet rose and wobbled. Luce grasped his arm, rising and steadying the frail man. Beth forced her eyes down again, fearing the welling would burst. A light chuckle shook her chest though, and Zoro pawed her face. Gosh, she wasn't human, was she?

"What's funny?" Blue eyes blinked.

"Dr. Pawl didn't bat at an eye at a talking cat or my freakish nature."

Zoro meowed. "He is an elder, Beth. Elders see a great many things, where others see just a house cat or a young woman. All animals have voices. Humans just have to listen correctly to hear us, or in your case, see what others don't."

Thanks, Dr. Phil.

Lucien returned. "You all right?"

Beth didn't respond as her heart rate soared. Her familiar and the man she loved weren't comfort enough to settle her down. Pain didn't help, but she had grown used to the rampant throbbing, and her lack of a human thyroid took precedence. "No, Luce, I'm not all right."

They were back in Lucien's car. "You shouldn't have let him do that." His forehead rested against the steering wheel. "If he tells the Mandate … the council …"

"He won't."

The x-ray had not looked good, but the vet said the doctor—he had handed over a new card— would confirm for a fee. With Beth's condition, he referred them to a doctor outside the Mandate. Between shouts of gritting pain, she had spoken little. Shoulders slouched a little more and her whole body ached as if strained through a wringer. Dr. Pawl took blood samples too against Lucien's protests to test her thyroid levels.

"Does it matter anymore who knows?" Luce turned the key, but she gripped his bicep. "Dr. Pawl needs my help."

"Hmm?"

"Let me help him." Lucien's eyes softened. He reached across the console, tucking a stray hair behind her ear. Thunder vibrated the car. Her thumbs twiddled on her lap, but his touch stilled the fidgeting. "What good is this power if I lock it away?"

"Bethy baby, you can't." She sniffled. "You've already given him enough evidence."

"Why not? Can't you speak to him?"

Rain pelted the windshield as the tears splashed against her cheeks. Lightning lit the sky, splintering and dancing along the horizon. Lucien gulped.

"Just this once." He opened the center console and withdrew a vile.

Beth blinked. "Why do you have a vial in your car?"

Luce drew a pocketknife from his pocket and ignored her question. "You ready?"

She nodded and glanced away, squeezing her eyes tighter. Cold air blasted her face as he pierced the tip. Beth never did enjoy the sight of blood. Years of donating hadn't numbed her to the reaction either. Hissing filled the car as Lucien squeezed her finger and allowed the drops to splatter into the vial.

"Don't have a bandage for that." The rain lessened, changing from downpour to a drizzle as he screwed the cap on. Years of this process and she could make out the sounds of each action without seeing. "Can I kiss you all better?" She gulped but held her finger up. Lucien swatted her hand away and kissed her tear streams as her eyes fluttered open.

"It's you, Beth, it's always been you." He flashed a grin and ran into the office before she could respond.

Zoro said, "You did the right thing." Didn't need him to say it to feel it, but something felt off.

She stared out the window, counting the raindrops. "I can sense his time shortening." Not just Dr. Pawl but Lucien too, both of them held wrongness, but could she save them both? The front door swung and her friend traipsed over the wet grass. He wasn't fast enough to dodge raindrops. Lucien slipped in the car and shook his head. Water splashed, and the cat growled.

"Hey, sunshine?" He squeezed her hand, but she didn't look at him. "Bethy, he'll be okay." He stroked her cheek. Could she still help them all?

"We need to talk about this more." Lucien pulled onto the deserted street. Rain and storms had sent everyone indoors. Streetlights emitted an odd hum, heard over the rain, and car engine. Yellowed lights flickered, and he slowed down, craning his neck forward. "Are you doing that?"

Hands twisted in her lap. "No?" Beth didn't believe any person could be responsible for the streetlights lights. He slowed down to a coasting crawl as they approached the intersection. The traffic lights blinked, strobing through their colors.

"C'mon sunshine, what's eating at you?" Her life, family, future, and past collided around her. Beth didn't know who to trust or believe. Things were simpler before. Lucien looked left and right and eased through the intersection. "Talk to me."

A deep breath packed her lungs. "What happens next?" The air sighed in a long steady exhale, but her hands wound in the fabric of her dress.

"We clear your name."

"After that?" Could she go home and pretend none of this ever happened? Beth glanced to Zoro snoozing on the back seat. What if they didn't have a home anymore?

Lucien shook her shoulder, stopping at an intersection. "Hey, I'm not going to let you be homeless. We'll figure something out." A small smile played at her lips. "You could always move to the cabin." And it disappeared just as quickly. "Seriously, Beth it ain't that bad." Arms crossed over her chest and she made a small noise. Luce chuckled and shook his head. "Whatever sweetheart, but would you rather the shack or the streets?"

She mumbled, "Shack."

"What's that?" He tugged on his ear, and she couldn't contain her amusement. "See that's what I thought. And you think I don't know you?"

"What if we can't clear my name?"

Lucien pulled into the driveway, pressed his code in, and the gate opened. He didn't say a word as he sped up the drive and tossed the car into park. The looming silence churned her insides and her heart hammered faster with each passing second. Dry lips parted and he shut his eyes. "Bethy there's a good chance I can't clear your name." A palm ran over his face, tugging his lip down. "I didn't know she kept a damned freezer of your blood."

Outside the window, the bushes bristled. "We're going to get you cleaned up first, and then we'll talk about this later." He faced her. "Hey, I'm sorry for lying to you."

Sweaty hands twisted a pamphlet she'd taken from the vet's office. "You didn't trust me." A shiver rolled over dampening skin. Frigid air rushed from the blower but it wasn't enough to cool the tension. "We were friends, Luce, and you shouldn't have lied to me." Teeth gnawed into her lip to stop the tears. "I'll always care for you." He opened his mouth, but she held up her hand. "The difference is I do understand why you hurt me and continued to do so. I don't understand what my family did." Her heart pounded as the words formed on her lips. "I don't know that I can trust you. Heck, Luce, I … I ran away from you. We aren't going to do anything, to be anything. I will clean up, and I will sleep alone. Tomorrow, I will see this doctor and answer everyone's questions. I alone am in charge of me."

He smirked, and she wanted to smack him clear across the face. "Well, well, sunshine or should I call you highness now?" Lucien chuckled and leaned over the center console. "Tell me princess, you plan on hobbling inside without my assistance? How are you going to make it upstairs to the shower?" His eyes rolled over her, and Beth stuck her chin into the air. "You're allowed anger, Beth. I messed up, but don't think for a second I'm giving up. I've known from the start you weren't involved, and I've tried reversing the damage." She snorted. Sure, the crazy talk and fat names had lessened, but his long ago rejections burned the scars. "I hadn't known about the party. Beth, I don't remember seeing you there, but if you say I was there, I believe you."

A shadow moved in the rose bushes, and her eyes widened. The shape of a man formed and walked right for his car. Words refused to form as the yellow eyes bore down on her. Beth tapped the glass, and Lucien cursed. A sinister smile rolled over the shadow man's features; she fought to breathe as her lungs failed to draw air. The locha came in droves. Everywhere she turned; they came out from the dark, and surrounded the vehicle.

"Draw your power forth." Beth cocked her head. "She didn't teach you that either? What the …"

"Huntress," they chanted in unison. The ground tremored in response and the rainstorm returned blanketing the car in a sheeting downpour.

"What do you want with her?" he demanded, smacking the dash. A crack formed in the plastic and she gulped.

They said, "Freedom." But the locha's eyes trained on Beth. Even through the buckets of rain, their glowing eyes flashed like lightning.

Zoro leapt in her lap and hissed. The car shook as they pushed from all sides and banged on the glass. The locks disengaged; Lucien hit the lock button. Beth trembled as her heart pounded faster than she could recall it ever beating. She looked to him, clutching Zoro, but he stared ahead. Her door opened despite the re-engaged lock, and the fiends dragged her from the car, kicking and screaming. Zoro dug his claws in and drew blood. Rain soaked through her, blending with the crimson gashes. Beth lifted her arms to the heavens and prayed. Lightning crackled and struck nearby.

"Center yourself," the vibrations sang. The locha pressed hands on her chest, but there were too many to fight free. "Find your light."

"My Lucien, my light," she muttered. Fingertips sparked; electricity poured into her being and illuminated the sky. Shards of cracked light drew from the earth, bushes, and even the flowers. Fire burned and scorched, scarring the ground.

Beth reached toward the locha and touched his face. The lightning outlined his form and for a blink, the monster of the dark solidified in hues of white-blue. Lucien gasped, but he remained out of her sight. Another locha, and then another, she touched them all. Their bodies vibrated with vivacity and pulsated. Inhuman creations, gained life and their yellow eyes smiled. Beth summoned the energy again; the lights in the Brown residence went out. The electricity coursed and hummed; her ears roared as if under water. Beth eased from the ground, ignoring the sharp pain in her ankle.

"Duck," she shouted over the storm and swallowed hard. A shaky hand lifted. "Lucien, get down."

Convulsions ransacked her body as the lightning unleashed. One by one the locha burned, screaming as their new bodies transformed into ash. All but one man fell. Rows of sharp teeth exposed sticky, foul jowls as they snapped, elongating into a massive beak.

"Free," the creature shouted as he danced upon the driveway. Beth collapsed, knocking her head into the concrete. Stars and rainbow lights littered her vision but she was empty.

Lucien yelled her name, sliding next to her by the time the words had reached her ears. Her arm lifted, and she pointed to the locha. "I see him, Bethy."

Her eyes closed and Luce shook her. "Stay with me." Her eyelids fluttered and again he roused her.

One by one, the creature separated into animals and joined the single dancing locha. Holding hands these fiends absorbed into one singular being again. Horns sprouted from atop its head, and long black hair cascaded into the no longer whispering wind and length-ened into a rainbow of feathers. A totem—a legend of myth—took form as the thunderbird.

Her breath staggered as Lucien drew her into his lap. Beth imagined Lucien's eyes were as her own, but she could not see if this was truth or inside her head. His heart beat its usual rhythm, and the steadiness of his hands gave way to a calm collective she hadn't possessed.

"Creator," it said to the sky and bowed before her. "You who have given life, creator wishes to thank you, Kolkohkafoosi the creator of storms."

Words would not form as her mouth hung open. The birdman nodded, and his eyes flashed with lightning. As his wings beat, thunder roared.

"You take her inside. She has done well." Luce lifted her as her belly flopped. "She killed many locha."

Lucien carried her inside, noticeable only when the rain gave way to dry, chilly air. Dana and James bounded down the stairs with eyes wider than saucers. "The locks wouldn't budge."

"I'm okay," Beth chattered. Dana removed her robe and draped it over her body. Warmth refused to penetrate her bones and Luce held her closer.

"Tea," the thunderbird said. She hadn't imagined him. Lucien carried Beth to the sofa, winding the robe around her body, and placed her swollen ankle on the pillows they'd left behind. Zoro—she assumed he had run off during the attack.

"I'll find him, sweetheart," Luce said, but James walked in with a drowned ball of fur, splattering water over the floor. Laughter shook his chest, but the sound died in this throat. "Now ain't that something."

"Shut it, iyyìnko." Zoro jumped from James arms and rushed into Beth's lap. He kissed her nose, sniffing for signs of harm. Deep scratches marred her arms, but the blood had dried into scabs. "I'm sorry. We aren't built for fighting locha."

Beth didn't hold it against Zoro. One tiny creature, even if he had the world's biggest attitude for a cat, he could not have stopped the locha from swarming. The kettle whistled as Dana excused herself. James' eyes trained on the strange creature standing before the fireplace but showed no outward signs of fear. Had he met such a creature before?

Red clay stained his bare feet. Lucien squeezed her tighter, but the shakes didn't cease. A spicy aroma wafted from the kitchen. China clattered and James hopped to his feet. Dana wasn't as iron willed as her husband.

Once everyone took their seats, they made introductions. Zoro rested wide eyed on her lap, and in a mechanical manner, she petted his silky fur. Her mind refused to function properly and if not for the others, Beth would have thought Emmanuel's presence impossible and nothing more than a hallucination. Had the spirits been a lapse of delirium? A tentative hand grasp from Lucien led her to believe he too had agreed with her assumptions.

"You fear me." Emmanuel did not pose the statement as a question, and Beth swallowed hard. The shiver had not left her body, and if her eyes closed, the brush of darkness dimpled her skin. He continued and spoke in the Muskogee language of her people.

"Locha lives in all of us. You hold no fear in your heart for you have saved life. I cast no judgments on brother or sister." 'Freedom' the shadows had chanted, but from what prison had Beth freed the thunderbird, and who had imprisoned him? Why did someone imprison him? "For many summers I have tried to reach you, but the wards on your house proved too great."

She glanced to Lucien and to his parents. "What is a ward?"

Mr. Brown rose and retrieved a book from the top of his shelf. He handed it to Emmanuel, and the heavy book dropped into his lap. *Native American Symbolism: A world of charms and healing through paintings and carvings in Early America.* He flipped the pages and stopped, motioning to the image of a circle with a black dot in the center and two arrows pointing inward.

"If you place the house center," Lucien said and flicked at the center dot. "The two out buildings and then the shrubs form sort of a circle."

The symbol was inside her house too. Downstairs in the basement … the mats and etched onto the weapons … on Auntie's apothecary labels. But wards hadn't stopped whoever attacked her in her room.

"Did you grab me the other night?"

"I watched you perform a strange dance with your curtain after whispering to you."

Cheeks burned. "Oops." Lucien chuckled and pulled her closer.

"You ran after that, but this one would not let me near." He motioned to Lucien. "You care for him."

Luce kissed her temple. "Of course she does."

She cleared her throat. "The water?" James and Dana echoed her word and leaned forward.

Emmanuel knelt and laid the book on the coffee table. "The locha did not want to let her go without their freedom. Some saw you as a threat. I told them you would free them." The thunderbird stood from his crouched position. "I sense your pain Bethany. You need medicine man. I leave now and watch over the night."

By the time any of them objected, Emmanuel transformed from man bird to an actual squawking thunderbird. Dana scurried to the front door and quickly let him out, scratching her head. "That was the oddest thing I've ever seen."

They nodded in agreement.

James called the doctor the vet had recommended, as it was still early. With all the excitement, she'd almost forgotten about her injury or perhaps it seemed unimportant compared to animal spirits turning into a thunderbird. Zoro ventured inside the house, exploring his new surroundings again, jumping every time Dana clanked something in the kitchen.

"If it weren't for your parents, Luce, I'd have sworn Dr. Pawl slipped us drugs." Her brow creased. What had all this meant? Fingertips danced over her teeth. Light, dark ... lies and truth seemed to collide at every angle. *Maybe they were just going a bit stir crazy.*

"We'll figure it out, sunshine." The phone receiver clicked and Lucien excused himself.

James said, "Doctor's on his way."

Lucien handed Beth a coffee. Steam wafted from the glazed terracotta mug, and a smile tipped her lips as he eased beside her. An arm slid around tight shoulders, and her head lulled against Luce's warm chest. The scene was almost perfect, and a life she'd once envisioned. A sigh stirred inside, but Beth swallowed it. Comfort seemed alien after the day's events. Running from the man she desired but was too afraid to face had been the beginning.

She sipped the perfect concoction of roasted beans, cinnamon, cream, and sugar. Heaven danced in her mouth, and her spirits lifted at the day's ending. Eyes closing for a moment, Beth willed the weariness aside. Each sip warmed her center; the warmth crept through her veins as if they were a valley of rivers.

"Mom said she can put you down here, so you don't have to take the steps." He scratched his neck, and Beth sensed a but rising in his throat. "I can carry you upstairs; you know … whatever you want."

The mug rattled against the saucer as Beth leaned forward, placing both on the coffee table. "Sorry."

Beth twisted. A blush rose in his cheeks, and he glanced away. The nasty words she'd spewed before the attack. None of those words changed the truth. Beth loved him. Lucien became her world when they were kids, and she wanted him to always remain in her life. But was now the best time to start anything new? On her hands and toes, she could check off reasons to wait. Her family, the investigation, the Green Corn Festival, her powers, she wasn't even human, a thunderbird, and shadow men had blind sided her. His love whacked into her like a sucker punch and knocked her on her ass. Could she trust him not to break her further?

Blue eyes shone, filled, and glistened with emotions. Breath blew as the sigh reared its ugly head. He fidgeted, and Beth covered his hand. One step at a time, one day at a time, one problem at a time, they would figure this out.

Opening her mouth to answer him, the doorbell rang. "Hold that thought," he whispered, brushing his lips across her wrinkled forehead.

Lucien led the doctor to her, introductions passed, and he handed him the x-rays. Dr. Haim held them to the light and pointed, speaking in hushed tones to Lucien. "Hairline, but still a fracture."

Beth's fingertips sizzled; her eyes widened as the lights flickered to the beat of her heart. Lucien's gaze slid to her, worry lines etched into his beautiful rugged face. Dr. Haim pointed to the area on her outer ankle. "Needs to stay immobile for six weeks before I can address the sprain and strengthen the muscles." That meant a cast, but he had not had the supplies on him. He whispered to Lucien about returning tomorrow and handed him a bottle of pills.

"How's your pain, sunshine?" She glared at him. "Figured as much, but you take one of these pills now, and you'll feel no pain." Lucien offered her a pill, but her gaze had not faltered. She would have rather dealt with the pulsating ache then lower her guard. "Bethy, I'd never do that to you." He palmed a hand over his mouth feigning defeat. "I'm a liar, there I admit it, but what you're think-ing." Lucien shook his head. "Maybe *you* don't know me at all." Beth snatched the pill from his hand and dry swallowed the medicine. "Good, now Momma said she'd help you bathe."

"No."

"You want me to help—"

"No."

"My dad?"

"Hell no."

"Doc said you can't put weight on your foot. You're stuck with one of them, sunshine." This should not have become a tough deci-sion, but Dana drove her bonkers. She sighed and met his amused gaze. "I've already seen all of you."

Her chin lifted. "That doesn't make it right, Luce."

"Maybe this'll change your mind, sweetheart." He bent down on his knee, smirking and holding his hands out in front of him. "Bethy, will you do me the honor of letting me take care of you," his brows wagged, "wash your tender parts, and with all the honor and integrity I own, make sure you don't fall and break your neck?" She'd have broken his neck if she could but whispered yes instead. "Will you spend the night with me? Like before, you know, let me hold you?"

"One step at a time, Luce." He nodded and asked if she was ready. Lucien cradled her in his arms and carried her into the bathroom. He sat her on the toilet and ran a bath, remarking that it would be easier but longer. Once it was half-full, he helped her out of her stinky clothes and no mirror was required for seeing her embarrassment between the stench and being naked in front of Lucien. In an answer to her turmoil, he kissed her, and reminded her he had not showered or used his toothbrush. "Kill two birds?"

"Well now sunshine, you're tempting the devil."

Lashes fluttered and the heat in her cheeks tripled. "I know you're gentleman enough not take my virginity in a tub." Years ago, she'd imagined lying under the star lit sky, the heavy moon shining down on the warm grass, and making love to Lucien that fateful night. Too young then and it was doubtful she'd have gone through with such a notion. He slipped from his clothes, and she leaned back, admiring the view. Embarrassment hadn't eluded him either, but Beth saw nothing he should have been ashamed about.

He lifted her again as if she weighed nothing, not two hundred pounds, and placed her gently into the steamy tub, raising her leg over the side to keep it elevated as the doctor had recommended. Lucien eased in behind her and started working on wetting her hair. Neither of them said much, whether shock or embarrassments were to blame, she hadn't known. Confusion swept over her thoughts though, searching her soul, mind, and even heart for a way to forgive him. Understanding did not heal the wounds. Grudges wouldn't have worked; she cared too much. Like before with his sharp insults, Beth would rather have hurt than felt nothing at all. The pain … could she live with his love instead?

Once they were no longer stinky, Lucien pulled her against his chest, and held her tight. "I could stay like this forever. Know that, and know I'll wait. No pressure, Beth." They dwelled together until the water had turned tepid, and their fingers and toes pruned.

Lucien slipped from the tub and wrapped a towel around his waist. The fabric hid nothing as the flap opened and closed. Beth tried her best not to stare, but curiosity caught her attention. He laughed, and life flared through her hot cheeks. "You make this …"

"Hard?"

"Baby, you have no idea." His arms lifted her with no effort from the water. One-handed, Lucien supported her as he reached for a towel. Taught nipples raked across his bare chest, the tingle spread throughout her body, pulling, tugging at her center, and her thighs squeezed together. Inside and out, Beth throbbed. Life seemed easier when she'd viewed him as her enemy, but now her old dreams and hopes rekindled. "Stay with me? Just you and me."

"Yes."

His brow rose. "No cat."

"No cat." She laughed and shook her head.

Chapter Seven

*L*ucien sat Beth on the bed and preceded to hand her new clothing he had bought earlier during his excursion into town. Pictures of them as kids hung on the walls where posters would have been normal. She gulped. Newer photographs of her sat on his nightstand. Luce must have taken them without her knowing, and Beth did not know if she should be flattered or offended.

Despite the late hour, she was not tired. The bath had reinvigorated her senses, and while the pill had dulled the pain, there were no sedentary effects. "I never asked you what you thought about the thunderbird."

Facing away from her, he dropped his towel. Beth's jaw bottomed out at how easy the man disrobed in her presence. Sure, he blushed from time to time, but it must have been a guy thing. Regardless of embarrassments, Lucien's cute butt looked good naked and in his jeans.

He said, "I don't know. The whole idea is crazy, but I've seen a lot of strange crap." She guessed finding out that she was not human topped that list. A hand scrubbed over his face reflecting in his dresser mirror. Blue eyes met hers and thick lips parted. Beth's gaze traveled south, following the lazy path of dark hair to … she averted her thoughts and chided herself for peeking. Footsteps creaked along the boards; his heat radiated and she knew he was close. "You don't make that list, and you're not crazy, Beth."

A nervous chuckle left her mouth. "Something's called to me for years." She tossed the t-shirt over her head, leaving her towel on underneath. Lucien dragged her hair free from the collar, but she did not look at him. Salty sweetness flared her nostrils, overpowering her senses. Beth cleared her throat, coughing into her balled fist. "None of it makes sense. Does it?"

"Some of it does."

Aunt Vivian told her only what she thought she needed, but Beth hadn't realized it at the time. Believing her lies was easier than questioning what she thought she'd been powerless to change. Lucien climbed on the bed, scooting behind her, and combed her hair. The tingling sensations relaxed her. Deft fingers braided and wrapped her hair. He pushed the plait to the side and kissed from her neck to ear.

Turning toward him, Lucien captured her bottom lip. Too quickly, he pulled away. "I wish you hadn't run, but I'm glad you did at the same time." His arms tightened as if she would leave him. No more running for her; running away had not solved her problems. At least she had answers now, but part of her wondered if he would have come clean otherwise. "I know it doesn't make much sense, but your smile is worth the trouble of tracking your ass through the woods."

Beth laughed. The shack had invoked a memory of their people, before they had converted to Christianity. More of a partnership than a love union, marriage was sacred, but not sacred enough. Envisioning him with multiple wives, lovers, the thought alone had intimidated her. Lucien scared her on a level she hadn't known. Before that moment, the fantasy of becoming lovers was just that, a fantasy. Reality shook her inside and out.

Like many women, Beth loathed her body. Her perpetual size fourteen shape remained a fraction of her self-hatred though. Lucien wasn't perfect either by any means, but for years, he had not judged her, not until the day their lives had changed. "What are you thinking?"

A long pause fell between them as she chewed on her lip. Lucien saw her naked and hadn't balked, but what if … if she couldn't please him, and he broke her all over again?

"Bethy?" Water filled her eyes. "Are you in pain?" Her ankle didn't hurt as much anymore, but medicine hadn't cured the emotional breakdown warring inside of her. "Don't cry." But no amount of chewing or biting could have stopped the whimper leaving her trembling lips. Hot tears burned her cheeks as she sniffled. Confusion swept in again and whispered between forgiveness and pride. But it was more than forgiveness because Beth had to let the past go and act as if he hadn't ruined those years of her life. The man tore her heart out, stomping on it for good measure. No books, television, therapy, or magic changed what he did to her; how he had made her feel worthless, ugly, and hated. She stared into his blue eyes, rimming with his own misery.

He broke her, and after years, the shards of her being had scattered into the four winds. Lucien knew it too; these tears were not for him but because of him. How could she move on? How could she forgive? *What type of woman did that make her?*

The wind replied, *"Weak."*

No, she wanted to cry back. Yet the answer formed from the gentle gust. Beth had to love herself and accept her for who and what she was. Then maybe someone else could love her … someone who didn't hurt or lie to her. Her tears dried, and her head set down. Eyelids grew heavier with each passing moment. Pain medicine won the battle or maybe Lucien's voice. The words jumbled in her mind, and she could not make them out, but the cadence lulled her.

The sun warmed her skin, as Beth lay out, surrounded by vivid wild flowers in the field. Rolling hills spanned for miles, and their grassy knolls swayed in the gentle breeze. No pain, emotional or physical, assaulted her. Birds flew and sang in the distance. Drums banded their tenor beat. Her eyes closed, and the scene changed. Lightning crackled and she awoke, shooting up in Lucien's bed, no longer in the field of dreams.

Emmanuel stood at the edge of the bed, and his feathered arms spread at his sides. Rain pelted outside, dinging and clanging upon metal and glass. Her trembling fingers reached toward him. Zoro hissed and growled at her feet, but Lucien snored at her side. A small smile played over the thunderbird's mouth, reflected only by the flashes of light.

"A wise one does not betray." Bolts reflected in his eyes. "Are you wise, or do you betray yourself?"

The cat lunged and struck him, but Emmanuel did not falter. Their exchange continued as if Beth hadn't awoken. Countless times her familiar lashed at the feathered man. Lucien had accused Zoro of something similar. She blinked and opened her mouth to ask why they argued, but words wouldn't come.

"She deserves to know." Emmanuel crossed his arms over his chest. "You tell Beth or I will."

She dragged the blankets back, but her hand went through the fabric. Stunned, she turned and gaped. Her sleeping body lain beneath her. *Had she died?* No, her chest rose with steady breaths.

Emmanuel frowned; his feet shuffled toward the bed, and placed his hands on her shoulders. Spectral Beth stared on unable to speak or move. Blue light flickered, jolting from his fingertips, and shocked into her body. She gasped, sucking in for air, and her spectral form sucked too. Wide eyes blinked. Blue eyes laced with concern, but Lucien's lips curled and snarled. "Get out."

Beth scooted her butt away. A sob rooted in her chest and swelled her throat. How would she make it out of his bed? "Not you, baby." He snapped his fingers, and she followed them to Zoro sitting at the foot of the bed. Her gaze rolled upward, catching the feathers shaped in the darkness, and settled on Emmanuel's eyes.

Pieces of the scattered dream reformed in her mind. Luce asked, "What happened?" Zoro jumped from the bed and fled the room.

"She projected." Lucien yelled, "She what?" Beth jumped, but he rubbed her back, soothing her. It didn't work. She reached for the nightstand, recalling a light, and blinked as the switch flipped.

"The huntress comes into her power. The nigh time is upon us—"
Beth said, "Stop the cryptic—"

"When?" Lucien cut her off, and she flinched as his hand flew into the air.

"The Festival." Fingers counted the days; two weeks remained until the Green Corn Festival—Posketv in Muskogee. What could have been important about that? People came from all over. Ritual fasting typically began the weekend before and lasted throughout the week. All men had to fast. The first day was the ribbon dance, but Beth had not participated before. The purifying dance was sacred to the Creek people and prepared the ritual area for renewal. Some Creeks still practiced the sapi too, which was bloodletting. Feather dances, Stomp dances, and large feasts took place each year, but only men took war names and partook in many of the festivities.

Emmanuel started for the door. "Wait what's happening to me?" Hazel eyes met blue, and both men nodded in a silent agreement she did not follow. Jaw popping, her arms crossed over her chest, alternating a glare. Neither man answered her.

"Find me soon." Emmanuel bowed; a screech pierced the silence, and she covered her ears as he disappeared through the open window.

"Ready for what?" Beth stiffened and pursed her lips. "Luce?"

"How's your pain?" He shifted away from her, rolling to his side. *Unusual behavior for him.* Giving him a tiny poke, he scooted over even more. "Tomorrow, sunshine, I'll tell you everything in the morning. You need to sleep."

Sleep refused to come. Confined to bed, Beth had only the light dancing from her electrified fingertips. She only put up with this crap because she could not run.

Zoro had stayed away too, even when she whisper called him to her side. The familiar knew something. Had it anything to do with Vivian or her family? Her blood? Emmanuel? Why her blood healed others but not her?

Numbers rolled over on the clock. Sheep jumped invisible fences within her mind. Beth tossed and turned through the remainder of the night. The sky lightened. She had decided that Lucien had slept enough. With all her force mustered, she shoved his shoulder.

He groaned and revolved onto his back. No amount of shoving or smacking worked.

Beth winced, dragging herself closer. Her ankle throbbed as it tangled in the sheets. The cry trapped in her throat and released as a gurgled whisper. Lucien still hadn't budged. Her lips skimmed his exposed shoulder, enjoying the taste of his skin. Bit by bit Beth made her way towards the base of his neck, watching the gooseflesh rise in her wake.

What she didn't expect was the reaction churning inside of her body. Her lips hummed, but made no sound, and the vibrations ran over her skin. Heat built beneath her surface and throbbed in time with her pulse.

Her tongue swept across his skin, tasting salt and soap. With a delicate grace and held breath, Beth hefted her leg over his body, wiggling and adjusting as her butt lowered down and pinned his erection. Lucien's eyes flew open as a blush eased over her face, and her hands splayed over his chest, tangled into his hair.

"Am I dreaming?" he asked running rough palms up her bare thighs.

Beth's braid flopped back and forth as her head shook. Unable to trust words she didn't speak. Lucien stared at her for the longest time, studying her reactions to the lightest of touches. Each tickle of his fingertips massaged her inside and out, and each sweep reached higher on her thighs.

"You have no idea how much this kills me. One moment you're in my arms, and the next you run away. You're still here … this must be a dream, sunshine."

A chuckle ripped through her body. Lucien cursed and gripped her hips. Every beat of his heart pulsed between her thighs, rubbing places she had never felt before, and sensations shivered in their wake, but she did not have a name for it. Air gasped from her chest, and her teeth nipped into her bottom lip, attempting to squelch the fire spreading through her veins. Fingers grasped his nipples and pinched.

"Ouch." Lucien blinked, and a smile tugged at her lips. "Okay, okay so you ain't a dream." He leaned on his elbows. "Why are you …?"

"I was bored." Beth faked indifference. Hips rolled forward and she laid flush with the heat of his body. Luce's lips parted; a pained expression creased his forehead, and Beth kissed the lines away, feathering a path over his nose and to his lips. Lucien's arms pressed her closer as he groaned against her mouth. He tugged her shirt, and she wiggled free of the garment. Tongues joined as he gently yanked her braid, drawing her closer, as he squirmed beneath her.

Blue sparks illuminated her closed lids as Lucien grounded the electricity coursing through her veins and releasing from her mouth. Flavors of oak and fire invaded her taste buds, and she could not seem to get enough. Rough palms smoothed over her back, and cupped her bare ass cheeks, as the air thickened with salty desire. Beth moaned, her body arching from the new shock rolling through her center. Without breaking their kiss or connection, Lucien delicately flipped her on her back and nestled between her thighs. Her ankle screamed as she gulped for air, but he would have stopped at the mention of pain, and she did not want to stop. For once, she wanted control and something good to happen, just once to make-up all the terrible of the past few days.

"I heard that."

Her thighs lifted, encompassing his waist despite the soreness, and held him hostage. His lips parted; a pink tongue teased across their surface. Beth slid her arms around his neck. Inky lashes blinked as his eyes seemed to glow in the grey morning light.

"Do you love me?" Beth nodded. "Say it then." Eyes glanced toward the door, face burning she chewed on her cheek. If they did this, would it mean the same to both of them? Would it mean anything in the morning or weeks from now once the dust on her life settled? Could his renewed love heal the pain his past left behind? A rumble sounded in his chest. "Beth."

Her watery gaze snapped; the same ache pooled in his blue eyes. "I don't deserve another chance." The pads of his fingers skimmed her lips, striking her insides. "But please sunshine. We can't do this if you don't forgive me."

"I want to say yes."

"But?"

"You know … I let you in, sleep with you, and you hurt me again." Saying the words that had haunted her since his return lessened the metaphorical weight drawing her shoulders down. "You're asking me to risk everything, and it's not fair, Luce. What are you risking?"

She had everything to lose.

"A lie is a lie, it don't matter I was saving your life? That's what you're saying?" Beth looked away again and wetness dribbled from her eyes. Did it matter? Lips trembled unable to utter the words. She was grateful, but it didn't change how he'd made her hate herself. The nights she had spent drowning in tears from the stinging verbal cuts. Beth choked as the sob wracked her body. Why didn't he understand? If he watched her, didn't he see her pain?

Beth whispered, "Yeah Luce." He had made the decision. Why should he avoid the consequences? "I can't go there again." She blinked at her words. Beth had never left *there*.

Lucien rolled from her body. "I think you accuse me of more than I've done in that mind of yours." He sat up, propping pillows behind his back. "I pushed you away and said despicable things to hurt you. For that I'm sorry." He took a deep breath. "All I can say is sorry, but there wasn't any other way." Luce yanked his hair, shaking his head. "Hurting you hurt me too. Every tear you shed, I felt, but I couldn't reach you."

"That's where you're wrong," she mumbled, hugging the blanket to her chin. "So wrong, Luce. I would have listened."

"Could have, should have, but I didn't, and for that I will I suffer the consequence for the remainder of my life. Isn't that punishment enough?" He left the bed and disappeared into the closet. Cracking bones reached her ears. "And I'm risking crap too. Do you know how much trouble I'd be in—my parents too—if the Mandate found out we love each other?" Not loved but love. Luce returned half-dressed and tossed fresh clothes at Beth. Without uttering another word, the bedroom door slammed behind him.

Her fingers combed through her dark hair, snatching the too long locks free of her braid. Why was forgiveness so hard? Luce's words rattled in her brain. Bitterness tainted her dry mouth, and she reached for a glass of water on the nightstand, chugging it in a long gulp. It didn't help.

She smoothed the cold mattress. The door creaked open, but Beth knew it was Lucien by his scent. "When we were children, before you got sick, I'd dream of our marriage. The older we grew, the more I thought about … us. Even after you hurt me, I often wondered what would have happened." Beth recalled the night her world had changed. Forgiveness wasn't her forte. Yet beneath everything he had done, she loved him and never stopped.

Lucien stroked her cheek. "I would've pursued you, loved you, and done anything to make you laugh. I mucked up the timing, but through it all, I never stopped loving you. Did everything because I love you more than life. Every time your family hurt you … Guess I ain't any better." Beth whipped her head toward him, mouth dropping in protest, but he pressed a finger over her lips. "See I drank your blood, Bethy and it bonds me to you. Every tear you shed, I felt. Stupid me thought it was guilt for the longest time, mine not yours." Lucien shook his head. "After we graduated, I saw less of you, but the feelings remained, and they grew stronger too. I would awaken in the middle of the night crying and clutching my chest. Took me a week to make the connection."

Those were her darkest days, and often she had tempered them with the idea of cutting his balls. "How'd you know?"

Lucien sighed stretching out beside her. Heat inched over her blanketed skin, and she bit her lip hoping he stayed on top of the covers. "One night the pain pulsed. Like a beacon and I couldn't fight it." A palm scrubbed his rough face. "It drew me to you like a magnet, and I stood there on your balcony, frozen, and unable to help as you thrashed and cried. Jemma held you until you fell asleep, but she knew. She saw me."

Beth had seen him too, but she had not known it was Luce all those times. Like clockwork, the shadow would arrive after sundown. For three years, all that had separated them was a curtain and glass.

"Jemma didn't tell me."

"If she hadn't of been there, I'd have busted through the door." He wasn't lying. "I've tried to make it right, but kept failing no matter how many letters, flowers, or gifts—"

"What?" Beth shot from the pillow. His eyes ignited; the blanket fell from her body. She scrambled to cover herself again and apologized.

Every muscle and vein flexed—Lucien jumped from the bed and faced the door. A twinge of guilt stirred her stomach as she eyed the photographs. Random shots of her in the yard or sipping a latte and a few of her sleeping lined the nightstand. Beth scooted toward him but remained on the bed, hugging his torso. Part of her expected Lucien to pull away. Instead, his hands squeezed back, and she clasped tighter, hefting herself up on her good leg.

"This is the most we've talked in a long time." His breathing changed. "First time you're naked and I'm not bathing you. Hard to think with your breasts pressed against my back."

Lucien bated her, and Beth fought the amusement tickling her ribs. "How hard?" She imagined his brow rising. He turned and cupped her face. Lips parted and crashed, tongues dove and swam, and rough hands dragged her closer. Lucien's erection was pinned between them, and he hadn't been kidding. . He was harder than steel even beneath his denim prison.

"Forgive me," he mumbled against her mouth. The motors ignited within her. Fingers feathered touches down his chest, and her palm ran along the softer ridges of his abs, halting just shy of his treasure trail. Lucien issued a rumble, half-growl, against her mouth as his belt clattered against the floor.

"You're burning every last ounce of my patience." A palm covered his mouth and hid his smile. "I promised you … you do things like that, and I'll break it." Attempting a sly and seductive stance, Beth eased onto the bed, reaching her desired effect as Luce's breath caught in a frozen hiss. A finger crooked, and Lucien's knees dropped in between her thighs.

"Bethy." Rough whiskers brushed against her kneecap followed by his lips. Inside her body hummed, and her belly tied into knots. Sweat reflected morning rays and trailed an audible shiver through Lucien. Her heart pounded against her ribs as the air stilled in the room. This part of her belonged to him and after nineteen years, she was ready.

Nipples hardened and heavy breasts swayed from quick breaths. Sweaty palms smoothed over her torso seeking their prize. Fire burned and built within Beth like never before. As if claws sunk into flesh and massaged instead of sliced, Lucien kissed the underside of her breast. Teeth scraped her skin, nibbling but not breaking the surface.

Fingers curled into the blanket as his tongue flicked her nipple. Her stomach clenched; breath caught as a spasm released through her body. Lucien moaned against her skin and renewed his assault. Beth's hands grasped his shoulders. Torn between his teasing touch and sanity she didn't know whether to shove him away or draw him closer.

"Luce." His name rolled like a breathless whisper, dripping with emotion she hadn't experienced before. Blue eyes lifted, sparking. An azure glow emitted from him, but the source wasn't his eyes. He was beautiful.

He kissed her nose. "Do you want me to stop?"

Beth's gaze widened and dark tresses tangled as her head rocked back and forth. "I need ..."

"Tell me, baby." Her body quaked as if being squeezed from the inside.

Beth averted her eyes for a second unable to hide the heat spreading over her skin. She took his hand and slid it between her legs. His nostrils flared again. A wide grin spread over his face, building as he explored her damp curls.

"At least I'm not the only one suffering." The pad of his finger skimmed over her bud, and her thighs clenched, holding him hostage. "More?" he asked, but words wouldn't form in her mind or lips.

Her gaze connected with Lucien's as he whispered to her, but even his words seemed alien over her ragged breathing and rapid heartbeat. Higher she climbed as pressure swirled around her nerves. Like bamboo, her spine bent into each stroke. Words like beautiful reached her ears, but the sounds releasing from her could have cut glass.

Tension built and welled at her center. Faster—her hips moved, and her eyes pinched shut. Toes tingled as lights flashed behind her lids. Her clenched jaw did little to ease the high-pitched squeal as pieces of her shattered and convulsed.

Lucien's hand withdrew as aftershocks rocked and pulsed from her epicenter. A hand stroked her neck and settled over her thundering heart. Fingertips crackled as power poured from their tips, but she didn't know if they'd done so the entire time. Maybe that was why Lucien appeared to glow blue. A delicious sigh eased from her parted lips.

Pressure and heat seized her entrance. Luce gulped; the bed shook from his unsteadiness. Beth opened her eyes to pinched brows. Teeth nicked her lip as he eased himself in, inch by inch. An odd sensation overtook her. Half-stretched but half-filled, and her hips tilted. Lucien wobbled, and sweat beaded on his brow. Kiss swollen lips parted, and Beth shuddered beneath him as he emitted a hiss. "I ain't going to last you keep that up," he said through gritted teeth, and she stilled. A curse flew from his mouth. "Bethy ... damn it."

"Luce, I'm not naïve. It's going to hurt, but I'll survive." A trembling hand cupped his cheek. "This part of me always belonged to you." She rubbed his palm over her heart. "I love you."

Sweat glistened on his forehead. Beth slid her arms around Luce's neck. He dipped toward her mouth, stared into her eyes, and whispered, "This part of me belongs to you too."

Beth cocked her head as he nodded. But what about the rumors she'd heard at school? "Just rumors and I didn't even start them." Luce kissed her nose. "Baby, it's always been you. The One Above made me for you and you for me."

Pieces of the walls she'd constructed crumbled. Blue eyes softened and there was no lie. Maybe he was right. In an attempt to heal and protect herself, she'd blamed Luce for far more than he'd actually done. Amber must've started those rumors. How could someone be so hurtful? What did she ever do to her? "Nothing," Luce answered her thoughts. "I love you and not her, so she lashed out at you, Beth."

She put a finger on his lips and shushed him. "Make love to me?" Dark brows rose and Luce's lips brushed against her mouth. Beth nipped him, and he growled low as the sound vibrated her chest. Her hips ground against him, pressing him through her final barrier.

A tear slipped through clenched eyes as the world exploded red and white. As Lucien thrusted he kissed her deeper, harder. His tongue did little to dull the pain, but her heart swelled. Her Lucien, his Beth, forever and no one could change the fact. They'd both made mistakes serving only to delay the inevitable.

Fumbled rhythm ensued as they rocked against one another. Their eyes remained open even as they kissed; neither wanted to miss a moment. Damp hands raked through his hair. Each bump of her nerves brought on rippling waves and soft moans. A low rumble resonated from his chest, and Lucien's breath quickened. Blue eyes bore into her as he'd promised.

Face-hardening, his body turned rigid. All too soon, their love-making ended.

A slow knowing grin flashed across his rough face. "You are even more beautiful when you moan." He kissed her nose. "Can we stay like this forever?" A scratch came from the door, and Beth twisted toward the sound. Zoro, she was certain. Lucien's sigh mirrored her thoughts, but as much as she wanted to remain in bed all day, there was too much to figure out. "Is this where you tell me he's a package deal?"

She groaned and turned onto her stomach. Her ankle had not hurt in the least bit, but had dangled safely off the bed during their tryst. Lucien, in no rush to let the cat in, molded himself against her back.

"I meant what I said. You know that, right?" He stroked her hair to the side and brushed his lips over her shoulder. "I love you, and I want us together. Nothing else matters to me except you."

Part of her wanted to believe him, but another part whispered, *"Why was he trying so hard?"* She shut up the naysayer devil. "We're about as together as two people can get."

"You know what I mean."

"Not exactly." If Beth could've moved, she would have. A kink formed in her neck from glaring at him over her shoulder, or maybe it was the throbbing vein in her neck from his beat around the bush bullshit. "You asking me out? Trying to prove this wasn't a hormone induced fling? Thought that was pretty obvious, but I'll spell it out for you, if you like."

Lucien scowled. "God woman you're a pain in my ass already." The scratching started again, and Beth sat up, contemplating on how to hobble. "I tell you I love you, and you accuse me of calling you a whore. What do you want from me? I've given you all I have … Bethy what else is there?"

Lucien grasped a pillow and threw it across the room. A hand brushed her neck, and the vibration of her heart increased. Trust was a two-way street and she'd made a wrong turn into the bad part of town. Beth didn't regret making love to him, so why would she say those things?

"Luce," she said and sat up. Veins thudded in his jaw. Soft eyes that didn't match the hardness turned on her. Beth motioned him closer. Lucien had saved her, helped her, and even cared for her. She'd been an ass to him far more than he deserved. Her stomach lurched at the thought, and she dry heaved, flecks of lights dancing in her vision.

Curses flew from his lips as Lucien carried her naked form into the bathroom down the hall. Luckily, no one but Zoro was inside the house. Supporting her thigh, he continued helping her through her routine, but something managed to eat at her stomach, and Beth knew the churning bile was her fault. For three years, she had blamed Lucien as often as she'd wished for kind words and longing glances.

He gave her his all, and she tossed it away like garbage. "I'm sorry."

"For what, sunshine?" Her neck and shoulders cracked. "I never blamed you." Whiskers grazed her shoulder as she brushed her teeth. "At least not for ignoring me."

She spat in the sink and rinsed her mouth. Their gazes met in the mirror as he closed the medicine cabinet. Deep scratches marred her face and purple and yellow bruises painted her bronze skin. Beneath it all, she was still plain. A finger brushed the deepest slice over her cheekbone. "It'll scar," she whispered.

"You're still beautiful to me." Beth leaned against his chest. Thunder boomed inside his chest. She was the lightning ... "I am your thunder," he finished her trailing thought.

Lucien dressed her in another sundress and carried her downstairs into the living room. Neither of them said much aside from please, yes, no, or thank you. His statement weighed heavily on her mind. Spirit Walkers controlled the elements and used them to help the tribes in times of need. But tales of thunder, lightning, water, air, and fire were more common than stories of the Spirit Walkers.

The cool air washed over her skin. Lucien phoned the doctor as she rested on the couch, wallowing in her memories of the legends. Zoro curled into her lap. "Tell me about the thunder."

"I didn't originate as a Creek but as Cherokee." Zoro kneaded her belly. "Aniyvdaqualosgi we called them, or the thunderers."

"I thought you were like me," Beth said and ran her fingers through his silky fur. "Why didn't you tell me?"

Zoro offered a cat smile. "You never asked."

"How different are our tribes?"

"Not too different. We spoke another language, but the stories are similar. Your people see thunder and lightning in the form of the thunderbird, who takes either bird or human form. My people saw them as spirits in human form, but thunder and lightning are controlled by different spirits."

"And thunderbird controls both?"

"So the legends say, but you control more than thunder and lightning, Beth. You control the whole storm." Her black brows rose at the cat as a sigh released. Why did The One Above limit what and when the guides could tell them about these matters? Was she or not a thunderbird?

Lucien flashed a grin and leaned against the wall. "He's right. You're more than a thunderer, more than a huntress of the locha."

Beth snorted at her birth rite. "I'm not even that."

"You slaughtered the locha last night with just a touch." Beth refrained from rolling her eyes. The lightning killed the shadow men, not her. She was a vessel, and Luce helped too. Quick steps brought him to her side. He shoved Zoro off her lap and grasped her hands. "You are too humble and I love that, sunshine, but it was you who saved us last night. The shadow men pinned me down and chased Zoro into the bushes. You, and you alone, defeated the darkness."

"Really?"

Lucien nodded and kissed her knuckles. "Imagine what you'll accomplish once you've healed and properly trained."

Zoro batted at her dress, playing with a dangling string. As an ancient spirit, he sure amused himself with the simplest of items. She changed the subject. "Hey, what happened last night?"

Beth recalled the strange dream and floating outside of her body. Spirit Walkers could walk between the planes of existence, but she had thought it a myth. Creek Indians believed in three planes: upper, middle, and under. The upper realm was for the Gods. Middle was for the humans and animals alive and deceased. The underworld was for the dark, but not necessarily evil spirits. Creek beliefs varied and much had changed, or evolved, due to translation too. Beth saw herself as spiritual, she read the bible, but she did not belong to a congregation. Aside from a few traditions and stories, she was not versed in Creek beliefs as Lucien was.

All three of them were there last night. Lucien paused, studying her from the kitchen doorway. Why did they all keep secrets? Zoro had argued with the totem man, who had formed into a thunderbird, but she saw the spirits that had joined inside of him. Where was Emmanuel now? The totem man seemed more and more like an enigma she'd imagined.

"Soon Beth. I don't want to overwhelm you." Luce reached for the clicker and turned the television on, switching the channel to her favorite show, *Little House on the Prairie*. Lucien started toward the kitchen again, and she started rising. "Keep that foot elevated. I'm going to call Dr. Haim."

Didn't he already call him?

"Iyyìnko, why not give her your blood?" Zoro licked his paw and cleaned his head. "It should heal her."

She whipped around and found Luce halted, mouth dropping. A blush crept into his cheeks as his lips closed, pressing into a tightened smile. Silence fell as his twisted face searched for an answer. Beth's eyebrow arched waiting for an explanation, as the boy from her dreams and the innocence she remembered broke through. The tough protector act crumbled, and a block of ice erected in its stead as he retreated into the kitchen.

"Zoro, what's going on?" she asked the cat.

Lucien handed her a steaming cup of coffee. Dry toast made an appearance followed by another dose of medicine. All morning he maintained a distance. Cold, quiet, and unreadable were the qualities she'd remembered from his teenage years. What changed? She blinked, stealing glances over her shoulder. A phone plastered to his ear but Luce managed to chat in a lower tone than she could hear.

He too eyed Lucien's activities. "Are you asking me to spy?"

"There's no need." Why did he act as if she had sprouted the plague again? Beth groaned as her face dropped into her hands. "You'd tell me if I needed to worry, right?"

Parting fingers revealed pale blue eyes blinking, and Zoro leapt into her lap. Soft fur brushed her hand and a small giggle jostled her. "Some secrets aren't mine to tell, Kolkohkafoosi, but if you are in danger or veer onto the wrong path, I would warn you."

She whispered, "Is he the wrong path?" Zoro glanced around her, and her breath held awaiting his answer.

"Not as of this time, but he too has a road to walk, but he must wander it alone. But you dream walked last night. Power strengthens within you. Maybe one day you will harness enough to save the world as you have wished."

"Don't encourage her," Lucien muttered, sitting by the coffee table and opening the book on symbolism. Cheers. She hefted the coffee cup, mock toasted his delicious backside as he leaned over the table, swiped the remote, and turned up the television show. *Little House on the Prairie* returned from commercial, and she immersed myself in their simple yet complicated lives, wishing she could have been like Laura. Besides her pretty, svelte frame, Laura had found true love in Alonso Wilder. Lucien did not speak and Zoro snoozed in her lap. At one point, he took her plate and cup. Their eyes met as their fingers brushed. Emotion stormed in his eyes and she had wished she were born an empath instead of a Spirit Walker. The modern name was not used on the Nenë Mvskokë—Muskogee Road. No one word encompassed her abilities, but she saw that as uniqueness. Maybe others saw it as a burden, as something uncontainable. Beth glanced at the television, hearing his footsteps carry him away. Maybe that was how Luce saw her too and now he realized he could not control her.

The pain pills kicked in quickly, and Beth battled the dizziness washing over her like a fog as the show continued. Eventually though she had lost the war with sleep, awaking a time later.

"How are you feeling?"

Lucien sat in the recliner a mere four feet away, but the words had not left his lips. Zoro peeked at her and yawned, digging claws into her belly. No dreams or leaving her body had occurred and she felt rested. Her nose crinkled at his fish breath, and Beth waved the stank air away. The breath from her mouth stunk too, but something about cat breath ranked up there with dog poo.

"Luce?" He stared off into space, but she could not pin point what held his attention captive. The television was off. No book in his lap or phone glued to his ear.

Slowly Beth transitioned to stand, removing the stack of pillows supporting her ankle and lowering the leg to the floor. Each movement stung worse than the last and the pain traveled, shooting through her leg. Still he stared off in a strange trance.

With all her weight on her good foot, she attempted to rise, but fell down courtesy of the fat feline in her lap. A quick shove at the ball of fur and he darted. She lifted herself again and wobbled, a tugging sensation much like a rollercoaster rushed over her skin. A rough hand grasped her arm, squeezing, and cold blue eyes narrowed in on her chasing her warmth away.

"About time," she mumbled, ignoring the stab, and his face softened a tiny bit but not enough. "What's wrong?"

Her finger grazed his rough cheek. The rugged look suited him and contrasted the blue eyes even more than his clean-shaven face. An urge to run her palms over his cheek surfaced, but Beth drew her hand away. He acted like the other Lucien, too cool and indifferent for Bethany Ann McCallister, and she swallowed hard having feared this moment.

A long second passed as they stared at one another. Not in the eyes, the emotions there were too intense for her to read. Her gaze brushed over his cheek instead. Pride battled within her, fought over the walls destroyed for him, and exposed the raw and delicate insides knowing how easily he could break her.

Luce said, "You're going to hate me."

Nerve-pricked laughter rushed out in a light chuckle. Lucien had brooded all morning because she might have hated him? Oh geez, what had he done now? What had he lied about this time? Her eyes wrestled their roll and narrowing. Beth slid her arms around his chest and squeezed, breathing in his fiery fragrance, and calming the internal battle. Whatever this was, they would clog through the problem together.

"It ain't what you think," he said into her hair as his fingers combed through the tangles. "But I haven't known how to tell you." Nothing in life was easy. "Remember when I said I couldn't read your actual thoughts?" Beth pulled away somewhat, but maintained a grip on his torso, and her injured foot raised. The drugs had yet to fully wear off too, and the room tilted, shifting and wobbling. Letting him go of him was not an option. Her brow rose, and she nodded. After all the lies, he had told what was one more. "Drinking blood connects me to you." Lucien scratched his neck. "I took a lot more than I should have … than I've ever had before … and ..."

The night the Mandate arrested her family he had drunk from her, and she had passed out. Beth had not felt right since as the dizzy spells attacked her senses. "Luce, just spit it out already."

"I hear you," he gulped, "loud and clear … thoughts … dreams too. Bethy, I can't block you out, and Lord knows I've tried." He grimaced, but his bronzed cheeks deepened with shades of red. "I don't know when it'll wear off … if it ever will." His tone softened. "I don't want it to end."

"That's what has you brooding like a hen?"

"If I could take it all back … Take everything back except the last week. I really did try, but you were never alone." Beth recalled the day before he had fallen ill. He'd spoken to her and stood up for her, but she ran away fearing it another one of his traps. "I'm an ass for not making you see, but I didn't know how or what to say."

Beth chewed on the inside of her cheek, and her voice shook as she said, "We've established that. Do you regret it?"

No fault in honesty, Beth reminded herself even though she did not like having him know her deepest thoughts, let alone her darkest desires. Lucien didn't answer, and she hid her gaze in the cavern of his chest. Heat rose in her own cheeks as thoughts drifted to the shack. *Crap.* He'd known then the affect he held over her entire being and heard him whisper her name. Beth back peddled, but the tears ached and welled behind her eyes. Such a fool she had been to trust him, to care, to …

"We got carried away, and it's okay if you changed your mind."

"No." He shook his head; his whole body stiffened along with his strained tone. "No, Bethy, I … we … you—" Her hands cupped his cheeks in her palm, and she silenced him, brushing her lips against his. A peck at first but it turned from sweet to sensual as she nibbled at Lucien's lips and forced them open. He melted against her, and his strong arms clutched her waist. In a quick swoop, he had lifted her.

For the first time Beth was elated to have been wrong. Lucien loved her; it was not a dream or game. Sighing as he moaned, their tongues entwined in a slow dance, and no regrets shadowed her mind.

She slid along his body, resting her weight on the good leg. Hands gripped his hair and dragged him closer. Was there such a notion as close enough? Luce made a noise that sounded like uh-uh. Soft against hard and smooth against rough, but the opposites attracted. Gliding her hands over the cotton, she dipped below his belt, and ran the palms over his chest.

Her forte was balance. Mental, physical, and spiritual balance all required practice and patience. *"Heles-hayv."* The word whispered on the wind as it shuddered against the glass. A chuckle broke their kiss, and Beth rested her head on his shoulder, not ready to loosen her grip. The wind spoke again, and she listened, knowing that was always the first step to understanding. Cedar wafted through the air and her eyes widened. Legends say to smell the cedar tree meant to smell the breath of The One Above. Tilting her head, she saw nothing out of the ordinary.

"What are looking at?" Her chin lowered and with it her gaze. Luce flashed his famous smile, and her lashes batted in tune with the flutter of her heart. In all the years, no one but he had looked at her that way. Maybe they were not supposed to see her as anything more than crazy Beth. Granted she was sane, but the townsfolk had not known about her Power or the locha. Just as she had not realized her family sold her blood for profit or that more had existed to being a Spirit Walker than she could have understood.

Sparks danced along her skin. Luce said, "I want to try something. Humor me?"

He sat her on the sofa again and disappeared into the kitchen. Lucien reappeared with a cat pawing at his frayed jeans and a glass of soda in his grasp. He smirked and shook his head at Zoro's wiggling butt as he prepared to pounce.

"Drink this." Zoro shook his cathead as if the human spirit arose and the cat spirit slept. "Won't hurt you, but you might refuse if you, well, you know." Luce handed her the cup, and his hands disappeared, shoving deeper into his pockets as his shoulders rolled.

Bubbles lined the glass walls. He was upset over soda? She inhaled notes of cola, sugar, and something metallic.

"Blood?" Lucien swallowed hard, curtly nodded, and her mouth spread into a smile. If others could drink her blood, why couldn't she have a taste of his? They had already shared more. His ice melted at her thoughts and she wondered if she would be able to hear his. "Esketv Hesaketvmese."

"Esketv Hesaketvmese," he repeated the blessing to The One Above.

The glass lifted, but she paused midway, and lowered the soda-laced blood. Zoro had alluded to Luce's blood healing her, but he did not seem keen about telling her why. All her life she knew Luce was special. Sweat reflected from his forehead and his heart beat quickened. The glass lifted again, and Beth took a deep breath. Lucien would not hurt her, she had to believe in him, and if it saved her from the doctors, all the better. But what had he said about sharing blood? Beth hesitated again; her hand trembled.

"Your blood is like mine, isn't it?"

Lucien grinned wider than the Cheshire cat. "It can be, sunshine."

"What else does it do?" The glass sweated in her hand and her grip tightened. "What does it mean for us?"

"Means I love you and I'm tired of seeing you in pain." Lucien yanked the cup from her hand; the liquid sloshed onto the floor. "Let it go. Dang it, now look what you've done."

"Iyyìnko," Zoro warned, and Beth sniffled. "Tell her the truth."

"I'm not a traitor," Luce snapped and shooed the cat with his bare foot.

Blue eyes bore into blue eyes. "But you are, in one way or another. Emmanuel knows it too."

"Ain't that grand. You want a can of tuna for ratting on me?"

"Luce." Beth reached toward him and folded their fingers. "Stop fighting with Zoro." Lucien yanked his hand away and stormed from the room. Keys rattled and the back door slammed. Moments later and the purr of his engine sped down the driveway. Beth reached for the glass and eyed her familiar.

"It won't kill me, right?" He shook his furry head, and she downed the glass. A draw built as if an invisible line connected her to Lucien. Feelings that were not her own pinched and stabbed her heart. Liquid poured from her clenching eyes. "He thinks I don't trust him."

"Are all inheritors like him?" Zoro chewed his foot, and Beth heard Lucien's thoughts searching. Images flashed—burnt and melted walls—papers scattered everywhere. "He's at my house."

Zoro asked, "How does your ankle feel?" Beth tilted and rotated her ankle with no pain. "Your bruises and cuts are gone too."

Beth lifted herself from the couch and gingerly applied pressure to her injured foot. Still no pain or swelling. *All that from his blood?* Zoro nodded at her unspoken question and returned to grooming his claws. She reached for the phone and dialed Lucien's number. Voice mail picked up and she left him a message as her fingers twirled in her hair. Pacing she called again and cursed herself for not having a way to text him. Beth cursed him too for not returning the phone calls. After the third call, she sat on the sofa and rested her head on her hands. If she felt him then he should have felt her too.

She bounded up the stairs and slid into his bedroom. The room smelled like him, and she clutched her stomach. "Luce." Beth choked, lurching forward and catching herself on the mattress.

"You are his biggest distraction." Zoro pranced into the room and leapt onto the bed as if he owned it. Luce would have had a hissy fit in a heartbeat. "They're not supposed to expose others to their world. Believe it or not, your kind almost hunted them into extinction."

"He's not an inheritor is he?"

"Half," Lucien said. "Get off my bed fish breath."

Beth giggled and Zoro grumbled. "Nice to see you too."

"You healed." But his thoughts hopped from her ankle and swept over the rest over her body, undressing the thin layers of cotton standing between them. The door closed downstairs, and she rolled onto her belly, ignoring his comment and racy thoughts. "Dad's home. I found him at your house. We're going to head back after lunch." Footsteps carried on the steps and the bedroom door's hinges squeaked. The lock clicked. "Beth, we need to face facts."

"Okay …" Wide eyes blinked, focusing on the wall. She became aware of every movement he made, but she'd always held that ability. The thought shook from her head, and she hid, fiddling her fingers, behind the dark curtain of hair.

"Will you look at me? I don't like talking to the back of your head." Thunder rumbled, but she did not spare a glance out of the small window. "Damn it, Beth. Talk to me."

"Lose the attitude first." Hours had passed and he could stew for a bit. Fair was fair. Coarse palms grazed the backs of her thighs, and a shudder tingled over her skin. Beth cursed under her breath as he the fabric of her dress shimmied up around her hips and exposed her commando-clad cheeks.

Hot breath skimmed her back as his lips traveled north. Lucien swept her hair and destroyed her wall, leaving her with nowhere to hide. "That's the point, baby." He traced her earlobe with his tongue, and she tensed as her insides clenched. "Ready to serve me lunch?"

Beth stammered, "What? Luce …" She scrambled to her knees as he captured her hips. "What are you doing? Let me go." Warmth gave way to cold. The fabric fell into place as she rose. But her fists balled. "Don't do that again, Lucien Brown."

"Hey." Luce snapped his fingers. "Don't be like that." The bed groaned as she leapt onto the floor, avoiding a grabby hand Lucien. Fingertips crackled, but he rolled his eyes. "You're sexy when angry." Beth glared at him and crossed her arms over her chest. "And I love when you shove your chest out like that too."

He eased his lanky frame over the rumpled comforter and stuffed his hands behind his head. Beth glanced to the closed door, but her arms and shoulders relaxed. "What did you find?"

A palm scrubbed his cheek. "What didn't we find? It isn't looking good."

It shouldn't have been this difficult to prove her innocence. But how did she prove what she should have known? "Let me talk to them."

"No."

"No?" She winced at his sharp tone and stepped toward the bed. Her palms lifted as her shoulders rolled. "Luce this is my life we're talking about. It's not your choice to make for me."

A breeze ruffled her hair. She blinked. The tiny window wasn't open. He stood before her and grasped her shoulders, squeezing. "They know your blood is different. They took it all."

"I want to see." Beth believed him, but the old saying about seeing and believing rang through her head.

"Yeah, we need to talk about that too, sunshine. But now that you're healed …" Her training would begin.

Chapter Eight

James and Lucien drove into town and left her home with Dana. She clattered in the kitchen preparing dinner. Beth stayed out of her way, sitting at the breakfast table while Zoro ate his fill of tuna flavored cat food. Dana's movements were quick and precise like those professionals on television. Chop, slice, dice, steam, and so forth. Beth tended to refrain from kitchens unless necessary. Anything cooking related was off limits, except for the coffee pot and teakettle. The house would burn down if she attempted to cook.

That meant Lucien would take over the cooking duties *if* they progressed that far. *If* she could clear her name because if they could not, she would go to jail. A breath whistled through her teeth as she rubbed her achy temples. His thoughts replied to hers, flashing through steel rooms and giants barred cages as a shudder ripped through her spine. No, they would lock her up and use her as a guinea pig. Beth chewed her lip and glanced to Zoro. Would that be so bad as long as she saved lives?

"Luce said your blood heals too? Does the Mandate know about inheritors?"

Her dark bun shook, but Dana did not turn around. "I don't know why we didn't think of blood sooner." Her tone said they had, but someone had not agreed. Was he keeping another secret? "Times have changed, Beth. New, younger Creek, form the councils without full knowledge of their ancestors. Some storytellers survive, but so many have passed away." The older generations typically told stories at the festivals and dances, but, in the family, the teaching fell to a mother's brother.

Dana stirred the pan as the purple hull peas simmered. Bacon and fried chicken scents filled the kitchen, and she could not stop the drool from pooling in her mouth. "We wanted to change that fact, but the townsfolk haven't been receptive." Her shoulders fell slightly as she took a deep breath. Dana twisted and faced her, but did not look at her.

"Beth, the world hunted us for centuries and killed many innocent Native Americans in the process. Many stopped telling the Jumlin story altogether." Her hands wrung in her apron. "We never intended to have Lucien, for fear they'd find out and harm him. He is rarer than an inheritor, but it is his place to tell you, not mine. Already I have said too much."

"He joined too though, despite requiring my blood." Vampire myths often had the bloodsuckers gorging on human or animal blood, but the inheritor did not need blood for survival like its co-creator the Jumlin. Luce's case was different. His healing blood could not combat the cancer growing inside his bones any more than hers could've healed her broken bone. The Creek turned to modern medicine, and so had Lucien's parents, but none of the treatments worked. Dana told Beth more than Lucien had shared, and she found all she needed was to ask.

A grim smile crossed her lips. "I objected, but he felt called to teach from The One Above." Her hazel eyes danced toward the ceiling.

With the whirlwind that surrounded them, Beth had not asked Lucien what he did for a living. From what life had she removed him? She stared at her hands, fingers shaking. Coming between him and his calling did not seem right. If The One Above wanted him to teach, then he should have been teaching, and not traipsing around, worrying about her.

As if reading her thoughts Dana answered, "He's teaching Muskogee language and heritage at the recreation center to children, and anyone else willing to learn. The Mandate pays him a small salary, but he's not truly one of them." She wiped her hands over an apron bib. "Truth is James called in a pile of favors to create the position, and Luce would've done it for free, but the money helps pay for his online classes."

Lucien and kids, who would have thought he would choose teaching? Aside from Zoro and James, he knew the old legends better than anyone else did. Water ran in the distance, and Beth shut her eyes, picturing the man in a suit and tie. He was handsome in any clothes, and without.

"He didn't want to go away for school?"

Dana's heels clicked over the floor. Her hand brushed Beth's fingers and stilled them. "He wouldn't leave you." *Lucien stayed because of her.* "You're surprised?"

Beth stuttered, "He's ... he's ... young is all."

"Have you forgiven him?" Her head shook and Dana changed the subject. "Vivian knew what he was. We realized then that she had to have known what you were."

She turned to the stove. "How did you know?"

"Do you ever wonder why Lucien calls you sunshine?"

"No."

"Those who originate from above hold the light of sister sun in their hearts. Those born below hold the glow of brother moon." The iridescence of Luce's skin came to mind, or how he absorbed her power and it reflected blue. "We can see one another, Beth. Vivian was born below." Beth opened her mouth to ask but Dana said, "It is not for me to tell you what she is, but you already know she is not a good person. Her mind and life fills with greed and malice, but I bet she was not always this way."

"What am I?"

"A walker of worlds," she whispered. "A creator of storms."

Beth stepped toward the pile of dirty dishes sitting in the sink. Had Lucien always wanted to teach? She soaped up a sponge and started scrubbing dishes. What had she wanted to become as a kid? A smile crept over her lips as she rinsed the dish, and Dana hummed a popular song. She had always wanted to fulfill her destiny and become a huntress. Was that, too, a lie? "How does one become like you?"

Dana's full lips dragged down. "Afraid it's not easy, Beth. We were all born, but the genes are in our blood." She pushed her away from the dirty dishes. "You're our guest. Besides, we have a dish-washer." Her fingers snapped toward the chair, and Beth sighed, but sat down. "It's not like Hollywood. We age slower after reaching adulthood, giving us baby faces, but we die like humans, and are susceptible to illness and injury."

Stiff shoulders rolled forward, cracking as the truth flared into the light, not about the dishwasher, or being her guest forced on the sidelines. Was there anything she did know? Elbows shook the table as the light flickered in the kitchen. Zoro paused, lifting his head in her direction. Beth buried her face in her hands, since her hair was not available. No future existed for her where Lucien would not have to sacrifice the life he had built for himself. Between his teaching and the little shack, she did not see room for her in his life. Especially not if the Mandate arrested her, she gulped, or turned her into a guinea pig. What had Lucien said about her options before? Stay and fight, run away, or hide. Beth couldn't fight.

Rain pitter-pattered against the windowpane. They tried hiding too. Thunder vibrated the floor. Beth had to run, to flee without Lucien. She couldn't ask him to give up his life. A fist formed and she bit into her hardened knuckles. The plan formed in her mind, but she needed vials first, to leave him enough of her blood to live a long life.

"Beth?"

She stared down at her hands; they glowed blue. The dish in Dana's hand crumbled to blackened dust. The phone rang and she answered.

"She's not responding." Beth blinked and lifted her gaze. "Nope, do what you need to do. Yes, Luce we're fine."

The phone beeped off. "He felt me didn't he?"

"He drank too much of you," Zoro said, purring between her legs. "The connection is sealed, and iyyìnko is your protector now."

She lifted the fluffy Himalayan into her lap. "You sealed the fate by having ... him."

Dana dropped another plate into the dishwasher, and the dish shattered. "You what?"

A hand flew to Beth's mouth, and her eyes widened. Heat ripped through her body and settled into her cheeks. She could not tell if Dana was surprised, angry, or ... just as embarrassed as she was. "I knew the two of you were serious, I'm not mad, and you're both adults."

Trembling hands petted soft fur, but even his powerful purr was not strong enough to calm her nerves. She had decided not too long ago, about how serious her intentions were.

"You're under suspicion ... I'd hoped you'd both wait till after the Festival." Dana released a heavy sigh. "This could go badly if they find out."

More secrets weighed her shoulders as her words echoed in her ears. Zoro's eyes reflected her pain. Mandate, or not, a relationship would not blossom between Luce and her. Carrying her familiar into the living room, Beth plopped down. No matter what she did or said, nothing seemed to work out for her. Everyone she had cared about found themselves in danger by mere association.

What could she do to fix it? Exonerate herself, yes, but it was too late for that. Why hadn't they come for her yet? She fulfilled his wishes of resting and seeing a doctor.

Dusk blanketed the evening sky as the moon lightened streaks shined. The chanting and calls had ceased since releasing Emmanuel. Beth stood at the back door. Dana was upstairs. Her hand hovered over the knob, her belly tight and churning.

"He will find you." She smirked at Zoro, cradled to her chest. Finding her was not a problem. Luce would not have allowed her to leave, or snoop around, when there was evidence to collect. As long as Beth could make it into her house, before he realized she had left, he would not stop her. Crossing her fingers and toes, she prayed for it.

"Now or never." The door creaked open, and they slipped into the muggy night. Gaze darting to the sky, the lightning danced on the horizon. Like a beacon, the storm approached, and the electric tendrils reached for her. Beth's heart hammered, and her pulse raced. Every crack or noise and her eyes followed, investigating and expecting an attack. Or Lucien, yet she sensed him, not close but not too far either. Just in case he showed up, she willed her mind to stay clear and unfocused as she ran, tippy toed across the dewy grass, keeping her eyes wide for signs of impending danger.

The shadow men did not return. Baby steps brought her to the fence, and Zoro squeezed through the bars. Beth gulped, staring upward at the tall iron fence. The slats were not wide enough for her curvy frame. That left climbing and she gulped again.

"You can do it," Zoro encouraged, and she began to scale the metal in a less than graceful attempt. The bars, still heated from the sun, burned her skin. Beth winced as the sensitive area between her thighs contacted the painted iron.

Lucien had cascaded the fence with such skilled grace that he'd made her look like a bumbling idiot. She was thankful cats could not laugh, but the amusement danced in Zoro's blue eyes as her ass landed on the grass.

Fear prickled her skin, and her hand rested upon her heart. Beth spun around but could find no source. Scooping Zoro into her arms, she sprinted toward her home. Efforts increased as she bounded through the sparse pines and across the front lawn, stopping only as the peel of tires and burnt rubber filled her nose. Headlights blinded her, and Beth shielded her eyes.

"Beth what on God's green earths are you doing?" Before she could respond, Lucien's warm hands cupped her face, and his lips consumed hers. For a moment Beth forgot why she'd run away from such a man. "You're as stubborn as a mule." Her mouth opened to retort his statement, but he only kissed her again.

When he pulled away, Beth finally found her voice. "I need evidence, Luce. I need to leave … run." Wetness splashed her cheek as she stared at his t-shirt. "I needed vials."

His brows touched. "Why?"

"You can't come with me," Beth whispered. "Your life—"

"You ain't ever listening are you? Baby, you are my life." His thumb rubbed her chin. "That's what we were doing today." Lucien folded his hand in hers and led them into the house. "'Fraid to say we didn't find much of anything inside. They took most of Vivian's stuff."

Large arms crushed her into his chest, and she squeezed back. "How did you learn about my blood?"

His unspoken question passed through his mind: How did she live in that house and not know? Lucien's mind flashed backward.

Vivian sat at the kitchen table sipping tea, facing the window, and she was on the phone. He froze in the doorway, white knuckles gripping the molding. Her words were muffled as she whispered, "I'm sorry you're having difficulties, but I have a business to run." Beth couldn't hear the other voice. *"The secret ingredient is costly and the demand is high, Jan."*

Costly? It cost them next to nothing to draw her blood. *"If I give it you for that price then everyone will expect a deal. It isn't personal. It's just business." Vivian hung up the phone and sighed.*

Dad said, "She'll die without Beth's blood."

"I know." Her fingers tapped on the mug. "We need to distance our-selves from the family and branch out more to make up the lost funds."

Lucien slipped from the doorway and plastered himself against the wall. His eyes clenched tight as a chair skidded. "I can only draw so much blood, Vivian. Beth is weak enough as it is."

"What about the boy? We could use his blood too."

"The Browns would suspect something. James is too close to the Mandate as it is without risking exposure." Lucien gulped and inched further away from the door. "Our bigger concern is what to do when Beth starts asking questions or leaves. You can't keep her here forever." Vivian snorted. "I'm serious. She's a smart kid and your little story isn't always going to scare her."

"We make the story a reality." The smile was evident in her voice and Beth gagged. *"Jan just may have earned herself another cure."* The *phone beeped. "Jan, I was too harsh. I have an idea on how you can earn the medicine."*

The scene faded from her mind, and she blinked. "Oh my gosh, Lucien." She smacked his arm. "Why'd you never tell me?" He could not have been more than fifteen in the vision. A hand covered her mouth as she gaped at him. "They actually did it … conspired …"

Bile swirled in her stomach at the hatred they held in their hearts. At least when she and Luce were not talking, she never stopped loving him. But what they had done was unspeakable.

"I told my parents that night what I'd overheard. They didn't believe me, not until Jan died months later." Jan … she could not recall the woman, but her grandson went to school with Luce and her. Bobby hated her with a seething passion, but they never spoke. He would just sit in the corner and sneer at her like everyone else.

"After she passed, I asked Bobby about your family, Beth. Vivian paid her in cure to have him and his dad dress in all black. She'd let them on the property at night, on specific nights when y'all were out late …"

Every time she wanted out, an attack would happen, or she would see something in the bushes. Vivian had reinforced the fear to make sure she never left. Beth leaned against him as her legs swayed, and her head dizzied.

"I didn't tell you because I didn't want to overwhelm you." He kissed her head. "There's more Bethy, but …"

"Tell me," she stared up at his pinched face, "Luce I deserve the truth."

"Let's go inside." He led the way into the kitchen. Disaster was an understatement. Hazel eyes scanned the destruction, some of it hers, but most of it from the Mandate's haphazard searches.

"Daddy is learning all he can about your case, but it ain't looking bright, sunshine. They know about your blood, and the question is whether making an example of you, or using you, will benefit them more."

Lucien drew out the same chair Vivian had sat in and Beth parked her butt. He filled the kettle with water and placed it on the burner, lighting the flame with a match. Cups clattered as he fished around in the cupboard and withdrew two mugs and a tea tin.

He continued, "Much of what I know is second hand from him, things I saw here and there, but I know Vivian left your blood out of her cures if a person couldn't pay."

"That burns me the most." Beth leaned backward in the chair. "She acted like it was something exotic that only she knew how to cultivate." A finger tapped her vein. "I mean the freezer had more blood than a freaking blood bank." Lucien chuckled but nodded as he sat beside her. His hand folded over hers and squeezed. "So what do they want?"

"They want the cure, meaning you sweetheart, but right now they have enough." Vivian had taught her there was never enough.

"Why haven't they come for me yet?"

"They think they have you." The kettle whistled, and Lucien retrieved it. The cabinet rattled as he closed the door. "I ain't letting them have you." She took a deep breath and held it. "If you're going to run, you need to do it for real. The Mandate allowed you to stay with us, because Dad promised them he wouldn't let you flee. We put our asses on the line."

"We?"

"It just came out that way, but you know what I mean." Fingers yanked through his black hair. "I wouldn't let you go at it alone, Beth." She rose, retrieving the honey and a spoon. "I love you, but they're my parents. Yours didn't give a damn, but mine do, and …"

"I get it. You don't want your parents hurt or to choose between me and them." It would be like her choosing between Lucien and Emma. Dana's words flooded into her mind again about the risks. Beth was bad news topped with a bright red bow. Lucien should have turned her over and let the Mandate charge her. Prison was not exactly a new concept to her, but at least she could save lives, and her own life would be worthwhile. Running wouldn't clear her name.

"They'll turn you into a science experiment." His voice dropped to a hushed whisper. "Bethy, you can't ask that of me. I'm an ass not a monster."

Every sci-fi movie flashed into her head. Cold metal gurneys, needles, and white, institutional rooms caused a shiver to roll over her body. But she had to face the facts.

"Your parents would have to run too. You can't ask me to ruin your lives."

A decision she didn't want to make, and certainly not one she would make for them. If she ran, the Browns would be in danger. Not just for letting her go but because her family knew, Luce was special. If they could exploit a child, they would hold no qualms over turning him in to save themselves.

James stepped from the shadows as Luce handed her a mug. "We'll do what we must, Beth. We'll do what is right, when it's right."

She spooned honey into her tea and stirred as the words set in. Who were they and why would they go to these lengths to save her? Luce lugged in boxes and James retrieved flashlights. Full dark had not set in yet, but the electricity did not work.

They had sorted through the disastrous first floor, piling papers and trash until well past eight. Dana called and James departed, leaving them alone. Zoro had disappeared shortly after their arrival.

"Momma says supper is ready."

Beth was not hungry. She stared at the mound of receipts retrieved from Vivian's shed. The evidence wasn't in her favor. Her initials appeared on every sheet, and her blood alone had filled the freezer. Beth could not blame the Mandate for jumping to the same conclusions. Even if she could somehow prove she did not know about it, they would have still wanted her blood, but a clean name gave her more leverage.

Her life had boiled down to the power of her healing blood. Beth pinched her forehead. Lucien rubbed her shoulders and kissed her cheek. "Baby you're stressing. C'mon let's go eat supper."

He handed her a flashlight and drew her chair out. None of this made a lick of sense. What was the Mandate waiting for? She would have brought her in already; if not for questioning them to make sure she couldn't run. Beth gulped and glanced out the window.

"What if they're watching us?" He cursed. What if they wanted to lock her away for good? Until they'd squeezed the last drop from her veins ... she turned into his chest. At least the Muskogee had not believed in the death penalty, but it was still a death sentence. Death of her future. Death of Lucien. Death of her spirit. Her legs buckled, but Lucien caught her arms. Death of them.

"It's my fault, Bethy." She pulled away and stared into his eyes. Hair fell forward and he combed it back into place.

"Don't blame yourself. I'm glad they were caught." An ache stabbed in her chest. Lucien brushed her cheek, fingertips lingering. Her lips parted sucking in precious breath. "I could fight."

"You're not—"

Beth leaned on her toes and brushed a kiss over his lips. "I was born to fight, Luce. Do they know about the Power?" He shook his head but maintained eye contact. "Then I have an advantage, right? We run and fight but we need to figure out the details."

"My cabin?"

"It's too close. Besides, they probably know it's there by now. No, I think we need to leave the town. We need to leave the state." Beth grabbed the empty vials and shoved them into a bag. Lucien did not say anything, but she wanted them in case. If anything happened to her, he'd have what he needed to survive.

As she scurried about the rooms, Luce sighed; his posture slouched as he braced himself against the kitchen window. Beth paused in the doorway as his reflected gaze caught her eyes and twisted her gut. She started toward him, a paper sack crinkling as it brushed her knee.

"The fault's still mine. If I hadn't gotten sick —" Beth punched his arm. "Ouch."

How could he still blame himself? This wasn't anyone's fault but her family. They used her and extorted other innocent people. She shook her head but he nodded.

"You listen real good." Lucien glanced away, rubbing his arm like a big baby. She pushed between him and the window, grasping his face in her palms and forcing him to look at her. "I don't blame you. Hell Luce, I don't even blame Vivian for saving your life. Losing you would've killed me."

At the mere thought, tears sprang into her eyes, and she choked them back. How could he blame himself for a sickness he could not control? His death would have crippled her then, and now.

"I lost you anyway, but knowing you were alive … not knowing it was blood and not my marrow … not once did I feel sorry for saving you. Not once will I ever regret saving you, because I love you no matter what pain you cause me."

Tears streaked along his face, splashing and rolling over her thumbs, and blue eyes glowed like stars in the darkest darkness. Beth had not meant to make the man cry but spoke the truth. No amount of deceit would have changed her mind. Even after all he had dragged her through, his life had continued to mean more to her than anything else in her existence. From the first moment she could remember, Lucien was her light—her hasi. Maybe hasi was the wrong word, but that was what she saw in him. An escape from her prison, a beacon of hope she ran toward when nothing else had made sense. When he'd turned his back on her, Beth lost all optimism, and each day a grapple for survival in the cage her family built for her

He wiped his face on his sleeve and forced a brave smile. "Gross. They make tissues." Luce brushed her statement off. She eyed the kitchen. It appeared smaller with all the boxes and bags of trash, but she no longer saw it as her home. Without the false warmth, it was only walls. Her eyes washed over emptied cabinets and drawers.

"I packed the basement earlier. The Mandate couldn't find the key." He yanked it from his pocket and rattled the chain. "Dad cleared the weapons and put them in my trunk." Her arms surrounded Lucien, and she kissed his rough, tear-dampened cheek. "The study and outbuildings were already trashed. But, can I ask you something?" He put the key in his pocket. "Why were the weapons phonies?"

"How would I know?"

Beth grasped his hand and yanked him toward her. Fake weapons … she stumbled as he swayed into her. Why stage the basement? He tripped and knocked her down, crashing on top of her. "Where's the fire, sunshine?"

Thick lips hovered close enough his breath tickled her face. A curse swept through his parted mouth, and her pulse quickened. Beth couldn't follow his rapid thoughts, but hadn't needed to as Lucien pressed his arousal between her outstretched thighs. Leave it to a man to be horny at a time such as this. Her hands inched, scooting backwards.

Dana's warning blared through her head, and she spun, scurrying away on all fours. A huffed growl resonated from his chest, and Lucien snared her hips. Salty fragrances overpowered the usual burnt wood as his zipper released. Torn between the tug of her insides and the repercussions, Beth froze as he lifted the fabric of her dress, and cool air dimpled her skin.

"Lucien we can't ... we shouldn't ... too dangerous."

Hands and lips caressed her skin as a moan released and speaking ceased. Taking on a mind of its own, her body pressed against his skillful teases. Fire spread, consuming her inside and out. A finger brushed over her bundled nerves, and she writhed, grinding her body into his touch. Lucien chuckled and smacked his palm against her flesh. Beth yelped more from shock than sting, but he soothed the ache with gentle kisses.

A breathy rumble rushed through him as he said, "Bethy, screw the ramifications. I love you, and to hell with anyone else." Legs trembled at his words, and their meaning as a grin spread over her face. "Nothing else is coming between us."

Shuffling sounds alerted to his movements, but Beth saw nothing beyond the pillowed fabric of her dress. Fingers eased inside of her, and she gasped at their invasion. "That's it Bethy." Muscles clenched and her hips rocked with his thrusts as the gentle hum built within her body.

Words refused to form as he encouraged her, and showered her thighs with kisses, teasing and working his way higher. Lucien's breath hovered above her bud; her breathing stilled, waiting for him to brush those thick lips over her, but all he gifted was teasing air.

Her spine swayed riding his fingers between cat and cow poses and flexing her pelvis toward his mouth. Light blinded her vision as the heat of him suckled her, and Beth exploded in a breathless fury, rippling and throbbing as the screams released.

Luce didn't stop; he sucked harder, twining the nub between his teeth. Her sparking fingers scraped and clawed into the hardwood floors. If thunder had rumbled, she could not feel the difference. Diving into her folds his tongue slid along her as her body spasmed once more, arching as high as the decibel of her scream. Only when the cries turned to whimpers did the devil release her.

Lucien skimmed upward, rising onto his elbows. "Turn around."

Beth came face to face with his hard length as she abided his gruff tone. A trembling hand wrapped around the girth; Lucien moaned, his hips mounting slightly off the kitchen floor, and pants clattering down as his belt scraped the wood. Her deep breath drew inward and she rubbed a thumb over his tip. Beads of white had already formed and they glistened in the moonlight.

"Slide your—" His words curled into a loud groan as her lips engulfed the head, and the velvety smooth skin pulsed beneath. Flavors blended and rolled over her tongue, neither sweet nor salty. Lucien thickened in her mouth. But her thoughts ceased as his mouth drew her bud into him again. Her sounds muffled and vibrated over the length of him. He grasped her dress and dragged her backward. Beth blinked, heat flooding her cheeks. Did she do it wrong or hurt him?

Frozen, she did not hear or sensed him move. "I'm not ready," Lucien whispered into her ear drawing her against his chest. "I was close." Teeth grazed her neck sending shivers rushing along her spine. The hardness rested in the clef of her ass. The hem of her dress jerked over her head, and he twirled her around. Beth searched his face, but the only emotion visible in his hungry eyes was lust. Her gaze dropped away, wondering if that ever changed. The raw carnal emotions were so new to her. Beth wanted more than the burn of fire.

Backing away, the cold door pressed against her naked flesh but did little to temper her heated skin. Sex heavy air strangled her lungs. Salt dusted her parched skin, and her arms hugged herself. Clattering teeth drowned out the thrum of her heart but not the racing sensation. As Lucien shuffled closer, her gaze would not lift. Beth had to let him go even if for his own sake. For her sanity's sake, they could not do this.

"Show me."

"Show you what?"

"Show me what's bothering you instead of locking it under your thoughts."

They had nothing more than teenaged lust. How would they survive the coming times without true love … how would they work together if he wanted to rip her clothes off all the time. This was not how she envisioned them together.

"Beth," Luce warned. That old vision resurfaced the one that never happened. A night much like tonight when the light breeze cooled the skin. Stars and moon shined, illuminating a secluded spot in the grass. No worries, no underlying anguishes, or pressures, tainted their love. All that had existed in the moment was Lucien and her.

Love and acceptance had filled vibrant blue eyes, and in their intimate moment, Beth would discover that there would never be another man for her. But the night had died a long and lonely death among her other dreams. Instead of making love on the grass, that night she'd wept and cursed her existence. The nightmare replayed often; one day she had shoved the vision into the grave, burying it alongside her love for Lucien. Or so she had told herself, but that was a lie. She never forgot.

Wind whipped her face as he scooped her into his arms. Beth stared into his eyes as he gently lain her in the damp grass. Outstretched hands ran over the blades tickling her palms. "Should've done this the first time," he said and tore his shirt free, followed by his jeans. "It should've been perfection."

Lucien rolled his body flush with hers and brushed those lips against hers. Fingers feathered through his hair as her legs skimmed powerful thighs. The sprinkler system started its cycle, and she shrieked as the icy water bathed over them. Lucien smirked, a dangerous glint flashing in his blue eyes. Her hand cupped his cheek and dragged him closer.

"I love you," he whispered. "But I don't deserve you. I never deserved you, sunshine." Lucien slipped into her to the hilt, sharing a gasp at the union. Tears glistened in his eyes as he rocked his hips forward. Hands intertwined and palms seared together. Bodies glided effortlessly, joining and melding as her tummy surged, mixing lust and love en masse. The crescendo inside her rose as his husky breaths came quicker.

Flexible hips met each drive as he ground against her body. Nipples hardened under the brush of his hair, and Beth leaned into his thrusts, needing to feel every inch inside and out. Lucien swayed on his heels, wrapping his arms around her; he brought her against his lap. A finger trailed across her flesh and dipped into her folds, stroking her delicate flower and increasing the speed of her hips.

"I need to feel you," he whispered, flicking his fingertip faster and alternating his mouth between her breasts. Beth gasped, moaned, and her legs trembled as her body climbed higher. "My cock is envious." Her stomach clenched at his words, and she bit her lip. Luce's assault didn't end. "Fuck, come for me, baby. Let me feel you."

Her walls dissolved; his pressure and thrusts increased until she saw nothing but stars. Moans replaced his dirty words, her screams replaced the moans; nails dug into flesh, clawing at his shoulders, and his skin bled as her body seized against him. He guided her head to the fresh wound.

"Drink me," he said, his words strained. Lips sealed around the scarlet brand, and Beth drew his life into her mouth. Thrusting again, Lucien cried out into the night. Breathless they tumbled through the slick grass fighting for desperate breaths.

Wide all seeing eyes focused on the stars above. His thoughts renewed, flashing through the pages of her old scrapbook, the one she'd thought lost. Lucien had stolen the book and left it at the cabin. Another shudder rippled through her as he said, "Marry me, Beth." He kissed her dewy forehead. "I can't think of any other way to prove how much I love you."

Six words most girls longed to hear from their partners. "Luce ..." Her fingers twisted; the disarray of her life posed a problem. Neither the past, nor pain, affected her decision. But she didn't know where her future landed. As long as they were together, she put his life at risk. More than his life, but his parent's lives too. They carried the burden of association like Jemma.

Alone was how Beth had lived her life and alone was how it would end. Somehow, she had known there was nothing else for her. Not in Abbeville, maybe not in Alabama, or in the country. Beth couldn't force him to stay away either, and she wasn't asking him to, but a marriage now?

"I can't."

"Why the hell not, sunshine?" Beth dashed inside and bounded upstairs. Footsteps echoed his fury, yelling and screaming as he stormed after her, but for once, she was faster.

She locked and fortified the bathroom door by shoving her vanity chair under the handle. Pounding rolled over the door. Beth eased into the icy cold shower. Teeth chattered, but the spray erased the salt, and Lucien, from her skin. A muffled voice carried over the cascade of water. "Beth don't shut me out. Tell me why so I can fix it."

But no one could fix her life. Only The One Above could have changed her fate, or the blood running through her veins. Her eyes shut against the water. What did he want her to do? Were his grand plans also to let others use her blood, selling it to the masses for an insane fee? Or should Beth take control and help those she found by the grace of her heart?

Water shut off and she wrapped the towel around her. Excess water dripped from her hair, splattering over the tile. Her reflection caught her eye in the darkened mirror, and she paused half expecting a change, but there Bethany Ann McCallister stood the same woman as before.

"Sunshine, open the—" Beth removed the chair and opened the door. Lucien was a mess, and she was to blame. Dirt and grass littered his disheveled hair, and mud smeared his chest. Beth motioned toward the shower and snapped her fingers. "I get the silent treatment now, is that it?"

Hazel eyes glued to the floor. One glance and her resolve would crumble into oblivion. She had to do this without him and, if she found a way out, then they could be together. Once the shower turned on, Beth slipped into clean clothes and her running shoes. Zoro, who she'd forgotten about, watched from the doorway with a wide stare.

"I'm going." He raised a paw, licking the surface, and dragging it over his head. "Zoro, you don't have to come."

"I will come."

Without another word, Beth shot into action. Clothing, papers, book, antiques … it did not matter. She needed money, and many of the items would fetch a fair sum. The floorboards groaned behind her, and a curse flew through her mouth; her hands lit up the bedroom, tendrils of lighting crawling along Vivian's walls as the wallpaper melted.

"Easy Bethy," Luce said naked, approaching with caution. His hands held out in front of him as he eased closer. "Let me take you home."

"I have no home," she snapped, clenching her blue hands into tiny balls.

His forehead creased, and Beth shattered, falling to the floor in a million pieces. The world she thought she knew … the dreams she thought she had … nothing fit into the future looming ahead. She could no more ask Lucien to come than she could leave him behind.

Zoro kneaded and purred on her thigh. All her life someone told her what to do, where to go, and how to live. Beth did not know up from down without the prison walls and wardens she despised. "I'm losing my mind, heart, and life all at the same time. Luce, I don't know what to do."

Lightning cracked, and her heart leapt into her throat. Zoro hissed, and Lucien's bones shook as footsteps thudded behind them. He spun her around and stood in front of her. Shrouded in the darkness and shadows of her old bedroom Beth saw a figure outlined.

"You will not take her from me," Luce growled, and electricity poured into his hands again. Whatever his other half was, it too harnessed the Power.

"Her destiny waits, as does yours, inheritor, or shall she call you by your true name?" The shadow stepped closer, feathers ruffling. Emmanuel had returned. "Your fates have entwined, and you must come now. She has healed."

What had he meant by Lucien's true name? He was an inheritor. "I'll explain later."

Beth shoved Lucien aside and poked a finger into his chest. "No, you'll explain right now."

"I'm a half breed."

"What's the other half, Luce?"

"He is estakwvnayv," Emmanuel said. "And that is his destiny."

"Hold-up." Her mouth gaped at the tongue-twisting name, but its definition was alien to Beth. "A what? Even in Muskogee that sounds like a face rolling across a keyboard."

"Half," Lucien repeated. "Daddy is a horned serpent, and my momma is the inheritor."

He had lightning too. He had thunder. Both he and his father appeared human. "I'm still me, Bethy."

She stepped backward, and he sighed. Beth cocked her head taking him in. Blue eyes blazed like fire. His tan skin shined in the light with a slight iridescent sheen across his forehead. Lucien was beautiful and unique, and he loved her. More so, she loved him. His arms stretched wide, surrendering himself, and his knees dropped to the floor. She glanced to Emmanuel, Zoro, and then Lucien. A dim cerulean shade glowed from his forehead.

"Iyyìnko," Zoro said as if reminding her of his nickname.

Beth held a hand up and shook her head. "Why didn't you tell me?"

The storm raged outside the window. It was not her alone creating them; Luce did too. "You didn't ask the right question."

"We must go. The trials must begin." Emmanuel shifted on his legs, but Beth ignored him.

Her feet shuffled toward Lucien, and she knelt in front of him. Cupping his cheek, her lips kissed his head. "You're still my Lucien."

But learning his other half didn't change the future. Beth glanced over her shoulder. "I need to leave."

"I'm not letting you go." His lips parted, and his breathing deepened. "Do you hear me?" Lucien tugged on her shirt. "I would leave this life for you," he said and rubbed his cheek against her face. "Everything I am, all that encompasses me belongs to you, Bethany McCallister, whether you like it or not. I am your protector and guiding light.

Chapter Nine

Lucien packed her a few suitcases full of clothing, shoes, and supplies then tossed them into his trunk. Returning to his parent's house was no longer an option, but he kept clothes for himself at the shack. Where he had stored them, she did not know. They bought maybe a few days with the Mandate. The risks would increase with each passing day.

"They'll know you helped her," Zoro said. "Your family is still at risk too."

Lucien shrugged his shoulders weighed down by the remaining bags. "My parents don't know where we are going."

"Luce, but what if they arrest your parents?"

A half-smile played at his lips, and he squeezed her hand. "Bethy, they'll be fine." They stepped outside, and the darkness blanketed the backyard. The moon had rested behind the tree line alerting her to a far later hour than she had realized.

Beth bee lined for Vivian's workstation. Needing to see no hope existed with her eyes one final time. The outbuilding lay in shambles too. Her burnt hole remained unscathed. Did they realize she did it? Careful to avoid the edges, she ducked through the opening. All the blood, the papers, everything her aunt had worked on had disappeared. She hugged her familiar tighter as a chill dizzied her.

"Emmanuel awaits us." Zoro leapt from her arms and darted from the building. Beth stayed behind, gaping in awe at the emptied shed that had saved and ruined lives, not the outbuilding itself, but her aunt's work and Beth's blood. Luce finished packing up valuables and heirlooms. Everything she owned the sale of her blood had tainted, but she did not want him using his money either.

"I wish I could just burn it." Luce's brow rose as he stepped in front of her. "Not just the house, but this place." She pointed toward the kitchen door behind her. "Daddy would draw my blood in there."

"Sometimes their just ain't any matches, but if it's a fire you want, I'll light this place up in a blaze of blue glory."

Beth touched her collarbone and chuckled. "Well now that's about the sweetest thing you've ever said to me." She bumped her hip against his. "But we're already in enough hot water without adding arson to the mix."

Zoro said, "And we've got company. We need to leave now."

In the distance, an engine revved. It could have been James, but she doubted it. . Lucien yanked her arm. Beth stared, like a frozen deer, at the yellow lights speeding down her driveway. "C'mon baby, we got to go."

Feet somehow moved, scurrying out of the building, and moving toward the property's edge. The engine cut and voices carried over the wind. They halted once they had reached the safety of the forest. Lucien placed their bags down as Beth caught her breath.

"Call the storm," Zoro said. "See it in your mind." The dang cat did not appear winded at all, but she heard the boom of his heartbeat.

A dog barked and bounded from the car. It had to be Claire. Luce said, "Rain washes our scent away. He'll track us, Beth. By your scent."

But she didn't know how to conjure a storm on the fly. They happened seemingly from her emotions, in particular her sadness and anger. "Well you need to get sad or angry real quick, sunshine." He glanced behind her. "You've got about five minutes, before she realizes we're not inside."

Beth spied Claire entering the house and cringed. As stupid as it sounded, Vivian would have blown a freaking gasket over a dog in her house. The thought shook from her head, and she closed her eyes. The tree frogs deafened the nightly sounds, and their cadence hummed over her skin. Wind brushed her dampened neck, but humidity hung thick in the air. In her mind, the dense clouds collected. Rough hands shook her from the vision, and she blinked into curious blue eyes.

Fingers snapped, thumbing toward her former home. Claire departed, her dog barking. Lucien's white knuckles gripped the bag. "Go with Zoro." He handed the sack to her. "I'll take care of her."

Clutching the duffel to her chest, she sighed. Luce grasped her face and kissed her, whispering words against her lips. Again, she blinked but this time Beth stared at an empty space.

Beth descended further into the woods at a light jogging pace. Heavy legs refused to move any faster, but she told herself she was saving energy. If anything went wrong, they may have to run for it. She did not know where they would run, but only that they must find safety as far from this place as possible. The old stucco walls called to her. Despite their insistence of boxing her in, but the house was the only home she'd ever had. Just as Lucien was the only man she ever loved. The bags clattered, crashing as they hit the ground. Shaky legs bounded toward the house. Zoro swatted at her. "Wrong way."

She could not leave Lucien behind and ignored her familiar's warnings. They were a team and she planned on them staying one for however long forever would be. Branches and leaves crunched beneath her feet, and she ducked under limbs. A dog yelped, crying out over the frogs' songs. She seemed faster than usual, and less clumsy, as she dodged and leapt. Her vision sharpened too, as her legs folded, sliding to the edge of the woods.

No dog barked.

No Claire.

Just Lucien's backside and outstretched hands, reflecting a glossy sheen, stood on her lawn. Had the sprinklers turned on again? "Beth turn around," Zoro whispered, "You don't want to see this."

Two crumpled forms lain at his feet. Her stomach lurched; a hand flew to her mouth.

"I told you to go, Beth." Her chin tilted as she rose from the ground, brushing the dirt from her trembling hands. A third form caught her attention. Bleach blonde hair sparkled under the moonlight. "Sunshine, it's not safe."

"Listen to him."

The wind hissed in her ear. Repeated words she had heard before like *unnatural* and *balance*. Shadow men did not come though. Beth did not listen to Zoro or Lucien and inched her way to Luce's side, glancing at her surroundings and calling his name.

"Go away," he said. Slouched shoulders moved slightly. Their heart rhythms synchronized. Why wouldn't he turn around? She loved him. He did not need to hide from her. Once again, he managed to save her life. "At the cost of three others."

She swallowed hard, placing a hand on his tense shoulder. Beth did not want to see the bodies. "Come with me, Luce."

His legs staggered backward; he crumpled to the ground. She looked to the bodies and to him. Tears streamed down his bloody face. Lucien Brown had murdered for her. Slick crimson marred his hands. Dark hair shook, and his twisted face shouted to the heavens. "She just wouldn't listen."

Thoughts poured into her mind like a raging waterfall. The scene unraveled.

Lucien strolled from the woods and met Claire halfway. Her dog snarled at Luce's feet. "Mr. Brown you're not supposed to be here."

"Beth asked me to check on something." The car door creaked, and Amber stepped out rubbing her arms. Lucien did not glance at her.

"The scene is sealed, and you're trespassing."

"The court unsealed it this morning." Lucien crossed his arms.

"You're still trespassing. This is private property—"

"Owned by the McCallisters and a McCallister gave me permission to be here. If anyone's trespassing, it ain't me but y'all. I can give Beth a call if you'd like to verify my statement, officer."

"Cut the crap. We both know she isn't a McCallister."

Amber laughed, leaning against the sedan. "She's a freak of nature."
Lucien's gaze snapped. "Shut your damned mouth. Why are
you even here?"

"Don't talk to my daughter that way." Daughter? So Amber was
bleached blonde. Did her posse know she was a Creek Indian
beneath her facade? Claire could not have been with Indian Affairs
without a hefty dose of Creek blood. Beth never understood the
shame some held over their heritage. She was proud of hers.

"Tell your daughter not to talk shit about my fiancé."

"Fiancé?" Lucien cursed. "Mr. Brown you can't—"

"Lucien how could you ... Beth? That's so gross."

*Hands covered his ears. The dog snapped again, but he was too
quick, grasping its neck, and twisting until it cracked. Claire drew
her gun; the safety clicked off. Amber shrieked. Crimson misted the
air and coated his body as Officer Claire slumped to the ground.
The shrieking blonde was next.*

Beth glanced away, staring at the bloodied masses dangling from his
hand. Scalped ... he had scalped them, because in the heat of the moment,
Luce had said too much about his romantic involvement. Chewing her
cheek, she nodded as if accepting this fate, but she did not approve of
the deaths. Lucien's head fell into his hands. Stiff shoulders rattled. She
could not recall hearing the screams, unless Amber had sounded like a
wailing dog. They were enemies, but she had not wanted to see her dead—
anyone dead for that matter. Beth knelt, her hand reaching toward him,
but he recoiled from her. A knife sliced through her heart as a gasp
released. Not an actual blade, but Lucien might as well have stabbed her.

Thunder rumbled; the air smelled of rain. Beth reached her pro-
verbial trigger and squeezed it. Clouds billowed over the full moon,
and stilled darkness surrounded her shut eyes. Wetness seeped from
above as drops pounded her head.

Blinking she opened her eyes. Lucien crawled further away, as if
she were a monster instead of him. Iyyìnko—traitor—Zoro's words
seemed fitting as the man she loved betrayed her again.

Beth locked out the world surrounding her. Engulfing her pain,
she bore the badge on her sleeve despite trying to hide it. Bare arms

reached toward the sky as lightning cracked, and the thunder followed as if chasing the sound across the heavens. Lucien was gone.

"Figures," she muttered and glanced at the three bodies. Steady rain washed their blood into the earth. Another rumble shook the ground beneath her feet, and the soil erupted, cracking, and swallowing the evidence. The Great Mother and Father Sky worked together, and once again, she had saved Lucien.

"That's what friends are for." Beth dusted her wet hands and turned around, marching back to the trees. She had lost Lucien all over again, but now was not the time to mourn his loss and crumble into dust. A time existed for everything in life. A time to love. A time to sow. A time to mourn. Laughter shook her chest. *A time for revenge.*

Beth saw Zoro huddled under a bush. The poor thing looked like a skinny drowned rat. A smile forced itself over her lips, but on the feline, the gesture was lost.

"Give him time," Zoro said. "He loves you."

Reaching down, she grasped the bags Lucien had dropped. Blankness settled over her mind and numbness tingled from her heart. Each step becoming easier than the last as Bethany Ann McCallister stormed away from her old life and toward a new one. Zoro led her deeper into the woods; over babbling brooks and downed trees she thrashed. Beth did not complain. She did not say a word, because there were no words to say that did not involve *him.* Admitting she still cared made her feel weak on the inside. She had nothing. Nothing left to her name except the sacks he had been carrying and the clothes on her back. It would trickle to the outside if she allowed her pain to control her. Too late—the storm was her emotion but was any of it Lucien?

They hiked, stopping to rest as needed, venturing outward into the unknown lands of the Creek people. Much of it had fallen into the hands of others before the Trail of Tears swept them west. Beth clutched the duffel bag in her hands, hugging it to her chest as she stepped over stony boulders or ducked beneath low branches. Spanning from the Mississippi River to the east coast and as far north as the Appalachians, her ancestors had worked, lived, and hunted these lands.

Zoro sat on her shoulder as she crossed a waist deep stream, the bags slung over the other. The warm water soaked her through, seeping into her sneakers, but she pressed forward. On the other side, she rested and removed the wet shoes. Still her mind stayed clear of whom she had left behind, but that too was a lie. Lucien would not leave her thoughts.

Time progressed as the cloud darkened sun rose, drifted, and arched into the sky. No rays befell her path as the perpetual storm cloud followed her, but no rain fell. Salty sweat crusted to her skin again, burning and itching from prolonged exposure. Flakes fell as her joints flexed leaving a salty trail behind her.

No beauty existed in this wilderness. None of it had ever existed within her. This journey became her own Trail of Tears, but she shed none, only the salty flecks would prove her trek.

Beth tasted stains in the air, and its soured odor turned her empty stomach. More than once, she halted, seeing movement out of the corner of her eye. Her heart skipped a beat, but nothing was there. *He was not there.*

Life seemed like meaningless survival; she pondered why it was worth living. Lucien Brown consumed her thoughts too, even though she did not want to think of the man who kept breaking her heart. *If he loved her, then why did he leave her?* Grey clouds covered the sun; it had not shined since he left her. Would her world see sunlight again? Branches rustled behind her, but this time she kept marching forward.

Red lettering caught her eye ahead. She slowed her steps. "Do you see that?"

"We'll stop there," her feline said. "We'll rest until night fall. It's too hot for you to travel during the day." Beth withdrew a bottle of water and downed the warm contents. "There should be a spring or pump nearby."

As a kid, she had explored more of Lucien's side of the joint property than her own. Her brow rose at how Zoro knew so much about her land. An abandoned building from her ancestors' time stood a few paces away, hidden behind brush and trees. A rusted pump jutted from the ground outside. Beth dumped the cool water over her head, and then proceeded to bathe her crusted skin free of the salt. For the first time in what felt like days, her skin breathed again, but a rash pricked her skin.

"What is that place?" she asked, dousing her head under the water pump. Zoro leapt onto the porch and disappeared inside. Beth drew a wooden dish from her bag and filled the bowl for her familiar.

"An old trading post," he called from inside and sneezed. "There's still stuff inside."

Beth eased in through the door, careful not to lean on the wood. The dirt floor was made of compacted earth. Shelves lined the walls. Lucien would know all about the building, but she shook the thought away.

Each breath twisted her gut. "Something's wrong." Swirls formed around her vision and a sense of falling overtook her.

Animals awakened, and their calls rippled through her. More than frogs or bugs reached her ears as the howling neared. Zoro spoke but his muffled words were lost on the wind. Where was she?

"We are not the only creatures," Emmanuel's voice boomed as snarls and growls replied. "Locha and Kolkohkafoosi can coexist, so can wolf and hunter."

Her steps slowed as she approached the glow of a fire. How did she get here? Bear, wolf, coyote, and all manner of wild creatures sat around the blaze. They were the same creatures she saw the night the darkness birthed Emmanuel. *This was a vision.* Beth glanced to Lucien. Zoro nibbled at a bowl of food. But the scenery was the shack. The shallow stream trickled under the clattering voices.

Luce halted at the fire's edge. Her heart pounded eyeing the wild creatures, or maybe it was him. Branches crashed and thrashed behind them. The world fuzzed again as the blood rushed from her head. She wobbled into the Browns but not Lucien.

Dana asked, "Beth, where's Lucien?"

"He's right here." Concern laced in her eyes, but Luce stood beside her staring into the fire. Didn't she see her son?

"Face your fears." The whispers returned. Her hands clawed at her heart, and the agony shredded the threads holding her together. Flashes overtook her mind, and Beth saw the stream bleed red. A dog barked and growled at Luce's heels, and a gun ripped through the night.

"No," Lucien said, and his words echoed through her lips. She blinked and stared at him, he clutched her hand hard enough it numbed.

"Bethy." Lucien stroked her face. "It was just a vision." His forehead touched hers. "I'm here, sunshine."

"She's getting closer," Zoro said. They were inside the trading post again. "We must find Emmanuel."

Luce ignored her familiar. "Talk to me."

Beth bit her cheek. A shaky hand raised and whacked him across the face, stinging her palm. Blood and blue sparks flew into the air, but Lucien chuckled. Steam rolled from her skin; her heavy breathing reminded her of a charging ox. All she had to do was stomp her feet. He reached for her, but she raised her hand again.

"Get away from me." When would she learn? She had to take a stand and stop letting him use her as a doormat. Her jaw relaxed. Luce was not dead, and they were in this mess because of her. If she had stayed put at his house—or at the shack—no one would have died. He had done the deed, but her hands were just as bloody as his were.

She wanted to hug him and smack him. At the simple thought, his arms engulfed her from behind, and she rested in his smoky cologne. A lump swelled in her throat, and Beth fought to swallow the obstruction. It sure as heck had felt real, as she had watched the scene unravel with her own eyes.

Loosing Lucien, even the thought of someone tearing him away, crippled her. He could leave her and one day, somehow she would get over it, but heaven help anyone who hurt him. Her heart rate settled, and the sick sensation returned, along with the sweat pouring from her palms.

But what was his fear? She could not read Lucien's thoughts. Had the blood bond worn off that quickly? Beth missed his jumping bean thoughts as they hopped between her and the strangest views.

"Losing you, sunshine. Haven't you realized that yet?" Beth spun in his arms and placed her hands on his chest. Her love for him made sense. Everyone loved Luce, but she did not think she would ever understand his love for her. She was not beautiful—at least Jemma had that going for her. Beth was not thin, smart, or funny either.

Lucien drew a heart over her heart. "That is why I love you, and you are beautiful, smart, and funny Bethany Ann. Thin is overrated." A finger pad tapped her nose. "You take my breath away, but when you're gone, there is no sunshine in my life."

She snorted. "That's the blood talking."

"Your blood wore off Beth, or else I wouldn't have symptoms. Can't you see that love and fate connects us, not your blood."

Then why did he push her aside and leave her at the house? *Wait what symptoms?*

"You didn't tell her," he said, scoffing at Zoro over his shoulder. The cat ignored him and batted a dried corn kernel. "Unfreaking-believable." Luce thumbed his chest as his brow rose. "And I'm the traitor?"

Beth cupped his cheek, and he melted into her touch. "You're burning up." Luce was running a fever. A fever meant infection, and Beth's heart sank. He grasped her hands and shook them. Dull blue eyes reflected the same pain as they had when he showed up on her doorstep. "No," she said shaking her head and stepping backward. "Luce …"

"The cancer spread a few months ago," he said, shrugging as if it was not a big deal. "Your blood ain't working anymore, not how it's supposed to." Just a drop he had told Beth, but the night he drank from her, he took far more than that. "Whatever days or weeks I have left, I want to spend them with you."

"But how?"

"Does it matter?" It mattered to her. How could God or The One Above have created such beauty and then poisoned it with cancer? Her dark brows rose higher as her lip trembled. How could he allow anyone to suffer through the terrible disease? Lucien grasped her shoulders and shook her from the thoughts. "After … taking a life has consequences," he gulped, "that's why I left … everything is in order now."

Lucien handed her a bag, but she stared at him, her head shaking again.

"The deed to my cabin is in there." Beth shut her eyes and turned her head as if not accepting his gift would change the future. He grasped her hand, smoothing his thumb over her skin. "You granted my last wish, sunshine, but I have one more to ask."

Beth leaned into him; his beard scratched her skin. "Anything, you know that."

Her eyes burned, and bitterness coated her mouth—his sickness tainted the air like Mr. Pawl's did. There had to be a way to save him though. Maybe herbal remedies were out of the question but what about medical advancements or chemo? Beth could force-feed him her blood if she had to; she would if it meant he lived and the other people needing her blood died. He shifted behind her; keys jingled in his pocket. Keys to a car she did not want without him driving it … a deed to a shack that would not be home without him. What good was saving others if she could not save the one person that mattered?

"Marry me, Beth. Everything of mine is yours, but I want it official." Hinges creaked and she opened her eyes to a velvet case. "It's not a diamond."

That was okay, she wasn't the diamond type. Her hand touched her pounding heart as a thin ray of sunlight bathed through the door and glinted off the stone. Inlaid on either side were pearls. "It's beautiful, Luce."

The sapphire stone glowed and flashed. He whispered, "Is that a yes? Please baby, we can be in Vegas in two days." She refrained from laughing, but he was so much like the old Luce, except he never called her baby. "Please Beth. I had the same dreams as you. Let me give you what I can, for as long as I can."

"What about your family?"

"I've spent nineteen years with them," he said, rubbing his nose against hers. "Besides they're waiting on me to call them before they fly out to Vegas." The smile reflected in his voice. "But we'll drive. They're still looking for you."

They meaning the Mandate and Beth groaned. Her arms tossed around his neck and squeezed. "Yes, but on one condition."

Luce held her tight, rocking her gently and drawing her closer. "What's that baby?"

"Let me try to save you." Beth stared into his eyes, their noses touching.

"Told you so," Zoro butted in, "she won't give up easily either." Beth would never give up on her Lucien, even if she had to live as a guinea pig. Electricity hummed over her lips. Her lashes fluttered, but his closed.

"Bethy," he brushed his lips against her cheek, "sweetheart, you can't save me forever. I heard the locha too. I'm disrupting the balance."

They could not have meant him. She drew away, shivering despite the stuffiness of the building. Rain pounded the thatched roof, seeping through in steady streams. All her life she wanted to fulfill her destiny, but she also needed Lucien. "You don't. I don't doubt you want me there, Beth, but you don't need me to survive."

But if there was a way and she didn't try … A lump swelled in her throat; her body shuddered, fighting the rising tide. "No." She smacked his chest, and he flinched. "No! I will not give up on you."

He snapped, "And I won't become a slave to your blood," and glanced away.

Beth gripped his shirt collar. Why wouldn't he listen to her? "Let me find another way." Lucien shook his head; his lips quivered, and he pressed them into a tight line. Did he want to die and leave her alone?

"You won't be alone." A sigh tickled her chest. She knew what he would say, but Zoro and Emmanuel could not have replaced her best friend and the love of her life. There would never be another Lucien Brown.

Beth handed him the velvet box. "I can't accept this." His breath caught, and the shudder rocked over his body. "Lucien, I love you, but you can't ask me to do nothing as you fade away."

Not when she was a cure, but she needed to make it permanent. The wind howled like her soul outside. Dirt swirled inside the abandoned trading post. Beth's emotions spiraled out of control, but she did not care. Lucien, Zoro, and Jemma were the ones who mattered to her, but out of them all, Luce was her light, her rock. If he wanted to die, he would have to do it on his own. He could not ask this of her. Ask her to do nothing and letting him die were not fair. Beth would have to live with the guilt for the rest of her life

… that she could have saved the one person that counted, but did not. She slipped outside. Raindrops or tears splashed her face; she did not know the difference anymore. Save him or save the world … weeks ago she would have chosen the world but, after all she had learned, Beth only wanted to save Lucien.

Where there was a will there was a way, right? A sigh eased from her parted lips. Beth could not save a man who did not want her help.

"Bethy, I didn't say that." Lightning splintered the sky, cracking and striking the treetops. What had he said that day, the day he'd stormed back into her life? "I asked for two weeks."

A sob caught in her throat as she leaned on a pine tree. Breaths came but the air did not help. Sirens blared in the distance: tornado warning. The sky swirled with colors of grey and green. What was so important about two weeks? "You said it only took a drop, but you received two doses, and you still were sick."

"You can't save me, Beth."

"How much?"

"Too much," he said, his breath whistling.

"How much?"

"I don't know, Beth, but you passed out last time, and I only took what I needed." Beth had given blood two days prior to that though. She did not know he would bite her, and he had not told her about her blood yet. "No, I didn't know."

How was he still answering her thoughts if her blood wasn't in his system? She turned away from him, hugging herself. They needed a doctor, someone who they could trust like Dr. Pawl, but for humans. Her head cocked. Was Beth even human? Everything was happening too quickly. She had forgotten about what he had told her. The images that had flashed through her mind, she had buried them.

Fingers tapped on her teeth. All roads came with risk, but the easy path was not the warrior's way. "Do you have your phone?"

Change jingled in his pocket, and he held out the phone. Beth's heart pounded, tapping the numbers on the screen. The phone rang as she touched the speakerphone button. Zoro sat in the doorway eying them both. On the third ring, his secretary answered, placing them on hold.

"Her plan isn't half bad," Zoro said to Lucien. "It might actually work if you take enough of her to alter your blood in a transfusion."

He sat beside the feline; Beth snuck side-glances from the tree. The storm settled, but the sun did not shine. She would let it shine again once Lucien healed for good. There had to be a way.

"Why do you call me traitor?"

Zoro closed his eyes. "Because that is the path you walk."

Luce whispered, "I don't want to be one." He glanced at Beth but she looked away, pretending not to eavesdrop. "I don't want her to risk—"

"But she will. You don't find yourself worthy." He shook his head. "Good because you aren't. I'm not either. Thunderbirds aren't like you, me, or humans, not inside or outside. We may all be Spirit Walkers, but we all walk separate roads. Yours is tainted. Mine was short. Hers is greater, but only if she has you."

Beth asked, "Why is Emmanuel fit and muscular if he's a thunderbird like me?"

"Because he isn't one." What was he then? Why all the spirits condensed into one body? She had seen them that night, fanning out and condensing into his body again like a totem pole. Zoro ignored her unspoken questions, but Luce's brow rose.

"Miss McCallister this is Dr. Pawl. How are you feeling?" She took him off speakerphone and strolled away from the men. While this plan involved all of them, Beth did not want to risk Lucien or Zoro butting in.

"I'm okay, but I had a few questions. Can I meet with you or is the phone okay?"

Dr. Pawl said, "It would depend on the questions, but if you would prefer in person—"

A million questions zoomed through her mind. "How does my blood work? I mean it helps, right, but it doesn't cure-cure diseases."

"In person will be best Bethany. Can you meet me at the library tomorrow? Say noon?"

They ironed out the details and said their good-byes. She would have to walk all night to make it back in time. Lucien's phone slapped against her palm as she chewed her lip. Beth glanced over her shoulder. The water and her bag were both by the pump. They would see her if she went back for them, and they would not allow her to leave.

Her chest ached, pinching and squeezing her heart. Wind brushed her neck, but it did little to cool the heat. Fall could not arrive soon enough. Beth stepped forward and crashed into Lucien's chest. "Where's the fire, sunshine?"

"Let me pass." She pushed past him, but Lucien was quicker, moving and pinning her against the tree. Leaning down his lips quirked as if he had won. Beth glanced away but her eyes trained back on him. Heat pressed into her as he closed the remaining gaps, and her breath held, waiting for him to make a move.

"This sure brings back memories," he whispered, trailing his hands along her sides. "Too many clothes though."

"Luce," she warned.

"Now, now Bethy get your panties out of a bunch and hear me out. You said your peace, and I listened. Besides you'd have to walk a mile away before I couldn't hear your conversation."

Beth held his gaze, tilting her chin higher. "Fine."

His fingertips grasped the hem of her shirt and tugged, ripping the stained garment over her head. "Oops."

"This isn't talking." Lucien popped the button of her jeans and slid them down. Beth tried protesting again, but his mouth seared her skin, trailing a lazy path down her neck. Teeth grazed her skin, digging, biting, but not breaking the surface. Her body welled, pooling into the pit of her stomach, and the climb was like an escalating roller coaster. Flexing, she arched into him, touching him from head to toes.

Rough hands gripped her hips, yanking and tearing her underwear. Kisses rained along her sweaty torso as she twisted in anticipation. A single thread held the flowery panties in place, but he tore the final strand, breaking it with his teeth. "Can I bite you?"

Without hesitation, she nodded and braced against the tree. Every muscle seized, waiting for the pain, but it did not come. A curse flew from her mouth as his tongue flicked her nerves. Beth's fingers curled into his hair, moaning as he sucked harder.

"Say yes." His voice filtered into her mind. She shook her head no. Luce's teeth nipped her thigh, pressing harder as his finger stroked her. Sweat cooled her brow as a wave washed over her tensing muscles. He drank, slurping as she writhed against the tree. *"Marry me and I'll take what I need, not a drop more, until we find a cure."*

Coherent words refused. Another wave grasped her middle, holding her hostage. Beth's head slammed against the tree as she shouted, "Yes."

Greedily he took what was his, drawing on her vein. She was always his. Whimpers released from her lips as the euphoria swept her sanity away. Breathing hurt and her heart rate increased. "Stay with me baby." His words were aloud. "C'mon don't sleep." He cursed, grabbing his hair as she slumped against the tree. "Zoro what do we do?"

"We wait, or you give her back what you took. She needs blood. Between her family and you, you've drained her."

"Damn it Beth. It isn't worth living if you die."

She muttered, "That's what I've been trying to tell you," and shut her eyes.

Chapter Ten

The sunlight filtered in through a window, and she blinked, her eyes squinting at the brightness. Days had passed since the sun last shined, but this was not her doing. Discomfort tore her body as if she had tumbled with the ground in a mocking dance. Bruises marred her wrists, but she did not recall falling. Beth did not recall leaving the woods either, but she had.

"Luce," she said, but the words did not leave her dry mouth.

A needle stuck in her arm, and her eyes followed the tubing to a bag hanging on her bed. Dull whooshing filtered in and gave way to a subtle beeping. One by one, her senses awakened as her vision sharpened. A deep breath soothed her, but the breath was not hers. Pale green tiles lined the floral wallpaper, and she surmised that the interior decorator needed a good whack upside the head. Hands curled into the blanket and drew it to her chin. A deep breath—this one hers—filled her senses with ammonia, and her nose curled.

"Hey there sleepyhead," Luce said, rolling over and stroking her cheek through the bed's railing. "We didn't think you'd make it there for a while." He was lying in the bed next to hers, and he had pushed it as close as possible. Or maybe someone else had. Blinking she noted the IV line in his arm and the machines too. "How do you feel?"

Like hell, but she did not answer his question. White blankets tossed into the air as he rose. Lucien yanked hers over and crawled into her bed, kissing her nose, and bathing her in tingly warmth.

Make it? Dry lips parted. "Where are we?"

"Hospital." Beth shot out of bed despite already piecing the scenery together, but Luce put a hand on her chest. "It's okay baby. Remember Dr. Haim that came to the house?"

She pulled at the needle and winced. Blood leaked from the site, the pooling crimson soured her stomach, and she glanced away. "Yeah, but—"

Lucien grasped her hands, and she stared at the trickling blood sliding along her forearm. "Focus on me sunshine. They don't know anything. We're in a different county, and I brought you in under another name. Dr. Pawl and Dr. Haim are helping us. Sweetheart you almost died."

Died? Lucien's last words repeated in her head along with her own. Call her crazy, call her codependent, but Beth loved him, and the world did not matter. Nothing mattered unless he was in it too. Her thoughts drifted to the day he'd showed up and the prayers she had made. As long as he lived, everything in the world would be all right, but if he died, she could not survive. They were not together yet, but a part of her knew Lucien Brown was destined for more than death. What—that was yet to be seen, but she believed in him.

Warm arms hugged her; rough kisses rained over her cheeks. "I love you, baby."

"I love you too, but what do you mean another name?" *Was it that easy to create a new identity?* "How did you do that?"

Lucien chuckled. "Sunshine Rousseau and it wasn't too difficult as long as no one digs around." Dizziness prickled her skin and her forehead dampened. A yawn escaped her lips as he kissed her brow, scratching her face with his five o'clock shadow. "I'll take care of everything baby, you just work on getting better." He pressed a button on her bed and it beeped. A crackling voice sounded in her room asking what the problem was. "She's awake, but her IV is damaged."

"Oh geez." Beth sighed and snuggled closer to him on the hospital bed, gripping him tight as if he would float away. Lucien ran fingers through her hair, and her eyes closed again. "How long have I been out? Why are you hooked up too?"

"A few days." Lucien wore a hospital gown instead of his usual jeans and t-shirt. Mindlessly she played with the chest hair sprouting around the loose neck hole and allowed his heartbeat to calm her. In any other place, the intimacy would have intensified in her, maybe him too, but Beth was far from feeling herself, and she doubted Luce was either with all the machines.

"What happened to me? I remember being at that place and calling Dr. Pawl. Why are you here too?" She recalled their fight and making up, or out, depending on how one looked at it. The ring graced her finger, and the blue stone reminded her of Lucien's eyes.

"I happened." The memories were fuzzy, but she recalled a tree, and he bit her. After that, she could not remember anything. No dreams, or nightmares, just nothingness touched her memories. "The staff thinks an animal attacked you which ain't so far from the truth ... That's the official report. Figured you'd need to know in case someone questions you. I already gave a statement to the game warden. Most is just red tape type stuff. Dr. Haim is taking care of the rest."

His voice trailed as she fell asleep. An awful beeping sound made a racket, but she could not find the source. Everything bathed in white as if four white walls surrounded her. "Hello? Lucien? Zoro?"

Was the hospital a dream? Hands pressed into each wall, and she smacked the surface with an open fist. "Let me out of here." She revolved between the four walls, pressing, hitting, and yelling but nothing changed, nothing moved but her. Each ticking second increased her pulse; her heart rate doubled its thumping as air refused to fill her lungs.

Nothing. No one. Beth was alone, and only the straight jacket was missing. Glancing left, right, up, and down, the walls inched toward her, pressing on her from all sides. Nowhere to hide and she had nowhere to run. This could not have been how her life ended. Her gravestone would read the girl who failed. She still had lives to save, people to rescue, and a life to live. Beth was nineteen not ninety-nine, and she screamed over the continuous beeping, "No. I'm not leaving."

"Come," Emmanuel said, but she could not see him. "There is no time. You must begin."

Beth spun, her hands feeling the walls again. "Begin what? Come where? Where are you? How—"

"Metamorphosis. Your rite of passage, Kolkohkafoosi. You will become a warrior."

A stranger's voice shouted, "Clear."

The light brightened around her, flaring and blinding her. Beth shielded her eyes, but it was not enough. She lowered her lids. "Open your eyes," Emmanuel said. "The light will not guide you this time. Face away from the light."

Arms slapped against her sides, and she forced her eyes to open. Light seared into her, burning and throbbing. On her hips, her hands cemented, rubbing toward the center as she lurched. "I can't."

"You must or you die."

Bile splattered on the floor. Beth heaved again, clutching her middle, but keeping her eyes peeled on the light. The strange glow pulsed, shooting toward her. A million particles glittered over her skin like diamonds in the sunlight. Beth gasped, brushing it away. "No, no, I can't get it off me."

"Fight harder," he said. "Or you'll never see him again."

Oh God, she choked on a sob, staring into the white light as the dots connected. The light was death. Her death approached. Lucien tried to tell her, but she ... the beeps ... the strange voice yelling clear ... it all connected. "I don't want to die." Her voice shook, and she swallowed hard. Fists balled; jaw clenched as the light crept closer. "I. Am. Not. Going. Damn. It." Beth took a deep breath and screamed, tossing her head against the wall, and clenching her eyes shut. It did not help; even with closed eyes, she saw the light.

"You're not taking me, you hear? I'm not going. You can't have me." With each shout, the light retreated, and the darkness skulked into the tiny space. It faded into the wall as she whispered, "And you can't have Lucien either. We're not ready, and we will fight to our dying breaths."

Beth's eyes opened and starred into a pair of grey eyes. Dr. Haim she assumed but could not tell underneath the mask he wore. Nurses fluttered around her bed. The beeping chirped steadily, but her chest ached. Dr. Haim held paddles in his hands, and she shivered, flushing red as her gown lay undone and open. Relief fluttered over his features as voices cheered and rejoiced. "Welcome back, Sunshine. You gave us a scare."

"Luce?" she whispered reaching her right hand through the bars. Tubes ran from his arms, red tubing connected to hers, and her brow wrinkled. Dr. Haim tapped above her head, and she followed the sound. A blood bag marked BAM hung from the pole. They were transfusing her own blood into her as she transfused her blood into Lucien too, but it cycled through her first. Why would they do that? Her lips parted as she glanced between Luce and the bag. Where did they find her blood? Had the Mandate come for them?

"James," Dr. Haim whispered and pressed a finger to his lips. Wheels squeaked as the machines rolled out and the staff's smiles disappeared. There had been two machines. He looked over his shoulder; the remaining nurse paused at the door, hovering as if needing instructions. He lifted a finger asking Beth to wait and closed the door.

Her observations turned, falling on Luce, and fingertips brushed his forearm. Peace nestled over his features and the rise and fall of his chest gave her pause. Two rectangle marks marred the surface. Feet squeaked over the tile. Beth did not hear the door, too engrossed in watching the man she loved. Eight years ago, she'd thought the fight for his life had ended. Boy had she been wrong.

"We tried to hold off, but after your heart stopped, Lucien's did too. He's special too isn't he?"

More than she was, but Beth did not say that. Their connection baffled her probably as much as it had the doctors and nurses. Could love weave the body and soul together? Beth had not thought about it before that moment. Seeing him hooked to machines again though, it sickened her stomach.

Wetness leaked from her eyes, and the doctor handed her a tissue. Small strokes were all she managed over his forearm, but she had to touch him, feel his energy and warmth against her skin. Never again had Beth wanted to see her Luce helpless or in a hospital bed. Dr. Haim rolled the gurney closer, and she reached for his tube-mangled hand.

"Thank you," she told Dr. Haim. "For everything. How did you know about the transfusion?"

"Lucien called me, showing up at my doorstep before we'd finished talking." He scratched his head. "It seems to be working. We did one transfusion after we stabilized you. Your body rejected regular blood, so James and Dana broke into the Mandate evidence hold." He pulled up a chair, and she cringed as it skidded. "I was skeptical, because I didn't know how it was extracted or stored but the human blood was only stabilizing you." He glanced out the dark window. "Lucien made me try." Beth chuckled, imagining just how she coerced the doctor into giving the blood. "Questions?"

"A million," she said. "Only one matters. Will he be all right?"

"Yes. He's stable, but the ordeal strained his body." Dr. Haim patted her leg. "You on the other hand ... You gave away so much of your blood that you developed hypokalemia." Her brows creased at the strange word. "Low potassium levels can cause it, but you'd lost so much blood we couldn't risk drawing a sample when he brought you in. The odd part was that you continued breathing. Most patients have to be incubated." Because neither she nor Lucien were human, not categorically, just freaks in human looking shells.

"As a man of medicine it goes against my oath to let anyone harm either of you. I'll keep you appraised every step of the way, but I want you to rest. Don't hesitate to call," he placed a card on her table, "if you have any questions."

*T*wo days later Lucien woke before her and stood by the window. They had not been awake at the same times and, although she wished to know how he was doing, Beth relied on the nurses and doctors. Aside from Dr. Haim and Dr. Pawl, the staff thought the young couple was already married.

"I'm in remission again." His tight face reflected in the dark glass. Blue eyes appeared to glow, and she took it as a sign. Luce should have been happy. Why wasn't he happy? "Because we can't do this again, Bethy. I've put you in more danger."

"Maybe we won't have to," she said, tossing the blankets aside and padding up behind him. The nurses had unhooked her IV that morning. Luce was not as lucky, but they were still giving him her bagged blood. Her arms encompassed his waist from behind, and she rested her head against his back, listening to the rise and fall of his breaths. "Maybe this is what we both needed, but if it wasn't enough, we'll cross that bridge later. All that matters is that we survived."

Luce grunted. "Did you see the light?"

Beth had wondered if he saw anything similar to her. The tingling warmth pricked her memory, but it did not compare to the love she received from him. A small smile played at his lips. "I'm an ass. How are you feeling?"

"About the same but Dr. Haim said it might take a day or two to feel better." Beth hated when he deflected to her, but his concern was genuine. "He tell you the same or are they giving you extra for good measure?"

"Good measure," he said, gulping.

All this fuss over her meant nothing; it was Luce who was special, not her. The horned serpents were rare, unheard of, and believed by fewer people every day. Hunted and tormented because of their healing horns, the old Gods intervened, so the legend said, and whisked them away to the other side of the mountains to live with them. That Lucien stood before her had proved the old myth wrong, but it did not make him any less special to her.

He sighed; she heard and felt the noise. "They arrested my parents. There won't be a next time. How long before they take in Dr. Pawl?" The Mandate could not touch Dr. Haim. He was not in their jurisdiction, but they could arrest the vet. Would they bother arresting a man so close to his final days? "We're hurting a lot of people just so you can keep me alive."

"We'll get them back." Beth did not know how to rescue James and Dana, but she could not leave them to rot, not after the kindness they had extended to her. Jemma too, she had to find out where they had sent her cousin. "I'm sorry, Luce."

Liquid plopped on her hands. His body shuddered and another drop fell. Beth kissed his shoulder, holding him tighter as he cried. Lucien twisted, yanking her hospital gown, and pulling her in front of him. "Don't be sorry." He sniffled and forced a smile. "I love you so much and don't want to leave you, but ..."

"Hush, we'll get them back." Lucien folded their hands together as his brows pinched. "What is it?" He shook his head. She warned, "Luce?"

"Emmanuel is waiting for you." He wiped his eyes and sniffled. "He came to me in the room of dark and light."

"He spoke to me too." Beth held his clean-shaven face. She had watched the nurse trim him that morning. Wisps of thick black hair stuck to his forehead. "Let him wait."

"It's time to become a huntress, Bethy. You have a destiny." She said nothing and gazed into his bright eyes. The dull blue no longer reflected in them, and he no longer smelled of the wrongness, but of smoldering ash leaves. Lucien's brows rose, straining his face further. "Isn't this your dream?"

Chewing her lip, she pondered his question and searched her heart. Was it still her dream? Beth glanced at her hands, shaking like a twig in a breeze. Her senses alerted. Lightning sparked on her fingertips as she willed the surge building in her veins. Darkness blanketed her mind like a thick fog, and she shook it aside, but it tiptoed in again whispering words like revenge. Beth's head flashed through the gory scene of Agent Claire, her dog, and Amber's death. How many more would die to protect their secrets? Even if she had not liked them, they had been innocent.

"Remember the options? You can fight back, run away, or give yourself up. I won't let you do the third, but if you want to run," he glanced over his shoulder, "sunshine, we'll get the hell out of dodge and never look back."

The people Vivian had been helping would die, but Lucien would live if they ran away. Even if she rose to her destiny and fought, they still might die. . *Save the one you love or save them.* She sighed because he would not agree with her answer—it went against every oath she had ever held sacred. Beth could not let Lucien go, but she could not turn her back on the people either. Two weeks ago, she would have still chosen him first over her people. Staying meant saving more lives, rescuing their families, hunting the evil locha, but, having to dodge the Mandate. Beth gulped as tears glistened in Luce's blue eyes again. The One Above made her different, he made Lucien different too, and he built these roads and obstacles for them to overcome. The greatest battle was his leukemia.

Scared—yeah Beth was trembling from head to toe, but she was not running. This decision did not affect only her though. Locha posed a real threat, one neither of them had dealt with before, but the Mandate was not something to laugh at either. Their reach was beyond her comprehension. Every reservation, every pocket of Native Americans living amongst the Americans … They stretched from Canada to South America and had ties to the governments.

Even then, they were not a great evil. Without them fighting for Native American rights their people would not have survived after the removal. She understood they too just wanted to heal the others. Lucien caught her chin, tilting it.

"You can't, baby. You cannot physically save them all without risking your life in the process." He ground his teeth. "It's only by the grace of The One Above that Vivian didn't kill you sooner."

"I took herbs daily to keep me in balance."

Lucien gasped, his mouth hanging open. "Why the heck did you keep letting them do it?" Not meant for her to hear was his unspoken question: why did he allow it to continue?

She leaned against his chest, listening to the gentle thunder of his heart. "They told me I had a rare blood type," she closed her eyes and let the tears flow, "I thought I was saving lives."

"You have no idea how close I was to loosing you," he said, fingers stroking her hair. "I didn't know what to do … I called Dr. Pawl, and he patched me through to Dr. Haim." Lucien shuddered. "Sweetheart, if I ever see Vivian again ..." Luce did not need to finish the sentence. "My hands are already bloody, what's one more?" Lucien cupped her face, swiping the tears away with his thumbs. "So, we leave this place, find Emmanuel and Zoro, and you become the warrior that I know resides inside of you. Beth you were born to fight. Courage, loyalty, and love command your veins. Screw saving people with your blood. That's not why the thunderbird exists."

"It isn't?" It wasn't the only reason, but why give them healing blood?

Lucien kissed her, lingering a moment, but drew away. "Of course not. Thunderbirds battle the dark forces of the world, but that don't mean natural illness. The lore says the blood heals so that the race could save each other, but," he scratched his head, "people hunted them, used them …"

Beth sat on the radiator and leaned against the cool window. "Drained them," she supplied what he did not want to say. "How is it that I exist or you for that matter? I keep thinking you're human, but you aren't."

Neither was she. In the grand scheme, it was unimportant. Not to her though. Beth wanted to know her roots, what to tell their children, if they could have children that was.

"There are legends in all tribes, but no one knows for sure." He knelt, resting his head in her lap. Beth ran fingers through his hair, noting he needed a trim. Creeks Indians did not wear their hair long like other tribes. "We don't seem to live long enough to find the answers, but Emmanuel might know something—whatever he is."

"Zoro said he wasn't a thunderbird, but what is he?" Lucien's breath tickled her knee. He didn't know either.

They arrived at the shack the following morning hoping to find Zoro or Emmanuel. A quarter of a mile behind the building was a hidden drive she had not known about, located off a back road lining the other side of his property. Sweat beaded her forehead, the air too thick for it to form crystals, and her steps were a bit shaky. The doctor however, had given them both clean bills of health. She leaned on Lucien's arm despite him carrying the bulk of their belongings, because he insisted, threatening to carry her if she didn't.

Her dress caught on the briars, snagging holes in the new outfit Lucien picked up for her. He had called a friend to retrieve his car and a change of clothing for him. The man was resourceful. She doubted anyone would have lifted a finger if they'd known crazy Beth was involved. Would his friends ever see her as a human being? "I never cared what they thought."

Her steps slowed, admiring the beauty of untouched nature. Soon the leaves would begin their shift as the cold months approached. Death and decay scented ever so faintly on the late summer breeze sparking the telltale signs of an early fall. Beth did not need his friends to like her as much as for them to stop making fun of her or spreading lies behind her back. Those barbs cut deep. They sliced her skin when Luce brushed off their words.

The worn path needed trimming, but it was the least of what twisted her gut. They had argued; the entire drive from Eufaula they had bickered. She didn't think it was wise to return, but Lucien pointed out that the Mandate didn't know about this place, and neither did his parents. He had only said that before because he thought she did not want to return. Still the risk existed. "Beth, they've probably given up for now. They still have a festival to run." She had let the argument drop.

"I still don't feel right about this," she muttered, scanning the area for signs of her cat. Birds sang joyful tunes from the safety of their lofty pines, but the unease would not settle in her stomach. "How far are we from the house?"

"Too close for a big fire," he said. But that was not what she meant, and he knew it too. "We'll be eating cold beans and dried foods for a while." *Double Ugh. No coffee?* "Sorry baby. But I can't risk them finding us."

Us meant her. *Them* meant the Mandate. She understood his protective nature but did not agree with the shack. Not coming here would have solved that, but she did not say it aloud. No need to start another fight that she would not win because he was too busy trying to be right.

Beth had not thought she would see the shack and its deteriorated walls again, Lucien was right. She hadn't wanted to either, but a smile touched her lips at the bundle of fur sitting on the wooden stoop as they rounded the corner. The ever-faithful Himalayan waited for her, amusement dancing in the cat's sky blue eyes, and he belted out a string of meows.

"Zoro," Beth gasped, running full speed to her familiar and scooping him in for a tight hug. Black birds scattered from the roof, taking flight to the canopy trees. He smelled awful, like a mixture of sweat and drowned rat.

He mewed and kissed her nose, purring louder than she had recalled. "I was worried." Zoro glanced to Lucien. "For both of you." He pressed a paw to his face. "You look better, iyyìnko."

Lucien had not told her everything that had happened during the hospital visit. Dr. Haim filled her in of course, but he did not know of the long discussions she had shared with him. They went over the signs, the little things that he would never tell her about, like the aches and fevers. But she had continued praying his battle was over.

Beth and Zoro sat on the ground, leaning against the wooden steps. The stream trickled filling her senses with a sense of peace at its bubbling, but she tried not to think of the last time she was in there either. Beth still had not come to terms with almost dying ... twice. Both times Luce played a role, but blaming him seemed pointless. No one could have known the locha were real or how much blood Vivian and her dad took from her.

"Where is Emmanuel?" Lucien asked.

"He comes tonight. You will need rest for this long journey, Beth." Zoro nuzzled her neck, and she kissed his head.

"Careful, a man gets jealous." Lucien grinned, easing himself beside the pair and slipping his arm around her waist. "Just kiddin' tuna breath." He held out his hand, and Zoro sniffed it. Beth's brow arched. These two never liked each other. "Compromise." Luce pawed his neck, and the cat let him. "I'm slowly learning what it means."

"Well, well so you can teach an old dog new tricks." Beth elbowed his ribs, resulting in a barking laugh. As if he could not be any sexier, Luce melted her with a single noise, and in that small moment, she did not think it possible to love him any more than she already had. Lucien called her sunshine, but as she returned his grin, she disagreed. All the light and happiness in her life came from him as if The One Above himself designed their union.

His laughter settled into a chuckle as she stared at him, smiling at her thoughts. Air sucked from her lungs as Lucien hovered inches away. The smile faded; his lips parted. Without his thick beard, he appeared young but not fragile. Blue eyes meandered like molasses over her face searching for what, she did not know, but the heat of his gaze flushed her skin. Thick lashes fluttered in tune with her heartbeat, and her free hand brushed his thigh, while the other played in Zoro's fur. Luce gulped, and in a strained tone he said, "Who you calling old? Zoro's the geezer here."

Beth glanced away, willing her heart rate to settle a notch or two, but the heat still flushed her cheeks. Air moved in and out of her tight chest. She changed the subject before losing her composure. "We were wondering about Emmanuel, like what is he?"

"I can tell you he isn't of this world, but then none of us are. Not even the humans who inhabit this planet." Zoro licked his tail, biting at the long coat.

"Planet?" Beth and Lucien exchanged a quick glance; hers lingered, studying the lines of his angular jaw and watching him swallow hard. How wonderful it would be if they did not have anything looming over their heads and could just be here in the moment with their mock family. He asked, "Like little green men? Aliens?" crooking his black brow.

"Heavens no, children don't be absurd." The cat shook his head and hopped from her lap. Lucien scooted closer, drawing her head against his shoulder, and playing with her hair as they listened to his explanation. "There are planes of existence and sometimes, for whatever cosmic reason, we stumble into the wrong one. That's why there are dinosaur fossils here and other abnormalities that are simply unexplainable, and it is true with those born magical, to an extent. Or they come from those of other dimensions here like the inheritor's creator."

That answer was not the one she had expected to hear. Lucien's scrunched brows echoed her thoughts. Little green men seemed more believable than multiple dimensions, but science was not her forte either. Coffee, yoga, and well, she had once thought there more, but now Beth was not so sure what she knew about herself was even true. He was right about the inheritor though; a medicine-maker summoned the Jumlin from another world, but most called it the spirit world. And how did The One Above factor into it? Wasn't he writing the paths and destinies of every living creature?

She gulped, cocking her head. What if there wasn't a The One Above? "Again you're being ridiculous, Beth. Of course, there is a God, but he created multiple universes. He did not tell everyone, just as The One Above does not give everyone Power. Why is it everyone jumps to conclusions?" Zoro snorted and tossed his head, wiggling his entire body in the process. "But even God and The One Above make mistakes, and for whatever reason—perhaps on purpose—there are doorways between the worlds. That is how you came to this world, by a simple mistake."

"Wait what?" Beth drew from Lucien's embrace and loomed over the cat. "You're telling me I'm not even from this world?" Her breath huffed as she paced, hands on her hips, the sun burnt grass crunching beneath her feet. Their eyes burned through her, but she could not look at either man or beast. Why could she not have one normal day where some truth was not plopped in her lap or someone was not dying or trying to capture her? "First Dr. Pawl tells me I'm a freak, and if that wasn't bad enough, you're telling me without a doubt that I'm from another dimension?"

"Your parents aren't your parents," Luce whispered. "They adopted you."

Like a sucker punch to her gut, Beth doubled over and gaped at him. Narrowing her eyes, she shook her finger, but the shaking had originated in her body. "You knew about this?"

"They stole her," Zoro snapped and so did her gaze. "They found you, yes, but they took what wasn't theirs and almost bled you dry."

"No, back up there buddy," she scolded. Luce continued staring off into the distance, settling on a small formation of rocks by the water's edge. They stole her. The McCallister family was not her family. Luce was not from this dimension either, but appeared peachy keen with the news that led her to believe that he dang well knew about her family not being her family. The sound of her heartbeat echoed in her ears; electricity sparked in her fingertips as the dark clouds scattered the once blue skies. "Look at me damn it."

Slowly his gaze shifted as the energy poured into her palms, and the lightning released into the sky, using her as the conduit instead of the ground. Ruffling breeze whipped her inky black hair into her face as her hands rose higher, and Zoro ran beneath the step; blue eyes peeked from the gaps.

"Not once did either of y'all say, "Hey maybe Beth would like to hear about this?" But nooo, she doesn't need to really know jack shit. Let's just keep her in the dark. Dumb and blind, crazy Bethy."

Lucien grasped her face and kissed her quiet, but she swung her leg, and kicked his shin. The glow of her current rolled through his body turning his tan skin blue. "Damn it, Beth. It ain't like we were even talking. Was I just supposed to come up and drop all this on you?"

Tears pricked her eyes. No, it was something else, something he buried. How many days did she see him and wish for a simple hello or how are you? To see him smile because of her or to look at her like a human being and not the monster she had not known she was. The tear sizzled, turning to steam as it splattered on her cheek. Thunder stomped as if dancing over the ground, and her legs trembled from the tremors.

Arms crossed over her chest and she said, "Yes, Luce you were. Because you know what? I would have done the same for you. Heck, I saw you every week, and it wasn't like your friends were always there. You could have pulled me aside, said hey I'm sorry—"

"Oh, so that's what this is really about, huh? I didn't say I was sorry enough or soon enough." Lucien cracked his neck, but the tension squared in his broad shoulders. The earth shook again as his jaw tightened. "Well baby, I am sorry. I'm sorry I was an idiot and tried to rescue you. I'm sorry I didn't tell you every little secret or how much I loved you every single day. Well you know what? I'm screaming it at the top of my damned lungs now, and it still ain't good enough for you. What else do you want? I've stolen, killed, and done God knows what else for you woman. When will it be enough?" Beth just stared at him, amazed at the emotion unleashed in his harsh words. Truthful words and he had been screaming too; she could not recall the last time he had yelled at her. His hands drew hers down, snuffing the wild lightning. The dark clouds stayed.

"Cat catch your tongue?" She did not reply as he invaded her personal space, unfolding her arms, and grinning from ear to ear. Lucien hooked his arms behind her back and she stumbled forward. "Well damn, finally won an argument." He shook his head. "But I do love you. You know that, right? No matter what, Beth, I love you."

Beth whispered, "Yes."

Booms rolled and echoed through the forest as he spoke. "I will kill for you. I will steal for you. Bethy, I will lie, even if it's to protect you from you, and whether you like it or not, baby I will die for you." Black hair whipped in the wind as her body shook. She was the lightning; he was the thunder. Opposites and pairs—even in nature one was never without the other even if she did not experience both.

"Yuh-huh, and you know what, you can't stop me. You've got your ways," he shrugged, "I got mine. Now, I've made mistakes, but don't you go stomping around here like you're Miss Perfect. Communication worked two ways, and it ain't like you even tried to talk to me either." That too was true. She had believed the rumors and taken them to heart. Lucien Brown was too good for her. "I'm tired of fighting. We never fought before."

A stray beam of light illuminated and shot from the clouds. Beth offered a small smile. "Yeah Luce, we did. All the time as kids, we were always bickering about something dumb." She had wished for those days often even if they were to argue.

"Guess you're right. C'mere."

She lowered her lashes, staring at his thick lips and the pink tongue running over their surface. "I don't think I can get any closer."

"I can think of a few ways." His whisper brushed her temple, setting her nerve endings on edge. Beth could think of a few ways too and pressed herself into their embrace as Lucien pulled her closer. Too many days had passed since they had last shared an intimate moment without the complications of life rearing their ugly heads. The belly stirring glances and electric draw would only increase with time, but the stolen touches, gentle kisses, and their future had to wait. Love was precious, but that meant all forms of love, from family to friendship. A groan vibrated from his chest as he followed her thoughts. Lucien sucked in a breath, squeezing her against him as if she would have floated away on the thick breeze, buzzing and whistling through the swaying trees. Their faces drew closer, either of them unable to let the other go. Her sweaty fingers curled into his back, gripping tighter. The world stilled. Sounds and surroundings filtered out. Nothing existed beyond him to her, and his mind told her nothing existed beyond her.

"I exist." Zoro coughed. "Are you two done bickering like an old married couple?"

"Shut your mouth," they said together, and the cat peered at them from beneath the steps, cautiously twitching his ears.

Silence fell between the trio, and even the forest creatures seemed quieter. Would they have one normal day? "The rest of today, baby. Go on in and rest."

"Too hot," Luce rolled his eyes, "Hey, you don't sweat crusty salt."

"Sunshine, what am I going to do with you?" He scratched his chin. "How about the lake?"

Beth did not have a bathing suit, or suitable undergarments, but did not want to ruin her new dress either. Chewing on her lip, she eyed the creek as Lucien stood behind her, drawing her hair to the side. The breeze touched her skin, but the shiver erupted as his lips brushed the surface, and her stomach tangled like the underbrush of the forest. Deft fingers untied the halter, but she caught the bodice, not wishing to expose herself to the cat.

"I don't care if he sees; he can't have you," he said, nibbling her sun kissed skin. Lucien drew her arms to her sides, skimming hands over her bare breasts, and pressing himself against her. Her heart thundered against her ribcage, aching with every breath as fire engulfed her, rekindling her insides. Gasps caught as he trailed kisses along her spine; her dress yanked down. Beth froze, dipping her head to her chest, and allowed her hair to shadow her face. She would never understand his attraction and hated that she questioned it during these moments.

Rough hands kneaded her ass, and a soft moan slipped from her lips. Lucien smacked her gently, and she yipped, biting into her lip. "Sorry." But he didn't sound it. "You should probably take your shoes off too."

They spoke of only their future as they waded in the water for the next few hours, but her mind still dwelled in the past as if there were some tiny detail that she was missing.

*T*weeting birds hung up their melody and gave the floor to the throatier croaking frogs as the daylight faded into nightfall. Beth could not stop thinking about her family and Zoro's accusations. It made sense though, if she thought about it. None of them were like her—magical.

Lucien handed her a protein bar and a canteen of water. After the hospital food, even it was appetizing.

Beth did not resemble the family aside from her weight. Was she even Creek? In her heart, the answer was yes, if not by blood, than spirit. Lucien slid his arm around her waist, and her head fell on his shoulder. The wrapper crinkled in her fingers finding her appetite fading after one nibble. She slowly nodded, accepting more truth she never thought to question. And why would she?

Lucien's fingers stroked through her hair. What she would not give for everyday normal like this, but she had the chance and ran from it. If she would have stayed ... Beth still wore her long black locks down and loose instead of the customary bun or braid. Were they her customs? Leaning into his comforting touch, she closed her eyes, reopening them as Zoro's paw touched her cheek, and his cold, wet nose pressed hers.

"It's okay," she told him. "I wouldn't have believed you." Beth chuckled at the absurdity but it was true. "I don't know if I believe you now."

"I'm with her." She heard the amusement in Lucien's tone. At least she was not the only one questioning the craziness. But Zoro's knowledge didn't change their circumstances or those innocents tied to them by love or blood. Beth's past was not a factor in their future. "For the record, I didn't know for certain. The dimensions come up in some Native American lore, but I thought of them like Heaven and Hell, not places we visit when alive."

"Jemma? Did she … is she …" The word stolen still sounded strange, leaving a bitter taste in her mouth like tea tannins at the bottom of the cup. What possessed Vivian to steal children? Was she the first? Would she have been the last if not for the Mandate?

"Scary thought," Lucien whispered lighter than the wind, weaving her hair into a loose braid, but he did not have ties or pins to secure it. Beth handed him her protein bar. "You need to eat."

"I'm not hungry." Queasy was more like it, but she kept the thought and churning bile to herself. No need to frighten anyone over a little tummy ache.

"Stolen too? Yes and she too will come into her powers soon," Zoro said as Lucien brushed his knuckles over her cheek, swiping the tear that had just blinked free. The cat curled on the blanket, yawning as the stars began their slow awakening in the sky. "You know Spirit Walker is the wrong word."

"I know," she said, "but I like it better because it has a deep meaning. We are all Spirit Walkers."

"You are a thunderbird, but your cousin is something else. I've watched over you both for years now, guided you specifically, while awaiting Jemma's spirit guide to arrive. The home she lives in … there is a stray that visits her."

Lucien asked, "How do you know this?" Beth listened, watching an owl swoop from a tree. In the summer, many animals awoke, feasting and hunting at dusk. Woodland creatures found the hours cooler without the sun beating on their backs. How many animals were the guides of others? Her stomach curled as she sought a balance between the lie she lived and the beauty surrounding her. What if they all held voices but humans failed to listen?

"We animals communicate. Not all are spirits of the departed, but the animal in us can reach across space, like whisper down the lane. Sometimes things are lost in translation, hence the strange behaviors shown by otherwise healthy animals like barking at leaves."

But the question remained unanswered. Was Jemma better off where she was? Would the new family nurture her gift or use her? A shudder attacked at the simple thought as she imagined her cousin tied to a chair with a needle in her arm. Would they have lied to her too about the special blood? Beth could not answer that question, but then who could? "This isn't the life she needs. She's a kid who needs love and protection."

But did Jemma need protection from the truth? What if the Mandate decided to test her?

Zoro nodded. "Jemma is out of the Mandate's reach, but they are not the sole evil either." He sat, glancing and blinking into the wilderness. "They aren't all evil but many are misguided into believing perverse truths under the guise of the old ways. Vivian, now she, is evil."

Vivian—she did not understand when or why her aunt became greedy. Maybe Beth never would understand, but she wanted to learn from their mistakes, and part of that was in taking a stand. She scooped the cat in her arms and rose from the stoop. "One day at a time. One problem at a time, but I think as long as we have each other, we will be okay in the end, so," she hissed. "As soon as it is safe, or she comes into herself, I want her by my side. We may not be blood, but she is my family."

"Hope is powerful, Kolkohkafoosi."

Lucien kissed her temple. "So are love and friendship."

Beth dusted her dress and meandered by the creek as the last of the orange and purple hues blended in the sky. Somewhere in another plane, her family, her blood, existed. Did they see the same beauty? The idea of dimensions confused her, but she was always drawn to the stars, wondering how, in such a vast universe, there were only humans, animals, and the Earth. Maybe Zoro did not have all the answers and little green men existed somewhere out there too. Lucien groaned, stretching behind her.

"Do you think they miss me?"

"I don't know," Luce whispered, stroking her bare shoulders. Aside from their bickering, there had not been another storm as serenity washed over her soul. Beth accepted that she could not change the past; the future, however, became their playground filled with dreams, hopes, and a brighter future. "But if they're anything like you, they've never given up searching or loving you."

"Tell me about the Spirit Walkers, Luce." Beth elbowed him, but she was stubborn. Misguided too. Always she'd sought the truth but had been too blinded to see it all around her. Vivian had covered her tracks well.

"The One Above created the Spirit Walker to transverse the dimensions. They right the wrongs caused by humans and police the spirits, but each one has a role to play, a job. You are a thunderbird, I am a horned beast, Zoro a spirit guide, but our jobs are different. You protect, I guard the truth, and he guides the Spirit Walker. Others exist and, they too, are all Spirit Walkers, but they have different responsibilities. Some touch dreams, some shape the future, and some will never understand their true destinies."

"Like me before?" He murmured his yes.

From fearing the night, to lying about the Mandate, to her blood, Vivian had lied. Luce kissed the top of her head. If not for the man standing behind her, she would have remained a prisoner until they'd bled her dry, and they had come close, as if they had known they could not have locked Beth away forever. Maybe that was why they had spied on her. To stay ahead of the game she did not know she was playing. Air filled her lungs, but her chest ached.

"I don't blame Vivian," she said.

"You should." His stroking halted as he gripped her shoulders.

"Luce, can you imagine your life without me?" He quaked and for good reason. He would have died at the age of eleven without her intervention. One kind deed out of who knew how many was not enough to erase her evil ways though. Beth patted his hand, and his grip eased. "Well I can't imagine one without you either." If Vivian had not taken her, if she had not brought and raised her in the Creek community, Lucien would have died. The lives he had, and would have, touched would not have received his gift of true heritage. "I wouldn't change any of my past because her deeds brought me to you."

He twisted her shoulders, wanting to turn her around, but Beth did not budge. "I love your heart and how you see the beauty in the darkest deeds. That you would risk living through the pain just for me … Damn it girl, you better marry me."

She laughed as tears sprung in her eyes. Beth twirled around, reaching for his face as she always did, and brushing his shadowy cheek. Easing onto her toes, she closed what little distance stood between them, and slanted her mouth over his parted lips. He would survive; she would marry him and stand beside him until her final breath. And she hoped it would be for a long time.

Every part of her life had flip-flopped on her in a matter of weeks. Soon the festival would begin   and, too soon, it would end. Time was never on their side. When the Mandate departed, they would whisk his parents away, and she promised him that they would find a way to save them, even if that meant breaking them out by force.

Chapter Eleven

"Crimes are forgiven at the festival." Zoro stretched at their feet. "It's customary and our best chance to strike, but they will be watched, likely in hopes to draw you both into the open."

Their brows rose and they sighed together. She did not need to read his thoughts, but they sounded through her head anyway. *Lucien did not want her to go. Beth was not ready. Showing up at the festival was too risky.* But she made him a promise and aimed to keep it regardless of the danger they faced. The problem was not her. Beth seized his face in her hands, holding him hostage. A quick quirk of his lips said he did not mind. The problem was going at it alone and making sure Luce stayed safe.

"Ain't a chance in hell," he said. "Besides, I'm quicker." To prove his point, she blinked, and he was gone leaving her with empty hands. "You can't jump as high either." Beth whipped around, but she did not see him. "Up here, sunshine."

Lucien knelt on the thatched roof and chuckled. Rising he puffed his chest and pounded it, and she rolled her eyes. Zoro squeezed from the steps, craning his body onto to two feet and gazed up at the idiot she called her fiancé pacing the roof as if it were made of concrete, not straw and mud.

"Get down before you …" Her voice trailed as he slipped; straw flew into the air. "Break something."

She found him sprawled out on the ground behind the shack. Lucien shook his head but appeared fine. "This is why women are superior. We don't show off and attempt stupid crap." Beth nudged him with her sneaker, and he groaned. "You better not be bleeding. Doctor said you can't have any more blood."

A hand scrubbed over his face. "I ain't bleeding, but man your trap is giving me a headache."

Her hands cradled her hips. "You sure it isn't from smacking your head against the ground?" Beth bit her lip, attempting keep a steady face. She pointed toward the woodpile, sliding her fingers to an inch. "You almost turned our firewood into sawdust you buffoon."

"Stop nagging and help me up." Beth reached for him, but he yanked her closer, and rolled her over. "On second thought," he pressed between her thighs, "this is better."

"Luce—"

"Shut up and kiss me all better."

"Emmanuel comes." Zoro trotted around the corner but halted. "Oh, apologies."

Beth blinked. When had he ever said he was sorry for interrupting them? "Rain check."

"Oh, you can bet the stars, baby, but we'll see how you fare after tonight." She crooked an eyebrow at his statement, but Lucien did not elaborate. He hefted himself from the ground, dusting off the debris. "Try not to make it rain, Beth. We have a hole in our roof now."

We and our: two words she would not have expected out of Lucien's mouth a few weeks ago. Two words that still sounded alien coming from her too. "What?" She liked the words. He cocked his head, sweeping his gaze from her head to toes. "You best get up, before I change my mind."

Beth did not budge as the heat crept in. He could have spouted off a grocery list and made her blush, but his commanding tone gave her pause and increased her pulse. Would that change as they aged? He flashed one of his charming grins and winked. "I sure hope not."

What if their attraction turned out to be nothing more than hormones, and he came to his senses? Luce groaned, shaking his head, as tendrils fell against his forehead. Even in the dark, she could clearly make out his features. "Not this again."

"Get out of my head then." Beth did not mean it, at least most of the time, but every now and then she wondered why her over all the other women. They were pretty, smart, and did not weigh two hundred pounds. Living in modern society fueled the questions. Zoro back peddled and disappeared from her sight. It was not that she did not think she was a good enough person either. Her heart loved easily and harder than most people did. She swatted at a bug and cringed at its guts on her arm. Lucien was right about how she saw beauty even in the ugliest of places. Beth did not believe in pure evil or something evil occurring without a greater purpose. But none of it answered why her out of all the girls out there ... why her.

"If it ain't one thing it's another. You were never this insecure as a ... oh." Lucien glanced away. "I did this to you."

As kids, they had often spoken of their future, especially after the cancer went into remission. They had five years of love and companionship, and she truly thought he would never hurt her, never leave her. Then he did. Dumped her like garbage on the side of the road, no explanation given but plenty of cold shoulder. For years she waited, took her lumps from him and the others, but waited as they had promised one another all those summers ago. One day she gave up hope, switching her focus onto the other impossible in her life: her future as a huntress. If she could not have love then she would have her revenge on the man who'd caused the pain in her life, but even if she had succeeded in fulfilling her destiny, Beth would not have been able to hurt Lucien as he had stabbed her in the back.

She closed her eyes and lay, sprawling, on the ground. He knew the pain he had caused, in some ways still caused, because letting the past go did not heal the wounds. Anything involving the past felt like salt and fire to her insides. Beth forgave him for the parts he had played, but some wounds took longer to heal, and her ego may never bounce back. He had made her promises all those summers ago, promises he snapped and splintered in a single day, and then he had continued to peel layers from her. Saying sorry did not fix it overnight, and it had only been a handful of days since he came clean.

Beth fought two battles, one against the Mandate, and another against the darkness that had lived inside of her for the past three years. Its voice still whispered poisons in her ear telling her she was not good enough, not to be a huntress and not for him. Lucien cursed, gathered a bundle of chopped wood, and disappeared around the corner.

He returned, dropping a sack at her feet. She asked, "What's this?"

"See for yourself, but come round front. Emmanuel can wait, you and me though...," he bit his lip, "we're settling this tonight." She squealed as he lifted her into the air, tossing her over his shoulders, and kicking the bag into his hand. "Yeah you know you like those skills too."

Beth laughed, squirming under his grasp. "You're impossible."

"But you love me, right?" Lucien swung her around as if she did not weigh two hundred pounds.

"Yeah, Luce, I love you." She would never stop.

He placed her on the ground and squinted despite the darkness, clutching the bag in his shaky hand. "I know it'll take time." Bolts of energy flashed in his eyes. "But I did try. Remember the letters and gifts I sent?"

"Yeah the ones I never received." She sat on the blanket, folding her legs to the side. "You found them?"

"In Vivian's room of all places. I brought them here for safekeeping. I thought Jemma was keeping us apart, but it was Vivian." He added a few more colorful words under his breath. But, why would Vivian care if Lucien sent her letters? "They're all opened. She knew I knew. I told you what I was doing in the letters, hoping you'd see the truth and understand." Luce scratched his head and paused. Blue eyes flickered as if he had realized something, but Beth could not be sure.

"What if ... nah." He waved the thoughts off, and she caught his hand.

"Luce just because I don't blame her doesn't mean I like her."

"What if all along she was changing my dosage? Like trying to get rid of me, but she'd known it couldn't be too sudden seeing as I hadn't been sick. The whole town knew about my leukemia. I mean it ain't like she could've hurt me any other way either."

Beth opened the bag and stared at the envelopes and boxes. His accusation sickened her stomach. After learning of her deceit, lies, and well, stealing of Beth and Jemma from their parents, she did not put it past Vivian to murder anyone standing in her way.

"So, you're thinking maybe her weak dosing was enough to bring the cancer back?" He chewed his lip. "I'm not saying you're right or wrong, but how come you got sicker after you'd had a heavy dose of my blood?"

Lucien stacked wood in a makeshift pit, brows furrowing and glistening under the moonlight. "I'm a guardian of truth and life, Beth. I thought it another myth. My daddy doesn't ever speak of his side, so I went by what I found." His scowl deepened, and she patted the blanket. "Karma is the easiest explanation. I killed without justification in the eyes of The One Above, and the sicknesses' return was my punishment."

What did he do as a kid? If his leukemia was a punishment ... "No, that was just bad luck. Coming out of remission was the Gods speaking or a The One Above. I do believe there's something up there." His eyes rose to the sky. "Something."

Split wood released a piney aroma that reminded her of Christmas. "Thought you said no fires?"

Maybe they could have a winter wedding like they'd once planned for as kids and Beth could wear ... She didn't have her real mother's gown, and Jemma wouldn't be there to stand with her either.

"I said no *big* fires." A branch cracked, and Beth's heart pounded. She glanced to Luce, but he appeared unfettered. Surely, he heard the noise too. Emmanuel strolled from the woods, a panting Zoro batting his heels. "I think we should have a ceremony in the winter, but I ain't waiting that long to marry you. As soon as we have my parents, we're heading to Vegas."

"Good thing no one listens to you." Beth watched the towering spirit man lumber across the creek, splashing and uncaring of the water running between them. His coat of multicolored feathers covered him from shoulders to toes, but the design appeared different. Before he had appeared like a man in a giant bird suit. In a way, he still did, but the spectral essences bled through and swirled around him like specters. Her familiar took the long path around, hopping and navigating broken branches. "I don't want to get married by Elvis in a leisure suit."

Rising from the ground, she felt Lucien's eyes on her. He grasped her hand, twining their fingers together, and issuing a charge of electricity over her skin. "I don't care if an alien marries us or what he's wearing. I don't even need the words or paper, baby, but I know you do."

Beth cocked her head, curious as to the strange events that always occurred when these two met, three if she counted Zoro, but more so to Luce's words. What did she want, beyond a happily ever after where she was not hunted and he was healed? Anything else was just icing.

"Then who cares about Vegas. I swear you don't know me at all sometimes, Luce. It isn't about your name, certainly not your money, but about love. You men think you know what we want, but just ask. Yeah I want to marry you someday, but I want to do it right, and the way I want it done, not some fly by night fat man in polyester with enough grease in his hair to oil a bike chain."

"You done picking a fight?" She ground her teeth and snorted. Lucien leaned back, striking a match. "Fine, I lied. I want the paper that says you are mine, and I am yours. Call me selfish or possessive, but we had dreams, Bethy, and maybe yours changed but mine did not. Plus you promised to marry me." He tapped the sapphire ring on her finger. "I know how you get with those promises."

"Compromise ... no Elvis?" Beth snapped her fingers. "Hey, what about your folks or Dr. Pawl? He's on the elders' council." But he might not live long enough to see another winter.

"No, I know what you're thinking, and the answer is no."

"I didn't say anything," she said, twirling her foot in the red dirt and adding, "what use is this Power if I can't use it for some good."

If it always came back to her blood, why could she not choose whom she saved? Beth did not live in a bubble. Her eyes ran over the shack. Okay so she did not usually live in a bubble. Her old house and its walls flashed through her mind.

"We don't even know if I'm truly cured." Translation: what if she saved someone else and Luce fell ill again, and she did not have enough blood to save him. Some bomb always dropped in her lap, and history told her the future would not prove to be any different.

"Bethany, Lucien, you are well. Good then we are ready." Emmanuel did not waste time, not even for a reply.

Luce still stared at her, and she fidgeted under the intense gaze. "I asked for one more night."

"Not possible. We have less than a week before the festival, and Beth has received no rites or training." Emmanuel looked toward the sky. The moon was almost full. "The rite begins tonight and lasts till the full moon ends." His grip tightened. "Beth, you must walk this path alone."

Her lips parted, but Lucien said, "No."

Emmanuel shifted as his face altered, flipping between the beings composing his body. "Beth must decide," the bear rumbled. "She cannot be forced."

"I ain't forcing her, you are," Lucien said, but his gaze did not falter. A shiver dimpled her bare arms, and he rubbed the chill away. Her hands cupped his rough cheeks, holding his face, and memorizing the lines wrinkled on his brow.

The pile of wood ignited behind them, and she jumped closer to Lucien. "It's dangerous," she whispered. "But I have to do this." Fire crackled, sputtering embers to the heavens, and her stomach ached. "It's only a few days."

Lucien grasped her hands and lowered them, but he did not let go. "Beth, don't go. We'll run …"

She glanced at the ground. "We are in this together even if in spirit." Her eyes closed as Lucien's thoughts danced between her and his parents. "I made you a promise."

Her protector, her guiding light through the darkness and without him, this job did not hold the same spark of her dreams. Deep down he was always by her side, even if in essence, but only if alive.

"Break it," he said, tugging her closer. "Shit, Beth it's you I can't live without."

But how long before he regretted the decision? How long before that regret turned into bitterness toward her? He could live without her now, if the process had worked, but that was not his fear. Lucien hid his fear beneath his hard exterior, and Beth could not find the source.

Emmanuel held out his hand. "Save him or save the world."

The animal's spirits rose from inside the man, separating and fanning around the fire. Past their physical forms as if they were particles of matter floating in the air, light shined from their hearts and glowed through their eyes.

She stepped backward as the same thing that had happened the night she freed Emmanuel from the locha began again. His lips moved and his brown eyes lit with a yellowed tinge much like the shadow men who tried to kill her, those she had killed with Power. Underbrush rustled as she gulped. Her eyes danced over the source, and her heart leapt into her throat as Lucien grasped her shoulders.

"What?" she snapped at him. Beth tore her gaze away, catching a blue glow emitting from her hands. The sapphire pulsed in tune with her heart; he had given her his life force. A squeezing sensation imprisoned her heart. His horn … she stared into his endless eyes … Luce had given her his horn. Fingertips brushed his third eye where the sapphire belonged, but only the smooth skin across his forehead met her touch. His life was forever in her hands.

"My blood isn't that special anymore," he lifted her hand, "but you are more special than life to me."

Emmanuel held up a lamp and repeated, "Save Lucien and remain with him, or come with me and save the world."

Her lips parted, and her hands rose into the air, palms up. "Hold up." Beth pointed to Emmanuel. "No. Just no. You don't walk into my life and demand ultimatums." Breath rushed through her clenched teeth. "Luce, I love you to pieces, but you can't give up your … what is this anyway?"

Luce released a bark of laughter. "Baby, it isn't the entire horn." She blinked at the word horn despite using it herself. Her fiancé had a horn … Oh Lord. Dizziness swept over her, and her eyes closed as her legs wobbled. "This is why I wanted her to have another day."

Beth held up a hand and waved them off. "I'm all right. I just need to sit." Lucien lifted her and carried her to the blanket, laying her down near the fire. Zoro promptly sniffed her, a curious one he was. "I choose Lucien."

Saving the world would not happen, maybe she could save some by touching their lives in a way no one else could, but no world existed for her without Luce. Beth had always said this. It did not matter if they were not a couple. As kids, she knew where her heart belonged.

"You disappoint me." The glint of firelight in his eye said otherwise as if she had made the right choice.

Beth smiled, allowing the full effect to overpower her face and radiate from her heart. "You don't know me very well. I'm selfish."

Lucien tucked her hair behind her ear, his fingers lingering. "No, you ain't Bethy. You're the most selfless person I know. Don't argue with me."

Instead, Beth snorted. If she took out all the ways Vivian interfered and all the attempts he made to save her, knowing her aunt could have pulled the plug on his treatment at any time … that made him the selfless one.

Zoro rubbed against her bare leg. "You are selfless, loving, and loyal even when it seems you are not." He brushed against Luce, purring. "You, I have wrongly named, but know I saw only one side, one truth of what happened in the past." His head dipped as Lucien crouched. "Forgive me."

Emmanuel took a copper kettle and sat it on the stones, awaiting the coals to smolder. "You have passed your first test. Love is an obstacle you will face, but loyalty is of the utmost importance to surviving."

The spirit animals murmured various responses in their native tongues. She whispered, "Do you see them?"

"All Spirit Walkers can see them," Emmanuel replied. "You however will see many of the Creek clans represented from turtle to bear."

Animals were loyal too. She rested against Lucien, holding her hand over his heart as the pulsating rhythm washed over her. As soon as this was over nothing would stand between them. But her destiny awaited her, a dream she once wished for as much as the man standing beside her. A hunter of the spirits, but the dream had changed. By her side would be the man guarding the truths of their heritage, and the cat who lead her. Could she have both her visions? A family with Lucien and hunt the locha terrorizing the people? Would there be any time to save those she deemed worthy? Time would tell.

"I will aid you, Beth." The bear slinked forward; his essence wavered like smoky haze, but she made out the clear lines of his large body and glowing yellow eyes.

"Think of locha not as black and white but as if they are grey." Emmanuel extended his hand to blanket the blazing fire. "Some spirits are harmless, stuck, and unable to move on until their business is finished." He motioned to Luce. "Some are great evils wanting only to devour and destroy, but then their offspring surprises even us too."

Jumlin would have destroyed all things living and much of his initial offspring too would have done the same if not for the hunters capturing and killing those they had discovered, but Lucien and Dana were not evil despite being descendants of a true monster. "I agree," she said smiling wider. "People and locha share that in common. Many are good but some are terrible, but then there are others who just survive."

Either way her job was to clean up. Beth gulped hard, swallowing the lump in her throat. When Emmanuel came through, so did other locha, but did she destroy them all? He shook his head, hanging it slightly. "You can never destroy them all. That is not your purpose. Like all paths in life, you must seek balance, or the raging storms will destroy them all."

One problem at a time. Her heart pierced. How many had she saved, albeit temporarily, through Vivian's deceit? The process drained her, and neither she nor Luce knew if it actually worked. His scans were clean, but even the tiniest drop could do that according to the doctor. Beth would like to undergo the transfusion one more time and save

Dr. Pawl. She had hinted at it as he said goodbye to her and Zoro, but the vet told her no, said he had lived a full life. A tear splashed against her knuckles. Beth sniffled, glancing around the small fire. The world had gone silent, not even a cricket chirping or a tree frogs song graced the airwaves. All eyes trained on her as lightning on the horizon caught her attention.

"Hole in the roof." Lucien coughed into his fist as the thunder followed. "Are you ready?"

No, she was not prepared, but she must press ahead.

The bear said, "Many actions out of fear affect the worlds. The decisions we make today have consequences for tomorrow," pointing toward the storm. "It storms in all worlds when the thunderbird calls it."

An owl flew from a branch and landed on her shoulder. "Day and night cannot dwell together and neither can sun and storm."

"We will be known forever by the tracks we leave," the wolf said. "Imprint your feet but never drag them."

One by one, the animals blessed their wisdom on her, and Lucien by proxy, but the ancient words touched and stirred her soul. They laughed and sang. Sitting by the fire, they shared tales and knowledge. Zoro curled into her lap, listening, but still intently watching her. As her familiar, he was her spiritual guide, but what did that make Lucien?

Zoro embarked the greatest wisdom of them all as he said, "He who would do great things should not attempt them all alone." Zoro had recited an old proverb. "Lucien brings his own strengths but he strengthens you too. Your paths have always crossed, Beth, but now they weave tightly as if creating a river cane basket. Cut one reed and the masterpiece unravels. That is your shared love. Both are strong when separate, but once bound, your greatest strength now becomes your weakness. This is why loyalty matters more than love."

Beth blinked as her fluffy familiar used his real name, instead of calling him a traitor. Luce snuggled closer, leaning to kiss her temple as the moon descended behind the trees. Their ancestors bore witness, twinkling in the sky. At least some of his could be, but Beth did not know about hers. If they shared the storms, did they also share the sky? Shivers washed over her skin and Lucien drew closer. A smile touched her lips, and his smoky scent blended with the warm campfire. Part of her expected this, and him, to be a dream—one she did not want to awaken from. The thought alone raced her heart.

"Different fears exist, Bethany." Emmanuel made a face at her name. What had her real parents named her? Did they miss her, search for her? Would she ever meet them? Her thoughts trailed and smashed into his words until she was nodding and smiling. "Founded fears such as burn of fire or pierce of arrow." He pushed his head back. "Then there are ignorant fears that arise from not knowing or understanding." Emmanuel scooped a handful of dirt. "Tears shed into this land and blood nourished the soil but do you understand why?"

"Greed," she said, her voice straining the word into a question, as if she were paying attention. Beth should have been, but with all that had happened in the past week and half, she could not focus on Emmanuel.

"For some but the true reason was fear. Settlers feared our ways because they differed from theirs. Our skin colors differed even though many Creek were of mixed races, including the European settlers that arrived far before the British. Our leaders were of mixed blood too. Many accepted us because they had no other choice, but the fear survived in their hearts. You young warrior must be fearless of the unknown."

Processing his words, Beth paused. The past nineteen years of her life were lived in fear. From the locha, to the dark, to losing Lucien, she still recalled the body numbing times when the bushes moved or the phone rang when he was in the hospital "Who are you?"

Thin lips pressed together as Emmanuel bowed his head. "Who I am is unimportant, but I am not ignorant to your questions. The ones you have not voiced. Zoro has told you much and so little, Corazon."

Lucien said, "Heart—was that her name?"

"No, but it suits her better than Bethany, and there is Spanish blood running through her veins. People often wonder where your people went, Corazon. The Great Drought came to the southwest and southeast. Tribes migrated, disbanded, died from disease or starvation, and some seemingly disappeared, leaving behind all possessions."

"I don't remember any just disappearing," Lucien objected.

"They did, her family did, but in truth they trekked through a portal to another land, leaving all worldly possessions behind, and they started over in the new world they discovered. Those are Corazon's people, the Apalachee fought against invaders to their land and way of life. They too were a part of the Creek Nation, but their spirits were no match for disease and constant encroachment. Many sought refuge; some relocated and upon this journey found new land in one of The One Above's worlds."

Beth swayed, leaning against Lucien on the blanket, clutching to him through the stories Emmanuel shared of her family. "But there are people of that bloodline still here today. Many more ventured the Trail of Tears."

The day marked great sadness for the Creek tribe spanning across the southeastern United States, but other tribes made the gruesome journey before, and after, their people too. The Chickasaw, Choctaw, and the Cherokee all walked the same ground heading west, escorted by armed U.S. Calvary. While many Native Americans survived the cross-country trek, many more perished from disease, attacks, and unknown causes both during and after the sale of their lands. More than two hundred million acres were lost to the settlers, and the McCallisters, albeit corrupt, held onto a tiny fraction by assimilating into the new America.

Zoro said, "Hasse Ola is correct. The Native peoples did move from their lands, and some tribes did disappear into the other world. But many returned, like your family Lucien. Have you ever asked your parents how they met?"

Luce shook his head, but Beth knew the story, overhearing it many years ago.

"They met in Florida. Dana was attending college and studying at the library late into the evening. She said the rain poured from the sky for days. She departed and your father stood on the steps, blinking, and spinning. He appeared lost, and Claire asked if he needed help. Their gazes met, and her body electrified as if struck by lightning. It was love at first sight."

Lucien and she had not share their fate, instead they were best friends, falling in love long before they had understood the word, but how she had described Dana and James' meeting was exactly how Beth felt every time she saw Lucien Brown. During their years apart that fact did not change regardless of the hatred and bitterness that brewed within her. It seemed so long ago, instead of just weeks. It served only to add to her confusion. Beth spent three years hating and pining for a man, but when he finally showed a lick of interest, she ran, or fought against it, because of what he'd done.

"And I'll never forgive myself for hurting her," he thought. *"That she still loves me ... I don't deserve her."*

Beth blinked at his thoughts. She still was not used to hearing him, unless he directed the thought at her, but she did love the connection and the depth they shared because of it. He said, "Me too, sunshine." Dry lips kissed her knuckles. "Like being sucker punched in the gut, but you can beat me senseless with your beauty and charm any day."

"Can I ask you a question?" she asked Emmanuel, and he extended his hand. "Can you tell me about the horned ones and their purpose here?"

Lucien warned, "Beth ..."

"No, I think you have a right to know." She did not need a definition to know he was special. "If the thunderbird creates balance among the locha, what purpose do other creatures bring? Isn't the thunderbird enough?"

"Where there is good there must also be evil; too much good and the balance sways. But sometimes the foulest of creatures do good for others just like man can be both good and evil. The horned one's job however, is to protect life where your job is to balance life. In the end, the thunderbirds slaughtered the horned serpents. I wondered if history would repeat itself as I watched your friendship unfold."

Beth didn't know about either aspect. No one ever told them they were destined to be enemies, and she wasn't going to start believing that now. Emmanuel smirked and her hand itched to smack it from his face. She found no amusement in his myth. "It happened long ago, but the world has changed from what they faced. We must move on."

Her mind disagreed. Why did the thunderbirds kill them? The spirits, Zoro, and Emmanuel ignored her unspoken question. A crack from behind caused her back to stiffen. Lucien whipped around, a low growl sounding from his belly. Her familiar's claws dug and burned her skin. Zoro gave new meaning to the phrase fraidy cat.

"If I were to say a bear approaches would you become frightened?" Footsteps continued as a slight tremor vibrated the ground.

"Yes," she said mid gulp. The idea of a real live bear quickened her pulse. Lucien stared at the woods, clenching her hand. Zoro's wide gaze peeked over her shoulder, but Beth couldn't bring herself to look, and clamped her eyes closed.

"Why?" Emmanuel asked as a breeze brushed her skin.

"A bear is a wild animal, viciously unpredictable, and territorial."

"So is man."

True. But man had empathy. "Open your eyes, baby." Beth shook her head. Luce reassured her again, promising it was all right. Her eyes opened.

A man covered in a bear pelt sat across from her where the bear spirit had shimmered. He said, "Are you still frightened?"

Sweaty palms gripped Lucien tighter as her pounding heart managed to beat even faster. How could there be a man— Beth believed in magic, but never had she witnessed anything this powerful. A shaky hand traced his outline, noting the nose, jaw, and pores. Not a spirit but a solidified man sat before them.

"Is this necessary?" Emmanuel nodded to Lucien. "Sunshine," he whispered into her hair. The bear man's beady eyes locked on her. All that sat between them was the dying fire. Beth buried her head in Lucien's neck. He rubbed circles over her back, trying to soothe her, but failing. "Sweetheart, nothing will hurt you."

Beth still did not know what attacked her aside from the locha, but the man materialized out of the freaking woods. Emmanuel claimed she had danced with her curtain, but something *had* grabbed her that night. Her throat constricted at the memory. Which was worse, the night in her room or the shadow man who attacked her here? Both could have ended her life, but Luce rescued her both times, and each time the shadows ran away.

"The unknown frightens you and makes you ignorant." Emmanuel waved his hand over the bear clad man, and his image disappeared. "This is not the way of the thunderbird. All fears of the unknown will hinder your duty. Questioning is natural, but you cannot judge with your mind alone."

The process repeated as he called forth more human-like spirits, but as each one came forth her fear lessened, and her pulse settled.

"You must disregard anything your family, or this Mandate, taught you about the darkness." Beth nodded as Emmanuel placed a hand on her stomach and cocked his head, smiling. "Rely on this. Instincts and knowledge will guide you on this journey, but fear starts here," he flicked her forehead, "fear will end you before the other begins."

The other begins? Her dark brow arched. But as she opened her mouth he added, "I will return tomorrow night, and you will receive the next blessing. By the third moon, you will be ready."

Emmanuel bid them a good night and placed his bird head on again. Fingers snapped; the fire died instantly, taking the spirits away, as he ascended into the air. Dampened fire curled her nose as she gagged from the odor. *What did he use to snuff it out, pee?* The three of them lingered in the darkness, Zoro fast asleep on her lap despite her heaving. Unlike most cats, he was not nocturnal. Beth always blamed his human spirit, but were they still human?

Lucien said, "I think we are. What makes a human … human?" She took deep breathes to calm her stomach.

The bag clattered as she lifted it; Luce took them from her and pointed toward Zoro. That cat slept through anything. Scooping him into her arms, he purred and mewed.

"Can you see?" Her eyes adjusted well in the darkness. Shadows scurried about the forest; twigs snapped. "Hook your arm through mine, so I don't lose you." Her hand slipped through his bowed arm, gripping his forearm. "It's all right, Bethy."

"I know," she said, but any minute now, she still expected her new life to be a dream. Not all of it was sunshine and roses, but there were parts she wanted to keep alive. But the bear and the spirit men … Beth shuddered, fingertips sparking as if reminding her she wasn't helpless. "Let's go."

Lucien saw her settled into the shack and left, retrieving the rest of their belongings and supplies from the car. Beth washed the campfire from her skin in the basin and unpacked a few items she needed for bed. Bending down made the dizziness worse and she grasped the wall for support. Zoro knocked over the sack containing the letters and packages. After scolding him, she fished out the letters, inched her way to the table, and clutched the chair. Deep breathes filled her lungs as she willed the queasy stomach away. Beth eased into the antique chair and it groaned under her weight. Lighting the second oil lamp, light bathed the table and kitchen.

She had not noticed it before, but there was a small potbelly stove in the corner. How had she missed such a quaint detail? Or the lace curtain hanging from the window facing the stream. Such charm existed within the four walls, and she had been a fool to miss the history. Her people may not have lived in this exact spot, but they were still a major part of the Alabamian history. Tapping feet filled the space with a constant rumble, but her legs would not steady.

"Aren't you going to read them?"

Beth chewed on her cheek, picked up a letter, but put it down again. "I want to," she whispered, "but I've had more than enough excitement tonight."

Her stomach fluttered, but the odd sensation was not like butterflies. Lucien had wanted her to have them. Beth reached and traced his handwriting with her fingertips. The postage dates lined the top, and some of the stamps were peeling too. Each envelope reminded her of the times he had ridiculed her. A sigh hissed from her lips, and she eased from the chair, retrieving her brush.

"Do you think the letters will change your mind?"

Beth shook her head, yanking the brush through her long hair, snagging and wincing on the knots. "I forgave him, but the wounds are still there. The scabs are light, and with time, I'll heal. I don't want to rip the scabs off now."

Getting over her fears would not occur overnight, but Emmanuel's advice repeated inside her head. Her family lied to her, and the Mandate turned its back on the old ways.

"Your momma said you were teaching at the community center for the Mandate." Lucien placed the bags on the floor, and sat removing his boots. Hands ran through his hair; shoulders rolled, releasing tension. "Why didn't you tell me?"

Luce chuckled, leaning forward and shaking his head. "We weren't speaking, sunshine."

"When you were better. I had to hear it from her not you ... actually I had to hear you were working for the Mandate from the officer." The one he'd killed and Amber's mother ... people would ask questions but they would not find their bodies buried deep on the McCallister property. "What were you teaching?"

Luce drew her feet into his lap and rubbed the soles, but her nails tapped the tabletop waiting for an answer. "Math, History, and Muskogee mainly, plus reading to a few."

Lucien cracked his neck. What had him all worked up? "Ready for bed?" Issuing a grunt, he removed his shirt as Beth petted Zoro.

"Sorry bud, but you ain't sleeping in my bed." Zoro turned his large blue eyes on her and frowned—at least she thought it was a frown. Luce rose, grasping the cat and gently tugging as she drew her familiar closer. "No way, Beth." He sighed and released her cat. Luce yanked his hair, spinning around and skulking toward the corner. "He's not sleeping in *our* bed."

Beth placed Zoro on the floor and prepared a makeshift bed for him under *their* bed. Lucien still did not answer her question about what was eating at him. The stress only made her tummy ache worse. Were all men this stubborn? Removing her clothes, she headed into the bathroom to change, holding her breath despite the lack of smell from the sawdust toilet. Aside from lack of space, it was her least favorite part of the shack. Luce waited, fingers tapping over the wall as she opened the door. . He was on her faster than a wolf on a wildcat, pinning her against the closed door.

Rough and hot, his mouth devoured hers as he pressed her against the pine boards. Groaning he ground against her, skimming her thighs, and pushing her nightgown higher. Beth could not catch her breath, and his thoughts spun through his mind faster than she could comprehend. Wildfire lit his eyes; she gripped his neck, clutching hold of his shoulders, and matching the speed of his feverish kisses.

Fabric tore as Luce shredded her panties. His belt clattered against the hardwood floor. A lamp by the bed lit the corner, but shadows bathed the rest of the cabin. "Bed," she whispered as the wood scraped her backside.

"Sorry," he muttered and put her down, drawing his pants around his waist. The cabin was too dark to see his reaction, but his tone laced with annoyance.

Beth shivered more from his attitude and the hot and cold behavior. Breath caught as she leaned against the wall. "What is your problem?"

"Don't even think about it," Zoro said as Lucien's fists balled. Inching along the wall, she made her way to the basin, placing as much distance between her and Luce as possible. His fingers uncurled but drummed against his thigh.

"I can't do this," he whispered and climbed into bed. The light dimmed as he cranked the dial down. Almost romantic if there had not been an annoyed ass hole. Lucien rolled on his side and stared at her as her fingers smoothed over the fabric of her plain nightgown. "What?"

One by one, her arms crossed over her chest. "You tell me what, Luce." A breath hissed through her teeth. "No, just forget it."

Her gaze swept the space. Share the bed with a frigid pain in her side or watch the stars? Beth opened the door and slipped into the night. The still air was warm and muggy. Light reflected from the calm stream lazily lapping its path. Tiny hairs electrified on her arms, but she willed them to settle. A slight increase in heartbeat altered her pulse as the shadows moved.

"Beth?" The door creaked. "Bethy, what are you doing out here?"

"I'm the queen of freaks, right? You're a wishy washy ass hole."

"Performance anxiety," he mumbled and shut the door behind him. The heat of him brushed across her skin, but Beth stepped away before he could touch her.

"Don't lie to me, Luce. Haven't you learned by now that I can hear it in your voice?" A hand lifted. "Your tone isn't steady." And his fists what was up with those fists? "Go to bed."

"I'm leaving in the morning, Beth."

"Why wait?" she whispered, her eyes stinging. "Zoro and I are fine. Go."

"Beth … come to bed." All day her gut twisted as if there was something going on that she could not see. A deep breath filled her lungs until no more air would fit, and it hissed through her lips. This was not happening to her.

"You're not coming back are you?" He was leaving her.

"If I can." Rough hands clamped her shoulders, and she stiffened. Burning eyes shut tight, blocking out the light, but she smelled him, felt him touching her. "You can't risk yourself for them."

His parents—why did he have no faith in her? She opened her eyes and stared at her empty hands fidgeting with her nightgown. Beth fought against the urge to turn into the embrace, to hold onto it, but she shook her head. Lips parted, shaking. "Just go."

The breeze caressed her skin, and Lucien was gone.

Chapter Twelve

"News?" Zoro asked as the sky lightened to fiery shades, and the dewy grass reflected the iridescent drops. Lucien left her. What news was there to tell?

"We can't stay," she said rising from the ground and wiping the tears away. Beth had cried from the moment he disappeared until the sun peaked on the horizon, but inside the tears hadn't stopped. Damp hands wiped over her dress as she smoothed the wrinkles.

The shack reminded her of him. From the smell to the belongings, she did not want these memories. Beth changed into a pair of jeans and a tank top and wound her hair into a high bun. Rifling through his drawers, she found a baseball cap. She emptied the tote bag containing the letters and tiny packages, sniffling as his handwriting reminded her of all he had done for her, but of all the lies he'd told too.

"Why would he leave you?" Zoro hopped on the bed and sat on the empty bag.

Specifics did not matter. Beth knew he was going after his parents. His speech rang clear. He would lie to her only to protect

her. He would die for her. He would kill for her. Did it not make
sense that he would have done the same for his family?

Beth sighed. Luce never promised to stay with her. She had
assumed and it bit her in the ass. A hand scratched her back as salt
flaked from her skin. "I'm going after him."

"You're not ready."

"I don't care. I'm not letting him do this, Zoro."

"Let me get Emmanuel first, please." Large eyes pled with her
and she nodded. "I'll be quick. Promise me you'll wait."

A curse flew from her lips. "I promise." Dang cat assumed she
would not go back on her word. That was not true. If Lucien had
made her promise, she would have broken it too. A hand rested on
her stomach; it tightened as she doubled over in pain. "Kolkohkafoosi what is wrong?"

Tears streamed and the pain ripped through her with every
breath. Nails scraped the wood siding. Hurt was an understatement;
her insides were tearing her apart as if fire or acid rushed through
her veins and settled into her belly. "Luce," she said, reaching out as
if saying his name would have made him materialize in front of her.

"Sleep now, Bethy. Stay … away …" She shook her head, forcing
her body upright. Feet stumbled over the steps; her feet urged her
forward as Zoro jabbered on her tail. His words blurred as each step
increased the pain. The world around her painted itself in shades of
crimson, dark like the blood she had bled for so many. Briars ripped
into her nightgown, snagging and scratching at her legs as they sank
their teeth into her warm flesh.

Beth was dying with each breath. Her own blood ripped through
her as she clutched the invisible wounds. *Emmanuel had said fear would
kill her.* She laughed, tossing her head backward in a fit of mania as
her familiar darted ahead, jumping from her sight. The sky did not
darken. The energy, her heart all but battered as she slumped against
the tree trunk. The light and dark cannot dwell at the same time.
She was light; he was dark. Her head rested between her knees as
her stomach heaved coffee ground bile. Beth had watched enough
television to know it was not a good sign, but it made no sense. She
had broken her ankle.

Pinching herself, she attempted to rouse from what had to be a dream. A trembling hand lifted, catching the light of the sapphire and she yanked it from her hand, chucking the meaningless bauble into the woods. Yesterday was a sham, a last hoorah to tear her to pieces before he walked off alone into the sunset. How could he have broken her again?

No—her dampened brow dribbled sweat. Beth quieted the whispers inside her head, but she could not muster the energy to retrieve her ring sparkling in the bushes. Luce would not have hurt her, not intentionally, and this was not her pain. A sob wracked through her body. It was his. The saltiness burned her dry lips as it grazed her mouth. Dizziness lit her eyes with stars, but as she shook them away more appeared. The light came like a thick fog, and a chill chased over her bare skin despite the heat. It lulled her, singing a song she did not know, in a dialect long forgotten.

Blood oozed from his scrunched brows as the breeze ruffled his hair. *"No Beth."* Muscular arms splayed, nailed to a pecan tree. His bronze chest displayed jabs, punctures, and leaking gashes. A woman twirled the knife, but she could not see her face. Beth breathed easier despite the gory scene in her head. Luce lived but for how long? *"Stay there, baby."* Lucien glanced to his feet. *"I love you. Forever, I will love you."*

"Like hell I'll stay," she whispered on the breeze and willed the element to carry her message. Maybe it was a trap. Maybe it was not. A knife sliced his flesh, cutting across his belly, and her skin burned. She raised her tank top. Red lines marred her tan skin, but no blood escaped the ghost wounds.

Her mouth dropped open, but no words came. No shouts or cries released from her shaky lips. A thud sounded behind her like rolling thunder.

Emmanuel said, "They have your protector."

"They're …" Her head shook, as the words would not form on her tongue.

"Your connection is stronger than I anticipated, Corazon." She would never get used to that name. Emmanuel knelt and reached toward her. Beth shied away from his hands as the lightning sparked at his fingertips. "You already have the heart; let me teach you the skill. Your family should have done this." Beth gulped and leaned forward. "Close your eyes."

"You are born with the instinct and knowledge, but it is dormant in your mind," Zoro said, brushing his wet nose against her hand. "Don't fight him."

But as he touched her skin, nothing happened. "That is wrong." Beth's eyes fluttered open and she cocked her head. "You already know."

Zoro glanced at Emmanuel. "Something the protector did?"

He chewed his lip, staring at her hand. "Where is the ring?" Beth lifted her hand and pointed to the brush. Emmanuel retrieved the ring and slid it on her finger. "Let me try again with the protector's spell."

"He's hurt," she whispered, wincing as another cut seared her ribs. "Someone's got him."

Wide brown eyes met hers. "You can see him?" Beth cringed and shouted, clutching her stomach. "And feel him?" He muttered about how she should not be that connected.

"She took his blood."

"Does not matter. It should not matter. I have not witnessed a bond such as this."

Their words filtered in, but she could not speak. Unconditional love was powerful. They had loved one another regardless of reciprocation. The sacrifices they had made for each other went beyond most relationships.

He killed for her. He lied. She delayed, took the lashes and lumps, but she still held on for him, clutching to her memories as if they alone were made of him. Beth would have waited until her final breath for Lucien. The scars were her courage. They reflected the broken soul that still reached for Lucien as if he alone were a bottle of glue. She was his cure, but he was hers.

Unstable legs propelled her from the ground. The white light faded as the wind swept it away and the dark clouds rolled in, blocking out the light. Blue hands lifted in front of her face as she gasped at the surging ball of energy in her hand, the same hand with his ring. She closed her eyes, releasing a tear that sizzled into salt. Lucien gave her his horn ... she couldn't figure out why before ...

"He gave you all of him," Emmanuel said. "Now we must go to him." He handed her a pocketknife and she stared at the leather-sheathed blade in her palm recognizing Lucien's knife. "He asked me to give it to you. How are you with bow and arrow?"

Beth cocked a brow. "Never shot one before," she lied. Luce and she had shot them all the time as kids, but she was terrible. He tried training her in secret, but she could not hit the target even with her sharp vision.

"Long or short?" he asked. Could everyone read her mind?

"Long." Her cheeks heated. "At least that's what Luce called it, but we were kids."

"Short bow might be easier. Your predator vision will not help you time a shot. You must understand what you hunt too. Learn how it reacts in nature."

"I assume it's a human holding him."

"Never assume," Zoro said. "A human being doesn't carve his victims, not even the Mandate is that vicious." But they were wrong. Humans could be if motivated.

"But it can't be the locha—"

"Locha aren't the only evil in this world."

"I know that," she snapped, placing a palm over her heart. Each thud reminded her that life was too short and fragile. Emmanuel grasped her arm, tugging her toward the shack. She had not traveled far and made out the roof through the trees. Beth glanced over her shoulder, taking a long look at the path Lucien had departed on—wanting to follow him—but what good was she to him?

"Time is not on our side, but perhaps fate will be our friend instead."

The past week and half Beth had wasted time on uncovering meaningless truths. Not one of them prepared her for fighting or becoming a huntress and that thought sickened her. Lucien's life was in her hands, and so were his parent's lives, but her selfish nature may have been their death sentence.

"They won't kill him," Zoro said, but she chewed her cheek. A month ago, she would have said no, but the world had twisted and distorted giving her insight on humanity. The lengths some were willing to go just to save their loved ones—she had understood. Beth would have done the same for Lucien. Stealing, imprisonment, torture, though she could not wrap her mind around those actions.

Emmanuel retrieved Lucien's bows and arrows from the shack, in addition to his tomahawk and war spear. Where had he hidden them? No space for any of them aside from the walls, but they were bare. Did Luce know? Did he have insight into the future? Beth wiped her brow.

The pain ended but she still felt him in her heart as she always had in the past. The hair-raising sensation was gone but he could not erase himself from her soul. Grey clouds blocked the light, but the temperature rose, soaking her clothing into a second skin. Bronze skin turned ashen, flaking and irritating her.

"Take your aim," he said holding her arm and the short bow, "draw back slightly." Emmanuel set up targets outside the shack, and she missed each one on her own. "See the wind? Adjust for the air."

Beth blew out a breath and clenched her jaw. Why not use her gift? "Because you risk others seeing you." For Luce it was worth it. "He would disagree," Zoro muttered. "The idea isn't to use your power on humans but the locha, Beth."

"Corazon, close your eyes." Her lids fluttered. "Hear and taste the nature around you; use your other senses."

Trickling water filtered in; birds tweeted as the rain drizzled, bringing needed relief to the heat, and the wind washed them with its hot breath. "See the target with sound."

Her eyes shot open. "What? How can I see with my ears?"

"Call on your senses, and let them make up for what you lack. You rely on sight alone, ignoring the whooshing wind or the taste of rain, and you fail. Bring all three together, but close your eyes first." Beth shook her head as a salty drop tickled her nose. She repeated the steps, allowing the arrow to fly. Another miss landed in the stream, and she tossed the bow down, crumpling to the ground in defeat.

Knees drew into her stomach as fists pounded the earth. "I'm useless." Four fingers wrapped around a rock, and she tossed it at the dumb target mocking her with its shining gleam, knocking the tin can over in one clean shot as a flock of birds took to the skies.

Footsteps drew away from her and she hugged her knees. They were right to give up on her. Beth sucked. A few moments later and they steps returned. Emmanuel dropped something by her feet and she opened her eyes. "A slingshot?"

"This was yours," Zoro said, pawing at her name carved into the handle. Luce had made it for her on her eighth birthday, but she had forgotten about it. Fingertips rolled over her name and flipped the slingshot, revealing his name opposite of hers with a tiny heart. A small smile drew her lips upward. How had she forgotten about all the summers? Half of the memories were of him but not of what they had done. What they had done did not matter to her. It was always about him, but he'd remembered.

Beth ran into the shack seeking any type of ammunition. The letters caught her eyes, and she grasped the bag—three years' worth of letters hugged to her body as she searched the cabin. "I'm coming, Luce. Whether you like it or not."

"You have two more days of preparations."

The letters fell from her hands, dropping and sliding over the bed. "I'm not waiting to rescue him." Beth did not know if the Mandate or some other yahoo had him. She shoved the slingshot in her pocket and stormed passed him. Ammo, she required ammo.

Rolling her pants up, Beth waded through the water, filling her pockets with large stones. She did not have time to make any from scratch. Even in the hot temperatures, mud balls would take days to cure because of the thick humidity. She slipped her shoes on and guessed at the time, wishing she had a watch. "You should listen to Emmanuel and wait."

Zoro sat in the grass, his fur blowing in the stiff wind. "No."

"At least wait for sundown and the guides. Hear their messages, learn their ways."

Her eyes shut, and she reached for Lucien with her mind. The pain had connected them before. But could she find him without it? Her brows twisted. "Pain connects us." Meadow grass tickled her cheek. "Scratch me."

"No, Beth."

"C'mon, you can do it."

Zoro glanced away, staring into the woods. Lights glowed like lanterns floating through the darkening forest. Beth cursed, grabbed the cat and her slingshot, and ran toward the battered path. She did not know where Emmanuel was and no time left to find him. They were on their own.

Muscles strained and her heart ached. No looking over her shoulder this time as she darted, bounding over broken branches. Each step brought her closer to Luce, and she clutched her familiar tighter. His little heart pounded as fast as hers did, and she bet his eyes reflected her alert gaze.

Her body quaked as thunder and lightning danced in the distance. Wobbly legs threatened to give way as dizziness distorted her vision. Beth halted, hooking a tree trunk, and deciding they had put enough distance for a short reprieve. Limbs pulsated, throbbing in tune with her heartbeat.

A branch cracked, and her gaze jumped toward the noise. Something moved in the shadows, and she braced herself against the tree, holding her breath. Zoro saw it too. *Do not be afraid. Do not fear what you don't know.* The advice rolled around in her head, but only in theory did it sound easy. In practice was another story. It spun around and strode further into the woods away from them. Beth breathed, sighing and relaxing.

"That was close." She agreed. It was too close whatever it was. "I can walk now."

"Sorry," she muttered, releasing Zoro to the ground. From head to toe, inside and out, her body burned, but she pushed herself forward, strolling instead of running over the damp forest. The rain like mist coated them, and even her cat looked more like a frail rat than a feline. "Sorry about the weather too. I can't—"

"Kolkohkafoosi, it can take years to master control over the elements. Lightning is the easiest these days because electricity is abundant, but rain, hail, and wind are stubborn." They arrived at a small clearing and another abandoned building made of stone. A tiny chimney jutted from the rooftop, but there were not any windows. "Are we close to what you saw?"

She did not know. What she had seen was Luce nailed to a pecan tree. "Where would the Mandate hold people? They don't have jurisdiction here because this is private land."

Beth smacked herself, halting mid-step, and gaped at Zoro. "They had no right to take Vivian either. How could I have been so stupid not to question this?" Her arm spread out as she twirled, spanning the area around her.

"But you said it yourself, they have a far reach, and local enforcement here is lax."

She scoffed. "It isn't that lax. Vivian committed a serious crime, heck I'd run out fingers before I ran out of federal charges, and that isn't including the local laws she broke." Beth stepped forward but stopped. Were they dealing with the Mandate or was it bigger than that now? Her throat swelled knowing the cat read her thoughts. "We can't take on the government with a slingshot."

"Don't jump ahead of yourself," he said creeping onward. "You don't know who has Lucien yet, and Vivian can rot for all I care."

Pecan trees. She closed her eyes and breathed in deeply. They had a subtle smell to the leaves, one ingrained into her from the groves on her property. The earthy scent had a sweet bitterness it wafted into the air. Beth was not supposed to play among the trees as a kid, but she used to use the nuts as ammo. Vivian used the oils in cooking and her cures. The contents of her stomach lurched and spilled onto the earth at the thought of her cures. Bile rose again and she choked, stumbling to the ground and eating a mouthful of dirt.

Fingernails clawed at the surface as she flexed and moved in a fluid line to standing. "He's in the grove." Dirt brushed from her clothes. "Vivian is free."

Chapter Thirteen

*E*mmanuel poked the fire, balancing on the balls of his feet. His feathered head tilted down. Cinders caught in the light breeze, dancing for a moment before turning into ash in the misty rain. Each living creature on Earth reflected those embers life span. They lived, sometimes for a moment, and then they died, returning to the earth to be reborn again in either Heaven or Hell. Some people still believed in reincarnation. But Zoro said it was a choice. Beth eyed the man she had trusted torturing the one she loved.

Zoro trotted behind her. Her fists balled. "You cannot ..."

"Tell me you knew about this, and I will skin you alive," she hissed as the lightning splintered the sky and charged her fingertips. Emmanuel danced, singing around the fire in Muskogee. Twirling and stomping the ground as if this were the Shaker Dance. The turtle shakers were all he was missing. Beth spat on the ground. *How dare he pray to The One Above.*

"Beth I didn't, I swear I didn't have anything to do with this." Beth did not glance at her cat as he stammered his innocence. The creature before her had all four of her friends: Lucien, James, Dana, and Jemma nailed to pecan trees. Firelight reflected her cousin's tear stains. If she had not known the truth, she would have wondered how Vivian could have done such an atrocity to her daughter. But she had stolen her too.

A pulse throbbed in her jaw, and she swallowed hard. The training, the excuses, all of them served as distractions. She had believed him, trusted him, but he betrayed all of them with his trickster ways. Somehow, he had done the same to Luce. Crouching lower, she watched trying to devise a plan that he would not have known about. "Beth, who hurt them when he was with us?"

"What?" She blinked, staring at the wide-eyed ball of drowned rat. He closed them and nodded as if reassuring his memories, but she did not understand.

"You were in pain earlier and seeing things when Emmanuel was with us." Zoro's words shook, rocking the realization, and nailing it into her head. The first time he was not there, but he had arrived for the second round as the visions started.

Emmanuel removed his jacket, folding it neatly, and placing it on a log. Piece by piece the disguise unraveled, revealing a man she did not recognize, not that she could have from his naked bottom. The back door slammed. A robed person stepped from her old house, strolling across the grass toward Emmanuel. Graying hair peeked from beneath her hood, and she handed him a garment. Vivian—she was almost sure of it.

Why was she free? Why did the robe have a fancy *M* embroidered on it? "Who exactly are the Mandate, Zoro?"

"They did not exist in my original time. The Cherokee were not a part of the Mandate." The cat shivered in the rain, and she hugged him against her for more warmth.

Her head cocked downward as he purred, vibrating her skin with calming energy. "I thought they were old though, like when the Trail of Tears happened. They formed to protect the Native American ways."

"Yes, but they don't rule over all tribes. Each tribe rules itself and has a mekko, Beth. The Mandate is a private group not a government. And old ways includes the old religion where some—not the Creek—sacrificed the horned ones and the inheritors."

Why didn't they fight back though? Beth knew what they were capable of, so how had they managed to subdue them? What about their Power? Beth's brows rose, scrunching as each question filtered into her mind. "Why have you never corrected me before?"

"I didn't realize you saw them as such, and you never asked. My job is to guide you, not tell you about the world, or what to do, but maybe I should have made an exception. There are rules for me, for what I can share because you must walk your path and make mistakes. Only then do you learn." Zoro paused. "As for how, that I cannot tell you because I do not know, but I would assume it was someone they each trusted. There is a lesson in that."

"Trust no one," she muttered under her breath.

Rain pounded the fire out. She needed a closer look just to believe what she was seeing and army-crawled the forest perimeter. Water dripped through the canopy of trees as she prayed there were not any fire ant colonies making their homes nearby. A bunch of ant bites in her nethers was the last thing she needed. Smoke rose from the large fire as it sputtered out, allowing her the cover of steam and smoke, and the roar of thunder and the crackle of lighting covered her noises. Still Emmanuel knew she would attack tonight. He knew Beth would rather die than see her friends— her eyes connected with Jemma, and she shook her head, mouthing for her to run.

"She still hasn't come into Power," Zoro said. "Why drain her?"

Beth understood why. Aside from Zoro, the Mandate held all she cared about. Save the world or save Lucien the bastard had asked her, planting the idea as if she could have saved the world. The truth smacked her across the face. What Emmanuel meant was save Lucien or become their blood slave again. James, Dana, and Jemma raised the stakes and, as if she had thought it herself, she saw their plan unfold. *They expected my rescue to fail. They wanted me to barter myself.* Her eyes narrowed. They had used her and Lucien to cement her as their prisoner for life.

Stiff shoulders slumped, rounding forward as she released a breath. "I can't free them can I?"

"Electricity?"

"I can't control it, Zoro. Luce is immune, but not the others." A tear slid down her cheek. Every second counted as they ticked to the throb of her heart. Vivian and Emmanuel waited, standing silently in the downpour as she continued her approach from behind. Moving from the forest's edge and into the grove of pecans was tricky. More space stood between each tree and there was not any underbrush to hide her body. She should have worn all black instead of the dark jeans and white tank top muddied the color of Alabama red clay. Leaves rustled behind her, and every muscle froze. Zoro darted, scurrying up the tree, as footsteps approached and voices carried over the wind.

She melded with the ground as flashlights shined and by the grace of The One Above, skipped over her. "She still hasn't showed?"

Vivian said, "No. Did you see her?"

"She wasn't at the house. Looks like she left in a hurry though." Lucien snickered, but they ignored him.

Vivian tapped her chin as the two robed people joined them. "Maybe you were wrong about her and the boy." Beth recognized that voice as her fake daddy.

Her fake momma said, "She'd come for Jemma."

"She loves the man," Emmanuel said. "She risked death for him, almost succeeding."

Vivian chuckled. "Yeah it's a good thing we let James take her blood, and we got two for the price of one, once we get rid of his parents."

"And Jemma?" fake–momma asked, gulping as her cousin strained against her bonds. "She's just a little girl. No one will miss her?"

At least she appeared to have some sense left in her, but no one answered her. Beth was not close to either of her parents growing up, and now she understood why. They did not know how to be parents, not like James and Dana who would have died for their son a hundred times to save his life, but for whatever cosmic reason only her blood worked. It did not matter why. Already she had wasted time pondering the questions of her past while her enemy nailed her future to a tree.

Fingertips glowed blue as she stared into the dark hood of Vivian McCallister. The woman from her vision had to have been her because she could not see her mother capable of physically harming Luce or anyone. The fact that they questioned Vivian gave her a tiny ember of hope, and it sparked in her heart, spreading through her veins.

Leaves rustled and pecans shook free, too young to have fallen, but the perfect size for her slingshot. She reached, grasping the green nut in her hand. Electricity flowed into the shell, and it glowed, emitting a blue light in the darkness. Silently she cursed, dropping it to the ground. She was not ready to give up her position, not yet.

Vivian tilted her head, staring at the treetops. "Zoro?" Emmanuel narrowed his gaze on the familiar and swept the surroundings, searching for Beth.

A small smile played at his lips. "Thunderbird is here." Flashlights skirted around the woods as he stared in her direction, gaze locking. Emmanuel did not give her up as the other three searched the woods. Their backs to him, he nodded at her, placing a finger on his lips. Confusion wrinkled her brow. Whose side was he on?

Another nod added to her growing curiosity as her fake family crunched through the woods. Beth's heartbeat hammered in her ears as she crawled closer, knowing better than to emerge. Heck, she did not know how to get them down without hurting them more. *Who nailed people to trees?* That was not the Creek way of execution then or now. Deaths by arrows or war club were the usual methods before assimilating into the Union. Sickos; she shook her head, rising at the back of a burly pecan tree wide enough to hide her body. A leg swung around the side, and she brushed Luce's calf, whispering, "I'm here."

"I felt you." He gulped. *"Baby, you need to run, call the police."*

The time for police had come and gone. Energy sizzled in her hands, pulsing in time with her heartbeat, as a renewed courage filled her heart. This was her family; this was her destiny. Beth was a Spirit Walker born to police the worlds. Maybe she could not save all The One Above's creatures, but she could and would protect these people from the hands of crazy tyrants. The Mandate would fall. Vivian would crumble.

Thunder echoed her footsteps and lightning lit the darkened sky. Spirits whispered in her ear speaking of revenge, but Beth pressed the lochas' words away. Caresses brushed her face, arms, and legs, mocking her for choosing love. What were they without loves touch? Even the animals loved.

Lungs burned; her breath wheezed in the misty cloud as the wind cleared the smoky fog, parting and clearing a path. Trembles rolled, threatening to freeze her, but she propelled through the fear of losing them all. Zoro peered at her from the treetop, nodding for her to continue. Beth leapt from the shadows; side stepped, and avoided the dagger whizzing her head, splintering into the tree trunk behind her.

Vivian stepped from the woods; her arm slung backwards, but again Beth twirled from the weapon's path as it thudded behind her. "You won't take me."

"Let them go."

Her aunt called to the darkness. Shadow men formed at the forest's edge, and their yellow eyes glowed like little lanterns—like the lanterns in the woods. A grim smile touched Vivian's lips churning into a sinister sneer. .

"You cannot win, Beth. The whispers tell me your every move." She removed her hood. "Did you think I didn't know?"

She had seen the same earlier. Beth gulped, but tilted her chin higher, and said a silent prayer. Her hand shoved into her pocket, retrieving a rock and her slingshot. Ignoring the locha, Beth aimed at Vivian, drew the rubber band toward her, and released the rock. Beth did not know if she had hit her until a string of curses released. Quickly, she scooped a pecan from the ground and poured her electricity into the wet nut before firing it in Vivian's direction.

The ground shook as the locha marched toward her. Luce stirred behind her; his mumbled words pled for Beth to run. Her shoulders straightened, rolling the tension along her spine.

"No, Luce." She grasped another rock and flung it toward Vivian as her parents appeared, flanking the traitor. "I am in control."

Beth glanced at the sky, calling to the storm. Holding the image in her mind, she formed hailstones, and willed them to batter her foes, but to not harm the innocent. As they plunked and blanketed the ground, Beth drew the current from the earth, blackening the terrain as the steam rose around her. From head to toe, the tendrils danced over her skin, returning and recharging from within the earth.

The locha kept advancing as Vivian chanted, willing them to attack her. "You are a silly girl who cannot control the Power. Draining your kind is the only way to protect this world."

Beth laughed inside but allowed the tiniest of smiles to play at her lips. "Liar. You did this to me for money." Her eyes narrowed on her aunt. "I know the truth. You stole Jems and me from our real families, with the sole purpose of draining us dry for money."

Lights flashed behind her, but she ignored the strobing red, white, and blue as the wind roared over the sirens. Someone had altered the police. Rain and smoke tainted the air as Beth drew more Power into her, granted by The One Above, until her skin had turned blue. Lightning encircled her as the blue-white tendrils coursed from the ground and were absorbed into her body. Bolts arced from her head and hands, stretching and feeding the electrical shield encompassing her and her friends. As the shrouded foes advanced, the lightning crackled, zapping their cloaked bodies to dust, and the Four Winds scattered their ashes.

"You will kill us all," Vivian whispered, but the gales carried her words. If it meant stopping them then she *would* destroy them all. She would sacrifice herself if the woman never harmed or stole another soul. Lucien cried out, but she did not risk a glance. James, Dana, and Jemma's voices followed, but she closed the distance.

"You lied to me," Beth said as a locha touched her shield. He exploded into black dust. One by one, they came, but the touch of the thunderbird's cage was deadlier than any weapon. "Death is almost too good for you."

"Beth," her parents warned, but they did not burn as they eased through her shield. Her teeth ground against each other. A low growl rumbled in her chest. They had drunk her blood too.

"Stay," she replied, flicking her wrist as the earth fissured at their feet, and trapped them in its claws. "*You* created me. *You* held me back from my true purpose." A deep breath energized her lungs. "*Your* biggest mistake was upsetting the balance."

A hand clamped on her shoulder, and she shrugged from its grip. "Corazon," Emmanuel said, gripping her shoulder again. "You are not a murderer of humans. Revenge is not for you."

"No." Luce stumbled forward, weakened from blood loss, and clutching his wounds. "But I am."

Black hair tousled in the wind as he shot a grin. Beth was not fast enough. Blood sprayed Vivian's dirty clothes and dripped down his face making her cringe.

"He's making it painful," Dana said. Emmanuel must have freed them, but she did not know why. Was he truly on their side? "She will suffer."

"She deserves it after what she did to him," Beth said, shivering at the indifference in her tone.

"Oh sweetheart, he's doing it for your pain not his own. Haven't you learned anything about my boy yet?"

Her legs staggered toward him, tripping her body rolled, screaming out as pain slashed across her arms, legs, and face. Blood splattered on her clothes and filled her mouth.

"Luce," she gurgled, reaching for him. Zoro cried, mewing and nosing her wounds. Emmanuel huffed as he caught up to them; her vision tunneled.

"Do not move," he said. Every inch of her body throbbed, but her skull pulsated. "Something hit her head."

Dots littered her eyes, and she closed them wanting to sleep, wanting to forget. "Lucien," she said, licking her dry lips. "I'm sorry."

"Hush now, sunshine. You hang in there." A rough tongue licked her head. Luce was not there despite her head playing games. Fingers snapped. "Stay awake."

But warm darkness cocooned her body. Floating through the sky, she drifted, searching for her Lucien. Images appeared like gliding watercolor strokes and dribbled away. The bear approached, stalking her, but Beth did not run. Death meant traveling to a new life and starting over. Bear stopped at her feet, rising and roaring, and she laughed.

"Huntress," he said, blinking his brown eyes. "It isn't your time." His meaty paw pressed against her forehead, and a sultry heat seared through her veins. "You have an option. Return to earth or the world you belong in."

"The one with my family? My real family?" He nodded as she chewed her lip. "If I go—"

"You will go alone. Lucien will survive, but he cannot follow." The bear wavered in the wind. "You alone must decide whether to remain here as a thunderbird or to go home."

A smile touched her lips as the grin widened. "But I am home. Lucien, James, Dana, Zoro, and Jemma ... they are my home, my family."

"This is good-bye, Beth. You were my best student." The bear bowed and shimmered away as she opened her eyes. Lucien's mouth covered hers as his hands pumped her chest. She gasped as his air inflated her lungs.

Shaky hands reached for his face, cupping his cheeks. Blue eyes shot wide open, glowing in the darkness. *"I love you."*

"You scared me, Bethy. That's three times you've died on me. I'm a sucky protector."

Sitting up, she searched the woods. The storm had cleared, and moonlight brightened the grove. Vivian lay on the ground, still alive as a paramedic and man in an FBI jacket stood watch. James and Dana secured her solemn parents, but Beth did not pity them. Jemma sat, hugging her knees to her chest, and Zoro sat at her feet. Her sobs evident by the shuddering shoulders, and Beth wanted to hug her, promise her it would be okay, but that would have been a lie. They had lived enough lies to last a lifetime.

"You're not sucky," she said grasping her hoarse throat. "But we work better as a team. What knocked me out?"

"One of the locha." Luce glanced toward the woods. "You didn't get them all. Emmanuel got away too. More police will be here soon and another ambulance, but she'll be finished for good." The FBI jacket man turned, and she blinked at James shouting into his radio.

"You didn't kill her." Beth glanced between her crumpled, bloody body and him.

"Sunshine, I've witnessed enough death. I'm sure we ain't seen the last of it either, but you trumped revenge," he placed a hand over hers and squeezed, "ain't nothing more important than my family, even if I don't deserve you." Lucien lifted her from the ground and steadied her as she wavered like bamboo in the wind against his bare chest. "Better have the ambulance check you out too. I gave you a little blood, but you're still woozy."

Red, white, and blue lights flashed around them. Beth leaned against Luce, shivering in the misty fog rolling through the forest. She did not tell him about the bear. Destiny did not matter when the Power evaporated. Pink fingertips mocked her, no longer glowing blue, but Beth smiled. A lifetime with Lucien was worth being boring and plain.

Chapter Fourteen

The FBI took her parents and Vivian away. Beth had given the injured blood and healed their wounds despite Luce's arguments. The small amount would not hurt her, but he refused to take any. The paramedics treated his wounds, cleaning and wrapping his palms in gauze before recommending he receive a tetanus shot too, but he denied further medical care.

"What happens now?" she asked James. The corners of his eyes crinkled. Did he know about the murders? Beth glanced away, catching sight of a fluffier and drier Zoro slinking toward her. "I mean … am I free now?"

"Assuming Vivian was the threat all along, yes. The locha are out there still and then Emmanuel is missing too." James ran a hand through his hair and cracked his neck. "For now I think we should call it a night. The festival starts tomorrow."

He motioned toward two black sedans. Men stepped from the car, and he shook their hands. They wore suits, and she pegged them as FBI agents. Luce picked up Zoro and handed him to Beth. She whispered, "Did you know about this too?" But he only purred.

Luce slid into the backseat, she followed, and a silent Jemma plopped next to her. Her cousin had not said a word. Beth reached for her hand, but she stared ahead, and did not so much as flinch. "Jems, I'm so sorry," no response to her old childhood nickname, "we'll take care of you."

Dana and James slid into the front seat and started the car. "You kids ready?"

Beth was more than ready to forget this part of her life.

*T*he Brown residence always had a warm and inviting feel, as opposed to the coldness of the McCallister house filled with its dated treasures. Beth would have taken no money over her fake family any day. They entered the house in silence, yet the coldness of their situation and ordeal floated away.

James disappeared, reemerging and motioning Beth and Lucien to follow as Dana attended to her cousin. Luce was not kidding when he had said they had a training room. Weapons and dummies cluttered the space. Instead of swords though, there were guns, bows, crossbows, and there was an empty spot about the size of her slingshot. James removed a large knife. A key pad hid behind the weapon, and he pressed in a code. The wall opened, and he ushered them through the doorway.

Photographs lined his walls, and an American flag hung in the corner. A large desk sat in the middle and took up most of the space. James pointed toward the chairs. "Have a seat."

The room burned her nose, courtesy of the dust and old books, but the underlying aroma of campfire came from Luce. She zoned in on him and allowed it to comfort her beating heart. He clasped her sweaty palm and waited for her to sit before taking his own seat by her side.

"Luce wasn't allowed to tell you," James began. "I've been working undercover since before he was born, Dana too." Beth gulped recalling how they'd met and wondered if that too was a lie. "We've been partners for years, posing here as a couple … we fell in love and well you know the rest." James waved his hand. "But that isn't important right now. What is important is that you realize the Mandate is essentially a cult posing as a Native American clan under the auspices of old traditions, natural life, and healing. It sucks people in, sick people with no hope, and it bleeds them dry. They have no affiliation with the real tribal leaders, and they spread themselves across the Americas, popping up and moving on before we've had a chance to investigate. This is why I had to lie to you and why Luce here lied too. Are you with me so far?"

Beth nodded. A file slid across the table, and he tapped the folder. "With the internet, groups stayed in one place longer, and reached a wider audience."

"But I made local deliveries too," Beth objected, toying with her muddy tank top.

"She had both local and online clients, but the burden is split between both of you. Because of your innocence, I've recommended you receive immunity in return for testimony."

Luce cleared his throat. "Is that wise?"

James' chair squeaked as his hands cradled his head. "It's a hard sell, and we may not need her testimony, but if we can't get anyone else to flip she'll be our only hope. I'll know more as we prepare for trial, but I want you on our list."

Her eyes closed for a moment and Beth nodded. "Whatever it takes … how did she know about the other dimensions?" How did Vivian know where to find such beings? Did the Mandate spread around the country do the same?

"We have followed them for over twenty years, infiltrating and tearing them down. Vivian's was the hardest because her cures worked. Dana and I stayed on, watching, reporting. We had no evidence that she broke the law until Luce told us about you and even then, the word of a child wouldn't have stood up in court." James leaned forward and stared at his tapping fingers. "We underestimated her reach in the community and its size. I … we thought it was just the McCallister family. We didn't know that the majority of this little town was on her payroll in either cold cash or blood.

At the same time we were grateful," he scratched his head, "without the Mandate we would have lost Luce."

"My men picked them up and detained Vivian, Billy, and Arden. Jemma was never in harm's way. I promise you. Until Vivian made bail that is. Dana had taken her to a friend's house out of town. The plan was for Lucien to extract you but ..."

"You wouldn't leave."

Beth glared at Luce. "You were sick."

"Yeah, I didn't expect that either."

She shifted in the chair. "And I didn't trust you."

"That too," he whispered, blushing.

"The Mandate regrouped, flushing out more members than I knew of in the surrounding area. I sat on their council, but let me tell you, I learned more in the past two weeks than I knew in the years of making my way through their organization. Vivian did a good job of keeping you hidden until Luce overheard their plans. Of course, he didn't know about me yet, so I had to lie to him too."

"How many of them know I am the source?"

"We think we've arrested them all, Beth, but we honestly don't know."

"What about the bodies?"

James eased in his chair and sighed. "Claire wasn't innocent," Beth opened her mouth but he held up a hand, "Amber was an unfortunate accident, but her mother knew who you were."

Claire had acted as if she was crazy.

"He's telling you the truth, Bethy." She gulped, closed her eyes, and turned away. Believing him did not change the fact that they were dead because of her. "It wasn't your fault."

Lucien stroked her cheek, running his knuckles along her neck.

James said, "He's right. Look I brought you down here to come clean. You have been lied to enough. I also have a question for both of you." Papers shuffled on his desk and drew her attention. "Dana and I want you to work for us. Let me finish before either of you answer." He held his hands up. "Neither of us expects an answer tonight. You both are young and in love, trust me," he chuckled to himself, "we understand. I'm retiring as soon as Vivian is behind bars, but we want to open a school for disadvantaged youth. Luce we'd like you to eventually teach history."

Beth did not understand how she would be involved. Hands twisted into her muddy top. She was not smart like him, but she would never stand in his way.

Most of her life Vivian had kept her hidden away, aside from going to school and work. The subjects interested her and she received decent grades, but served as nothing more than an escape. She succeeded because she did not want Vivian to pull her out. The moment she had started speaking of college, her aunt had threatened to home school her, so she stopped talking about leaving. Then this fiasco had exploded around her.

One by one, she could have added the incidents that had escalated since she had graduated high school, expanding the events of the past two weeks to extend almost a year into the past. Vivian had known Luce knew the truth. Did she know about James and Dana too? Had she truly thought she could have taken over the FBI or turned Beth against them?

What would she do now that the threat had mostly passed? Teaching was not for her, that much she knew, unless the children were Spirit Walkers. "Dana wants you to go to college, Beth. You can attend classes or go online if you don't want to leave. Commuting is an option too."

"I ... I don't know what to say, James. Thank you, but I ..."

He patted the air. "No rush, Beth. Think about it. You too Luce. Your momma wants you to get your degree too. Think about what you would do or want to do, and you let us know." She swallowed hard and dipped her head. "We'd also like your permission to adopt Jemma, if of course she wants us too. You aren't of blood relation, but if you want custody, we'll not stand in your way."

"Dad, I don't think she's thought about it—any of it."

"Right, we should be celebrating. The witch is captured, the girls are safe, you two are getting married, and here I am going over mundane details." James leaned on his knuckles. "We love you both," Beth choked at his words, and Luce's arms encompassed her, "what did I say."

She cried on his shoulder, squeezing him as the tears fell. Until Lucien and his family, no one had ever said that to her. Not Billy and Arden—she couldn't recall ever hearing those names—certainly never Vivian, and she wondered if anyone had ever said those words to Jemma.

Her chair skidded across the room as she tore from Lucien's arms and screamed for her cousin. Muscles burned as she raced upstairs, falling twice. A teary-eyed girl waited, sniffling, and she tossed her arms around her, squeezing her tight. "Jems, I love you so much." Beth rocked her cousin as Dana's arms joined in. "I don't care what they say. You are my cousin, and I love you, Jems. Don't you ever forget it."

"There are our girls, Lucien. They're fierce fighters; don't ever let the tears fool you," James said. Beth held onto her for a few more minutes, letting her eyes run dry.

"What now?" The past two weeks were a blur of running, fighting, learning, and loving.

James and Dana hovered over Jemma as she sniffled. She joined Luce at his wallflower position as Zoro snored on the couch. The last few days had been the roughest on her, but especially difficult for the housecat.

"We need a vacation." Beth arched her eyebrow. "I hear Vegas is beautiful, like a special woman I know."

She glanced at her hands and blinked as a tiny spark emitted. "It came back." Luce folded his fingers around hers and drew them to his lips. "I thought ..."

"Beth, what are you talking about?"

"The bear said I could stay here with you or go home. I thought staying meant giving up Power."

"Baby," he held her face, "sweet sunshine, you will always be you. The Power is in your blood like mine. We'll pass it on but never lose it."

"Pass it on?"

His nose touched her as he glanced at her mouth. "Surely you know what happens when a man and woman ... you know ..." Beth bit her cheek to stop the laughter, but her chest shook. "See now you made me turn all red. Why you got make it …" Lucien palmed his neck, and she loved watching him squirm. Sometimes he could forget, and be in the moment with passionate kisses and words, but deep down beneath all the layers, he was still the sweet little boy she had always known would steal her heart. "You know what I mean."

"Hard?"

The choice did not belong to her. Beth realized that after her family's plans evaporated. Emmanuel never showed his face, and she would not learn how or why he was involved. "I thought I could make a difference," Lucien said interrupting her thoughts. "Maybe people would like to relearn the histories and language of our people. There were a few who came to the community center."

"Luce, I'm not about to tell you no. You have to follow your dream." She let go of his hand; the return of Power had changed her though. Hunting the locha was her future. Someone had to police the spirits. "I have to follow mine too." She nodded to herself, swallowing hard as he cocked his head. But locha were not the only evil in the world. "Do they teach criminal justice?"

He smirked, snaking an arm around her, and drew her against his chest. "Going to argue the law?" Beth smacked him. "Sorry, sunshine, but you could argue the pants off a man any day."

She glanced at the ground as the heat touched her cheeks. "I want to help people, Luce. I don't do blood, so I thought maybe … just forget it."

"I ain't forgetting shit. Whatever you want, we'll find a way. Teaching doesn't pay much, but I will figure out a way—"

"Lucien Brown, if you think I give a rat's ass about money then you don't know me at all."

"Rousseau." He licked his lips as she blinked at him. Rousseau was the name he'd used in the hospital for them. A Cajun name at that … "Brown was Daddy's cover name. I'm Lucien Alcee Rousseau and seeing as you didn't know," he knelt on one knee, "I'm asking you for the …" He shrugged and extended his hand. "In front of all these people to marry me and become Mrs. Lucien Alcee Rousseau because you fill me with light, sunshine, and hope that nothing else in this world can tear us apart. Not bad people and not cancer, only death itself will separate us."

Their shared family gathered round. "Technically it's the fourth time you've asked and seeing that I've already said yes, well then, yes Lucien I will marry you." Beth jumped as hoots and hollers rattled her brain. "Now get up already. You're filthier than a wallowing pig and getting your momma's clean floor all cruddy."

The End.

Thank you for reading. Please help others find this book, and let them know what you think, by leaving a review.

Also available by Rae Z Ryans

Constricted: Beyond the Brothel Walls

Valkyrie Rising

Chivalry and Malevolence: Alfheim Book One

For news and updates sign up to the mailing list at
www.raezryans.com

About the author

Rae Z. Ryans is a member of the RWA and RWA Fantasy, Futuristic, and Paranormal chapter. She currently resides in Alabama with her family. Published since the age of fourteen, Rae enjoys writing romantic, erotic, fantasy/paranormal stories and poetry. Her name pays homage to her brothers: Specialist Ryan D. Rexon and Zachary U. Berthot.

She is currently working on Beyond the Brothel Walls #2: Altered. This post-apocalyptic paranormal romance is emotionally driven, dark fantasy.

Contact Rae or get news and updates about new projects or upcoming releases at her website ot on facebook.

www.raezryans.com

www.facebook.com/raezryans

Acknowledgements

First, I would like to thank my early readers, Beth and Aimee. Your insight and advice helped tremendously.

Vicki, you supplied Zoro with his name. If not for the whimsical addition, he'd still be stuck with my placeholder name.

To my family for putting up with me as I talked endlessly about Beth and Lucien.

To Valerie and her family, you're always in my thoughts and prayers.

To the Native American Creek tribe whose culture, both past and present shaped this story. While I am a quarter Chickasaw, I hope you won't hold it against me. Our tribes were once neighbors.

To the fictional Bethany Ann McCallister, I hope to see you again in the future, but if our paths don't cross again, I hope you walk the path of love and light.

Finally, to my readers, thank you for your continued support and insight.

www.ingramcontent.com/pod-product-compliance
Lightning Source LLC
Chambersburg PA
CBHW020555180626
46810CB00007B/2514